Then Came
LOVE

The Bradens & Montgomerys
(Pleasant Hill – Oak Falls)

Love in Bloom Series

Melissa Foster

ISBN-13: 978-1948004022

THEN CAME LOVE

Cover Design: Elizabeth Mackey Designs
Cover Photography: Wander Aguiar Photography

WORLD LITERARY PRESS
PRINTED IN THE UNITED STATES OF AMERICA

A Note to Readers

I have been excited to write about Jax Braden since I first met him years ago, and I knew that with his meticulous nature, he would tell me when he was ready to settle down. Little did I know he'd holler it in my ear when I was writing Nick Braden's book, HOT FOR LOVE. Everything about this story took me by surprise, from the premise to the soul-deep connection between Jax and Jordan. I don't usually write about heroes or heroines who are involved with others, but when Jax met Jordan, he knew she was *the one*, and he wasn't going to settle for anyone else. When Jordan whispered in my ear that Jax was meant for her, too, I knew they were soul mates. I let their hearts carry this story, and I hope you love it as much as I do.

If this is your first Love in Bloom book, all my love stories are written to stand alone, so dive in and enjoy the fun, sexy ride. You will find a Braden family tree included in the front matter of this book.

The best way to keep up to date with new releases, sales, and exclusive content is to sign up for my newsletter and join my fan club on Facebook, where I chat with readers daily.
www.MelissaFoster.com/news
www.Facebook.com/groups/MelissaFosterFans

About the Love in Bloom Big-Family Romance Collection

The Bradens & Montgomerys is just one of the series in the Love in Bloom big-family romance collection. Each Love in Bloom book is written to be enjoyed as a stand-alone novel or as part of the larger series, and characters from each series make appearances in future books, so you never miss an engagement, wedding, or birth. A complete list of all series titles is included at the end of this book, along with previews of upcoming publications.

Download Free First-in-Series eBooks
www.MelissaFoster.com/free-ebooks

See the Entire Love in Bloom Collection
www.MelissaFoster.com/love-bloom-series

Download Series Checklists, Family Trees, and Publication Schedules
www.MelissaFoster.com/reader-goodies

Love Audiobooks? I've got you covered
www.MelissaFoster.com/audio-books

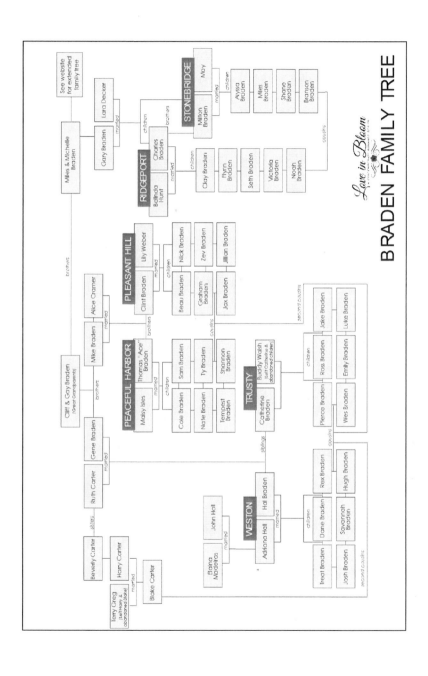

BRADEN FAMILY TREE

Chapter One

WEDDINGS WERE SUPPOSED to be joyful, bringing families together and celebrating the future on what should be the happiest day of a woman's life. But for Jordan Lawler they were bittersweet, making her long for the family she'd lost. She stood at the edge of the dance floor, trying to push that longing aside, just as she'd done nearly every day for nineteen years, and focused on enjoying the beautiful spring evening and the wedding reception of her close friend Trixie and Trixie's new husband, Nick.

She took in the glittering lights on the enormous barns and rustic wooden fences of their Pleasant Hill, Maryland, ranch. Lanterns dangled from tree limbs, and roses and wildflowers added a country touch to elegantly set tables. Trixie was a beautiful bride in a white strapless gown with exquisite pearl embellishments on the fitted bodice and a ruffled skirt that was long in the back and above the knee in the front, showing off her gorgeous legs and cowgirl boots. Her burly husband was equally handsome in dark dress slacks, a matching vest, and his ever-present cowboy hat. Jordan watched them chatting with two of Trixie's brothers and a handful of Nick's siblings and their parents. She had been introduced to so many Bradens and

Jerichos tonight, it was hard to keep them all straight. Nick reached for Trixie's hand, pulling her close with so much love in his eyes, Jordan was sure everyone around them felt it.

She looked away from the painful reminder of what she would never have with her fiancé.

"A beautiful woman like you shouldn't be standing on the sidelines."

Jax Braden's voice coasted over her shoulder, as rich and enticing as dark, decadent silk, bringing rise to goose bumps and wild flutters in her chest. Jordan had seen Nick's younger brother, a famed wedding gown designer, only once before the wedding. That was eight months ago, when, on Trixie's suggestion, she had met with Jax to discuss having him design her wedding gown. Jordan had left that meeting weak-kneed, with a heart-thrumming crush on a man she barely knew.

She'd postponed her wedding for a fourth time later that day.

She thought she was over the attraction to Jax and had finally chosen a firm wedding date, but as Jax stepped in front of her, her heart raced, and she wondered how she could escape before her legs stopped working. But she couldn't even look away from the tall, lean, and supremely beautiful man who looked at her like nobody else ever had, with reverence, curiosity, and whispers of *trust me* and *kiss me*.

She was in big trouble.

"Where's the lucky man who put that ring on your finger?"

The same place he is every time we have plans and he breaks them at the last minute. "He got tied up at work and couldn't make it." She'd moved back to her hometown of Prairie View, Maryland after college, while her fiancé, Todd Karns, had moved to New York to start his career.

Jax's brows knitted, and a sexy smile curved his lips. "His loss is my gain. Shall we?" He put a hand on her back, eyeing the dance floor.

"Actually, I was just getting ready to leave."

"And waste that Hervé Léger dress? Not a chance, sweetheart."

As he guided her onto the dance floor, she tried to calm the thrills scampering through her. Her fiancé rarely noticed what she wore, much less cared who made it. Jax drew her into his arms, gazing into her eyes as they slow danced. His alluring masculine scent of danger and sweetness enveloped her, making her even more nervous.

He held her tighter. "Now that you can't get away, we can talk."

"Is that what this is? A trap?" That shouldn't be so tantalizing, but she always felt like she was clawing for time with Todd, so she soaked in Jax's attention.

"Most definitely," he said coyly, their bodies moving in perfect sync. "How have you been? How were your holidays?"

How do you tell someone that the holidays had lost their magic decades ago? "Okay. You?"

"The holidays are always big, fun events with my family, but this year my older brother Zev and his childhood sweetheart, Carly, got married, which made it an extra-special celebration. But to be honest, I've been a little off my game for a while. You see, this incredible woman came into my office to discuss her wedding gown, and I haven't been able to stop thinking about her."

A pang of jealousy moved through her. "*Uh-oh.* Did she marry someone else?"

He lifted her left hand from his shoulder and glanced at her engagement ring. "Not yet."

She was stunned speechless.

"I was shocked, too. Nobody has ever had that effect on me. But what can I say? You're unforgettable."

Her heart stumbled, and she stilled. *"Jax…?"*

He held her tight against him, helping her sway to the beat. "Don't worry, sweetheart. I'm not going to try to steal you away from your man. But life's too short to hold the important things in. I didn't know if I'd ever see you again, and now here you are, like a gift." He leaned closer, lowering his voice. "I haven't been able to take my eyes off you since you walked in."

His honesty nearly bowled her over. Nobody had ever said such sweet and meaningful things to her. She opened her mouth to speak, but no words came.

"I didn't mean to make you nervous. I just want you to know how you affected me."

"I…" *You had the same effect on me.* "I don't know what to say."

"You don't have to say anything."

They danced in silence for a minute, and she tried to process all that he'd said. Her mind spun, but it was her heart that had her holding him tighter. The song ended, but they continued dancing into the next song.

"Who did you hire to make your gown?"

She blinked several times, trying to clear her head. "I didn't hire anyone. I postponed the wedding."

"Really?" A devilish glimmer sparked in his eyes. "You were hung up on me, too, weren't you?"

He twirled her so unexpectedly, nervous laughter bubbled out, and when he drew her into his arms, his smiling lips were a whisper away. She wondered what it would be like to kiss him.

"Go on, *Jordy*, admit it. You had Jax on the brain."

"Jordy?" She couldn't stifle her amusement, but it came with a warm and slightly painful memory of her childhood nickname.

He arched a brow. "Be honest. How many cold showers did you have to take after we met?"

She gasped, but she was grinning like a fool. "Would you *stop*?"

"Sorry. I'm just having fun with you."

And I'm liking it way too much. He'd been just as charming and funny during their initial meeting, but he hadn't flirted with her. He hadn't had to. The air between them had been electrified, and the way he'd looked at her had turned her inside out.

"You're obviously still engaged, so why did you call off your wedding?"

Because I couldn't stop thinking about you. "Scheduling issues. My fiancé is a portfolio manager for RZS Wealth Management in Manhattan. He works all the time, and it's hard for him to get away."

"Sounds like an impressive job." He leaned closer, his scruff tickling her cheek as his husky voice rolled into her ear. "If you were mine, I'd never put work ahead of spending time with you."

Now she was all fluttery and nervous again. "I thought you weren't trying to steal me away from my fiancé."

"I was just stating a fact. It's not like I challenged him to a duel at midnight."

Another song began, and he continued holding her. "Have a drink with me."

She wanted to say yes more than she wanted her next

breath, but she didn't want to lead him—or herself—on. "I can't. I have to go."

He held her gaze. "Have to, or want to?"

"Does it matter?" came out before she could think to stop it.

"Yes, what you want matters."

It had been so long since anyone had made her feel like what she wanted was important, it took all her willpower to skip over his question and say, "Thank you for the dance, Jax." She stepped out of his arms, but he caught her hand, his piercing dark eyes rooting her in place.

"Come by my studio tomorrow at three. Let me make your dress for you."

"Jax…"

He stepped closer, still holding her hand. "Please let me do this for you. I promise I won't do anything inappropriate."

What did it say about her that she was a little disappointed by that? "But the wedding is less than three months away. There's not enough time to design and make a gown."

"I'll make it happen."

"But you don't see clients on Sundays. Or at least you didn't when I made my initial appointment."

"For you I do. Three o'clock?"

She was breathing so hard, it was difficult to think, but the din of the wedding broke through. "Your relatives are in town. Don't you want to spend time with them?"

"I will. We're all having brunch tomorrow before they take off." He gently pulled her closer, making her pulse quicken again. "Say yes, Jordan."

I can't hung on the tip of her tongue, but "Yes" came out, and she silently chided herself. "But *no* flirting."

A slow smile spread across his handsome face. "You're the

boss. Let me walk you to your car."

"*No*" flew from her lips. "Sorry. I'm just…I'm late for something. I'll see you tomorrow."

"I'm looking forward to it." He leaned in and pressed a tender kiss to her cheek.

Her heart thundered as she hurried away, wondering if she was making the biggest mistake of her life.

LETTING JORDAN WALK away was the toughest thing he had ever done. From the moment he'd first set eyes on her, the intensity of their connection had been inescapable, and he'd have bet she'd felt it too when she'd cut their initial meeting short and had flown out of his office like a frightened bird. He had plenty of beautiful women at his beck and call, but there was something about Jordan that made him want to know her in ways he'd never taken the time to know other women. It was much deeper than physical, although she was stunning, with delicate features, a slightly upturned nose, long blond hair he'd like to tangle his hands in as she lay beneath him, and gorgeous legs he wanted to feel wrapped around him as he loved those frightened shadows she thought she hid so well out of her beautiful blue eyes.

He watched her talking with Nick and Trixie and caught a narrow-eyed glare from Nick. Jax gritted his teeth, holding his brother's stare.

Nick was one of only two people he'd told about being so taken with a bride-to-be that he hadn't been able to concentrate. The other person was his petite, burgundy-haired twin,

Jillian, who was stalking toward him with an incredulous look on her face. He steeled himself for an onslaught of questions and turned away, catching sight of his older brothers Beau and Zev and their wives, Char and Carly, fawning over their cousin Tempest's new baby girl, Penina Jane, who they called PJ, after Tempest's husband Nash's late brother. Their little boy, Phillip, was dancing with Jax's mother. Beau and Zev had also suffered a loss that had affected their whole family for a long time, and it was good to finally see them happy again.

Jillian stepped into his line of sight, glowering. "Oh my *God*, Jax."

"What?" She was as pushy as he was laid-back. When they were younger, she could rile him up like no one else ever could, but he'd learned that if he remained calm, eventually she'd back down.

"Don't *what* me. I saw you dancing with Jordan, and *holy frick*. I'm surprised the dance floor didn't go up in flames."

Good to know he wasn't the only one who'd felt it.

"I've never seen you look at anyone the way you looked at her. It's Jordan, isn't it?" she whispered harshly. "*She's* the one that's had you tied in knots so badly you almost missed a deadline. How did I not know this?" She paced, brow furrowed. "You know her wedding is back *on*, right?" She froze, eyes widening. "Are *you* the reason she postponed it in the first place?"

I wish. "If I were, do you think her wedding would be back on?"

She sighed. "I guess not, but, *Jax*, what are you doing?"

"I'm trying to enjoy my brother's wedding."

"Yeah? Well, *that* brother looks like he's ready to kill you."

Nick, their largest and gruffest brother, was striding toward them, his serious dark eyes locked on Jax. "Stay here," Nick growled at Jillian as he grabbed Jax's arm, pulling him a few feet away.

Jillian scoffed and stomped over to them. "I'm *not* missing this."

Nick ignored her, his angry eyes boring into Jax. "I saw you dancing with Jordan, and she was all flustered when she left. Tell me you didn't proposition her."

"Back off, Nick. Of course I didn't, and this is none of your business."

"She's Trixie's friend, which makes it my business," Nick barked. "If you didn't proposition her, then what did you say that got her all wound up? Jesus, Jax. Didn't you see that rock on her finger?"

He'd seen the damn rock. It was a fucking solitaire, about as common as rings could get. She deserved a one-of-a-kind stunning creation made just for her.

"He knows she's engaged," Jillian snapped. "She came to him for a wedding gown last summer."

Nick's eyes narrowed, and Jax saw understanding dawning on him. "Aw, hell, Jax. Seriously? It's *her*?"

"Relax. I just offered to make her dress."

"Make it, or take it off?" Nick challenged.

Jax threw his shoulders back, stepping closer. "What kind of asshole do you think I am?"

"I don't think you're an asshole," Nick gritted out. "But you're a Braden, and we stop at nothing to get what we want."

When it comes to Jordan, truer words have never been spoken.

"Okay, *down*, boys." Jillian stepped between them, pushing them apart, and looked up at Nick. "You know he'd never cross that line." She turned a thoughtful gaze on Jax. "It's too bad she's engaged. I think her fiancé is a bit of a jerk, and you'd be cute together."

Nick glared at her. "*Don't* encourage him."

"Don't bark at me," Jillian snapped. "I've spent months working my matchmaking magic behind the scenes and talking him up to all of Trixie's single girlfriends, some of whom will be at the bachelor auction." She had talked Jax into taking part in a charity bachelor auction next month. "But he didn't give *any* of them a second look, so put that snarl away and let me talk to him." She huffed out a breath. "As I was saying, Jax, you'd be cute together, but Jordan *is* taken, and considering how she's made you all *gaga* over her, and you lost your freaking mind for all these months, making her dress might not be the best idea. Why don't you let me make it?"

Jillian was a phenomenal fashion designer, but she specialized in dresses, not wedding gowns, and her style was far more outlandish than Jax's. "No. I want to do this for her."

"I don't know, man." Nick's jaw clenched. "I saw the way you were looking at her when you two were dancing."

"He's right," Jillian said. "Tempting fate might not be a good idea. What are you thinking?"

That she should be mine. "That I'll take every minute I can get with her until she walks down that aisle."

Chapter Two

JORDAN CALLED TODD on her way out the door Sunday afternoon and tried her best not to sound annoyed when the call when straight to voicemail for the fourth time since she'd left the wedding last night. "Hey. It's me again. I'm about to meet with the designer about my dress, and I was really hoping to get your input. I know you're busy, but please call if you get a chance."

She put her Kate Spade tote bag on the passenger seat and drove to Jax's studio in Pleasant Hill, the next town over. She'd spent all day thinking about the things Jax had said to her and how it had felt to be in his arms, to be *wanted* instead of made to feel like an imposition. As she drove, she found herself trying to remember if Todd had ever said the type of sweet things Jax had said to her or the last time he'd made time for her spur-of-the-moment, as Jax had. But after coming up empty, she stopped comparing them, because it wasn't fair. She'd been with Todd for seven years and had probably forgotten those moments. Wasn't it normal for couples to cool off and take each other for granted after so many years together?

She pushed those thoughts away, focusing on the pastures and spring flowers lining the road as she drove out of Prairie

View and into Pleasant Hill. Pleasant Hill was a charming, upscale small town with tall buildings, fancy shops, brick-paved sidewalks lined with flowering trees, and cute wooden benches on every corner. She parked behind Jax's studio, noticing his shiny black Lexus in a reserved spot.

A classy car for a classy man.

Butterflies swarmed in her belly. She'd talked herself in and out of showing up today about a hundred times, but she kept coming back to how happy she'd been last night. Despite her nervousness, she'd had more fun in the short amount of time they'd spent dancing than she'd had in years. And didn't that just tell her something she wasn't ready to admit to herself? But she deserved a little joy, even if he gave her butterflies, didn't she? They were both adults, and they'd already set boundaries. She trusted herself and Jax not to cross them.

She glanced in the rearview mirror, her nerves flaring as she gave herself a quick once-over. She'd changed her clothes several times and had finally settled on her favorite skinny jeans and Jimmy Choo Metz Charm 100 sandals, a white boatneck shirt, and a white blazer, which she pushed up to her elbows. She'd worn dangling silver earrings to match the charms on her sandals and had pinned her hair back in a low ponytail, leaving a few wispy bangs framing her face with the hopes of covering the thin white scar above her right eyebrow. She'd gone easy on the makeup, except for the pop of red lipstick that matched her nail polish. She hadn't worn red lipstick in a long time because Todd thought it was too racy. It felt good to wear it, like she'd rediscovered a piece of herself she'd been ignoring.

Satisfied that she looked chic but not overdone, she grabbed her tote bag. She'd brought her own wedding gown designs, but now she felt a little silly. Jax was a world-renowned designer, and she was just a girl with a love of all things fashion who had never finished her fashion degree. But if she was going to have a gown designed, shouldn't it at least include some of the elements she wanted? She felt a familiar knot in her stomach. It had been there a lot lately when she thought about marrying Todd. But she didn't have time to get lost in those confusing thoughts right now.

With a deep breath, she climbed out of her car and headed around the building, which was surrounded by the most glorious gardens. Jax's studio was directly across the street from a beautiful park in the center of town. Even from the outside, it looked like a diamond among gemstones, with a rich, green storefront that was so dark it bordered on black, giving it an elegant feel, with JAX BRADEN DESIGNS in large, simple gold letters over expansive, paned windows, through which she could see the leather chairs in the lobby. The first time they'd met she'd seen only the lobby and his office, both outfitted with dark wood and sumptuously soft gray leather. She was curious about the rest of his studio. What did his work area look like? Everything about him seemed a step above the rest, and she'd been as taken with his offices as she'd been with the man himself.

The studio door opened, and Jax stood before her, striking in a fitted white dress shirt, windowpane-plaid gray slacks, and black dress shoes. Their eyes connected with such magnificent force, she swore the temperature spiked by fifty degrees.

"Good afternoon, Ms. Lawler."

"Hello, Mr. Braden."

"Won't you come in?" His gaze swept appreciatively down the length of her, and as she walked inside, he said, "Killer outfit."

"Thanks. Fashion is my guilty pleasure."

He closed and locked the door, making her heart race. "I'd like to be *your* guilty pleasure."

Her cheeks burned. *Holy cow.* "*Jax*, you said you wouldn't flirt."

"I'm not flirting. I was merely stating a fact." He closed the distance between them and took her hand. "If I were going to flirt"—he kissed the back of her hand—"I'd say something far less brash."

She wanted to know what he'd say, but that was a road that she had a feeling would lead to trouble, so she didn't dare ask. "Then we need another rule. No more stating facts."

He laughed. "Okay. Lies it is. But for the record, I despise lies more than anything in the world."

"So do I," she said softly, mentally noting another thing they had in common.

"I like a woman who appreciates honesty *and* the finer things in life."

"I'm really not materialistic."

"As noted by the fact that you were willing to buy your wedding gown off the rack."

He didn't miss a thing, did he? "Yes, well, I didn't expect you or any other designer to have time to make a dress. But for the record, I don't buy nice clothes or accessories to be flashy. I do it because I feel good when I wear them. For *me*, not for anyone else."

"Not even for your fiancé?"

"Todd's too busy to notice anything like that."

"I hope you mean he doesn't recognize brands and not that he doesn't notice you."

"No, I mean all of it. He doesn't often notice what I wear."

Jax's jaw tightened, his brow furrowing. "It would be a sin to be with a woman as beautiful as you and not notice every little thing about her. It's one thing not to know brand names, but to miss that you took the time to pair the perfect earrings with your heels, or your nails to your lips? That would be as much of a crime as missing the scar above your right eyebrow."

Shocked, she reached up and touched the wisps of hair she'd thought had covered it.

"I noticed it the first time we met. You shouldn't cover it up. Scars tell a story, and I'd like to hear yours sometime. Can I get you something to drink?"

She was still stuck on him noticing her scar. "No, thank you."

"Why don't we sit down and talk?" He put a hand on her lower back again, sending a tingling sensation through her as he guided her down the hall, passing what looked like a fitting room. "You can tell me all about your *guilty pleasures*."

"Jax." She laughed softly.

"I was talking about your love of fashion." With a wicked glint in his eyes, he said, "But if you'd like to share your other guilty pleasures, I'd most definitely like to hear them."

"Do you talk like that to all your clients?"

"Absolutely not."

She tried to calm her racing heart and caught sight of what looked like a showroom at the end of the hall as they entered his office, which was even more luxurious and welcoming than she remembered, with a high coffered ceiling, light bamboo floors, and warm, textured gray-blue walls with white accents, complementing the elaborately carved dark wooden desk and shelves. A gray leather sofa and two matching armchairs created an inviting nook in front of the nearly floor-to-ceiling windows overlooking magnificent gardens. The last time she was there, she'd seen a single framed photograph of his family on his desk. Now it was gone, and a new one stood in its place.

"I like your new picture. You have a beautiful family."

"Thanks. We take one every Christmas. Did you meet everyone last night?"

He picked up the picture, and she looked more closely at it. His parents, Clint and Lily, were standing arm in arm, his mother's head resting on his father's shoulder. The men were tall and handsome, like their father, and Jillian was petite and beautiful, like their mother. Trixie and Nick stood with their arms around each other, bright smiles on their faces. His other brothers were with attractive women who she assumed were their wives. But her gaze was drawn to Jax. He stood out from the others. He had his father's smile, his mother's kind eyes, and he exuded a certain confidence and surety that set him apart. Some of his brothers' eyes weren't quite as unfettered as his, and she wondered about that. But there was so much love in the picture, it felt tangible.

"I met so many people, I'm sure I did, but I don't know if I remember everyone's names. I know Jillian and Nick, of course, because of Trixie, and I met your parents, who seem wonderful." When she'd met them at the wedding, they'd embraced her so warmly, she'd wanted to remain in their arms and soak in their comfort. "I'm sorry, but I don't remember the others' names. Where do you fall in the lineup?"

"That's okay. There are a lot of us, and we had a lot of cousins in for the wedding. This is my oldest brother, Beau, and his wife, Char. They run an inn in Colorado and live there for half of the year. Nick is next in line. Then comes Zev. This is him and his wife, Carly." He pointed to the shaggy-haired man who had his arm around a cute blonde. "They're the ones who were married over Christmas. They're treasure hunters, and Carly also owns a chocolate shop in Colorado."

"*Real* treasure hunters?"

"Yes, believe it or not." His brow knitted, but just as quickly that tension eased. "They recently discovered the remains of a pirate ship off the shores of Silver Island."

"Wow, that's amazing."

"Yeah, it's pretty wild." He paused, as if he were thinking about what he'd said. "Jilly and I are next in line, and we're twins."

"I never would have guessed you were twins. Other than being designers, you seem quite different."

"Tell me about it. She's a firecracker, and I'm more like a steady flame."

"More like a raging inferno." As the words left her lips, she realized she'd said it aloud and snapped her mouth closed.

He chuckled and pointed to a younger version of Beau, standing behind a hippyish blonde with his arms around her middle. "Graham is the youngest, and this is his wife, Morgyn. Graham runs an investment company that specializes in eco-friendly businesses, and Morgyn is an artist. She recycles old things and makes them into art, clothing, and jewelry. She's really talented. They have a tree house here and a tiny house in Oak Falls, Virginia, but they travel a lot."

"A tree house? Like *Swiss Family Robinson*?"

"Something like that, only nicer." His smile reached his eyes, and boy did she like it. "I'll show it to you sometime. It's spectacular." He set down the picture and motioned toward the couch.

She set her bag on the floor by her feet as they sat down. "It sounds like you're all talented. Are you close with everyone? Now I see why you said holidays are always fun."

"We're all pretty tight, and holidays are wonderful, but it wasn't always that way."

"Why? Didn't you get along?"

His brows knitted. "We've always gotten along great. But Beau's long-term girlfriend, Tory, was killed in a car accident many years ago. We'd all grown up together. She was Carly's best friend, and she was like a sister to the rest of us. Beau and Zev had been out drinking that night, and Beau never heard her call for a ride home from the airport. As you can imagine, he was devastated, and Zev felt guilty. Zev quit college and broke up with Carly, and he and Beau took off right after the funeral. They were like the wind for more than a decade, working, traveling, and rarely coming home. We never knew when we'd see them again."

Her heart broke for his family. "That's awful. Seeing you guys at the wedding, I never would have imagined they, or the rest of your family, had suffered in so many ways. How did they heal and move on from that?"

"Char's love for Beau brought him back to life, and Zev…" He shook his head. "He never stopped loving Carly, and I guess when he saw her at Beau's wedding, that was it for him. He was determined to win her back. We spent so many holidays missing pieces of our family, now we treasure every day we get together."

Tears burned her eyes, and she blinked them dry, willing them not to fall. She hadn't cried in so long, she didn't know where the emotions were coming from. "As you should."

"But that's enough about my family. Tell me about yours. You didn't go into detail last night. Were you with your family over the holidays?"

"I was in New York with Todd. His family has a Christmas party every year. It's kind of a work thing. His father is also in finance, and they host a few hundred people. Todd invites his clients, and they spin deals over drinks. It's one of their most profitable gatherings."

His brows knitted again. "Did they have a separate family celebration?"

"No. His parents always leave right after the party and go to Cabo for Christmas."

"That's *different*. Did you do all the fun Big Apple holiday must-dos? See the Christmas tree at Rockefeller Center, go ice-skating, take a romantic carriage ride through the park?"

She shook her head. "I've never done any of those things."

"Really? Is your family in the city? Did you get to see them?"

"No. Todd and I celebrated together, and then I went to my aunt and uncle's in Ridgeport, Massachusetts."

"I have relatives in Ridgeport. It's a nice town. Todd didn't go with you?"

"No. He usually spends Christmas working on the deals he negotiated the night before, so I go by myself."

Jax's jaw tightened. "Excuse me for saying this, but holidays should be about love and family and building traditions that have nothing to do with business."

"It's okay. We've been together since we were in college, and I know how hard he's worked to get where he is. He got a promotion last year that requires more of his time and attention." The rationalization came so easily, she barely noticed she did it anymore. But Jax's thoughts on holidays were so different from Todd's, it magnified what she was missing.

19

"That's noble of you to understand, but no woman should come second to anything in her man's life, especially over the holidays."

Jax looked like he wanted to throttle Todd and take *her* in his arms, and that made her feel vulnerable, which she never allowed herself to feel. She sat up a little straighter, reminding herself that she didn't need to be taken care of.

"You didn't mention the rest of your family. Did they meet you at your aunt and uncle's?"

"They are my family. They're all I have left."

He put his hand over hers, holding it tight. "I'm so sorry. When did you lose your parents?"

"They were killed in a car accident when I was nine."

"You were so young," he said softly, eyes full of pain.

"It's okay. My aunt and uncle raised me after I lost them, and they were good to me."

He moved closer, and her pulse quickened. "It's not okay, Jordan. Losing your parents is never okay, no matter how old you are, unless they were harmful to you."

"They weren't. They were wonderful."

"Then you must have good memories of them."

So many memories. She nodded, trying to swallow past the lump in her throat.

"You must miss them terribly, especially during the holidays."

She lowered her eyes to try to keep her emotions in check. "I do. And my little sister, too." The admission surprised her. She rarely talked about her family and had learned never to mention her sister.

"Aw, *babe*. You lost her as well?"

She nodded, and when she met his gaze, the torture in his

20

eyes was so different from the annoyed expressions Todd wore when she talked about her family, it nearly drew tears. Not that she talked about them much anymore, but Jax's emotions were so genuine and raw, they loosened the chains keeping hers at bay.

"I am so sorry, Jordan. I know how devastating it was when Tory died. It affected everyone who knew her. I can't imagine how it would feel if it were my parents and sibling."

Her tears sprang free, and she turned away, wiping her eyes. "I'm sorry."

"Don't be." He drew her into his arms and put a hand on the back of her head. "It's okay to cry."

She tried to stop her tears, feeling weak and embarrassed, but at the same time, he felt safe, and he was so kind to her, she wanted to stay right there and give in to the sadness she repressed so often. He didn't just share his mother's warm embrace. His was warmer and so powerfully reassuring, the way he cradled the back of her head with one hand, keeping her close with the other, the steady beat of his heart against her chest calming the frantic pace of her own.

But embarrassment won out, and she sat back, wiping her eyes. "I'm sorry. I don't know where all of that came from."

JAX WAS BEGINNING to understand the shadows he'd seen in Jordan's eyes, and it crushed him. She obviously wasn't used to others accepting her sadness, and knowing how she'd spent Christmas, he didn't have to look far to figure out who'd caused that. He bit back the things he wanted to say about the man who sure as hell didn't deserve her. *He* wasn't Jax's concern, but this incredible woman was, and his protective urges surged.

He gazed into her sad eyes and brushed a tear from her cheek. "It came from your heart, and matters of the heart should never be withheld or apologized for." He gave her hand a reassuring squeeze before going to his desk to retrieve a handkerchief. He handed it to her as he lowered himself to the couch.

"I have tissues." She reached for her bag so quickly, he knew she wasn't used to being taken care of in this way, either, and wondered if that was because of her fiancé, or if this was her own resilience shining through.

He touched her hand. "Use mine."

She sighed, her shoulders dropping. "Thank you." She dabbed at her eyes.

"You don't have to tell me how you lost your family, but I'm here if or when you want to talk about it."

"Jax, I came to talk about a wedding dress, not cry on your shoulder."

"In order to design your gown, I have to know who you are, how you think, what you want and why, and I can tell from what you've already told me that your family plays a big part in who you are. So please don't be embarrassed for being sad. My shoulders are good for a lot of things, and crying on is one of them." He was afraid she might try to leave, and he wasn't ready for their time together to end. "I have an idea."

He rose to his feet and reached for her hand. She looked at him curiously as she took it, and he helped her up. "Do you have any food allergies?"

"No. Why?"

"Because you're in for a treat." He kept a hold of her hand

and headed out of his office, earning the smile that was both cute and sexy and had been in the forefront of his mind for months. She had bright white, straight teeth, save for the tooth to the right of her two front teeth, which was crooked, and that uniqueness made her even more attractive.

"*Jax*," she said with a laugh as they walked outside, and he locked the door behind them. "Where are we going?"

"Emmaline's."

"I *love* Emmaline's."

They headed down the street and into the café, greeted by the savory scents of fresh-roasted coffee and warm baked goods. Emmaline's could put anyone in a good mood, with yellow walls boasting beautiful paintings from local artists and an enormous chalkboard announcing today's specialty coffees in pink, desserts in green, and bright yellow starbursts with inspirational sayings like *Share your smile. It's free and contagious!* and *Create a life you love!* Customers sat at round tables on the first floor, and toward the back of the café, a spiral staircase led to a loft with additional seating.

Several women were checking Jax out. He put a hand on Jordan's back to ward off the oglers and stepped into line behind a customer Emmaline O'Connor, a vivacious brunette, was ringing up. Jordan peered into the pastry display cases, her eyes dancing with delight, and *man*, he liked that look on her.

"Which one are you thinking about?" Jax asked.

"An easier question is which ones I'm *not* thinking about. I have a mouth full of sweet teeth. What's your favorite?"

You. A slow grin spread across his face.

She tilted her head, eyes still gleaming. "Do you *ever* turn the charm off?"

"Apparently not around you."

"You are a *major* flirt," she said as they stepped up to the counter.

"You must have Jax confused with someone else." Emmaline winked at him and lowered her voice. "He doesn't need to flirt. Panties magically melt when he walks into a room."

Jax chuckled, and Jordan rolled her eyes.

"See for yourself." Emmaline lifted her chin in the direction of a table of three women who were eyeing him up.

Jordan followed her gaze, then set a coy smirk on Jax. "I can invite them to sit with us, if you'd like."

He added that snark to the growing list of things he liked about her. "I'd much rather give you my undivided attention." Acutely aware of Emmaline listening to their conversation, he added, "So we can discuss your wedding gown without interruption. I was thinking we'd take a walk after we get our order. How does that sound?"

That smirk turned into a sweet smile. "That sounds nice."

"What can I get you guys?" Emmaline asked.

Jax arched a brow at Jordan. "Do you trust me?"

"That's a loaded question. *Sure.*"

"We'll take two of my special lattes and two almond croissants to go."

"Your *special* lattes?" Jordan asked. "What's in them?"

"A gentleman never tells."

She looked at Emmaline, but Emmaline shook her head. "Sorry, Jordan, but I've been sworn to secrecy."

As Emmaline went to make their drinks, Jordan said, "Do all women do as you ask?"

"Talk about a loaded question."

"I don't think I've ever met anyone quite like you, Mr. Braden." Her brows knitted, and she studied him for a moment.

"Why didn't you bring a date to the wedding?"

"I told you I've been off my game lately."

Emmaline returned with their order. They paid, and Jordan took a sip of her latte as they headed outside.

"*Mm.* This is delicious." She took another sip. "Is that chocolate and coconut? Caramel? Baileys? What am I tasting?"

He remained silent as they headed down the sidewalk and into the park.

"You're really not going to tell me?"

"Sorry, sweetheart, but some things are sweeter when left up to the imagination." They followed the path until they came to a bench and sat down to eat their croissants, which were covered in powdered sugar.

He handed Jordan a napkin, and she spread it over her lap at the same time he spread one over his. "Finally, someone who won't roll their eyes at me."

"I roll my eyes plenty at you." She broke off a piece of the croissant and popped it into her mouth. "But my dad taught me the value of taking care of nice things when I was young."

"I'd like to hear about your family and where you grew up. Unless you'd rather not share."

Her brows knitted. "I don't talk about them often, but this is a good memory. I grew up in Prairie View, and when I was little, I *loved* fancy dresses. The fancier the better, and I'd wear them everywhere, even to the park."

"A true fashionista."

"That's what my dad called me. His little fashionista. He would troll eBay looking for fancy dresses, and the two of us would spend hours hunting down yard sales on the weekends. I loved doing it with him." She ate as she spoke, her expression thoughtful.

"I think I would have liked your father."

Her eyes lit up. "You couldn't help but love him. He was a great dad, and he didn't mind that I wore those dresses out to play, because he believed kids should be kids. But he had rules. It was my responsibility to take care of them. He taught me tricks, like covering my lap when I ate, and—don't laugh—tucking a napkin into my collar to protect the front of my dresses when I was eating something especially messy, like ice cream. I must have looked ridiculous to other kids, but the only thing I cared about was that my *dad*, a rough and tough construction worker, had found me pretty things to wear."

"I don't think there's anything quite like the relationships we have with our folks."

"I agree. I loved him so much, and he adored us." Her eyes were glassy, but she didn't slow down. "He used to do things for my mom that didn't mean much to me back then, but now I see how special they were. Like after it snowed, he'd shovel the driveway and clean off her car before he left for work in the mornings, and he'd call her every day at four o'clock to see if she needed him to bring home anything for dinner or for us. My sister and I used to run to answer the call, and my mom would light up when she spoke to him."

Jax felt her missing them like a thickness in the air. "What was his name?"

"Craig."

"And your mom? What was her name? What was she like?"

"Her name was Sara, and I look just like her. She was soft spoken, but she was like a bright light, always telling us that we could do or be anything. She was hope personified, and she called us her little doves, because doves are a symbol of hope. She never yelled. If we did something bad, she'd press her lips together and shake her head, like this." She pressed her lips into a hard line, and her brow furrowed as she shook her head. "I can still hear her saying, 'Please don't do that.'"

"Did you listen?"

Jordan shrugged, smiling. "Probably sometimes. She's the reason I love fashion. She used to pore through fashion magazines. She loved looking at them and sketching designs, but wearing fancy clothes wasn't her thing. She liked pretty clothes, but not fancy. But she was really talented. I have all of her old sketchbooks."

Jax had so many questions, but he loved her enthusiasm, and he didn't want to interrupt her.

"She used to sing us to sleep, too."

"Did she sing a special song?"

"Yes. 'My Girl' by the Temptations, and she had the prettiest voice. My dad called her his angel. They were high school sweethearts, born on the same day, believe it or not."

Sadness rose in her eyes, and he knew she was thinking that they'd also died on the same day. "What about your sister? What was she like?"

"Casey," she said wistfully. "She's five years younger than me, with golden-brown hair that was always tousled and a little frizzy. We're total opposites. She was always tough, and I'm more of a girly girl. She hated dresses as much as I loved them, but she liked to pick out pretty outfits for *me* to wear. She wanted to be just like our dad, and she wore sweats or leggings, T-shirts and flannels, and work boots. My dad loved that about her. She was *always* getting dirty, running through puddles or digging in the dirt. I'd be twirling in the grass in my princess dress, and she'd be making a mud castle." Her expression softened. "She's still out there. I can feel it."

Jax's heart ached for her. He set his food and drink aside and moved closer, putting his arm around her. "I'm sure your parents are watching over you, too."

"I know they are, but it's more than that. I want to tell you something, but I've learned that some things can make people look at you differently, and I don't want that to happen."

"Your secrets are safe with me, whatever they are."

"I believe you." She seemed to think about that for a second. "Casey wasn't killed in the accident. She's missing."

"I don't understand."

"She was in the car with my parents when they were killed. They were on their way to pick me up from camp, driving through back roads in West Virginia. It was raining, and I don't know why, but the car veered off the road and hit a tree. When the rescuers found them, my parents were dead and my sister was gone. It's like she vanished into thin air."

Holy hell. "They must have searched for her."

"They did, with dogs and everything. But they never found a trace."

"Jesus." It made him sick to think about anything happening to a child, but for Jordan to lose her entire family in such a devastating way was almost too much to take. "She was four?"

Jordan nodded. "Yeah."

"That's awful. How did you get through that?"

"I *couldn't* wrap my head around it. When my aunt and uncle picked me up from camp with the police, they told me what had happened, and I didn't believe them."

"Of course not. It's too much for a child to fathom."

"It really was, and everything after that is a blur of police, funerals, and endless crying. I had nightmares about my sister all alone in a cold, dark place. I slept in her bed after the accident, praying every night that they'd find her. Shortly after the funerals, I moved in with my aunt and uncle in Massachusetts, and they got me into therapy, and eventually they had to sell the house in Prairie View. The first couple of years were...I don't know. I looked for Casey in every little girl I saw. But after a while, the therapist and my relatives urged me to let it go. I don't talk about Casey with my aunt and uncle anymore, either. They just want what's best for me, and to them, that's letting Casey go."

"But you can't." Lord knew he wouldn't be able to.

She shook her head. "She's my sister. How do you just turn off those feelings when you've had no closure?"

"You don't. Did your aunt and uncle hire a private investigator?"

"They worked with a detective for a long time, but there weren't even any clues. There were a lot of different theories about what happened to her. Everything from alien abduction to being picked up by sex traffickers or being holed up in some crazy person's basement."

"Don't think like that. What about your fiancé or his family? It sounds like they have the means to hire someone to search for her. Have they tried?"

"I would never ask that of them," she said softly. "Todd thinks I need to let it go and accept the very real possibility that she's gone. But I can't. I think I'd feel it. I'd *know*, and I can't shake the feeling that she's still out there somewhere. That's why I went to college in Maryland and moved back to Prairie View right after graduation. I know if Casey is out there, the chances of her remembering anything about me or our lives here is slim. But if she *is* alive and somehow finds her way back to Prairie View, I want to be there waiting. That's one of the reasons I put off my wedding so many times."

"Because Todd doesn't support your belief that she's alive?"

"Partially, yes. We also agreed that I would move to New York after the wedding, and I just don't know if I can do that."

Why would he want her to? What kind of man disregarded the emotions of the person he loved? "But your wedding is back on. Jordan, I'm sorry for asking, but why are you marrying this guy if he doesn't support your beliefs?"

"Because maybe he's right and I need to move on with my life. Maybe I'm the reason he works so much, because Casey takes up a lot of space in my head and in my heart, and it's probably not fair to expect him to accept that."

"You shouldn't have to choose one or the other."

"Maybe not, but maybe I should. We've been together so long, he knows what I've been through and he's stuck by me during some trying times. He protected me in college and helped me to make friends and fit in. I'd just come back to Maryland, and I was a little lost and alone. I knew not to talk about my sister, but that always made me feel different from other kids my age. He shielded me from situations that were overwhelming and made sure I never felt alone. When I wasn't sure which way to go with my education, he helped me figure that out, too. I know I've told you some things that probably seem unfair, like him not coming to see my family for Christmas, but we had a plan and that included his working hard to get ahead. *I'm* the one who's breaking our plan by wanting to stay here."

"But for good reasons, and true love has no timeline."

"But long-distance relationships are hard enough, and I've postponed our wedding *four* times. It's amazing he's still with me. I'm starting to wonder if I'm hurting our relationship by holding on to the hope that Casey is alive. Besides, I'm sure things will get better after we're married and I move to New York."

But what if they don't? "You just said you might not feel comfortable moving there."

"I know, but maybe it's time. You must think I'm crazy, postponing my wedding so many times and holding on to the hope of finding Casey after all these years."

"I absolutely do not think you're crazy." *But I think you're as confused about your relationship as I am.* "Casey is your sister, and if you don't hold on to hope, then who will?" He paused, letting his words sink in. "I think you have a lot of important decisions to make, and I'm a firm believer in following your heart and listening to your gut instincts, wherever they may lead you."

He gazed into her eyes, feeling her struggle and wanting to find out the truth about her sister to give her closure in whatever form it came in. He wanted to be there for her, to show her what it was like to truly be loved by a man. But he was getting in too deep, and he needed to break the spell he was under before he crossed a line he'd promised he wouldn't.

He withdrew his arm from around her, putting a little space between them. "*My* instincts are speaking very loudly right now, telling me it's time to enjoy our croissants and lattes and this beautiful afternoon."

"I like your instincts. They're far less confusing than mine."

If you only knew how wrong you were.

They kept their conversation lighter as they ate, discussing Nick and Trixie's wedding and how beautiful it had been. Jordan gushed about Trixie's wedding gown and how meaningful their vows were, and they both raved about the dinner and wedding cake. They laughed over silly things, and the more they talked, the more Jax wanted to know about her.

"You said you have a mouth full of sweet teeth, so what's your absolute favorite food?"

"Anything sugary. That croissant was delicious, but this is like heaven to me." She touched her finger to her tongue, then dabbed it into the pile of powdered sugar on the napkin in her lap and held it up to show him, before painting her lips with the sugar and licking it off with an adorably mischievous expression.

He wanted to kiss that sweetness off her lips. Heat slithered through him as he imagined her body painted with powdered sugar, tasting his way down her breasts and over her luscious curves, all the way down to her promised land, her long legs draped over his shoulders.

"What's yours?" she asked, snapping him from his fantasy.

"*My...?*" He tried to wrangle his desires into submission, but his mind was hung up on pleasuring her. He'd bet his life her inattentive fiancé couldn't please her the way he could.

"Your favorite food. Is it sweet or savory?"

"Both." *Because I know damn well that's how you'll taste.* He needed to move before he said or did something he shouldn't. "Let's take a walk. There's a lake just over that hill." He collected their trash and threw it in the garbage can.

They headed down the footpath, and he tried to get his mind off kissing her. "What's your favorite color?"

"Pale pink. What's yours?"

Like your Kate Spade bag. "It *was* steel blue, but pale pink just rose to the top of my list."

She bumped him with her shoulder. "No flirting, remember?"

"Right." As if he could help it.

"This is fun. It's been a long time since I've gotten to know someone like this. What's your favorite movie?"

"That's a hard one. I'm not sure." He knew damn well what it was, but it was too embarrassing to tell her. "What's yours?"

"That's easy. It's *50 First Dates*."

"The Adam Sandler movie? What do you like about it?"

"I love how he loves her. The way he makes every day special, and the newness never wears off. That's how I remember my parents' relationship."

He found it odd that a woman who wanted that kind of love was willing to play second fiddle to her fiancé's job and move away from the place where she longed to be.

She stopped walking to take in the lake in the distance. "That's beautiful."

He couldn't take his eyes off her. "Sure is."

She turned, catching him staring, but he didn't look away. Their gazes held so long, heat coiled around them, drawing them closer. He didn't think as he touched his fingertips to hers, whispering her name. Her lips parted with a sigh, and his heart told him to kiss her, but his head knew he shouldn't. Caught up in a maelstrom of right and wrong, he could do little more than stare at the woman he felt like he'd waited his whole life to meet. Her phone chimed, breaking their spell, and the air rushed from her lungs. She stumbled backward, and he put his hand protectively on her lower back as she pulled her phone out of her pocket. He saw Todd's name on the screen and knew he shouldn't look as she read the message, but he couldn't help it.

Sorry. I've been in and out of meetings all day. I'll call you later tonight.

Disappointment rose in her eyes, but she quickly masked it with a feigned smile as she slid her phone into her pocket.

"Wow, can you believe it's already after five? Where did the time go?"

"Time flies when you're in good company. What are you doing tonight?"

"I have a date with a bowl of cereal and the Fab Five."

"As much as I like the *Queer Eye* guys, we're breaking your date. Tonight you're having dinner with me, the Fab *One*." He guided her back the way they'd come.

"*Jax*, I've already wasted enough of your time."

"Spending time with you is not a waste. It's dress research. We'll talk about it over dinner. We just have to make one stop along the way."

"*Jax...?*"

"Save your breath, Jordan. One way or another, you're mine tonight. Do I have to put on the charm?"

"As if I'd stand a chance if you did?"

You don't stand a chance anyway. "Glad you agree."

Chapter Three

JORDAN PROBABLY SHOULD have refused Jax's dinner invitation, but she hadn't wanted their day together to end. She couldn't remember the last time she'd talked so openly about her family. It was cathartic, as if she'd finally allowed herself to expose a dirty secret that had been eating away at her. Only it wasn't a dirty secret. It was the most important thing she thought about day and night, and Jax had treated it as such. He hadn't tried to hurry her along or shut her down the way Todd or her aunt and uncle did.

She glanced at him as he turned off the main road, and the flutters in her chest that had stuck with her all day turned to something deeper. Sure, he was strikingly handsome, but that's not what she saw this time. She saw the caring man who encouraged her to hold on to her hope. The man who had looked gutted when he'd learned the truth about her family and had held her when she'd needed it, so different from what her life with Todd had become. But Jax had called her noble, and she wasn't. She was selfish for putting her hopes ahead of her relationship.

Jax glanced over as he turned down a residential street. "You okay?"

"Mm-hm." He pulled into the driveway of an enormous brick and stone manor-style house. "Whose house is this?"

"My parents'. I need to pick up my dog, Coco. It'll only take a few minutes. She usually stays with a nanny while I'm at work, but it's Sunday, so she got to be spoiled by Grandma and Grandpa instead."

"Your dog has a nanny?"

"Of course. Would you leave a two-year-old home alone?"

"We *are* talking about a dog, right?"

"Yes. But she gets lonely when she's home alone, and with Heidi, her nanny, she goes on walks, plays with other dogs, and gets lots of love."

Who was this man that worried about his dog being lonely? Todd was so busy at work, he didn't even know where Jordan was most of the time, much less asked if she got lonely. "I think it's great. I've just never heard of anyone having a nanny for their dog."

"That's because you don't live in a booming metropolis like the Big Apple or LA, where everyone's dog has a nanny. The way I see it, Coco will only live for ten to fifteen years, and it's my job to make sure every one of them is as good as it can be."

That makes you a little irresistible. She caught herself as the thought hit and added, *As a friend. Geez...* "What kind of dog is she?"

"An Australian retriever. Nick's golden retriever had a tryst with his neighbor's Australian shepherd, and Coco is from that litter."

He climbed out of the car and came around to open her door. As she took his hand and stepped out of the car, she said, "Coco is lucky to have you."

"Thanks, but I think it's the other way around." They headed up to the front door. "Do you have any pets?"

"No. I always wanted a dog. Even more so after losing my family because they symbolize hope. But my uncle was allergic, and Todd said it's too hard to have a dog in the city, so I never got one."

"I know plenty of people who have dogs in the city, but to each his own."

"Do you ever feel guilty for working long hours?"

As they climbed the front steps, he said, "I don't usually work many evenings or weekends, and I'm pretty sure once Coco meets you, she won't mind the exception."

He opened the front door, and as they walked in, Jordan's nerves prickled. What would his parents think about them going to dinner together? Just as the thought hit, an adorable fluffy tan and white dog bounded down the hallway.

"There's my girl." Jax scooped up his pooch, letting her lick his face. "Were you good for Grandma and Grandpa?"

"Jax, she's beautiful. Can I pet her?"

"Absolutely."

"Hi, sweetie." She nuzzled against Coco's fur, enjoying her puppy kisses. "No wonder your daddy spoils you. You're the cutest girl around."

"Did I hear someone call my granddog spoiled?" his mother asked as she came down the hall, casual in jeans and a navy sweater, her straight blond hair brushing her shoulders. Jax set Coco down, and she trotted over to his mother, who petted her.

"I didn't mean it in a bad way," Jordan reassured her.

"I was only kidding, honey. Jax's little princess is most certainly spoiled." His mother hugged her. "What a lovely surprise, seeing you again."

As his mother embraced him, Jordan was struck by how

warmly she'd welcomed her. Todd's parents were kind but chilly, and she and Todd would never show up at their house unannounced. Todd considered it a rude intrusion. She'd never really thought much about that until now.

"Our meeting ran a little late, so I convinced Jordan to have dinner with me. I thought we'd go to Travilla's and take Coco with us." Travilla's was an old farmhouse that had been converted into a pet-friendly bed-and-breakfast and outdoor café on the outskirts of town.

"The café can be crowded on Sundays. Why don't you join us for dinner?" his mother suggested. "We're having one of your favorites: spareribs with mint sauce and grilled vegetables, and we have three-berry tart pie and vanilla ice cream for dessert."

"Sounds delicious. What do you think, Jordan? My mom is a great cook."

"I don't want to intrude on your family dinner. You stay. I can call an Uber to take me home. I have a spare key there, and I can come by tomorrow to get my bag from your office."

Jax shook his head. "You're kidding, right?"

"Don't be silly, Jordan," his mother said. "The more the merrier. I've been cooking for Nick and Trixie all day. I have plenty of extras."

"Oh, did they change their plans? I thought they were having an at-home honeymoon and trespassers would be shot." Trixie told her that she and Nick were going to hang a HONEYMOON IN PROGRESS sign on the door and not come out for a week other than to take care of their animals.

"They are, but do you really think those two lovebirds will remember to eat?" His mother shook her head, but her smile told Jordan she was all for their love nest. "Someone has to provide sustenance for them. But they gave me strict instructions to leave the food by the front door, ring the doorbell twice, and leave."

"That's because clothing is optional on their at-home honeymoon," Jax said with a chuckle.

Jordan couldn't imagine what it would be like to have Todd's undivided attention for a few hours, much less a week. He checked his phone incessantly, even on the weekends, so as not to leave his clients hanging. That's why they were delaying planning their honeymoon until the fall, when he hoped things would slow down at work.

"Well, good for them, and good for us that you two are here for dinner." His mother put her arm around Jordan, guiding her down the hall with Coco on their heels. "Clint is out on the patio grilling vegetables. You and Jax can hang out with him while I finish up in the kitchen. It shouldn't take long, and we can get to know each other better over dinner."

"Are you sure you don't want some help?" Jordan offered.

"She's sure." Jax took Jordan's hand, pulling her toward the patio door.

His mother flashed an approving smile.

Coco trotted out the door with them and darted into the yard.

"I thought I heard an unfamiliar voice. It's nice to see you again, Jordan." His father embraced her and clapped a hand on Jax's shoulder. "Are you sticking around for dinner?"

"We are," Jax answered.

Coco pushed a basketball onto the porch with her nose and sat at Jax's feet, panting up at him.

"That's my good girl. Thanks, baby." He bent to love her up and picked up the basketball. Coco trotted over to a lounge chair by the basketball court and made herself comfortable.

His father said, "Does his dog know him, or what?"

"I didn't know Jax played basketball."

"Just a little here and there," Jax said coyly. "Do you play?"

"No. I'm too uncoordinated for sports."

His father arched a brow. "Maybe you just haven't had the right coach."

"No, I'm seriously bad at all sports."

"Let me show you a thing or two. Do you want to borrow a pair of sneakers from my mom?"

Was he really going to make her do this? "No, it's okay. I'll just take these off."

"You might want to lose your jacket, too," Jax suggested. "It's too restrictive for the court."

As she took off her jacket and heels, Jax shrugged off his shirt and hung it over the back of a chair, revealing planes of lean, hard flesh and ripped abs. Her pulse quickened as he picked up the basketball and dribbled, his muscles flexing with his movements as he closed the distance between them and said for her ears only, "Careful, sweetheart. Wouldn't want you to get drool on your pretty white shirt."

She clamped her mouth closed, stealing a glance in his father's direction, relieved to see he was busy grilling.

With a hand on her back, which was starting to feel familiar, he led her on to the basketball court and said, "Love the stars."

It took her a second to realize he was talking about the white stars painted on the red polish on her toenails. "My mom used to paint them on our toenails. Casey loved them so much, I guess it makes me feel closer to her."

His expression turned thoughtful. "Now I like them even more."

His voice was so honest, his expression so genuine, it tugged at her heartstrings.

"Ready to show me what you've got?" He spun the ball on his index finger.

"I haven't even touched a ball in so long, I probably won't hold it right."

His smile turned a little bit wicked. "Don't worry. I'll put your hands in all the right places."

"*Jax!*" she whispered. "You are *bad*."

He stepped closer, eyes darkening. "I promise I'm *incredibly* good."

She had no doubt. "What happened to *not* flirting?"

"Once again, I'm not flirting. I'm just stating a fact." He handed her the ball. "Come on, beautiful. Show me how you handle the ball."

She rolled her eyes, but she was enjoying the banter, and she began dribbling.

"A'right. Looking good. You've got it."

"That's because I'm standing still. I can't dribble and move, and I can't shoot worth a darn."

"I don't believe that. Let's see you take a shot."

She turned toward the basket, feeling ridiculous as she aimed and threw the ball. It arced high and dropped several feet in front of the basket. "I told you I suck."

"You definitely did not use that word." Those dark eyes hit hers, full of desire. "But it's good to know."

Her cheeks flamed, and she looked for his father as Jax retrieved the ball, but the grill was closed. Clint must have gone inside. Jax carried the ball over, and she said, "You know I'm engaged."

"Yes, I'm aware of that rock on your finger."

"Then please stop *stating facts* like that." *It makes it hard to keep my own thoughts in line.*

"As you wish."

Wow, that was easy. "Thank you, and I told you I was horrible at sports."

"You aren't. We just need to make a few minor adjustments."

"Like having someone else throw the ball?"

"I think you mean *shoot* the ball, and no. You're going to do it." He handed her the ball and moved behind her. His chest pressed against her back as he reached around, putting his hands on hers.

"What are you doing?"

"Showing you how to hold the ball. Focus, Lawler. Your hands are small, so you want to sort of cup the ball with this hand and guide it with this one…"

As he talked about finger positions, traction, and pushing with one hand while guiding with the other, she could barely concentrate past the feel of his warm, hard chest against her back and his enticingly masculine scent.

"They didn't teach it like this in gym class." *And my gym teacher sure didn't look like you.*

He laughed. "That's probably why your form needs help. The right partner makes all the difference."

She looked over her shoulder at him, and the amusement in his eyes brought a smile.

"Stop checking me out and pay attention," he teased.

"You're too much."

"I've heard that before."

Stifling a laugh, she leaned back. *"Jax."*

"Careful putting your body all over me like that."

She futilely tried to glower over her shoulder, but she couldn't stop smiling. "You're impossible."

"With a ring on your finger, you're right. But without one...I'm very possible."

Her jaw dropped.

"Focus, will you? Geez, you're always flirting with me. Look at the ball." He waited as she turned her head, his warm breath skimming over her neck. "When you take the shot, bend your knees a little, and then push off."

He held her hips, pushing her down so her knees bent around his, and then they rose together. He was gentle, yet firm and in control, and it was such an intimate position, her mind tiptoed down a naughty lane and she got hot all over.

"Okay, Lawler, you've got this."

He stepped back, and a rush of cooler air washed over her. *Come back...*

"Take your time, practice the move, and remember, the power comes from your shooting hand—the other is just guiding the ball."

She was all revved up, and he expected her to get the ball in the net? She closed her eyes, trying to center her thoughts, but she could still feel his hands on her hips, his chest against her back. The heck with it. She opened her eyes and shot the ball. It flew in a straight line to the basket, hit the backboard, circled the rim twice, and dropped through the net.

She squealed and leapt into his arms, both of them laughing as he spun her around. When he stilled, their eyes collided with the heat of a thousand suns, turning their laughter into heavy breathing. Their lips were a whisper apart, their hearts thundering to the same frantic beat. In his arms, she felt on top of the world. The urge to kiss him was so strong, she could barely breathe. But she *had* to breathe. She had no business wanting to kiss him.

"*Jax*" fell apologetically, *painfully*, from her lips just as "Jordan" fell from his, mirroring her emotions as he set her on her feet.

The patio door opened, and his mother said, "Dinner's ready."

Coco bounded inside.

"Coming. Give us a second, please." Jax's eyes remained trained on Jordan. His mother closed the patio door, and he stepped closer. "Jordan—"

"Maybe I should go." She was so confused. In all the years she'd been with Todd, she'd never wanted to kiss any other man, until she'd met Jax. She'd spent eight months getting over that heart-racing feeling every time she'd thought of him, and in the space of twenty-four hours it was even stronger than before.

"Please don't leave." His eyes implored her. "This is *my* fault. I'm sorry I made you uncomfortable. I'm not usually like this."

She gave him a *yeah, right* look.

"I'm serious. You can ask anyone who knows me. I just have so much fun with you, it's hard to hold back. But I promise if you stay, I'll be on my best behavior."

But can I be on mine?

"I know I said this already, but you can trust me this time," he said earnestly. "I promise to keep us in line."

"Okay. I will, too."

As she put on her heels, he said, "And if I mess up, you can always spank me."

She glared at him as she grabbed her jacket and he put on his shirt.

"I'm kidding." He sidled up to her. "Unless you're into that type of thing."

Lord help her. If she weren't engaged, she'd be on him like white on rice.

JAX HAD PROMISED himself he wouldn't come on too strong, and he'd blown it. He'd never been a blatant flirt, but Jordan brought out his primal instincts, and he was having a hell of a time trying to rein them in. He looked at her, loving up Coco on the way to the table, hugging his pup despite the fur clinging to her clothes. Giggling as Coco licked her face and neck. If she married that twit in New York, he'd better get her a dog. At least that way she'd get the unconditional love she deserved. She'd already been let down in so many ways, he refused to add to that disappointment and vowed not to break his promise again.

Jax pulled out a chair for her, earning that slightly shy smile that underscored that heart-stopping moment they'd shared outside. He sat beside her, across from his parents, and she whispered, "I love that your parents sit beside each other like mine used to."

He fought the urge to put his arm around her and kiss her temple, whispering, "They always have," instead.

Coco settled in at Jordan's feet, which was surprising, since she usually stuck to him like glue, and his father poured them each a glass of wine.

"Did Jax teach you a thing or two out there?" his father asked.

"Yes, he did." Jordan laughed softly. "I even made a basket, and I've never done that before."

"See? It's all about having the right coach." His father nodded at him. "Jax was a star player in high school."

"That was a long time ago, Pop."

"Were you Homecoming King, too?" Jordan asked.

Jax shook his head. "No. I didn't go to the dance."

"Couldn't get a date?" she teased.

"I had better things to do." *But if I'd've known you were right around the corner, I'd have given up my plans to take you.*

"He always had a gaggle of pretty girls vying for his attention," his mother said. "But it was LA's Fashion Week, and he didn't want to miss it. He watched all the Fashion Weeks from the time he was a little boy."

"Really?" Jordan's eyes lit up. "I thought I was the only weirdo who did that."

She had to be kidding. "You missed school dances to watch Fashion Week?"

"No," Jordan said. "But I've watched them from the time I was a little girl."

His father eyed him curiously. "Well, aren't you two peas in a pod?"

Yes, we are.

"When I was young, my parents made a big deal of it for me. My father always bought me a fancy new dress and sketch pads and pencils so I could draw while we watched. They'd set up Christmas lights around the living room, and my father made enormous homemade pretzels with my mom's famous honey-mustard dipping sauce, which was delicious. We'd have pigs in blankets and Hawaiian Punch in champagne glasses. The whole meal felt extravagant, and for dessert we'd have lime gelatin salad with Cool Whip mixed into it. I thought that was the most decadent dessert." Jordan's enthusiasm was contagious. "We'd all sit on the couch and eat and talk about the clothes. Casey called them yucky, because none of them were flannel, but the last year we watched together, she let my mom put flowers in her hair, which she *never* did. I think she only let her do it because I asked her to." Her expression softened. "Gosh, I haven't thought about that in the longest time."

Jax felt a tug in his chest and couldn't resist giving her hand a gentle squeeze under the table. She smiled appreciatively, but he was quick to pull his hand back, so as not to renege on his promise.

"Your parents sound wonderful. Is Casey your sister?" his mother asked.

"Yes." Jordan took a bite. "This is delicious. Thank you for inviting me."

"You're welcome anytime." His mother sipped her wine. "I'd love to know more about your family. Where are you from?"

"Prairie View." Jordan ate a forkful of vegetables.

"That's right around the corner," his mother said. "Does your family still live there?"

Discomfort rose in Jordan's eyes, and Jax said, "Jordan lost her parents when she was young."

"Oh, honey, I'm so sorry," his mother said.

"Thank you. It was a long time ago." Jordan took a drink of water.

"That must have been very difficult for you and your sister," his father said empathetically. "Did you have other family to stay with?"

"Yes, my aunt and uncle in Massachusetts."

"That's good, but it must have been awful hard to be up-rooted after such a tragedy," his father said. "Has your sister returned to the area, too, or is she still in Massachusetts?"

Jax wasn't sure he should divulge what Jordan had told him, but at least he could try to change the subject. He opened his mouth to speak, but Jordan beat him to it.

"I don't often share this because it can make things awkward with people that I've just met and because I don't want it to define me. But I told Jax, and I trust you to keep it between us. My sister has been missing since my parents' car accident nineteen years ago."

"Missing?" His mother's brow furrowed, and then sadness rose in her eyes. "Oh, honey. Did the accident happen in West Virginia?"

Jordan's eyes remained trained on her plate as "Yes" slipped softly from her lips.

Jax took her hand, holding tight this time.

His parents exchanged a tortured glance. "That was a horrible tragedy," his father said. "My brother, Ace, and I went to West Virginia with a number of other friends and neighbors and helped with the search for your sister. Is her real name Cassandra?"

"Yes." She squeezed Jax's hand and met his father's gaze. "Thank you for helping them search for her."

"We all kept our kids closer after that," his mother said. "I'm sorry they never found Casey."

"Me too, but I'm hopeful that one day I'll see her again."

"You hang on to that hope, honey," his mother said. "You never know what kind of energy travels through our universe."

"I am, thank you." Jordan's grip eased like a sigh of relief.

They ate in silence for a few minutes, and Jax thought about what it must be like for Jordan, not knowing if her sister was alive or dead, being cared for or harmed. That was a heavy weight for anyone to carry, but without the support of family or her fiancé, it was unimaginable. He was starting to understand how strong Jordan Lawler really was.

His father glanced at Jordan, and Jax recognized the paternal ache of the man who had watched his sons suffer and had taught him how to love. He knew his father wanted to take her into his arms and tell her everything would be okay.

Join the club, Dad.

"So, Jordan, did you retain your love of fashion through the years?" his father asked.

Jax sent him a silent *thank you* for trying to put Jordan at ease. "Did you see her dress at the wedding?"

Jordan smiled sweetly, and as much as he wanted to continue holding her hand, it felt too good, and he reluctantly let it go.

"Yes, and she looked beautiful. But you know me, son." His father smiled at Jordan. "Despite my stylish children, I know nothing about fashion."

"I think you dress nicely. My father's idea of fashion was flannel shirts and jeans. And to answer your question, I did retain my love of fashion." Jordan sipped her wine. "I even thought of making a career of it. But after my first year of college, I took the safer route and went into health administration and marketing."

"Trixie mentioned that you're the director of volunteer programs at Pleasant Care Assisted Living," his mother said. "That must be very rewarding."

"It is. I love my job, and Rising Hope has been a big hit with our residents." Rising Hope was Trixie's miniature horse therapy business. Jordan eyed Jax. "I can't stop thinking about you missing Homecoming for Fashion Week. Is that when it all started for you?"

"Heavens, no," his mother said. "Jax's love of fashion started *way* before that. The first time he saw *Cinderella* he wanted to be the Fairy Godmother, so he could magically turn scrappy dresses into gorgeous gowns."

"Really?" Jordan looked amused. "I would have pegged him for Prince Charming."

Touché. "With a little effort, any man can be charming, but very few can make a gown that makes a woman feel like a princess." And if ever there was a woman who deserved to be treated like a princess, it was the woman beside him, hoping to find her sister and spinning tales of being happier if she broke her own heart and moved away.

"Clint, remember when Jax was four and refused to believe mice couldn't sew?" his mother asked.

His father chuckled.

"I don't think we need to tell this story." Jax drank his wine.

"Now they *have* to tell it," Jordan said.

His mother leaned forward like she was sharing a secret. "Once he got it in his head that mice could sew, he decided to make a princess dress for Jilly and convinced Nicky and Beau to catch field mice so they could help him make it."

Jordan giggled. "You weren't the brightest tool in the shed back then, were you?"

"Hey." Jax bumped her with his shoulder.

"I think he was pretty darn smart to convince a six- and seven-year-old to do the dirty work for him," his father said.

"Good point. I take it back. That was very clever of you," Jordan agreed.

"*Backpedaler*," Jax teased under his breath.

"Did they catch any mice?" Jordan's smile reached her eyes, and Jax was glad to see her tension dissipate now that they'd steered the conversation safely away from her family.

"They did," his mother said. "Clint taught them to make mousetraps out of cardboard boxes, sticks, and string, and they caught four mice. Jax immediately began planning a gown for Jilly. Meanwhile, the mice got busy, and a month later we had twenty-eight mice."

"*No way*," Jordan exclaimed.

"Yes, ma'am," his mother said. "And Graham felt bad for them, so our precocious three-year-old set the mice free *inside* the house."

"*Oh my gosh.*" Jordan laughed.

"Two exterminator treatments and three hundred and fifty dollars later, we were finally rodent free." His father shook his head. "All because Jax wanted to make Jilly a dress."

"At least he meant well," Jordan offered.

"Want me to reimburse you, old man?" Jax pretended to reach for his wallet.

"Son, dollars can't take away my gray."

His mother looked at Jordan and said, "Our Jaxon has a big heart, and when he sets his mind on something, he doesn't let it go until he's accomplished it. Once he realized we were telling him the truth about mice, he was pretty upset. In his four-year-old mind, only mice could sew dresses. I don't know why I didn't think of doing this before the mice fiasco, but I took him into town to meet a seamstress, and bless her heart, she worked with him for a month, and together they made Jilly a dress. In fact, I have a picture of their first fashion show. Excuse me for a moment." His mother hurried into the living room to retrieve the picture.

Jordan said, "That's the cutest story I've ever heard."

He wished her parents were still alive so he could hear their stories about when she was younger, too.

His mother returned with the framed photograph of Jax and Jillian holding hands, caught midstride on the makeshift catwalk their father had built. They were wearing dark sunglasses, and Jax's hair was parted on the side and slicked back. He wore a black blazer with a red handkerchief in the pocket, a white dress shirt, black skinny dress pants, and white high-tops. Jillian was wearing a denim jacket over the black dress he'd made for her. It had a sequined bodice and a black underskirt covered by several layers of tulle. Her hair was long and windswept over one shoulder. A red handbag hung from her wrist, and she wore white sneakers.

"This is priceless," Jordan exclaimed. "Is Jilly wearing lipstick?"

"No, honey," his mother said. "Her lips were cherry red from a lollipop, which I told her was nature's lipstick."

"You're brilliant." Jordan studied the picture, grinning from ear to ear. "I can't get over this. Look at you two working the runway. Where did you *get* a runway?"

"Our dad made it."

She looked at his parents. "You're amazing parents, the way you support your kids' dreams."

"I don't know about amazing, but we do our best," his mother said.

Jordan covered her heart with her hand. "This is so special. I would love to look at more pictures after dinner and hear more stories about Jax and the others."

"Yes, let's do it!" his mother exclaimed.

Jax glanced at his father and said, "I have a feeling it's going to be a *very* long night."

NEARLY TWO HOURS and too many embarrassing stories later, after loads of laughter and good-natured ribbing, they were finishing dessert. Jax watched Jordan eat the last bite of her pie and sit back with her hand on her belly, wearing a contented expression. Damn, she was beautiful.

"That was the most delicious home-cooked meal I've had in a long time," Jordan said. "And the pie was absolutely scrumptious. If I keep eating like this, I won't fit into a wedding gown."

"Where are my manners?" his mother exclaimed. "We were having such a good time, I forgot to ask about your wedding. Tell us everything. When is your big day? Where are you getting married?"

"The wedding is the last weekend in August, but we haven't chosen a venue yet. My fiancé lives in Manhattan, and it's hard for him to get away. He's coming to town next weekend, and I'm hoping to get all our big decisions made in one fell swoop. I've booked all day Saturday with visits to venues, meeting with the florist, and our cake tasting."

"That's a busy day. Are you working with a wedding planner, or is your aunt helping you?"

"I'm planning the wedding myself. My aunt is a painter, and she has a number of big commissions right now. I didn't want to put her through the stress of planning a wedding, especially since she's done so much for me already."

"That's thoughtful of you," his mother said. "I'd be happy to help in any way I can. My family has owned Hilltop Vineyards forever, and I planned their events for years."

"And let's not forget the dozens of parties and events you planned for our kids," his father added.

"It must have been crazy busy but fun raising so many kids," Jordan said.

"It was controlled chaos at all times, but I loved every second of it, and I can't wait to have a house full of grandchildren."

Jordan smiled. "I bet. I appreciate your offer to help, but I think I've got it under control."

"Okay, honey. Have you chosen a caterer?" his mother asked.

"Yes. On Trixie's recommendation, I hired the same person who catered her and Nick's wedding, Finlay Whiskey."

"Finlay is wonderful," his mother said.

"You don't have to tell me," Jordan said. "I've had to reschedule twice at the last minute, because of my fiancé's work schedule, and she's been so nice about it. I'm glad Trixie referred me to her. She gave me a referral for flowers, too. Isla Redmond at Petal Me Hard. Our interactions over the phone have also been great so far."

"Isla did a great job for their wedding. But your big day is only three months away?" His father eyed him. "Someone's going to have to put their nose to the grindstone to make a gown that quickly."

"I *know*," Jordan said. "I was ready to get a gown off the rack, but Jax insisted on making it."

"I want Jordan's wedding to be everything she's ever dreamed of." *Even if she's making a mistake by marrying a guy who doesn't appreciate her.*

"Did you make any progress today?" his mother asked. "What kind of gown are you thinking about?"

Jordan looked at Jax in embarrassment, and they shared a laugh.

"We haven't even started talking about the gown yet, Mom. I wanted to get to know Jordan first. Tomorrow evening we'll get into the nitty-gritty."

"We will?" Jordan asked with surprise.

"If we want to get your dress done, we will. I figured you could come to my office after work. I'll bring dinner in, and we'll put our noses to the grindstone, as my father said. What time do you get off?"

"Six."

"Great. It's a date." Jax pushed to his feet, and Coco did, too, as he began collecting the dirty dishes.

"I'll help you," Jordan said.

His father stood. "I've got it, Jordan."

"No, really—"

"Let them be, honey," his mother said. "Or you'll undo years of training." She winked, and Jordan looked at Jax, who grinned.

"If you want to raise good boys like me, you might want to start taking notes." He and Coco followed his father into the kitchen.

"I'll wash, you dry." Jax put the dishes by the sink and pulled out his phone, thumbing out a text to his cousin Josh, a fashion designer in New York. *Hey, cuz. Can I get that PI's number from you?* He pocketed his phone, rolled up his sleeves, and began washing the dishes.

"Sounds like Jordan's had a rough go of it."

He handed his father a plate and grabbed another to wash. "You can say that again."

"She's a nice girl."

"Mm-hm."

He set the dry dish on the counter. "Attractive, too."

"Yes, she is." Jax handed his dad another dish, glad he was talking quietly, and wondered where the conversation was headed. His father never beat around the bush unless he was trying to figure out how to say something. "And…?"

"I was just thinking about how many women you've brought over in the last decade."

That would be none. "We came to get Coco. Don't overthink it."

"Yes, that's what you told your mother. But I keep asking myself when the last time was that you worked on a Sunday or took on an extra client when you were already booked. I don't recall either, but I get it. Trixie is family now, and Jordan's her friend, so you're helping her out."

"Exactly." *Plus, I want her in my arms, in my bed, and in my whole damn life.*

"The thing I keep coming back to is when was the last time you took Coco on a dinner date with a *client.*"

Jax handed him a dish and began scrubbing a pot. He'd be lying to himself if he didn't admit he'd been thinking about the same thing. They could have gone to any number of restaurants in town and left Coco with his parents. But he'd *wanted* Jordan to meet Coco, which was probably also very telling, and he had a feeling he'd wanted his parents to see him with Jordan so he and his father could have this very conversation.

Talk me out of it, Dad. Tell me to back off, because nothing else is working.

He handed his father the pot and grabbed another dish. "Would you believe I was hungry for Mom's cooking?"

"No, but we can go with that if you'd like." He leaned against the counter as he dried the pot, wise eyes on Jax. "You know, everyone thinks I worry about Jilly getting her heart broken more than any of you boys, but that's never been true. You and Jilly are the most sensitive of our kids, but Jilly won't allow a man to hurt her. That's why she's found something wrong with every man she's ever dated. She's not ready for love. But you, Jax. You've been ready since you were fourteen and fell head over heels for Audrey Hepburn."

Jax smiled. "I sure did. She was graceful and classy, but there was also something real and relatable about her. She seemed so different from the girls I'd met back then, and the women I've met since." *Until Jordan.* "I didn't think anyone could hit me the way Audrey did."

"I didn't think a teenager could fall so hard for a woman who'd already passed on and was several times his age. But you set that bar high, and you wouldn't settle for anything less."

Jax was surprised at how spot-on his dad was.

"I've been worried about you since last summer."

"Why? What'd Jilly tell you?"

"She didn't have to tell me anything. I'm your father. I see *you* and sense everything you go through. You have always been so driven and focused, nothing and no one has ever been able to distract you from your work. You are relentless in your pursuit of never letting anyone down, creating impeccable gowns for famous people, and you put that same effort into gowns for the girl next door. That's admirable, son."

"I'd never half-ass a gown."

"Maybe that's why I noticed you've seemed different these

last several months. You haven't half-assed anything as far as I know, but your attention span and enthusiasm have seemed off."

He didn't even try to deny it.

"I've been racking my brain trying to figure out what was going on. Then you walked outside with Jordan, and just like that, my boy was back. Only you aren't the same person you were before you started acting different. You shine brighter with her by your side. When I saw that, *that's* when it hit me, and I remembered that you canceled dinner with me and your mother to meet with one of Trixie's friends about a wedding dress last summer, and after that is when things changed. Was that Jordan?"

Jax slid his hands into the front pockets of his slacks, meeting his father's gaze. "Yes."

"She's taken, son."

He gritted his teeth against that hard truth, his entire being readied for a battle, and suddenly the desire to have his father talk him out of wanting Jordan went out the door.

"In a few months, she's going to be another man's wife," his father reminded him. "And I didn't raise you to be a home-wrecker."

"No shit, Dad. I'm not going to lie to you and say that I don't wish it were different. But damn it, there's something real between us. I felt it the moment I first met her, and yes, I've been messed up for months because I couldn't get her out of my head. I can't—I *won't*—walk away and act like there's nothing there, and I'm sorry if that disappoints you. It hurts me to say that, because I respect the hell out of you, but it's the truth." He took his hands out of his pockets, straightening his spine. "I won't make a move on her, and I will *not* ask her to end her engagement, but I'll be damned if I'm going to stand by and watch her marry the wrong man without treating her how she deserves to be treated and showing her what real love looks like."

"You're playing a dangerous game, son, and I worry that you're going to get hurt."

"Then so be it. At least I'll know I've given it my all."

Chapter Four

EARLY-MORNING RUNS had always helped Jax clear his mind so he could focus on work, and this morning it was vital that he had his head on straight, because his first task was dropping a bomb on his team about the deadline for Jordan's dress. But as he and Coco ran through the park, his thoughts were a tangled mess.

He couldn't shake his conversation with his father or the disappointment he'd seen in his eyes. That had cut deep, but not deep enough to sever his feelings for Jordan. He'd taken her back to her car last night after ten o'clock, and her fiancé still hadn't called. He didn't know if the guy was genuinely busy with work or if he had *extracurricular* activities keeping him from reaching out to the woman he was supposed to cherish, but it didn't matter. What mattered was that Jordan must be in love with him in order to put up with it, and Jax couldn't do a damn thing about that.

It was those thoughts pushing him to run faster and harder than he had in years. Coco kept pace with him, as she did every morning. She was the most loyal of companions, although she'd been so taken with Jordan, she'd jumped into her car as if she'd belonged there, and Jordan's eyes had glittered with delight.

Jordan's voice whispered through his mind—*I've always wanted a dog, but my uncle was allergic, and Todd said it's too hard to have one in the city*—fueling his fire. How could anyone deny her the joy of a loving companion? He couldn't believe he was asking himself that about a guy who didn't seem to know what those two words meant.

As they ran out of the park, he caught sight of a blonde walking into Emmaline's, and his heart beat impossibly harder, but in the next second he realized it wasn't Jordan, deflating his excitement.

He slowed to a walk, reaching down to pet Coco. He'd made a promise not to flirt with Jordan, which he intended to honor, but he sure as hell was going to keep the promise he'd made to himself and give her so many reasons to smile, she couldn't help but think about him.

He pulled his phone from his armband and called Emmaline's cell phone.

"To what do I owe this honor?"

"I need a favor…"

"READY BOSS?"

Jax looked up from the email he was reading. Glenna Moore, his efficient and organized office administrator, stood in his office doorway wearing one of Jillian's designs, an above-the-knee sleek gray sheath with an asymmetrical V collar, capped sleeves, and a black-and-gray cheetah-print belt. Her side-parted pixie-cut revealed a pen tucked behind one ear. How she balanced it with her black-framed glasses, which matched her hair, was a mystery to him. "Yes. Come in."

"The design team is waiting in the conference room, and your ten o'clock call is confirmed with Penelope Price." Penelope Price was an A-list actress who was getting married next spring.

"Good. How about my video call with Amber and Dash at two?" Amber Montgomery was Graham's wife Morgyn's sister, and Dash Pennington was her fiancé. They had originally planned on getting married in the summer but had changed it to a fall wedding earlier this year, stating something about acorns, which had given Jax a head start on the gown.

"Also confirmed. I'll make sure the gown is in place for their viewing."

"Excellent."

"Alisha Drexler is coming in for her fitting on Thursday afternoon, the crystals for Karen Esso's dress are shipping today, and the Thrashers are emailing their thoughts on the designs you sent."

"I saw the email. I'll get back to them this afternoon."

"Great, and there was a message from Jacqueline Santana. She has a layover in Baltimore this evening and asked if you were free for dinner."

Jacqueline was a model he'd met and had spent a night with while at a fashion show in Milan last February. They'd had a great time, but as with the other women he'd entertained over the years, she was fun but hadn't left him longing to see her again, the way Jordan had without even as much as a kiss. "I'm not available. I have a dinner meeting here at six thirty."

Her brows furrowed. "I didn't see an appointment on the calendar. Who are you meeting with? Would you like me to stay?"

"I'm meeting Jordan Lawler, and thanks, but there's no need for you to stay."

"Why is that name familiar?"

"She came in last summer."

"*Right.* Trixie's friend. I thought her wedding was earlier this year."

"It was supposed to be, but she postponed it." He pushed to his feet and walked around the desk. "It's in August, and I'm designing her gown. That's why I called the meeting this morning."

"*August?* You do realize it's almost June. Is that even possible?" She followed him down the hall toward the conference room.

"If it weren't, I wouldn't have offered to do it." He stepped aside, letting her enter the room first.

"This should be fun," she said as she walked past.

As she took a seat at the table with the design team, Jax said, "Good morning, everyone." The team consisted of Emiko, an exemplary Japanese seamstress in her midfifties who had worked for a top designer in Japan for twenty-eight years, Franco, a fastidious dressmaker with more than thirty years of experience and a dry personality, Jonathan, an exuberant tailor who came to Jax with only three years of experience, but his attention to detail and meticulous nature had won Jax over, and Roberta, a middle-aged, bespectacled blonde with ten years of seamstress experience on Broadway and a penchant for taking care of everyone around her. They were as different as they could be, but they worked together like a well-oiled machine.

"Good morning," they said in unison as Jax sat down.

"Emiko. How close are you to finishing the handwork on Amber's gown?"

"Ten day? Maybe two week?" Emiko had come to the States to be closer to her children after her husband passed away several years ago, and though her English was spotty, her handwork was unparalleled.

"Perfect. Franco, where do we stand on Tracy Dwyer's dress?" They had several dresses currently in the works, and Jax knew making Jordan's dress would tax them all, but he'd make it worth their time.

"We are on schedule, as planned." Franco had a thick Italian accent.

"Wonderful. We have a new project. A wedding gown for Jordan Lawler, a friend of my sister-in-law's. Her wedding is at the end of August, and—"

"*Next* August?" Roberta asked.

"No," Jax said firmly. "This August."

Jonathan fanned his face. "I feel a panic coming on. Does anyone have a Twix? Snickers?"

Jax pulled a Twix from his pocket and tossed it on the table in front of Jonathan. "Breathe, Jonathan. I have faith in you."

"*Ah.* He slays me, and then he heals me," Jonathan said dramatically as he opened the candy wrapper and took a bite. "No wonder you're Paulo's hall pass."

Everyone chuckled. Paulo was Jonathan's husband, and Jax's hall-pass status had been their running joke since the first time Paulo had met Jax and had called him *a tall glass of champagne* that he'd like to *dive headfirst into*.

"There will be no passes of any type this summer, for me or anyone else. I know you're already stretched thin, but I also know what you're capable of, and each of you will receive a hefty bonus if we can make this happen."

"You know my motto. *Leave no bride behind,*" Roberta said.

"I'll make the time."

Jonathan waved. "I'm in, too, but, Glenna, can we please double up on our candy orders for the next couple of months?"

"Already noted," Glenna reassured him.

"I will do this, of course," Franco said.

"I can do, too," Emiko agreed.

"Thank you. I appreciate it."

"Excuse me, Jax," Glenna said. "Should we get Jordan's measurement session on the books?"

"I'll speak with her about it this evening." His cell phone rang. He pulled it out of his pocket and saw Reggie Steele's name on the screen. "I need to take this. Thank you all again. I'll report back once we have a concept on the gown. Excuse me."

He put the phone to his ear as he headed for his office. "Hi, Reggie, thanks for calling me back."

"No problem. Sorry I couldn't return your call last night, but I was tied up."

"That's okay." He closed his office door behind him. "I don't know if what I'm going to ask of you is up your alley or not, but Josh speaks so highly of you, I figured you were the best place to start."

"If I can't help you, chances are I'll know someone who can. Whatcha got?"

"A friend of mine's sister went missing nineteen years ago, Cassandra 'Casey' Lawler. She was four at the time." He relayed the details Jordan had told him and added the information he'd found online.

"Damn. Nineteen years is a long time, Jax. Do you know how slim the chances are of finding her at all, much less alive?"

"I have a pretty good idea. But her sister, Jordan, believes she's still alive and out there somewhere."

"The family always does. I'm really sorry for your friend's loss, and I'll do what I can, but you probably shouldn't give her too much hope."

Jax knew Reggie was right, but Jordan had enough people trying to quash her hope, and he wouldn't be one of them. He had a blessed life, surrounded by the people and things he loved, and he'd give it all up if it meant Jordan could finally figure out what happened to her sister.

"Thanks. I'll keep that in mind, and, Reggie, I don't care what this costs. I want to exhaust every possibility, get her name out there again, and do whatever it takes."

"I understand, but before we do that, let me see what I can dig up on the case, and then I'll be in touch."

As Jax ended the call, a text from Jordan rolled in. He'd had Emmaline send her a chocolate croissant and a special latte this morning with a note that had said, *Dear Ms. Lawler, welcome to Jax Braden Designs. I look forward to getting to know you better and making all of your bridal gown dreams come true. JB. PS: Not flirting. Just stating a fact.*

He opened and read her text. *Dear Mr. Braden, thank you for such delicious welcome-aboard treats. I thoroughly enjoyed them. Do all your clients get the same treatment? PS: Not flirting. Just asking for facts.*

"Not on your life, princess." He thumbed out, *Dear Ms. Lawler, only my VIP clients. PS: Feel free to flirt. There is no ring on my finger.*

He waited anxiously for her response, which came a minute later. *Dear Mr. Braden, I'm honored to be on your VIP list. PS: There is a ring on my finger. Not flirting. Just stating a fact.*

He fought the urge to tell her she was at the top of his fantasy list, too, but honoring his promise, he thumbed out, *Dear Ms. Lawler, the pleasure is all mine.*

JORDAN HAD BEEN on a dead run since the moment she'd arrived at work, for which she was glad, because it had kept her semi-distracted from thoughts of Jax. She had just enough time before the end of her workday to update the program board in the recreation room. As she reached for her whiteboard markers, her phone vibrated on the desk, and her aunt's name appeared on the screen. She set the box of markers down and answered the call.

"Hi, Aunt Sheila. How are you?"

"Hi, honey. I'm sitting on pins and needles, waiting to hear how your meeting with Mr. Braden went."

She'd spoken to her aunt the morning after the wedding and had told her about Todd canceling and Jax's generous offer. "It went well. I'm meeting with him again after work."

"That's wonderful. I wish I had known. I could have made arrangements to go with you."

"It's okay. I didn't want to take you away from your artwork for this."

"Honey, I never mind putting work aside for you. What's it like working with the man who designs gowns for the rich and famous? Is it intimidating?"

"Not at all. He's not like you'd think. He's easygoing and kind and thoughtful."

"Well, that's unexpected, and it's a good thing. You have enough pressure from Todd's family. You don't need to be working with a difficult designer. But you sound tired or hurried. Are you okay?"

"I'm fine. Just trying to finish up here so I can leave on time." What she didn't tell her aunt, and could barely admit to herself, was that she'd debated calling off her wedding today as many times as she'd thought about canceling her appointment with Jax. She was more excited to see Jax than to talk about her wedding, and that was just the tip of the problematic iceberg. She felt guilty for wanting to be around the man who had not only made her laugh more than she had in a very long time and had asked thoughtful questions and had actually *cared* about her answers, but had also sent the sweetest text last night: *Just making sure you got home safely. Thank you for trusting me and my parents with all you've been through.*

She couldn't remember the last time anyone other than her aunt had checked on her well-being like that or had thought of her first thing in the morning, much less thanked her for her trust. But after what his family had been through and spending the evening with his parents, it was easy to see where he learned to be so thoughtful. His parents were very much like her own had been. She'd felt embraced by their comfort. She'd almost forgotten how good that felt.

"Okay. I won't keep you, but just one more thing. Are you and Todd all set for this weekend? Because I can book a flight right now and be with you in case he cancels."

"I appreciate that, but we're all set. He's arriving Friday afternoon, and he's promised not to cancel."

"Good, sweetheart. It sounds like it's all coming together just like you wanted. *Right?*"

Jordan had already put her aunt and uncle through enough wedding plan cancellations. She wasn't about to tell her she was having doubts again. "Yes."

They talked for another minute, and after Jordan ended the call, she looked out the window at the beautiful afternoon, hoping she was doing the right thing.

"Knock, knock."

Jordan turned around and found Ari Lexington, a portly bald man with deep laugh lines and a heart of gold. He was one of her favorite residents, and he was carrying a small white bakery box with BAKED WITH LOVE and his initials on the side, tied up in a red bow. He'd taken up baking last year for his eighty-seventh birthday, and he'd been wooing Bess Ayers, another resident, with delicious sweets ever since. The personalized boxes were a gift from his great-niece.

His glasses lifted with his smile. "Good afternoon. May I come in?"

"Yes, of course. How are you?"

He shuffled into her office in his khakis and sneakers. "Mighty fine, thank you. I'm glad I caught you before you left for the day."

"Is that for Bess?"

"No, this is for you. Two slices of chocolate cake." He handed her the box. "For your anniversary."

"I'm sorry, Mr. Lexington, but I think you've mistaken me for someone else. I'm not married yet." She had seen many residents' health and cognitive abilities decline over the years, and it broke her heart every time, but this would be the first indicator with Mr. Lexington.

"I know your wedding is this summer. At least the last I heard it was."

"It still is."

"That's good, dear. But this is to celebrate your two-year

anniversary as our director."

She was touched that he remembered. Just that morning, when she'd received the surprise delivery from Jax, she'd had her own little celebration. "You are the sweetest man to think of me. Thank you."

"You think of us every day, Jordan, and now that I'm baking, I have a way of paying you back."

"You know I love working here. There's no payback necessary, but I will enjoy eating this later." She set the box on her desk. "I'm heading down to the hall to update the program board. Would you like to walk with me?"

"I'd love to." He offered his arm, and they headed out of her office. "You're on the cusp of such a thrilling time in your life. You must be excited about your wedding."

"I think I'm too nervous to be excited."

"Being nervous is normal. The month before Rosa and I were married, she was so caught up in the preparations, I thought she'd lost her mind, running here and there, worrying over every little thing. But I loved her even more for it."

Some days she wondered if Todd even noticed the little things she did. He used to call to ask how she was, but now he usually just called to pass on information or returned her calls hours or days after she left messages, and always did so with due haste. "How long were you married?"

"We had fifty-two wonderful years together before God took her from me. And you want to hear a secret?" They stopped outside the recreation room. "Before she passed, we looked back at our life and realized we never needed any of the hoopla of our wedding, birthdays, or any of that stuff. All we needed was each other. But I think all that hoopla was important. It was a way of telling the world that we held each other's hearts, and there's value in that. I was proud to be her husband, and I'd give anything to have her back by my side and hear her scold me for leaving the toilet seat up or leaving a dish in the living room."

She and Todd had lived apart for so long, she no longer missed him. How could that be when this man had lost his wife years ago, and he *still* missed her? Last night she'd realized that she'd shared more with Jax about her family in one day than she'd shared with Todd about her life in the last year. But she'd made a promise. Her wedding was *on*, and when she moved to New York, their relationship *had* to get better.

"I know you miss her. I'm glad you have Bess to keep you company."

"Bessie is wonderful, but my heart will always belong to Rosa."

"Does Bess know that?" she asked carefully.

He smiled. "Yes, she does. It's all about perspective. Bessie wants to be loved, and I have love to give. Not like I did at twenty-five, but I bake for her, and we talk, and sometimes talking is better than all that other stuff anyway. Life is much shorter than you think, Jordan, and it goes by quickly. Rosa would want me to have friends and spend what little time I have left being happy, and as long as Bess knows where we stand, there's no harm done."

And there it was, the answer she hadn't realized she'd needed. All she had to do was keep perspective and maintain a friendly, professional relationship with Jax, so as not to lead him on. "Well, I think Rosa and Bess are two lucky women."

"And your man is lucky as well. Hang in there, honey. Once you get past the jitters, you'll be starting a family and building a full, happy life. Just don't leave us all behind."

Jordan felt a pang of guilt. She liked the people she worked with so much, she hadn't found the courage to tell her boss or the residents that she was moving to New York after the wedding.

Three vivacious besties, Ruth, Gloria, and Sophia, came out of the recreation room giggling up a storm in matching red cardigans. They were members of the crochet club, the Crafty Crocheters, and they were known for stirring up trouble. But they also made the cutest hats for newborns, which they donated to a local hospital.

"Hello, ladies," Jordan said. "I'm glad to see you're having so much fun this afternoon."

"We were just torturing Jacob Castello." Ruth, the leader of the pack, with short white hair and a wild sense of humor, said with another giggle.

Sophia, a pistol at eighty-two, said, "He blushes so easily, we couldn't help ourselves."

"Ari, how do you like our shirts?" Gloria, the youngest of the three at sixty-eight, opened her sweater, and the other two ladies followed suit. They all had I'M A KNOTTY HOOKER emblazoned across their chests in pink. Below that were two crochet needles that formed an X and two balls of yarn.

Mr. Lexington laughed. "You *do* know how to make a man blush. Jordan, if you don't mind, I think I'll be on my way."

As he shuffled down the hall, Ruth called after him, "Come to the next Knotty Hooker meeting! We'll show you how to handle your balls!"

"*Ruth!*" Jordan chided her. "You cannot shout that here. You'll get reprimanded again by HR."

"Ha! At our age, we've got to make our own fun while we still can." Ruth exchanged a confident nod with her friends. "Please be sure to put our new club name on the board."

They stripped off their sweaters and turned around, show-ing her the backs of their shirts, which read PROUD MEMBER OF THE KNOTTY HOOKERS CLUB.

Jordan tried not to laugh. "Oh *my*. I…Ladies, you know I can't put that on the board."

"Come on, Jordan. Take a risk," Sophia urged.

Thinking of her meeting with Jax, she said, "I'm taking enough risks right now, thank you. Please put your sweaters back on. I don't want you to get in trouble."

"Trouble is our middle names. But for you, we'll cover up." Ruth nodded to the others, and they put their sweaters back on. "One day we're going to reel you into our mayhem, and you're going to thank us by teaching us all about style."

"You're the swankiest woman we know." Sophia eyed Jor-dan's outfit, which happened to be one of Jordan's favorites.

"With the exception of those naughty shirts, I think the three of you always look nice. I'd be happy to chat fashion with you, but let's skip the mayhem."

"We'll think about that," Ruth said. "Shall we, ladies?"

As they strutted away, Jordan felt another pang of longing. She was going to miss them when she left.

She updated the program board and went back to her office to gather her things. As she grabbed her purse, her cell phone rang. She was surprised to see Todd's name on the screen. They'd texted briefly after she'd gotten home last night, and he'd said he was going to be tied up in meetings for the next two days and may not have a chance to check in.

"Hi. Did your meetings end early?"

"No. We just got a short break, and I thought I'd check in. I had lunch with my mother today, and she's thrilled that you're working with that Braden guy. Apparently he's a big deal. You tell him that money is no object and have him make a dress fit for a queen."

She chewed on the fact that he'd made time to have lunch with his mother but had told her he may not have time to touch base. But she kept that to herself, because she wouldn't want him to think she was trying to come between them. She'd learned early on in the relationship that his mother was very possessive of her time with Todd. "You know I don't want a fancy dress."

"Jordan, you only get married once."

It made her happy that he had so much faith in their marriage.

"I'm so glad you're finally ready to move forward with our lives," he said warmly. "But you didn't want to have the wedding in the city, which means I can't invite my clients because they don't have time to travel, and my parents can't show us off to most of their friends because they live in the city, too. I am trying to respect your decision, but my family is kind of a big deal, and when clients come into my office, or into my father's office, or my parents' home, I want them to see pictures of my beautiful bride in her extravagant designer gown, so they know how they can expect to be treated. You live in that Podunk town, but once you become a city girl, you'll realize how important all of this is. I hope you'll reconsider and wear a fancier gown."

Appalled, she tried to figure out in what world that made sense, and she wondered when he'd gone from protecting her and helping her make decisions to telling her what was best regardless of her feelings.

"I have to go, but I know you'll make the right decision. Thanks, babe."

The line went dead.

And so did a piece of her heart.

Chapter Five

JAX WAS AS nervous as he'd been the first time he'd shown his gowns at a fashion show. He wanted everything to be perfect for Jordan, and he'd had to pull a few favors to make it happen, but she was worth it. He walked out of the conference room and headed up front just as Jordan walked through the door, and *damn*. She looked like she'd walked off a runway. Her hair hung like spun gold over the shoulders of a double-breasted burnt-sienna blazer with cream buttons, which she wore over a cream blouse with dark buttons, and had paired with tan tweed slacks. She carried a small white box with a red bow around it in her hands and a large red leather tote that matched her heels over one shoulder, bringing back to him the subtle reminder of all she'd lost painted on her pretty red toenails.

Her eyes found his, a flicker of heat rising to the surface, but just as quickly, he noticed a hint of trepidation, cutting him to his core. *Don't worry, sweetheart. I'll keep my feelings in check and focus on making you the gown of your dreams.*

She blushed. "Why are you looking at me like that?"

"I'm sorry. I was just admiring your outfit. You look incredible."

"Thank you." She looked down at her clothes. "It's one of

my favorites."

"I can see why. You have a great eye for fashion."

There was that sweet, appreciative expression again, making him want to tell her how beautiful she was apart from the clothes, so he could learn each and every one of her expressions, of which he was sure there were many. He'd tell her that her skin was as smooth as mulberry silk and her cornflower-blue eyes made him want to know her thoughts and feel everything she felt. He'd tell her that she resonated the strength of wool and the softness of cervelt and that he wanted to wrap her in his arms when she talked about her family and hold her hand on however many paths it took to find the answers she sought. But as her eyes swept appreciatively over him, he kept his promise and said, "I thought we'd have dinner and talk in the conference room. Would you like to get started?"

"Sure. I brought dessert." She handed him the box. "It's chocolate cake. A resident made it for me."

"Most clients try to get on my good side by lavishing me with praise. I'll take a client who shares her sugar with me any day." He winked, earning another beautiful smile. His hand was drawn to her back, but he forced himself to lower it. "Did you have a nice day?"

"Yes. How about you?"

He held her gaze as he opened the conference room door. "My job rarely feels like work, so most days are good."

"You're luck—" Her voice fell away as she stepped into the conference room, her gaze trailing over the platters of enormous handmade pretzels with homemade honey-mustard dipping sauce, pigs in blankets, and lime gelatin salad. "*Jax*," she said just above a whisper, full of disbelief.

He set the box on the table and held up his hands in surrender. "I didn't do this to flirt." He lowered his hands and his voice. "I did it because usually when I meet with a bride, a member of her family or someone who's as close as family comes with her. Since your family can't be here, I thought it would be comforting to have something familiar in the room, so they didn't feel so far away."

Tears welled in her eyes. "I'm sorry. I *can't*." She walked out of the room.

He went after her. She was halfway down the hall, digging a tissue out of her tote, her back to him. "*I'm* sorry, Jordan. I obviously overstepped."

She shook her head, wiping her eyes as she turned to face him. "It's not that. It's just...You keep making my feelings a priority, and I'm not used to that."

His relief was tempered by what her confession meant, and it was hell keeping his thoughts about that to himself, but he managed to hold it in. "Jordan, your wedding is going to be one of the most momentous occasions in your life. Your feelings should be a priority every step of the way. I probably should have asked your permission instead of surprising you."

"You *shouldn't* have. This is the best surprise I've ever been given, which is why I'm tearing up." She wiped her eyes. "I must seem like a ridiculous mess to you."

"No, you seem perfect to me."

She lowered her eyes. "I'm far from perfect."

"I don't mean perfect as in free from faults, and for the record, if you were that type of perfect, you wouldn't have lingered on my mind for eight months. What I meant was that you're *real*, and that's a rarity these days. Everyone wants to look and act the way they think others want them to. It's hard to know who or what to trust, which is one of the reasons I live in this area instead of one of the fashion hubs of the world. But with you, it's easy, because you cry when you're sad and laugh when you're happy. You blush and you try to scowl, although I haven't seen you accomplish that yet, and you set up expectations based on what you need to be comfortable. That's *real*, Jordan, and I hope you believe me when I say that I had that dinner made for you without any ulterior motive."

"I do believe you, because I knew I could trust you the first time we met, too." She breathed deeply.

He was dying to explore that further, but once again, he kept that to himself. "Well then, I think we should take our real, trustworthy selves into the conference room and enjoy dinner while we talk about your gown." He heard Jonathan and Emiko coming downstairs from the studio. "But before we do, I'd like to introduce you to two of my dressmakers. The others have already gone for the day."

"I was going to ask if you design and make the gowns yourself," Jordan said.

"I wish I were that talented, but I'm afraid I fall short in the sewing and handwork departments."

She held his gaze, a small smile playing on her lips. "I have a feeling you don't fall short in any department."

He was *this close* to making a comment he shouldn't when Jonathan and Emiko came around the corner. Jonathan's sharp features, flawless skin, and impeccably tailored suit gave him a modelesque vibe, while Emiko's always-a-little-tousled short black hair, skin mapped with deep grooves that made her look older than her fifty-six years, and loose linen dress gave her an understated, motherly appearance.

"I thought I heard voices other than the nagging ones in my head," Jonathan said loudly.

"Jonathan, Emiko, this is Jordan Lawler, the bride-to-be I mentioned to you this morning."

Emiko offered her hand. "Congratulations on your wedding."

"Thank you." Jordan shook her hand. "It's a pleasure to meet you both."

"You must be frantic, working on such a short timeline. But don't you worry—you're in the best of hands." Jonathan ran an assessing eye over Jordan. "You have beautiful bone structure. Are you considering a strapless gown?"

"Possibly," Jordan answered.

"How are you wearing your hair?" Jonathan asked. "Up? Down?"

Jordan looked amused. "I haven't thought about that yet."

"Honey, the summer will pass like this." Jonathan snapped his fingers three times. "And before you know it, you'll be walking down that aisle. It's *decision* time." He leaned closer. "I'd go with an updo and show off your long, swanlike neck. You'll make all the ladies jealous."

"*Okay*, Jonathan. Let's give Jordan a little breathing space." Jax was used to Jonathan's theatrics, but he knew he could be a bit much for others.

"My apologies," Jonathan said. "But if you need a hairstylist, Chicki Redmond or Sarah Whiskey at Chicki's Salon in Peaceful Harbor are absolutely magnificent. Sarah works wonders with makeup, too."

"Sarah Whiskey? Is she related to Finlay Whiskey?" Jordan asked.

"Yes, they're sisters-in-law." Jax turned his attention to Jonathan and Emiko. "If you'll excuse us, we were just about to sit down and eat dinner."

"I will be honored to work on your gown," Emiko said.

"Thank you," Jordan said. "It's an honor for me to meet the people who make the magic happen."

Jonathan peeked into the conference room. "What on *earth*? Is that Jell-O and *pretzels*?"

"Yes, now get out of here." Jax ushered him down the hall, and Emiko followed.

"Are we in financial crisis?" Jonathan whispered. "Has the world as I know it ceased to exist?"

"*No*, now go, please, and lock the front door behind you." Jax laughed as they headed out. "Sorry about that."

"He's a riot," Jordan said as they went into the conference room.

"I'd like to say he gets punchy at the end of a long day, but he's always like that."

"He must be fun to work with."

Jax handed her a plate. "I'm lucky to work with a team of talented professionals and one talented jokester."

They loaded up their plates and sat down to eat.

"This was so thoughtful of you. Where did you have this made?" Jordan pointed her fork at him. "And don't say a gentleman never tells."

He arched a brow. "I'm very well connected in the culinary world."

"That was a very coy answer, Mr. Braden." She spread a cloth napkin over her lap.

"Might I remind you, Ms. Lawler, we're here to talk about your gown, not my ability to trade favors." He filled their champagne glasses for a toast. "Here's to new friends and beautiful gowns."

They *clinked* glasses, and Jordan took a sip. "Hawaiian

Punch. You don't miss a thing, do you?"

"I guess we'll see."

She broke off a piece of a pretzel, dipped it in the sauce, and took a bite. "*Mm.* This is good."

"As good as your parents' recipes?"

"Well…" She wrinkled her nose, and they both laughed. "I'm kidding. It's delicious, but I'm not sure anything could taste better than food my parents made just for me and Casey."

He'd thought a lot about how much she must miss hearing her family's voices and seeing them. But he hadn't thought about how much she probably missed the little things he took for granted, like being able to enjoy his mother's cooking and popping in for a visit whenever he felt like it. But they'd already had such serious talks. He didn't want to bring it up and put a damper on her good mood.

They made small talk and joked around as they ate. Jordan dipped the pretzels and the pigs in blankets in honey mustard and told him stories about a phase she'd gone through when she put honey mustard on everything. Even pancakes.

After they finished eating, she sat back with her hand on her stomach, as she had the night before. "That was *so* good. I'm stuffed."

"Should I put the gelatin and cake in the fridge?"

"Don't you dare." She laughed. "I just need a few minutes for my stomach to settle, but I definitely want to devour them."

He liked that hint of fierceness and bit back the urge to make a comment about wanting to devour her. "I'm glad you're not afraid to eat the things you enjoy. Women worry so much about their weight, but beauty has nothing to do with size and everything to do with who a person is and how they treat others. A pretty person can be a jerk, and that makes them ugly, no matter what their size. Then take someone like yourself, for example. You could gain two hundred pounds, and you'd still be beautiful."

"Says the man who not only is going to get up onstage to be auctioned off, which takes supreme body confidence, but also probably only dates gorgeous women and works out seven days a week."

"Being in the auction doesn't take confidence. It takes my sister and her friends browbeating me until I agreed to do it, and beauty is in the eye of the beholder. I've gone out with women of all shapes and sizes, and for your information, I only work out *six* days a week, and that's for my sanity, not vanity."

"You're awfully defensive."

He chuckled. "Okay, maybe vanity has a little to do with it."

"Mm-hm. I thought so," she said sassily.

"You should come running with me and Coco sometime."

"I'm not a runner."

"You said you couldn't play basketball, either."

"That was a fluke of a shot, and you know it."

"I don't know that. But I'm serious about going running with us. We go early, before work. We could do a short run. A mile or two? There's nothing more invigorating than a jog through the park as the sun comes up."

"Did you know sunrises and sunsets are signs of hope?"

"I didn't know that, but it makes sense. That's another reason you should come with us. You can start your day with a dose of hope."

"I don't even own running shoes, and I'd probably end up walking most of it."

"Then we'll walk."

She seemed to mull that over. "That does sound fun. I'll think about it."

"Great. Let's talk about your wedding. When I design a gown, I like to get an idea of the bigger picture. Do you have a theme? I'd imagine you've been dreaming about your big day since you were a little girl."

"Then you are imagining wrong. I've never dreamed about my wedding."

"Really? That's surprising, given your love of fashion. You said you've been with Todd for several years. Surely you must have thought about what it would be like to walk down the aisle."

"I have, in a general sense, but I've never dreamed of it the way other girls dream of their weddings, picturing every minute detail. Then again, I learned a long time ago that my dreams are nothing like other people's."

"What do you mean?"

"When I was a kid, I dreamed about designing fancy dresses to wear to school or playdates, but not wedding gowns. And after losing my family, my dreams were replaced with night-mares. When those finally subsided, my dreams became mostly about finding Casey."

"It must be difficult trying to plan a wedding and think about moving forward with your life when pieces are missing."

"That's *exactly* how it feels. Like pieces of me are missing."

"I've been thinking a lot about Casey. I could help you hire an age-progression specialist and get her face all over the internet to see if somebody recognizes her."

She looked like she might cry, but she pressed her lips into a fine line and shook her head, her expression turning deter-mined. "You have no idea how much it means to me that you would even suggest that, but I promised Todd I'd stop chasing my *sister's ghost.*" The last two words came out soft and a little spiteful.

"But if there's—"

"I know. Please don't say it. I've already put my aunt and uncle and Todd and his family through enough. I made a promise. And Todd is right. I can't live in limbo forever. I need to move forward."

She sounded like she was trying to convince herself as much as she was trying to convince Jax, and that bugged the hell out of him. But this was her life no matter how much he wanted to show her she was doing the wrong thing with it. "Okay, moving forward it is. Do you have an idea of the style of gown you're interested in?"

"I have an idea of what I like, and I've made a few sketches."

"Great." Many brides showed him drawings or pictures of gowns and asked him to create something similar. "Can I see them?"

She pulled a sketch pad out of her tote and handed it to him. "The gowns are toward the back, but they're not very good."

Jax opened the sketch pad, admiring page after page of elegant gowns and dresses. Trumpets, sheaths, empire waists, and A-lines, all with notes calling out fabrics, threading, and embellishments. There were simple gowns with touches of lace or beading and more elaborate gowns with meticulously detailed embellishments and layered skirts. Every dress had its own unique flair, many reminiscent of older classic gowns worn by famous actresses throughout the years. Others were unlike anything he'd ever seen. But they weren't wedding gowns. They looked more like gowns worn to awards ceremonies and other special occasions.

He lingered on a formfitting sleeveless and belted corded black lace gown with an above-the-knee underskirt and flowing lace panels hitched at one hip. He turned the page and was blown away by a V-neck tulle gown with embroidered shooting stars on the skirt, the tails of the stars made from clear sequins and gold threading. He continued turning pages, admiring a gown with glittery fabric, billowing silk sleeves, a plunging neckline, and an open back, and lingered again on a white silk sleeveless knee-length dress with a fitted bodice that was embellished at the back with distinctive cutouts and a low neckline, just like Audrey Hepburn's famous *Breakfast at Tiffany's* black dress. But the rest of the dress looked nothing like the famous frock. It was even more striking. The waist was cinched, and the full skirt had two rows of black lace cutouts, giving it a sexier edge. The crowning touch was white elbow-length gloves with black lace cutouts on the forearms. He imagined Jordan in the enchanting gown, her glossy hair trailing over her shoulders or pinned up, with tendrils skimming her cheeks. Man, he'd love to see that.

As he leafed through more of her designs, he found outlandishly loud and fabulous gowns and dresses. The type worn at haute couture shows.

JAX HAD BEEN quiet for so long, Jordan feared the worst. "Are they that bad?"

He looked at her with wonder. "No. Quite the opposite. I think you've done a great injustice by taking the safe route into health care administration instead of following your heart into fashion design."

She gave him an incredulous look and glanced at the open sketch pad. "Now I know you're kidding. Those aren't even wedding gowns." She reached over to turn the page, but he pulled it out of reach. "Come on, Jax."

"Jordan, these are exquisite, and show such diverse talent. I'm in awe of you. Are the dresses that are similar to the old classics ideas for your maid of honor and bridesmaids?"

"No. I'm not having bridesmaids. I don't have those kinds of close friends."

"What about Trixie?"

"I really like Trixie and your sister. We've gone out a few times, and I enjoy their company. But Trixie works with our residents, and I try not to step too far over that thin gray line between personal and business relationships. Your cousin Tempest also works with me, and she's one of the sweetest people I know. But that work connection keeps me from reaching out."

"I understand, but I know Trixie and Tempe well enough to believe they'd keep your personal and professional relationships separate."

"Maybe so, but I'll be moving soon anyway, so why get too friendly?"

His jaw tightened. "What about kids you grew up with or college friends? Are you still in touch with them?"

"Not really. I had friends, but I always felt a little like an outsider because of what I'd been through. When I was younger, if I opened up about my family, girls treated me differently, like they had to be careful about the things they said and did. You know how kids say they're *dying* to do something or jokingly say they'd *kill* someone? It never bothered me much, because I knew they didn't mean it that way, but there were lots of things like that, that made relationships awkward. It's just easier to have more superficial friendships than to make other people uncomfortable or try to justify my belief about Casey."

"That must be difficult for you."

She shrugged. "I'm used to it. But I will admit that when I saw Trixie with her girlfriends at the wedding, I was more than a little envious. She has a group of women she feels safe with, and I bet they share all of their secrets and keep them close to their hearts. I wish I knew how to make that happen for myself, but I've never been able to accomplish it."

"I think it happens naturally, but you have to be open to it."

"That's something I'll have to work on when I move to New York." She didn't want to think about moving away. "Gosh, how did we get so far off track?"

"We didn't. This is all important, but we were talking about your sketches. If they're not bridesmaid gowns, what are they for?"

"I don't know. I sketch all the time while I watch TV. It's like doodling. I have dozens of those pads lying around. But if you turn to the back, you'll see my ideas for wedding gowns."

"I will in a minute. After seeing these *doodles*, I'm curious about why you didn't think you could make it in the industry."

"They aren't that good, Jax."

"How about you let the guy who designs gowns for the stars form his own opinion?"

Was he flirting or serious? "You really think they're good?"

"Better than good. I think they're captivating and unique."

"Are you serious?" His expression turned even more serious. "Oh my gosh, you are. I don't even know what to say." To hear that from not only a professional designer she admired but also a man she admired was a lot to process. "Thank you. I was afraid to show you my wedding gown drawings. I didn't even *think* about those other dresses."

"Knowing you're *doodling* while you're watching television and not spending painstaking hours poring over each design tells me that you have a rare, innate ability, which makes me even more curious about your decision. Did something happen that made you think you'd be better off in healthcare administration?"

"Not specifically. One of my professors hammered into us how difficult it was to break into the industry and how we'd have to live where fashion was born, in New York City or overseas. You know how that is. You mentioned not wanting to live in those places earlier. I don't know how you got started, but I knew there was no way I'd ever make it in fashion living here, and my heart was where my family had been. So *yes*, I took the safer route, but I also followed the bigger part of my heart."

"And do you enjoy your job as much as you like designing?"

"How can I answer that? I've never truly designed anything for anyone else. But I do love my job and the people I work with. For a girl without much of a family, I sure feel like I have a lot of grandparents."

"That makes me happy."

"Me too. In fact, one of my favorite residents, Ari Lexington, is the one who made that cake for my two-year anniversary as the director."

"He must really appreciate you."

"I think a lot of the residents think of me as family, too, and that's the greatest feeling."

"Yes, it is. Had I known it was your anniversary, we would

have had champagne." He lifted his glass. "To your director-ship. May you continue to enjoy it more with every passing day."

She melted inside and lifted her glass to toast. "Thank you."

They sipped their punch, and as Jax set his glass down, he said, "Do you still have an interest in designing?"

"As a career? I can't go back to school."

"You don't have to go to school. You just need to work with someone who can help guide you and teach you about the industry."

"Is that how you broke into it?"

"Yes. My cousin Josh is a fashion designer, and I studied under him while I was in school. He saw my potential and let me take the lead on a gown for a prominent client, and luckily, she loved it. She was all over social media and the society pages, and I was blessed to have my career take off after that. You've probably heard of Josh's company, JRBD?"

Her eyes widened. "That's your *cousin*? Isn't JRBD a hus-band-and-wife team? They're not just designers; they're world-renowned."

"Yeah, they're pretty big." He laughed. "Josh and Riley have been designing together for years. They've got an adorable three-year-old daughter named Abigail, and Riley is a few months pregnant with their second child."

"Do they live in New York?"

"They split their time between Weston, Colorado, where they grew up, and Manhattan. You'd like them. They're really down to earth."

"I guess that's a family trait. See? You had connections that I couldn't even have dreamed of."

"I was lucky that Josh allowed me to work with him, but I'd

like to think that you have a fairly good connection in the industry now, too."

That made her feel good all over.

"Let's take a look at those wedding gowns."

He looked at the sketches, making comments about the elements he thought would be flattering and complimenting her design choices. When he turned to the last page of gowns, her two *favorites*, he laughed.

She couldn't help but laugh with him. "I *know* it's ridiculous to want a wedding gown like Audrey Hepburn's in *Sabrina* or the one she never got to wear that the Fontana sisters made when she was engaged to that British guy, but I've kind of always had a girl crush on her. She was so stylish and graceful, but she also had a childlike charm, and I *loved* those dresses. I mean, Givenchy knew what he was doing, and I know the other dress is plain and simple, but there's a certain elegance to that, and I made modifications to spruce it up a little."

"I'm not laughing because it's ridiculous. I'm laughing because she was my first crush."

"No *way*. You're just saying that."

"I'll prove it." He pulled out his phone, poked around on it, and a second later it was ringing on speakerphone.

"Hi, Jax," a man answered.

"Hi, Dad. What was the name of my first crush?"

Jordan's eyes widened in embarrassment.

"First attainable crush or first crush?"

"First crush," Jax answered.

"Didn't we just talk about this? Aubrey Hepburn. Why?"

"No reason. Thanks, Dad. I'll talk to you later."

"Okay, love you."

"I love you, too." Jax ended the call, grinning like a Cheshire cat. "You'll learn that I always tell the truth."

"I can't believe you called your *father* or that you crushed on Audrey." They really were two peas in a pod. "That's so coincidental."

Holding her gaze, he said, "You call it coincidental. I think maybe we were fated to meet."

Her pulse quickened, and she didn't even believe in fate. If fate were real, then it was an evil bitch to have put her parents on a road that would steal her whole family from her.

"Fated to meet so I can make your gown, of course," he quickly added. "But I'm not going to design your gown, Jordan."

Her heart sank. "You're *not?*"

"No," he said solemnly. "*We* are going to design it."

"We…?" Was he talking about his team?

"You're too talented not to take the lead in the design process."

Her heart stumbled. "You want to design it with *me?*"

"Absolutely. I think we'd make a great team. What do you say?"

Her mind spun. "I don't want to disappoint you."

"It's your wedding gown, Jordan. You can't disappoint me."

"But I have to work."

"We'll get together in the evenings."

Seeing Jax every night was dangerous. She liked him more every time they were together. She shouldn't do it, but gosh, she wanted to! "I can't on Friday or Saturday. Todd's coming to town, remember?"

"We can work around your schedule and still get the dress done. Don't worry. *I* won't disappoint *you.*"

Why did she have a feeling he meant that in a bigger way

than just the dress? And worse, why did she want to find out for herself? She'd thrown caution to the wind more times in the last forty-eight hours than she had in her entire life, and she knew she was walking a tightrope. The trouble was, she wanted to take that chance. She might not believe in fate, but the way he was looking at her, like he was waiting for her answer with bated breath, made her want to believe in destiny. "Okay. Let's do it."

"*Great.*" His smile broadened. "After we eat dessert, I'll show you where the magic happens."

She had a feeling he could make magic happen anywhere he so desired. "Designing with you is a really big deal for me." *For many reasons, including some I'd rather not think about.* "I'm too nervous to eat."

"It's a big deal for me, too. Let me put the desserts in the fridge, and then we'll go up to my design studio."

A few minutes later she carried her sketch pad upstairs to his studio, which was everything she'd dreamed of as a little girl. Sunlight flooded in from enormous windows, spilling over drawing tables covered with sketches. Mannequins were draped in partially finished gowns and bodices—winter white, soft ivory, sky blue, and black-and-gold. Fabric and lace were draped over the tops of, and pinned to, enormous fabric boards on wheels. Inspiration boards lined the perimeter of the room, with dozens of pictures and sketches pinned to them, and running down the center of the studio were long tables littered with measuring and sewing accoutrements, pencils, books, and more sketches. Beneath each table were dozens of rolls of fabric stacked on shelves.

"Wow, Jax. Your studio is amazing."

"Let's be honest. It's a mess in here, but I have several designs in the works, and I learned a long time ago not to suffer over my surroundings."

"I don't see a mess. I see creativity coming to life." She walked over to the sky-blue gown. "Is this a wedding gown?"

"It will be."

"I've never seen anything like it. Is it for someone famous?"

"Yes, but unfortunately I'm not at liberty to disclose who it's for."

"I understand. I wasn't asking for you to breach a confidence. It's magnificent." She walked around it, admiring the pearl and lace embellishments. "When I think of wedding gowns, I think of white, but I can see a bride wearing this for a spring or summer wedding, or even a winter wedding. *Ooh*, that would be gorgeous. And this one..." She made her way over to the black gown. The bodice was embellished with gold threading and sequins.

"That's for a bride as well."

"I would think a black gown would feel goth or give off a dark or sad feeling, but this is elegant and feminine. It's magical."

"Thank you. I hit a few snags, but it's getting there."

She turned to look at him, so handsome in a black button-down and slim-fit plaid trousers, both of which looked like they were custom made for him. Which, she realized, they probably were. "Okay, it just hit me."

"What did?"

"Todd's mother and my aunt are starstruck about me working with *the* Jax Braden, but you're so laid-back, I don't think of you like a celebrity. But you *are* one, and deservedly so. Somehow in my head, the designer Jax Braden is separate from the Jax I've been getting to know, which sounds weird, doesn't it?"

He laughed, shaking his head. "No, it sounds about right. I'm just a guy who designs wedding gowns, and in some circles I'm a pretty big deal. But I'm glad you don't see me as an arrogant designer."

"I never said arrogant."

"It kind of goes with the territory. Those women probably imagine a guy who puts on airs and expects people to kowtow to him."

"Yes, I think that's what they expect you to be like."

"They wouldn't be wrong." He closed the distance between them. "I do have to put on airs at fashion shows and other events, but there's only one place I expect anyone to kowtow to me."

"Where is that?"

Wickedness rose in his eyes. "In the bedroom. *After* I satisfy them, of course."

Her mind sprinted to the gutter, and she imagined kissing him and unbuckling his belt as she sank to her knees before him. *Ohmygod. Stop!* "Oh, *um*, that must be nice for you."

He raised his brows. "Trust me, it's good for *all* parties."

I bet it is.

"Are you ready to get started?"

She tried to drag her mind out of the gutter, but it was like quicksand. *"Mm-hm."*

He chuckled.

Shoot! "Yes. Sorry. *Designing.* Let's design. Where do you want me?" *Ugh. Ramble much?*

"That's a dangerous question, especially when you're looking at me like I'm the dessert you haven't had a chance to eat. Not flirting. Just stating a fact."

Holy crap! Jordan Lawler, get it together. "Well, your facts are incorrect, Mr. Braden. I'm looking at you like you're a big-time designer."

"My apologies for misreading you, Ms. Lawler." He pulled out a chair for her at the drawing table and waved her into it. "The clock is ticking."

Her head told her to walk out the door and never look back, but apparently her head was no longer in charge.

As she sat down and he settled in beside her, that ticking clock felt like a time bomb.

Chapter Six

JORDAN WAS ON cloud nine Tuesday morning as she worked through program reports.

She and Jax had spent hours designing her gown last night, and other than her momentary naughty mental blip, they'd kept things professional. Well, more friendly than professional, considering they'd laughed as much as they'd talked, but they hadn't blatantly flirted, which was good. Jax had shared stories about when he was interning, telling her about mistakes he'd made and how his cousin Josh had been the greatest mentor he could have ever asked for. A couple of hours into designing, they'd taken a break to eat dessert, and she'd discovered that Jax was as much of a sweets-lover as she was. They'd eaten the lime gelatin on the cake, like ice cream, and had both devoured it. Coco's nanny had sent Jax texts with pictures of Coco's evening walk, and he'd shared them with Jordan. She'd had a great time and had learned more about designing in one evening with Jax than she had during her first year of college. Jax scheduled an appointment to have Jordan's measurements taken today during her lunch hour by someone named Roberta, and since he had a five o'clock meeting with a bride, Jordan was looking forward to seeing him at seven.

Kelly, Jordan's loyal assistant, a petite, opinionated brunette, walked into her office carrying a vase of pink roses and set them on the desk. "It looks like Todd is stepping up his game. Breakfast yesterday and roses today? What special favors have *you* been doing?"

Jordan hadn't told her that the croissant and latte were from Jax. "Planning the wedding, I guess." Todd hadn't sent her flowers in years.

"He doesn't want you to postpone it again." She plucked the card from its holder and handed it to Jordan. "You're not going to postpone, are you? I mean, this time you're actually getting a dress, right?"

"Yes. Jax Braden is designing it."

"Get out of here! You're *so* lucky. My sister's best friend got married two years ago, and Jax made her the most *gorgeous* gown. Isn't he hot? I know you're engaged, but you're still human."

If the way her mind had veered off track last night was any indication, she might be a little *too* human. "He is good-looking." *And sweet and funny and patient as the day is long.* She opened and read the card.

> *Jordan, happy belated two-year anniversary. I won't miss the date next year. Jax*

How did he even remember that after everything they'd talked about?

"What does it say?"

She shoved the card back into the envelope, thinking fast. "Thanks for handling the wedding preparations. Just like I thought."

"And he's sincere about it," Kelly said. "That's what pink

roses mean. Sincerity."

Thinking of Jax, she said, "Yeah, I know he is. Thanks for bringing these in. I have a call to make. Would you mind closing my door on your way out?"

Kelly waggled her brows. "Thanking him in private. I like it. Go, Jordan."

She closed the door behind her, and Jordan read the card again. It was professional, not flirtatious, and they were friends, so remembering next year wasn't inappropriate.

So why is my heart racing?

Her answer came with a heavy dose of confusion. Jax knew she was moving after the wedding and wouldn't be celebrating a third year as the director. She looked at the flowers and told herself she was overthinking, and he was just being nice.

She grabbed her phone, pacing as she thumbed out, *Thank you for the gorgeous flowers. You didn't have to do that.* She bent to smell the roses. How long had it been since she'd smelled fresh roses? She smelled them again, warming at the thought of Jax picking them out for her. Had he known what pink roses signified, or was sincerity a coincidence?

His voice whispered through her mind. *There's only one place I expect anyone to kowtow to me…In the bedroom. After I satisfy them, of course.*

She swallowed hard. She had a feeling he did everything with purpose. Her phone vibrated on the desk, startling her. She picked it up, and her pulse kicked up as she opened and read Jax's message. *Half the fun in life is celebrating our accomplishments, both big and small, and two years as director is no small feat.* She read it again, because it felt *that* good to be noticed and thought about.

Everything he did made her feel seen and special. If he put

that much effort into her, she could only imagine what he did for the women he went out with.

Another text popped up from him. *I was up early working on your design, and I think it'll be helpful if you try on different style gowns tonight. I'm not sold on any of the necklines we were thinking about last night.*

She'd been mesmerized watching him sketch last night. He was a true artist, taking her ideas and making them even more unique, less like a copied version of the classic dresses she adored. She typed, *It's a good thing I'm having my measurements taken today.*

His response rolled in seconds later. *I've been doing this a long time. I knew your measurements the minute I saw you in that Hervé Léger dress. I've already set aside the gowns I'd like you to try on. I'll bet you a morning run together that I guessed your size perfectly.*

Knowing he'd looked at her close enough to figure out her measurements was as thrilling as it was intimidating. Until she remembered their conversation about women and weight. Did she want to go running with him through the park and watch the sunrise? Heck yeah. Should she? The angel on her shoulder said no, while the devil said go for it. She didn't like extremes, so she decided to listen to the voice in between. The one telling her that there was no harm in being happy as long as she didn't cross any inappropriate lines, and she typed, *You're on!*

THE AFTERNOON FLEW by, and Roberta was a joy to chat with while she took Jordan's measurements. Jordan had hoped to see Jax while she was there, but she hadn't been so lucky. Now it was nearing seven thirty, and she was standing in the most luxurious dressing room she'd ever seen, wearing a gorgeous Jax Braden original wedding gown and having a panic attack. Her chest felt like there was an elephant sitting on it and the dress wasn't even zipped yet. She turned away from the mirror as a knock at the door startled her, and she froze.

"Jordan? Do you need help with the zipper?" Jax asked.

No. I need an ambulance. She closed her eyes, breathing deeply. This was just cold feet. That's all it was. It was normal, *natural.* Tons of women probably freaked out the first time they saw themselves in a wedding gown. "Yes, but I need a minute, please."

"Sure."

Glad he didn't push, she forced herself to look in the mirror again. The strapless gown could make anyone look like a princess, but she didn't see a princess in the mirror. She saw a woman who had so much baggage she wondered how she'd lug it down the aisle, and that wasn't the worst of it. Todd wanted her suitcases open and empty for him to fill as he wished, which meant all of her belongings, everything she cherished, would fall out as she made her way down that aisle. But she'd made a commitment to him, just as he'd made one to her all those years ago, when she was scared and alone, and he'd told her that she'd never be alone again.

But she *was* alone.

Reality slammed into her like a Mack truck. It was *her* fault she was alone. She'd put off the wedding all those times, and *she* had stayed in Maryland. Todd hadn't broken his promise. He was just waiting for her to keep up her end of the deal.

She lifted her chin, determined not to give the oppressive

feeling in her chest too much weight. It was only fear, wasn't it? Fear of moving away from the area and the job she loved? Fear of letting go of the hope that she'd find Casey?

Yes, that had to be it. With another deep, cleansing breath, she slipped her feet into her heels and headed out of the dressing room.

JAX HEARD THE dressing room door open and turned to see Jordan walking out in the strapless gown he'd chosen because it was most like the column dress and full, detachable train from *Sabrina* that she loved so much. He couldn't look away from the woman who had claimed a part of him eight months ago and even more of him since Nick's wedding. He didn't want to miss a second of her beauty. He'd seen hundreds of brides-to-be in their gowns, and never once had he felt like he was making a mistake.

Until now.

He was dressing the woman he was certain was meant to be his future wife so she could walk down the aisle to another man. He was starting to understand how much it had hurt Zev to walk away from Carly all those years ago. How his love for her had consumed him, growing more with every passing day for a decade until he finally got his girl.

Only Jax wouldn't get his girl in the end.

But he'd made a promise to design Jordan's gown, and he wasn't going to let her down.

"You are exquisite." He stepped behind her to zip the dress, inhaling the sweet scent of lavender. "Do you use lavender shampoo?"

"I do. You're as good with scents as you are with clothes. Lavender is a scent of hope."

He loved knowing that, and it made sense that she'd surround herself with things that represented hope, since the people closest to her didn't share her feelings about Casey. He gathered her hair over one shoulder—smooth as silk, just as he'd imagined—and his gaze fell to the most beautiful shoulders he'd ever seen. They were dusted with freckles, a smattering of them spilling down her spine like raindrops frozen in time. He wanted to kiss each and every one of them. Stifling that desire was like trying to wrangle a runaway bull, but he forced himself to remain focused on making this a memorable experience for her and zipped the dress.

"Let's take a closer look." He took her hand, leading her toward the fitting stand, and helped her onto it. She was surrounded by six full-length mirrors, but as he fixed her train, he noticed she kept her eyes downcast. "What do you think?"

"It's a beautiful gown." Her eyes remained trained on the floor.

"Take a look in the mirror." He waited for her to do as he'd asked, but she didn't. "Does it feel uncomfortable?"

She looked at him, eyes wide, as if he'd said something awful. "No. It's perfectly comfortable."

"Then why aren't you looking in the mirror?"

"I will." She feigned a smile, inhaling deeply before looking in the mirror. That feigned smile quickly disappeared, and the color drained from her face. She fanned herself with her hand. "Is it hot in here?"

"Not particularly."

She lifted her arms. "I'm sweating. Can you unzip it please

so I don't ruin your dress?"

"Of course. Is it too tight?" He unzipped it.

"No." She fanned her face again.

"Jordan, come off the platform." He took her hand as she stepped down. She wobbled, and he put his arm around her, drawing her against him. "Did you eat anything before coming here?"

"Yes, a little dinner."

"Do you feel sick?"

"No, just overwhelmed."

Me too, wondering how I'm going to let you go. He struggled to push that reality aside and focused on helping her find her footing.

"That's not uncommon among brides. Let's go sit down."

"No." She clung to him. "I might not make it over to the chairs."

"Okay. I've got you, sweetheart." *I'd rather you were in my arms anyway.* "Take a few deep breaths and blow them out slowly." She breathed deeply. "Attagirl. There's no rush. We have all night."

"This is so embarrassing."

"It shouldn't be. Lots of brides get overwhelmed or have cold feet."

"I've had cold feet for so long, I think they're nearly frozen."

Doesn't that tell you something? He wasn't going to be a dick and try to talk her out of marrying that dolt, no matter how much it killed him. "Getting married can be scary, and moving away and starting a new life in an unfamiliar place adds to that. Plus, you're leaving a lot more behind than the typical bride does. But you'll be *fine*, Jordan. You're a smart, strong woman, and I am one hundred percent certain that there is *nothing* you can't do for the man you love." Those last words tasted bitter.

Her brows knitted, and she looked like she wanted to say something, but she pressed her beautiful, kissable lips together and let go of him, drawing her shoulders back. "You're right. I'm just afraid of the changes that'll come after the wedding. Starting over *is* hard. And finding a new job in a new city where I don't know anyone *will* be scary."

"With a new husband," he reminded her, steeling himself against the reality that he'd no longer even have the chance of running into her in town.

"He's not new," she said softly. "But the husband part is."

Open your eyes, Jordan. This is where you're meant to be. By my side, in this area, with a man who would do anything for you. The color was coming back to her cheeks.

"I think I'm okay now. Thanks, Jax. I just needed a little perspective."

"That's what I'm here for."

"Does it ever get tiresome talking brides off ledges?"

"No." *But I've never wanted one of them to be mine before.* "It's all part of the job, and I get it, you know? Life changes— going to college, starting new jobs, moving to new cities—can be frightening, but handing your heart over to someone and trusting them to treasure and protect it for all the years to come? I'm sure, for some people, that's terrifying."

She lifted her eyes to his. "You have no idea how terrifying until you're standing in a gorgeous gown staring down that future. Everyone talks about how exciting weddings are, but nobody prepares you for the fear that comes with them. I'm glad you understand, and I know I'm just being silly. *Overthinking.* It's a bad habit of mine. Let's talk about this gorgeous gown."

She held out her hand, and he led her back to the fitting platform. Holding his gaze, and his hand a little tighter, she said, "Thank you for being so great about everything."

"Of course." He stepped back, freeing his hand, because holding hers made it too easy to pull her close.

She watched him in the mirror as he fixed her train again. "Roberta did a good job with my measurements. This fits perfectly."

"I never saw Roberta's notes."

Her eyes widened. "Are you kidding?"

"Would I kid about something that ends with us going for a run?"

She grinned. "I told you I suck at running."

"Coco and I don't mind walking. Don't even try to cop out of our bet. You don't want to be known as a *bet copper*."

"Is that even a saying?" She laughed softly.

"It is now. What morning works for you?"

"I don't *know*. Pick one."

"Friday. It might help stave off withdrawals since I won't see you this weekend."

"I can't do Friday. I have to go into work early. I'm leaving at three since Todd is coming into town."

"Thursday morning it is, then. Five forty-five?"

"Are you *sure* you want to do this? I'll definitely slow you down."

"I could use a little slowing down."

"You're not going to let this go, are you?"

"Nope. Do you want us to pick you up, or would you prefer to meet us at the park entrance?"

"I'll meet you there, and I'm making a mental note not to make any future bets with you." She ran her hands over the skirt of her gown. "What do you think?"

"I think you could make any gown look glamorous, but what matters is what you think and how you feel in it."

Her smile warmed. "There's that Braden charm again."

"I'll try to rein it in."

"Please don't," she said sweetly. "It's nice to be charmed sometimes."

Damn, he loved that.

She shifted her gaze to the mirror again and touched the straight neckline. "You said you weren't sold on the necklines we were thinking about last night, and this was one of them. I think you're right. It might be a little *too* straight. It kind of makes me look like I'm wearing a sports bra."

"That was my worry. You have beautiful curves, and this neckline doesn't accentuate them." He stepped in front of her. The platform brought them nearly eye to eye, and he realized she had rings of gold around her pupils.

"What?"

"Sorry. I didn't mean to stare. I thought your eyes were blue, but they have gold around the pupils. I've never seen that before."

"Casey had it, too. There's a name for it, but I can't remember what it is. My dad used to tell us that only really special kids were born with gold in their eyes. He said we were the *chosen ones* and that we wouldn't know what we were chosen for until we were older. When Casey went missing, I was convinced that it was because of those gold flecks. Like she'd been marked from birth to be taken away from us. The night of the accident, I was so sad and angry, and I felt so lost, I went outside and I just ran, screaming and crying, 'Take me! Bring her back and take me!' I remember my aunt and uncle chasing after me, and I tripped and hit my head on a rock." She touched the scar above her eyebrow, her eyes dampening. "I had to get stitches."

He brushed her hair away from the scar, his heart aching. "It's your Casey scar." He wanted to press a kiss to the thin white line, but he held back and simply ran his fingertip over it.

She whispered, "My Casey scar."

"I wish I was there when you went through that." He brushed his thumb over her cheek, wiping away a tear.

She lowered her gaze. "You couldn't have done anything."

"I could have run with you, cried with you, and held your hand when you got your stitches."

She lifted her eyes, more tears spilling from them. "Please stop noticing things about me and saying nice things. I don't want to cry every time I see you."

"I've tried to stop, but I can't. So how about if I just try to keep what I notice to myself?"

"*Deal.* Thank you." She wiped her eyes, turning back to the mirror. "Back to the dress."

The dress. Right. "If you like the straight neckline, which is perfect for highlighting your shoulders and collarbone, we could create a visual by following a path from here"—he touched the area where her neck joined her shoulder on either side and ran his index fingers at an angle down to just above her breasts, wishing he could kiss along those same paths—"to here." Her breathing quickened. "Then cut a narrow V down the center like this." He dragged his fingers lower, between her breasts, showing her what he meant, earning more lustful breathing as he brought them together just above her waist. "Creating an illusion-inset neckline."

"I like that," she said breathily, desire brimming in her eyes.

"Me too." He fought the urge to lean in and take the kiss he longed for and stepped aside, putting space between them before his willpower faltered, trying to distract himself with talk of her gown. "I have a few other ideas, which is why I chose more gowns for you to try on. But before you do, I wanted to ask about the column dress and detachable train. You liked them a lot last night, on paper. How do you feel now that you have one on?"

"The column dress," she said absently, blinking rapidly, as if she were trying to clear her head, too, before looking in the mirror again and studying her reflection. "The gown is gorgeous from top to bottom. I love the full skirt and the cinched waist. I can't believe I'm going to say this, since I loved Audrey in this type of dress, but I think I'm too *hippy* for a column dress after all." She turned, looking in the mirror over her shoulder at the train. "Do you like it?"

"You have a gorgeous figure, and I'd like you in anything." *Or nothing.* "But I agree that there are more flattering styles to suit your curves. More importantly, I don't think this gown is special enough for you. I actually don't think any of these will be, which is why we're designing something."

"What do you mean? Did I come across as snobby?"

"Not at all." He arched a brow. "I'm going to tell you something that I noticed about you, but only to help with the design process. Is that okay?"

"Yes." She shook her head. "I shouldn't have said anything."

"I'm glad you did. I want to know your boundaries." *In and out of the bedroom.* "And I didn't want you to think I was noticing too much when I said that you exude a certain softness, a grace and elegance that's all your own. I'd like to create a gown that allows the real you to shine through, not a modified version of someone else's gown."

She turned to the right, shading her eyes with her hand and peering around the room. Then she turned to the left and did it again.

"What are you doing?"

"Looking for whoever you just described, because we both know I'm a hot mess with all this wedding stuff."

"You're definitely hot, but I don't think you're a mess. I told you what I see, regardless of your state of mind at any given moment."

"Then we can agree to disagree. Are you thinking of a more elaborate gown?"

"No. Bells and whistles would detract from your natural beauty." He paused, letting that sink in and enjoying the bashful appreciation in her eyes. "I think we should go with simple and elegant, like the old classics, with a touch of small-town charm."

"*Ah*, the Jax Braden touch," she teased. "I like that idea."

You have no idea how much I want to touch you.

He wished like hell she'd read his thoughts, which meant he was losing it. He needed to get his head on straight, or designing together was going to be torturous. He tried to redirect his thoughts by focusing on the gown. "Now that we have a direction, as you try on gowns, we'll see what you like, and then we'll put our heads together and see what we come up with. Do you have any other thoughts on this dress?"

"I don't think so. I'll try on another." She reached for his hand, and he helped her off the platform.

Jordan tried on gown after gown, and every time she walked out of the dressing room, Jax was blown away anew.

As they picked apart each gown, discussing the pros and cons of various necklines, styles, and types of lace and embellishments, they both loosened up, and he got to see a whole new side of Jordan. She strutted like she was on a catwalk, and he fell into the game as the announcer. She wiggled her hips and arms to see how it felt to dance in each gown, and Jax took her hand, teasing her over needing to make a quick getaway at the wedding, and they ran across the showroom, both of them laughing. He'd never had so much fun doing what he loved.

"I'll go try on the last dress. I'll be right back," she exclaimed.

She was adorably sexy, dancing across the floor toward the dressing room. He couldn't resist stepping in and twirling her, just as he'd done at the wedding, earning more of her addicting laughter. As the dressing room door closed behind her, he grappled with how the universe could be so cruel, putting her in his path *twice* when she couldn't be his? Was there a lesson in this that he was missing? Was he being punished? Hell, even that didn't seem right, because this time with Jordan was anything other than a punishment, and it was likely all he'd ever get with her.

"Jax?" She peered out of the dressing room door, holding the front of the high-neck, open-back gown against her chest. "I was able to unclasp the collar, but the zipper is stuck. Would you mind helping me?"

"Sure." He stepped into the dressing room behind her, and as he moved her hair over her shoulder, his gaze fell to those tempting freckles trailing down her back. "We should definitely consider an open-back gown."

"With all my freckles? I'm not sure."

"Yes, with all your freckles." He traced those sexy freckles down her warm skin to the base of her spine, where the zipper was stuck, and heard her breathing catch. He reveled in that sexy little sound as their eyes met in the mirror. "They're one of the most beautiful things about you."

Her lips parted in surprise, giving her an air of innocence. Not innocence as in naïveté, but as if she was hearing some of these things for the first time ever and didn't quite believe them. If that were true, it was a tragedy. But he couldn't afford to get lost in that, in *her*, because he knew it was a point of no return, so he set his attention on the zipper. "Let's see if I can work this free."

"I'm sorry I got it stuck."

"Helping you take your clothes off is *not* a hardship."

"*Jax Braden*, might I remind you that I am here to design my *wedding* gown?" Her tone was sharp, but her eyes told another story. One he didn't think she even realized she was conveying.

"I wasn't flirting. I was—"

"Just stating a fact," they said in unison, and they both laughed.

He freed and unzipped the zipper, revealing the edge of pink lace panties. If that wasn't enough of a temptation, just above them were two of the sexiest dimples he'd ever seen. He wanted to get his mouth on those sweet indentations so badly, he could taste them. He gritted his teeth and tore his gaze away, catching hers in the mirror. That metal-to-magnet effect took over. He told himself to look away, but she bit her plump lower lip, and he desperately wanted to kiss it free. He knew he wouldn't stop there. He ached to wrap his arms around her and grind his hard length against her ass until she begged to be touched. To peel that dress down and fondle her breasts with one hand, pushing the other into those sexy pink panties, teasing her as he sealed his teeth over her neck, making her come so hard, her legs would give out.

But he wouldn't stop there, either.

He'd take off those panties with his teeth and bury his face between her legs, devouring her. Then he'd take her in his arms, breathing new life into her lungs as he made love to her the way she deserved to be loved, with every ounce of his being.

Fucking hell.

Now he was hard, and her eyes bored into him with as much confusion as heat, snapping him out of his fantasy, and he realized he was clutching her waist. He released her, swamped with emotions and a good amount of self-loathing.

"I'll be out there if you need me." He made a beeline out of the dressing room before he got them both into trouble and paced, giving himself hell. That could *not* happen again or he'd have no choice but to back out of designing her dress and hand the job over to Jillian…and he sure as hell didn't want to do that.

"I *love* the way this hugs my waist and hips, but it's too tight at my knees," she said nervously. "Am I too tall or—"

He turned, and for the tenth time that evening, she took his breath away, and a vision appeared in his mind like a movie. He saw her walking down the aisle in the most divine dress he'd ever seen, and standing at the end of that aisle, he saw himself.

"What's wrong, Jax?"

"Absolutely nothing." A laugh bubbled out. "I've *got* it! I can see it!"

She looked down at the dress. "See what?"

"Your gown. I *know* what it looks like."

Her face lit up. "Tell me!"

"I'll show you. *Come on.* We have to go up to the studio." He took her hand and ran toward the hall.

"I can't run in this! It's a fishtail!"

He scooped her into his arms, and she squealed, throwing her arms around his neck as he carried her into the hall.

"Jax, I'm too heavy!"

"You're perfect."

She beamed, both of them laughing as he ran up the stairs with her in his arms, but in his heart, he was weaving a different ending to their story.

One that looked a lot like this, only she was *his*, and the threshold he was carrying her over wasn't to his design studio.

Chapter Seven

JORDAN HAD NEVER been so sore in her entire life.

She grimaced with every step as she headed down the hall Friday afternoon to check in with the Crafty Crocheters before taking off for the day. She'd met Jax yesterday morning for their run, which had turned into a walk/run, and she'd had a great time with him and Coco, but she hadn't realized she'd be this sore. She smiled to herself, thinking about when Kelly had walked into her office Wednesday morning with a box of running shoes that had been delivered for her with a handwritten card from Jax that read, *No excuses, Ms. Lawler. Looking forward to tomorrow's run. JB.*

She couldn't believe he'd remembered that she'd said she didn't have running shoes. But after designing with him until nearly eleven o'clock each of the last three nights, she'd learned that he *really* never missed a thing. He was meticulous and patient, and while she'd expected to simply give her two cents about his designs, he'd actually wanted her to sketch her ideas in conjunction with his. It was amazing how well they worked together. Their styles complemented each other's, and they were coming up with new concepts that surprised both of them. That patience and attention to detail had carried over to their run.

He'd timed it perfectly, and they'd watched the sun rise over the mountains from the crest of a hill that was covered in daffodils, another sign of hope. He'd thought to pad his calculation to include time for her to warm up and stretch, which she hadn't even considered, and walking some of the way instead of running. But despite warming up and stretching with him, she was still sore.

She paused by the program board and saw that someone—Ruth, she was sure—had crossed out "Crafty Crocheters" and written "Knotty Hookers" above it. She chuckled to herself as she walked into the craft room, where Ruth, Gloria, and Sophia were chatting up a storm with five other ladies, their needles hard at work.

"Good afternoon, ladies." They greeted her as she went to their table and put a hand on the back of Ruth's chair. "You wouldn't happen to know who changed the program board, would you?"

Gloria clamped her mouth closed, eyeing Ruth and Sophia.

"I didn't notice anything," Ruth said. "Did you, girls?"

Four other ladies shook their heads, sharing guilty expressions, but Carla, who was ninety-two and showing signs of Alzheimer's, said, "You did it, Ruthie. And you call *me* forgetful. *Pfft.* I guess we're all getting old."

Jordan gave Ruth a disapproving look. "Ruth, you know we can't have that club name on our public board."

Ruth rolled her eyes and held up a limp wrist. "Go ahead. Give it a slap, and then take a seat and we'll show you the hats we've made."

"I'm not going to slap your wrist, but please respect the rules." Jordan winced as she lowered herself into a chair.

"Hemorrhoids?" Sophia asked.

MELISSA FOSTER

"What? *No.*" Jordan laughed.

"Did your man come to town early and make up for lost time?" Ruth waggled her brows.

"*Ruth.* No, he did not, and if he had, I wouldn't discuss it with the queens of *Gossip Central.*"

"I think he's in town," Sophia whispered, and the other ladies giggled.

"He did *not* arrive early. I went running yesterday morning with a friend, and I'm feeling it today."

"That's not nearly as fun as I'd hoped," Ruth said.

"Who needs enemies when your friends are willing to torture you like that?" Sophia asked.

"I actually enjoyed it," Jordan admitted. "It was nice spending the morning chatting with someone and moving my body instead of going through the same old morning routine before work. He brought his dog, and we watched the sunrise. I'm sore, but I had a lot more energy yesterday."

"A good man can get all those endorphins pumping in a much more enjoyable way," Ruth said, and the other ladies agreed.

Jordan wasn't about to tell them that making love with Todd had never left her as happy as spending the morning running with Jax and playing with Coco had. But that was another thing she could barely admit to herself.

"Before we show off our hats, we have a little something for you." Ruth reached into her bag and handed Jordan a small box wrapped in silver paper.

"What is this for?"

"For being you." Ruth smiled. "You might be a bigwig director to everyone else, but to us, you're sweet Jordan, our surrogate granddaughter and the woman who makes sure we have full, exciting lives."

"Even if we do try your patience from time to time," Gloria added.

A lump formed in Jordan's throat. "Thank you. That means a lot to me."

"Open it, honey," Sophia urged.

Jordan looked at the kind faces around the table as she unwrapped the box. When she lifted the top, she found a gorgeous pair of thin, crocheted-lace fingerless gloves that hooked around the middle finger, forming a V over the back of her hand to her wrist, under which they were secured with two pearl buttons. Her first thought was how much she loved them and the women who had made them for her. Her second thought was that she needed to text Jax a picture of the gloves so he could find a way to match them to her gown, but on the heels of that thought was the reality that Todd might not like them. He wasn't big on anything that didn't cost a fortune. That had always irked her, but it had never seemed as big of an issue as it did right then. But it wasn't fair of her to assume the worst. He'd surprised her before, like when she'd first rented the cozy house in Maryland. She'd thought he'd hate it because it was older and not as flashy as some, but he'd said if it made her happy, he loved it, and it did make her happy. It reminded her of her childhood home with three small bedrooms and a fenced backyard.

She looked up, her throat thickening as she met their eager expressions, and vowed to wear the pretty gloves no matter what Todd thought. "I love them. Thank you so much."

"Quick, show her the baby hats before she cries," Sophia urged. "Because if she cries, Gloria will cry, and then we're done for."

Jordan was relieved when they reached into their sewing bags and pulled out tiny crocheted hats. She put the top back on the box, mouthing, *Thank you*, to Sophia, who winked.

They passed the adorable hats around the table to Jordan. There was a white bonnet with scalloped edges and a pink flower on the side, a blue one with navy trim, a green and white striped hat, a pink one with rainbow stripes, and several others, including a little gray hat with a tiny brim and a yellow-and-black bumblebee on the side.

"These are the cutest ones yet." Jordan imagined tiny newborns wearing them. Like her gloves, knowing how much love went into every stitch made those hats even more special.

"One day we'll make hats for your babies, too," Gloria said warmly.

Jordan's chest constricted. She didn't want to think about how much she'd miss them when she moved away, much less how she couldn't even think about starting a new family when she was still missing pieces of her old one.

"There you are," Kelly said as she hurried into the room. "Hello, ladies. I'm sorry, but I need to steal Jordan away."

"Fun sucker," Ruth teased.

"I guess I won't be invited to join the Knotty Hookers anytime soon," Kelly said.

"You got any pull with *this one*?" Ruth motioned to Jordan. "We want our new name on the board."

"No, she doesn't," Jordan said. "Thank you again for the lovely gift. I look forward to wearing the gloves. Have a great day, ladies." She winced as she pushed to her feet.

"The only way to get over the pain is to go running again," Kelly said.

"I can barely *walk*," Jordan said as they headed back toward her office.

"No pain, no gain. Mrs. Nicholas Braden is holding on the phone for you."

"Trixie?"

"Yes, but she said you must now address her as Mrs. Nicholas Braden."

"She's so funny." Trixie was a funny, sharp businesswoman, and from the few times they'd gone out to dinner together, Jordan knew she took no guff and hid behind nothing. As Jordan walked into her office, she thought about how Jax had called her *real*. She'd had only fleeting moments of feeling real these last few years, and most of them had been with him. But the rest of the time, she always felt like she was hiding behind a cloak of secrets.

She picked up the phone. "Hello, Mrs. Nicholas Braden. Aren't you supposed to be honeymooning?"

"Oh, we *are*. We're honeymooning in the bedroom, the living room, the bathroom, the barn—"

"Okay, okay. I'm thrilled for you, but don't rub it in. I only get to see Todd once a month, and this weekend makes *seven* weeks since I've seen him because he's been so busy lately." Trixie's sex life sounded exciting. Jordan could only imagine the horror on Todd's face if she ever suggested having sex in a barn. Todd wasn't a particularly creative lover, and that hadn't bothered her in college. She'd only been with two other guys, and sexual fantasies hadn't been high on her priority list. She'd heard other girls talking about having to fake it with their boyfriends, and she assumed that was normal. But after college, when they saw each other less often and she had more time on her hands alone in the evenings, she realized she could make herself orgasm multiple times. She'd tried to spice things up and seduce him into fooling around at his office once, but he hadn't been into it, and she hadn't tried again. But the way she practically turned inside out around Jax had her mind wandering down darker paths, piquing new, thrilling curiosities, and she was having a heck of a time trying to ignore them.

"Sorry, that *is* a long time. But he's coming this afternoon, right?" Trixie asked.

"Yes. He should be here around five. I can't wait to see him. It feels like it's been six months." She was secretly hoping that seeing him might silence her loneliness and temper the attraction she had to Jax.

"Good! I will definitely *not* call you tonight. But Todd *is* the reason I'm calling. I thought we could all go out to dinner Saturday night. I'd love to meet him, and Nick is so protective of all my friends, he said he needs to check out your man."

"What do you mean, check him out?"

"It's a guy thing. My brothers would do it if you lived in Oak Falls. They protect people in their circle, and you're in ours."

"I am?" She couldn't hide her surprise.

"Of course you are. We thought we'd meet Todd at our wedding, and since he wasn't able to come, we don't want to miss our chance to get to know him. Unless you want that time alone with him, which I'd understand."

Trixie couldn't know how much that meant to her. Or how it made her feel guilty for keeping certain parts of her life a secret. But then another thought crept in. Jax was so thoughtful, she wondered if he was trying to facilitate a deeper friendship between them. "Did Jax ask you to invite us to dinner?"

"No. Why would he? I haven't even seen him since the wedding."

"We were talking about friendships the other night, and…never mind. It's not important. We'd love to have dinner with you and Nick." She'd have to clear it with Todd, but he was social, and she was sure he wouldn't mind.

"Great!" They made plans to meet for dinner tomorrow night, and then Trixie said, "Now, for the *other* reason I called. At our reception, Jax told Nick he was designing your wedding gown. How's that going?"

"Better than I ever imagined. Jax is incredible, and he asked me to design it with him."

"I think that's pretty standard, right? Don't all brides give input on what they want?"

"Yes, but he asked me to actually design the gown with him. I sit beside him at the drawing table, both of us sketching our ideas as we discuss them, and then we blend the parts of each of our drawings that we like into one. I never mentioned this to you, but before going into hospital administration, I studied fashion design."

"Holy cow, woman. That's *big*. I've never heard of him co-designing a gown. You must be *really* good. Why did you change fields?"

"Job security, mostly." She felt a pang of guilt glossing over her answer, but explaining was a whole *other* conversation. "You can imagine how shocked I was when Jax asked me to design it with him. We've been designing together all week in the evenings and texting with new ideas during the day and late at night. You know he's a brilliant designer, but I'm in awe of his artistic eye, and it's so much fun being around all that delicate lace and sparkling tulle, lustrous satin, and elegant chiffon."

"Oh my God, you sound like a designer. *Lustrous satin.*"

Jordan laughed. "Hey."

"I'm only kidding."

"I know. I met Emiko, who does the beadwork, and I just about died when she showed me Amber Montgomery's dress. I mean, *wow*. That woman deserves an award."

"She's so talented, and don't you just love Jonathan?"

"Yes! I want him as my best friend. He's hilarious."

They both laughed.

"I want to see your wedding gown designs," Trixie said.

"I'll text them to you right now." She grabbed her cell phone from the desk, navigating to the sketches she and Jax had drawn and texting them to Trixie. "Todd and his mother want me to have an extravagant gown, and you know I want something simple."

"It's your wedding day. You should wear the dress *you* want."

"I'm going to. I talked to Jax about it, because I want Todd and his family to be as pleased with my gown as I am, and we think we've nailed it with these designs. Jax called them *demure elegance*."

"I love the sound of that. Let me put you on speaker while I look at them." A second later, she said, "Ohmygod, *Jordan*. I *love* the first one. It's sexy *and* classy."

Jordan looked at the picture of the mermaid gown with a Queen Anne sweetheart neckline and lace cutouts along her ribs that widened at the bottom, giving the illusion of a heart on her chest. The lace from the cutouts continued over the white satin down to her hips, then trailed inward, giving it an extra dose of femininity.

"Jax and I love it, too. Who am I kidding? We love all three! They all have open backs and—"

"Wait! The other two pictures just came through. Oh, *Jor-*

dan. The off-the-shoulder one is like a fairy-tale gown with that flowing skirt and deep neckline."

"I know! I love it so much. The skirt would be hand beaded so it sparkles."

"That sounds gorgeous. I love the row of beads that looks like it's floating above the neckline and the way the three rows come together on each side and rest just off the shoulder. Okay, hold on. Pull back on the reins. The last one you sent is to die for! But if you wear that one, you'll have to get married on a beach, because the bodice looks like a seashell with the embellishments you've drawn, and the fishtail is stunning as is, without any embellishments. You've got the body for it, too." The gown had an intricately beaded strapless bodice that rose in the center and a long fishtail skirt.

Trixie's enthusiasm made it even more exciting to talk about. "I would *love* to get married barefoot on a beach or in a simple garden wedding."

"Why don't you? You haven't chosen a venue yet."

"Todd and I talked about it. His family doesn't like the idea of anything too simple, and I don't want to be too pushy and start our marriage on a bad note. We've already had to compromise on a number of things, like getting married here instead of in the city. You lucked out with Lily and Clint. They're so easygoing."

"I know I did. You haven't said much about his parents. They're not nice?"

"They are, but they're big-city nice." She winced. "Did that sound mean?"

"No, just honest. I think I'm starting to understand your cold feet."

Unfortunately, so am I.

They talked for a while longer, and Jordan finished up for the day and then headed home, excited to see Todd. She stopped to pick up a bouquet of daffodils, because a little extra hope for a romantic weekend wouldn't hurt. When she got home, she straightened the living room, putting away her lavender- and peppermint-scented candles, even though they were also symbols of hope, and lighting Todd's favorite applewood-scented candles instead, which she'd bought to use the weekend of Trixie's wedding. She put the daffodils in a vase on the dining room table and set the sketches of her bridal gown around them in a pretty display. She hadn't told Todd that she was designing the gown with Jax. She wanted to surprise him.

She placed tomorrow's itinerary, which she'd prettied up using Photoshop, adding wedding bells and garland, on the table and retrieved the gift box with the gloves. As she set it by the drawings, she remembered she hadn't texted a picture to Jax, and she did that quickly. Then she showered, primped, and dressed in the new lingerie she'd bought before Trixie's wedding, cream slacks, and a sexy wrap sweater. She was putting on her makeup when her phone vibrated with a message from Jax. *What a thoughtful gift. Let me play with the designs tonight and see what I can come up with.* A call from Todd rang through, and her heart skipped. "Hi. How close are you?"

"Pretty damn far."

"Oh no. Traffic?"

"No, babe. I was two hours into the drive when I got a call from a client whose life has basically imploded. He's being sued and divorced and all sorts of shit. I just got off the plane in Atlanta to meet with him and his lawyer."

"Atlanta?" The pit of her stomach sank. "So you're coming

tomorrow morning instead?"

"No. I'm sorry, babe, but I'll be here until at least Monday."

Anger clawed its way out. "But we've had this scheduled for *weeks*. You promised you'd make it. We have the venues to look at, and the cake tasting, and—"

"Jordan, for Christ's sake. This guy's entire world is crumbling around him, and you're worried about *cake*?"

"It's not the cake," she seethed. "It's everything. You cancel on me all the time, and I know your clients are important, but what about me, Todd? What about us?"

"We *both* knew what we were getting into when you chose to stay in Maryland. If I had it my way, you'd've moved to the city with me right after college, so cut me some fucking slack. Do you think I like being yanked around like a damn puppet and working a million hours?"

She blew out a breath, trying to calm herself down. "*No*. I'm just disappointed. I feel like we never see each other anymore. We're finally moving forward with the wedding and I'm doing it alone."

"My mom offered to help with the arrangements. Do you want me to get her a flight?"

God no. "No, thanks. This is *our* wedding, and I thought you were excited to be part of it."

"I am excited, and I hate disappointing you, but work has to come first. You know I trust your judgment, babe. It's just cake and a roof over our heads while we say our vows. Five years from now we won't remember what flavor the cake was or what the damn venue looked like, and I promise I'll make it up to you."

She was gutted by his cavalier attitude, but she was sick of begging for time, and she didn't have it in her to argue for what should be a given. "Mm-hm."

"I mean it, babe. I know I screwed up by missing your friend Tracey's wedding."

"Trixie."

"Who names their kid Trixie?"

She rolled her eyes, hating that judgmental side of him. "Her parents, obviously, and she and her husband were excited to meet you. We were going to have dinner with them tomorrow night."

"Well, hell. I'm sorry about that, too. But I'll make it up to you. Why don't I book us a weekend in Cabo next month?"

"So you can cancel that, too?"

"You're right. I won't make promises I can't keep. That's not fair to either of us."

Despite how upset she was, it wasn't fair to put all the blame on him. "One promise breaker in the relationship is enough, and I think I've got that covered after putting off the wedding so many times."

"Don't sweat that, babe, and mark my word. I'll more than make up for all of my cancellations on our wedding night. I'm going to make you come so many times you won't be able to walk the next day. I've got to go, babe. Love you."

He ended the call, and she stared at the phone, thinking about their wedding night, and the promise that he had no idea he was incapable of keeping.

JAX DIDN'T KNOW what he needed more: a kick in his ass by one of his brothers or a stiff drink, but he definitely needed something to get his head on straight. It was a little after nine, and he was in the studio working on the designs for Jordan's dress. At least he was trying to, but it was slow going. He couldn't stop thinking about her in the arms of another guy.

He gritted his teeth as his conscience corrected him. *In the arms of her fiancé.*

Coco pawed at his leg.

He reached down to pet her. He rarely brought her to work because he didn't want to chance getting dog hair on the fabric, but tonight he'd needed the company. "We'll go home soon, baby."

She barked, her tail wagging.

He'd just taken her out ten minutes ago. "It won't be too long. I just want to get this done."

She barked and ran out the studio door.

"Coco!" He pushed to his feet and heard Jillian talking to Coco as she came up the stairs. They had keys to each other's offices, and while Jillian made good use of hers, he'd never used his.

"Why aren't you answering your texts?" Jillian strutted into the studio looking ready for a night out in one of her signature minidresses and maroon knee-high boots. "I thought you were dead."

"Really, Jilly? That was your first thought?" He crouched to love up Coco.

"*No.* It was my third. It's Friday night, so I figured you were either busy with a woman and hadn't come up for air in the last two hours, in which case, *go you,* or that you were avoiding my calls, in which case, *what the hell?* But then I saw your car out front and the lights on, and you never work on Friday nights, so my mind took a detour."

He kissed Coco's head and pushed to his feet. "I'm working on the designs for Jordan's dress, and my phone is in my jacket. I must not have heard it." His jacket was hanging on the back of his chair, and he'd turned the ringer off because every time he'd gotten a text, he'd hoped it was Jordan, and it had driven him nuts.

"Speaking of Jordan, how's that going?"

"See for yourself." He motioned to the designs on the table.

She looked over the three gowns he was working on. "Wow. These are gorgeous. Seriously, some of your best work." She picked up the picture he'd printed from Jordan's text of the gloves. "What's this?"

"A few of the residents at Jordan's work crocheted them for her and she wants to wear them at the wedding."

"That's so sweet. They must really love her."

"Yeah." He'd been thinking about that and how much his sensitive girl would probably miss seeing them when she moved.

Jillian looked between the picture of the gloves and the drawings. "I see the tie-ins now. That's brilliant."

"I think she'll like them."

"No smart-ass comment about how brilliant you are?" Jillian studied him with narrowing eyes. "What's wrong?"

"Nothing."

"You can't bullshit your twin."

"You thought I was *dead*. Your twin powers are not what they used to be."

"If I really thought you were dead, would I have come in here alone, or would I have called Nick?"

"Fair point." He knew she wouldn't relent, and the truth was, he could use someone to talk to. When they were young, Jillian had been his confidant, because Nick and Beau had been more brawn than sensitivity, and Zev and Carly had been joined at the hip, while Graham was younger and had been more interested in swinging from tree limbs than talking about anything real.

Jax held up his hand, palm out, fingers spread, as they'd done when they were younger. "Twin talk?"

"Uh-oh, this is bad." She pressed her hand to his, and they laced their fingers together.

"To the grave," they said in unison.

Jillian climbed onto a chair at the drawing table. "I knew it wasn't a good idea for you to work that closely with Jordan."

"I needed to do it, and I'm glad I am. I'm discovering so much more about her." He reached for Jordan's sketch pad. "Take a look in there and tell me what you think."

He waited as she analyzed the sketches, brows furrowed. She lifted her gaze to his a few pages in. "Who drew these? They're not yours."

"They're Jordan's. She called them *doodles*."

Her eyes widened, and she laughed. "If I could doodle like this..." She admired a few more pages of dresses.

"So it's not just me, right? She's talented as hell. I saw it the second I looked at her sketches, but I thought maybe it was just because I like her so damn much."

She set the sketch pad on the table. "You already know the answer or you wouldn't have shown them to me."

He paced, too agitated to stand still, and Coco sat up, watching him. "She's designing her gown with me, which is probably why that's some of my best work, because it's not just mine. It's *ours*. I swear it's like a sign."

"You don't believe in signs."

"No shit, but I need to believe in something. She's here

every night until ten or eleven, and damn it, Jilly, we're so fucking good together. *Too good* not to be meant for each other."

"*Jax*," Jillian warned. "Just because she's got an eye for design doesn't mean she's got an eye for you."

"It's not just that. We are on the *same* page with everything." He didn't want to divulge Jordan's secrets, so he said, "We just click. She had a fucking crush on Audrey Hepburn, for God's sake. If you could *see* us together, if you could hear our conversations and see the way she is with me, you'd get it. She's open and trusting, and she's funny and sexy, but it's so much deeper than that."

"You really are gaga over her."

"I don't even know who I am anymore. I feel incomplete when she's not with me, and I know that's crazy, but it's *real*. You should see how she looks at me. I *know* she wants me as much as I want her. I feel it in my bones, and I have since the day we met."

"Jax, you're designing her *wedding gown*. I think you're seeing what you want to see."

"No, I'm *not*. She's postponed the wedding *four* times."

"Do you know why?"

"It doesn't matter why. If he was the right guy, she'd be married and living in New York right now. But she's *not*, because he doesn't respect her time or her beliefs, and God knows what the hell he was doing in the city instead of being here with her at Trixie's wedding. She needs to dump his ass."

"That's not your decision to make." Jillian pushed to her feet, speaking sternly. "Jax, look at me."

He stopped pacing and met her gaze.

"I'm worried you're going to get hurt. Have you told her

how you feel?"

He nodded. "At the wedding."

Her expression turned empathetic. "And she's *still* getting married. I think she's given you her answer, and you're too caught up in her to see it. You need to face the facts and accept that she's marrying another man."

"I fucking know she is, but I can't believe it. In my heart, she's supposed to be mine."

"Oh, *Jax.*" She wrapped her arms around him. "I hate this for you."

"*Yeah*" came out as tortured as he felt. "I just can't seem to let her go."

She stepped back with a serious expression. "Which is why you should let me finish designing her gown. This is bigger and more powerful than you, and I'm afraid you might do something stupid."

"I won't do anything stupid, but I made a promise, and I need to see it through."

"What you need is a sign to let her go. Why don't you come with me to Whispers tonight and get your mind off her? I'm meeting Emmaline and a few other friends." Whispers was a nightclub in Peaceful Harbor, the next town over. "We'll have a few drinks, chat up some unsuspecting hotties, and maybe we can break that spell she's got you under."

He scrubbed a hand down his face. He had no interest in flirting with anyone other than Jordan.

"Come on, Jax. This isn't who you are. You don't sit around pining for women. You're just caught up in the idea of being with her. Let's break the cycle. We haven't been out together in a long time."

"Maybe you're right, and I'm too caught up in her to see

things clearly."

"I really think you are."

He shrugged. "It's worth a try. I'll meet you there. I want to finish up these designs, and I need to run Coco home."

"Want me to stay with you? Or take Coco home?"

"No. Thanks. Go meet your friends. I won't be long."

"Okay." She leaned closer and whispered, "Have you gotten my birthday present yet?" Their birthday was next weekend. Nick and Trixie were hosting a family barbecue to celebrate their thirtieth.

"Wouldn't you like to know? Did you get mine?"

Jillian smirked. "It's in the works."

After Jillian left, Jax worked on the designs for another half hour. When he was done, he took out his phone to text Jordan, hesitating at first because she was with Todd. The Neanderthal in him wanted to send a message that would bug the hell out of her asshole fiancé, so he would at least know that someone was watching the way he treated her.

But Jillian was right. He needed to start accepting the facts.

He thumbed out, *Just finished the revisions and thought you and Todd might want to see them.* It killed him to even type the guy's name, but he was pretty sure "the dickhead" wouldn't be appreciated. *The gloves are important, and I'd like to see them as part of the design rather than an afterthought. I've tried incorporating matching lace into each dress, and I think it really pulls them together with the gloves. Let me know your thoughts when you have time. No rush. Good luck tomorrow.* He was about to send the message when he decided to rip the bandage off and added, *If you want to bring Todd by to see the designs in person, I'll be around.* He sent the message, along with pictures of the sketches and notations about the changes he'd made.

Maybe if he put a face with the name, it would help sever the connection he felt. He shoved his phone into his pocket and tried not to think about how long it was taking for her to respond as he drove home. But as he drove up the private lane to his four-bedroom home on three beautiful acres and parked in the circular driveway, she was still front and center in his mind.

Coco bounded out of the car and into the yard as Jax headed up to the wide front porch. His phone vibrated. He hoped like hell it was Jordan, and at the same time, in that split second before looking at the screen, he hoped it wasn't. He knew it would set him off if she texted about how great her evening with Todd was going. Yeah, that made him an asshole, but it wasn't like he had any control over it.

Jillian's name appeared on the screen. *Damn it.* He read her message. *Don't even think about standing me up.* He thumbed out, *Just dropping off Coco.* As he hit send, another message bubble popped up—this one from Jordan. His pulse ratcheted up as he read it. *I love all your ideas. Todd didn't make it, so we won't be stopping by. Thanks for the offer.*

He clutched the phone, calling Jordan, his other hand curling into a fist. That fucker didn't deserve her. In an effort to tamp down his anger, he watched Coco playing with one of her toys in the grass.

"Hi," she said a little tentatively.

"Hey, sweetheart. Are you okay?"

"I'm *fine.*"

He heard the pain she was trying to mask. "No, you're not, and you don't have to pretend with me."

"I'm fine, really."

"Jordan, you took off work early and planned an entire day

to make decisions about your wedding, and your fiancé stood you up. Only an unfeeling person would be okay with that, and you are anything but unfeeling."

"It'll be easier to make decisions by myself anyway."

Bullshit. "You're not going to do it alone. I'll come with you. I'm great at eating cake."

"Don't be ridiculous. You have a life, and I've taken up enough of it with my dress."

He noticed an uptick in her energy, despite her argument, so he took a different approach. "Do you have any idea what kind of clout my name pulls in this area? I can get you great discounts."

"Jax."

He heard the smile in her voice. "What time is your first appointment?"

"Ten, but I'm not going to take up your time for *my* wedding. I can handle it."

"I won't argue that point. What are you doing right now? Why don't you meet me for a drink?"

"Thanks, but I'm already in my comfy clothes, and I don't really want to go out."

"Your *comfy* clothes? Now, that's something I need to see for myself." He wanted to drive over to her house, but he didn't trust himself, so he pushed the FaceTime button and sat in a chair on the porch.

"Jax," she complained.

"Accept the video call, sweetheart. Let me see for myself if you're okay."

Her beautiful face appeared on the screen. Her hair was pulled back in a ponytail, and a reluctant smile stretched across her cheeks despite her red-rimmed eyes. He'd like to give that asshole a piece of his mind.

She covered her face with her hand, clutching his handkerchief in her other hand. "I can't believe you did that."

You wanted to see me, or you wouldn't have accepted the call. "I was having withdrawals." *And you're using my handkerchief. I was on your mind, too, sexy girl. Don't deny it.*

She laughed, lowering her hand. "How do you always know how to make me smile?"

"That's easy. I never want you to have a reason not to."

"I don't know how women resist that Braden charm."

"You seem to be resisting it well." He didn't want to pretend or play games. "I would come over with comfort food and watch movies with you, but I don't trust myself not to accidentally charm your pants off."

"Jax!" Laughter bubbled out. "You are too much."

"You have no idea how right you are, but you should stop flirting with me. I'm mentally dating an incredible woman and officially off the market."

"Ohmygod. I'm hanging up now."

"Wait. You haven't even shown me your comfy clothes yet."

She nibbled on her lower lip, looking adorable. "Promise not to make fun of me?"

"I promise, but now I'm even more curious."

"I can't believe I'm doing this." She angled the phone down, showing her white tank top, which had TIME TO WINE emblazoned across her chest, her nipples straining against the thin material, and cute white shorts with a wine bottle on the left and red ruffles on the hems, covering the tops of her beautiful thighs. When she pointed the phone at her face again, her cheeks were pink. "Don't tease me. I know they're silly."

"Don't apologize. Silliness looks sexy as hell on you." That earned a sweet smile, and he wanted to see more of it. "I have an idea. Do you have wine at your place?"

"Yes. Why?"

"I've had a long night, and I could use some company. Let's have a glass of wine and watch a movie together. You there, me here."

She wrinkled her nose. "I don't know…"

"From the looks of your smile, you're not hating this video call, right?"

She shook her head.

Coco bounded onto the porch, and Jax petted her. "You want to say hi to Jordan?" He turned the phone so Jordan could see her.

Jordan's face lit up. "Hi, Coco. You're so lucky to have her to cuddle with."

"Want me to bring her over to cuddle with?"

"Yes, but *no*. That's not a good idea, as you pointed out earlier."

"I take it back."

She smiled, shaking her head. "Too late. I've already heard it."

"Then watch a movie with us over FaceTime. I promise to behave."

"I don't think behaving comes easily to you."

"You've got that wrong," he said honestly. "With the exception of in the bedroom, and when I'm around you"—which he hoped would be one and the same one day—"I'm usually very well behaved." She didn't look away, despite the crimson spreading over her cheeks, and he knew how much courage that took. What he didn't know was exactly how to interpret it, but he wasn't going to take the time to dissect it and risk losing the chance to spend more time on the video call with her. "We don't even have to talk. I just like being around you, and I have a feeling you shouldn't be alone tonight, either."

Her gaze softened. "Are you sure you want to do this?"

Short of being right there beside you, "There's nothing I'd rather do. You can even choose the movie."

"What if it's a chick flick?"

"I like chicks and flicks."

She smiled. "Okay. How about *27 Dresses*?"

"You're a James Marsden fan. Good to know."

"He's super cute, but I love how he and Katherine Heigl have so much fun together. It always puts me in a good mood. Kind of like you do, but don't let that go to your head."

Too late. "*27 Dresses* it is. Just give me a minute to bring Coco inside and change into my own comfy clothes." He pushed to his feet and unlocked the door.

"What does a designer wear to be comfortable?"

"*Nothing*, but since that's not appropriate, I'll be wearing sweats and a T-shirt."

"I think I'd better hold you to that *not talking* offer. Do you want to get settled and call me back?"

"And give you a chance to change your mind? Hell *no*. I don't usually bring women home with me, but for you, I'm making an exception."

"You're so funny. Does that mean I get to see your house?"

"Sure." He flipped the camera around and cleared his throat, putting on his best Realtor voice. "As you can see, the foyer opens into a great room with a cathedral ceiling and stone fireplace."

"I love the built-in bookshelves, and look at all those French doors."

"They lead to a patio." She *ooh*ed and *aah*ed over the rich wood floors and commented on everything from the shelved half wall that separated the foyer from the dining room to the warmth of his study and the veranda overlooking the heated pool and basketball court. He couldn't show her the gorgeous gardens or stellar views in the dark, but he hoped to one day.

After showing her the bedrooms, he set the phone on his dresser, strategically leaning it against a bottle of cologne while he changed his clothes so she could see him from the waist up— so as not to embarrass her, because if it were up to him, she'd get an eyeful of every inch of him.

"Why did you build such a big house?"

He set sweats and a T-shirt on the bed and stripped off his shirt, enjoying the way she checked him out. "Because I don't plan on ever moving, and I hope to have a family of my own one day. So I built an upscale bungalow large enough to raise a family in, luxurious enough to feed my appreciation of nice things, and homey enough to welcome sticky fingers and dirty paws."

She was quiet for a long moment, looking at him like she was puzzling something out. "Do you ever get lonely in that big empty house?"

"It's hard to be lonely with Coco around." He moved the phone so she could see Coco lying on the bed, then turned it back toward himself. "Do you get lonely?"

She held his gaze as "Yes" slipped from her lips.

How could one simple word make him ache to be by her side so badly? "That's why you need me in your life." He stopped short of saying something he shouldn't. "To entertain you on video calls and keep the loneliness at bay."

"I'd say lucky me, but seeing you shirtless isn't helping."

"*Damn*. Sorry about that." He pulled on his shirt and

changed into his sweats. "You could have looked away."

She rolled her eyes.

They each got a bottle of wine and a wineglass, and Coco snuggled in beside him on the couch as they settled in by their televisions. Jax texted Jillian to let her know he wasn't going to make it to Whispers and told her he was turning off his phone and going to bed so he wouldn't have to deal with a dozen texts from her trying to talk him into coming.

He and Jordan angled their phones so they could see each other, and she tucked her legs beside her and draped a blanket over them. It took everything he had not to tell her how much he wished he was there. He propped his feet up on the coffee table, ankles crossed, enjoying the way she made a little nest of pillows around herself, and as Coco rested her head on his lap, he wondered if Jordan built that nest for the contact, to feel less lonely.

He held up his glass. "To good friends."

"Here, here. It's been a long time since I've had one. Thank you for talking me into this."

They sipped their wine and watched the movie. She stole glances at him, catching him watching her every time. They didn't talk, and that was okay, because seeing her smile and hearing her laugh was better than banter any day.

As the night wore on, she lay on her side, pulling the blanket over her shoulder, her eyes at half-mast. Her eyelids got heavier by the minute, and eventually she nodded off. She looked peaceful and a thousand times happier than she had when she'd first answered the call.

Jax turned off his television, but he left the FaceTime call rolling and whispered, "Good night, sweet Jordan. See you soon."

Chapter Eight

JORDAN SNUGGLED DEEPER beneath the blanket as wakefulness tiptoed in. She'd slept better than she had in so long, she wanted to linger in the warmth and comfort of being well rested. But the sound of the television broke through her reverie, bringing last night rushing back, and she realized she was still on the couch and couldn't remember ending their call. She bolted up to a sitting position, frantically reaching for her phone. Her stomach pitched at the sight of Jax's smiling face looking back at her.

"Good morning, beautiful." His hair was damp, his scruff perfectly manicured, and he was wearing a crisp white dress shirt, reminding her that she was still in her pajamas. "It's kind of unfair that you can wake up looking so good."

She snagged the blanket, holding it against her chest as she caught her reflection in the phone. Her eyeliner was smudged, her ponytail was falling out, and there were tangled wayward hairs sticking out everywhere.

"I'm a mess. Have you been watching me all night?" She was mortified. Did she drool? Fart? Talk in her sleep? She didn't want to know, and quickly added, "What time is it?"

"It's eight thirty-five. I made us coffee." He held up two

steaming mugs.

"Coffee? But I'm here, and you're....*Never mind.* That was sweet, but I'm late. I have to get ready to go." She jumped to her feet, clutching the phone. "I can't believe you stayed on FaceTime the whole night. I'm sorry I fell asleep. It must have been the wine. I almost never drink, despite what my pajama top says."

"You had a rough day and needed the rest. I was glad to know you were safe."

Safe? She didn't know what to make of that. "That was fun last night. I mean before I fell asleep, and I'm sorry to run, but I have to leave in forty minutes, and I'm going to be late if I don't get in the shower."

"No worries. I'll see you soon."

She ended the call and hurried through a shower. She and Todd had been together for years, and never once had they done something like watch a movie together on FaceTime or stay on the phone all night—awake or asleep. As she dried her hair and put on makeup, Jax's voice trickled in. *Good morning, beautiful. It's kind of unfair that you can wake up looking so good.* Did he always say what he felt, or was he just being nice? Whatever the reason, she felt prettier than she had in a long time and decided to wear a cute pale green minidress with a cream-colored flower petal print. It tied between her breasts, making the top clingy and the rest flowy and flirty. It showed a little too much cleavage, but she was feeling good, and Todd wasn't there to tell her she shouldn't dress so provocatively. She put on a pair of dangling gold earrings with three linked circles and a matching necklace, then slipped her feet into her comfortable Stuart Weitzman wedge-heeled cream espadrilles.

Her stomach growled as she threw her phone and wallet

into a small cream clutch with a crossbody strap so she wouldn't have to worry about holding it. She hurried into the kitchen for a breakfast bar and shoved it into her clutch, snagged her keys and her itinerary, and headed out the front door. She nearly tripped over herself at the sight of Jax standing by his car, drop-dead handsome in a pale blue blazer over a dark blue dress shirt, with white jeans and loafers, holding a cardboard sign that read, MS. JORDAN LAWLER. Her pulse spiked, happiness blooming inside her.

"*Hi.* What are you doing here?"

"This is your big day. You should have a handsome guy on your arm." He held his hands out to his sides. "Need I say more?"

Why, *oh* why, did everything he do make her giddy? "You don't have to come with me."

"Friends don't leave friends hanging."

He eyed her appreciatively as she came down the walk, making her glad she'd chosen such a cute outfit, but a little self-conscious about the cleavage-bearing neckline.

"Especially not gorgeous friends. We'd better hurry if we're going to make that appointment." He opened the car door.

"Are you always this pushy?"

"I liked it better when you called me charming." He guided her into the car. He did something in the back seat as she settled into the front, and then he leaned in, smelling like man, musk, and every woman's dream come true as he put a basket on her lap.

She peered into the basket and saw a muffin on a real plate, garnished with sliced strawberries and a sprig of mint. Beside it were silverware and a cloth napkin.

He handed her a to-go cup. "This morning's latte is French

vanilla, and the muffin is banana nut."

"Jax, you're spoiling me. Do you treat all your friends like this?"

"Only the ones I like as much as you."

"I bet there are a lot of women lining up to sit in this seat." She felt a pang of jealousy.

"I wouldn't know. I told you I'm mentally taken."

Guilt swept in like a gust of wind. "You deserve so much more than a mental relationship, but selfishly, our friendship makes me happy."

"Me too." He winked and closed the door, walking around to the driver's seat. "Where to, Ms. Lawler?"

She smiled as she spread the napkin on her lap. "The Davenport Estate. Would you like to share my muffin?"

He gave her a sly grin as he drove away from the curb. "Hell *yes.*"

There was probably some kind of sin wrapped up in enjoying their time together, but as she cut the muffin and handed him half on a napkin, she didn't care. Because there had to be some kind of sin in standing up your fiancé twice in one month, too.

"THIS IS EVERY bit as impressive as I'd heard it was," Jax said as he parked in front of the Davenport mansion, a sought-after French-style country estate.

"It's too over the top for my taste, but Todd's mother suggested we look at it."

"Don't underestimate the value of pleasing your soon-to-be

mother-in-law. This place definitely makes a statement." He climbed out of the car and came around to open her door.

She took his hand, noticing again how big and warm it was as she stepped out of the car, and realized Todd never opened car doors for her unless they were attending an event. She wondered if that was a habit because they'd been so young when they'd first started dating. How many nineteen-year-olds opened car doors for their dates?

"Why don't we lock your bag in the trunk so you don't have to carry it?"

She'd bet even at nineteen, Jax had opened car doors for girls. "Thanks."

He placed his hand on her lower back as they made their way inside. She was getting used to that intimate touch.

The marble-floored reception hall was so luxurious, it was intimidating. An enormous chandelier hung from the two-story coffered ceiling, which was painted off-white with steel-blue accents and trimmed in gold. Enormous paintings with substantial, intricately carved frames decorated the stone walls, the bottom third of which were covered in dark wood. At the other end of the reception hall was a wide marble staircase leading up to another elaborately decorated area.

Jordan leaned closer to Jax, speaking softly. "Why do places like this make me feel like I have to whisper?"

"Because it's like a museum, and that's how we're taught to act in museums."

A tall, thin brunette with pin-straight hair cut severely below her chin walked in through an arched opening. "You must be Jordan and Todd."

Jordan recognized her Chanel suit, and boy did she wear it well. "Oh, no—"

"That's right." Jax slid his arm around her waist, holding tight as he offered his hand to the woman. "And you are?"

Jordan shot a questioning look at him, but he just held her tighter.

"Felicia Withers. I'll be showing you around. If you'll follow me, we'll take a tour of the mansion and then walk the grounds."

As they followed her, Jordan whispered, "*What* are you doing?"

"Saving you from having to make an awkward explanation. Just go with it."

She didn't know whether to thank him or straighten him out. But as they followed Felicia around the estate, Jax was his charming self and asked all the questions Jordan didn't have the presence of mind to think of. How could she when he held her hand the whole time, calling her *honey* and *sweetheart* and asking for her opinion? She was just as charmed by him as Felicia was.

"You can let go now," she whispered as they followed Felicia toward a door that led outside.

He pulled her closer, speaking into her ear. "I'm supposed to be Todd, and I don't think he would let go."

You couldn't be more wrong. She kept that to herself, soaking in this glorious man's attention as they went outside.

Lush, expertly manicured lawns spilled out before them, with two rows of stone planters leading to a dome-topped stone gazebo. On the other side of the gazebo was a large reflecting pool and fountain, and just beyond the fountain was an elaborate stone colonnade.

Felicia motioned to the grassy aisle between the planters. "You're such a radiant couple, it's easy to picture you walking down the aisle."

"Thank you." Jax took Jordan's hand, gazing deeply into her eyes. "Jordan makes us look good."

He pressed a kiss to the back of her hand, stealing her breath. He made affection look effortless, like they'd been together forever, and *oh* how she wanted to feel like that every minute of every day.

"Most couples say their vows in the gazebo," Felicia said, pulling Jordan's mind back to the conversation. "But if you prefer, you can hold the ceremony in the colonnade."

Jax drew Jordan against his side. "What do you think, sweetheart?"

I think my heart is racing over the wrong man. "I don't know. But we can talk about it later. We don't need to take up any more of Felicia's time."

After wrapping up their conversation with Felicia, they headed back to the parking lot, and Jax said, "How did you like it?"

"It's immaculate, but it's more Todd's style than mine. I wouldn't be comfortable getting married there."

"Okay. One down, two to go. Now for the real question. How did I do channeling my inner Todd?"

I'm such an idiot. You were role-playing, and I bought into every second of it. "You did great, but you were nothing like Todd."

"I'm sorry if I missed the mark. What's he like?"

"He's nice, but in those situations, he can be a little more pretentious and less"—*attentive*—"chatty."

Jax's brows knitted. "I can up my pretentiousness, but I make no promises about what comes out of my mouth."

Role-playing, she reminded herself. *He's just role-playing.*

IT WAS COMICAL watching laid-back Jax trying to act pretentious at the next venue. Apparently in Jax's eyes, being pretentious went along with looking down his nose at people. They'd laughed all the way to the third venue, where he'd said it was too confining trying to be someone he wasn't, and he introduced himself as Jax Braden, Jordan's wedding gown designer and friend standing in for her fiancé, who had been called away for work. He was funny, devastatingly debonair, and his hand still found its way to her back. She noticed that he was protective of her, and it was nice being out with him and not feeling guilty for having fun.

They ate a late lunch at a café in Prairie View before heading to Peaceful Harbor to meet with Isla Redmond at Petal Me Hard. Peaceful Harbor was a cute seaside town with mountains on one side, the ocean on the other, and rows of beachy storefronts in between.

Jax opened the flower shop door for her, and as she walked in, he said, "I know Isla well. You'll like her. She drives a motorcycle and likes getting into trouble. She'll take good care of you. That's her over there."

Jordan was curious to know if Isla had *taken good care* of him. She followed his gaze to a petite girl who looked to be in her early twenties talking with a customer. Her blond hair fell in a thick, wavy mane to the middle of her back, and she wore knee-high black leather boots, cutoffs, and a flannel shirt with the sleeves rolled up to her elbows, revealing several colorful bracelets and a tattoo just above her wrist. Her legs were to die for, and when she looked over and saw Jax, her eyes lit up beneath thick dark brows and she flashed a killer smile. The kind of familiar smile that told of shared secrets.

Jax waved, and Jordan tried to ignore the niggle of jealousy clawing at her.

Isla held up her index finger, indicating she'd be with them in a minute, then turned back to her customer.

"I bet you can get a great discount from *her*" came out before Jordan could think twice about it.

Jax looked amused and stepped in front of her, blocking her view of Isla. "What was that, sweetheart?"

"Nothing." *I'm just losing my mind.* "I was just thinking about what you said this morning."

"I can wrangle a discount, but not because of the reasons you think." He leaned in, his chest brushing hers as he spoke low and authoritatively. "She's a beautiful, rebellious girl, but I prefer to be with a woman closer to my age *and* my experience level." He leaned back with a coy grin. "Any other misconceptions you'd like me to clear up?"

"I didn't mean it that way."

He gave her an *I'm not buying it* look.

"Okay, I *did*. It's just...I thought I saw something in the way she smiled at you." There was *no* excuse. "Never mind. I'm shutting up now."

He opened his mouth to say something, but Isla walked up behind him and said, "Am I interrupting?"

He turned around. "No. How are you?" He hugged her.

"Fanfuckingtastic," Isla said. "I've got a wad of cash saved for the auction. I'm *not* getting outbid this year." She waggled a finger at him. "You're going to be mine for a night, Jax Braden, and I'm taking you for a ride, so go buy a fancy helmet that's monogrammed or glittered, or whatever you need, because you're getting on the back of my bike." She smiled at Jordan. "And how rude am I, hitting on you in front of your friend. Hi, I'm Isla."

Jordan was dying to know who had won Jax in last year's auction and what kind of a good time he'd shown that person. But she had to stop thinking about those things, so she focused on the firecracker before her, who was very much like she had imagined Casey might be at that age, and that did the trick. "Hi. I'm Jordan. We have an appointment to talk about flowers for my wedding."

"Oh, *shoot*. Is it four o'clock already? I need two minutes to get my things from the office and tell my co-worker she's in charge. You two can make yourselves comfortable in our meeting area." She pointed to an area set apart from the store by a half wall. "I'll be right there."

As Isla hurried away, Jax's hand pressed against Jordan's back again, as he guided her toward the meeting area. "Still think I'd jump in the sack with her?"

"I like her spunky personality. I think Casey is probably like her. Her own person, you know? The type that says and does what she wants. Gosh, I envy that sometimes."

"You didn't answer the question."

They walked into the meeting area, and he pulled out a chair for her. "It was none of my business, and I was out of line with the comment. You've spent hours going all over creation looking at places with me for my wedding, and I've had the greatest day. I just got weirdly protective of my *friend* or something, that's all. But I'm over it."

"You think so, huh?"

"I"—*hope*—"know so."

An hour later they walked out of the flower shop with a

tentative selection of arrangements. Jax helped her into the car, and when he settled into the driver's seat, she said, "I had no idea you knew so much about flowers."

"It's my job to know everything that goes into a wedding, and I love it all."

"You're a rarity, Jax Braden. How did you make it this far without getting snagged by some lucky woman?"

"I've been *snagged* by plenty of women. But I'm a designer. I'm waiting for the right fit. Better to be single than marry the wrong person."

His comment stuck like chewing gum on a shoe.

He started the car. "Where to next?"

She wished she was supposed to meet Finlay now, so Jax could go with her, but Finlay hadn't been available until later. "My appointment with Finlay isn't for another two hours at someplace called Whiskey Bro's, so why don't you take me home, and I'll go by myself when it's time."

"Whiskey Bro's is on the main drag toward the bridge out of Peaceful Harbor." He drove out of the parking lot. "Which gives us just enough time to go see *my* wedding venue."

"*Your* wedding venue?"

"What? Can't a guy dream of a white wedding?"

"Yes, but I've never met a guy who did."

"Now you have."

They chatted about the venues they'd seen on the drive back to Pleasant Hill, and she asked him where they were going, but he refused to tell her. He followed quiet tree-lined roads up the side of a mountain and turned at a HILLTOP VINEYARDS sign.

"Is this your family's property?"

"Yes, it is. I used to come here with my mom when she was managing events."

A massive two-story stone and cedar mansion came into

view, with enormous windows and acres of vines as far as the eye could see.

"This is beautiful. Do you want to get married at the winery?"

"No." He drove around the packed parking lot and turned onto a narrow road that wound up the mountain, continuing down a long driveway before parking in front of a beautiful house.

"Whose house is this?"

"It belongs to a pretty great guy. We're just going to walk around back."

"Will he mind?"

"I think he'd be happy about it." He climbed out of the car and laced his fingers with hers as he helped her out. "Come on. It's this way."

The air felt crisper on the mountain, and as they walked around the side of the house, the grassy lawn turned to a stone path between sprawling flower gardens that led to the rear of the property, spilling down the hillside and giving way to a breathtaking view of the vineyard.

"Wow. I've never seen anything so beautiful. The vineyards look like a painting, and these gardens." She turned around, taking in more colorful blooms and gorgeous plants, surrounded by lush lawns. She saw a pool, a veranda, and a basketball court, and last night's tour of Jax's home came rushing back. "I recognize this. It's *your* house."

"It is."

"You want to get married in your house?"

"No. I want to get married in my gardens overlooking the vineyard."

She couldn't believe it. "You want a garden wedding?"

"Yeah. Something simple, with family and close friends."

"Why not at the vineyard?" She had to know if Trixie had said something to him, or if their hearts were really that aligned.

"I fell in love with weddings while watching them take place at the winery, and when I was younger, I thought I wanted to get married there. But as I got older, I realized something bigger and more important. I fell in love with *love* each and every time I witnessed a wedding, but it wasn't just because of the vineyard. It was the looks on the bride's and groom's faces that first second when they saw each other at opposite ends of the aisle. I want *that* every day of my life. If I get married at the vineyard, I'll think of that moment often, but if I get married *here*, then every time I'm outside, I'll relive those moments with my wife and our kids, our families. And I know those memories will get better every year, as we raise children together, overcome trials and tribulations, and walk them down their aisles. When we're gray and wrinkled, I'll remember those young eyes full of hope and brimming with love, and if I've been the best husband I can be, then with any luck, I'll see even more of both looking back at me."

She wanted that, too. *All* of it. To be looked at the way he'd described, to feel the love he'd spoken of wrap around her like a warm blanket, and most of all, to stop feeling the bone-deep loneliness she'd felt for the past year.

She swallowed hard, admitting to herself two hard truths. She'd felt lonely for quite a bit longer than that, and she hadn't felt a second of loneliness since Jax had come into her life.

"What are you thinking, sweetheart?"

That my heart is racing over a man who isn't mine, and I don't want it to stop. Disheartened by what that said about her and too confused to think straight, or even to know if she wanted to, she freed her hand from his and managed, "That we should go, so we're not late to meet Finlay."

Chapter Nine

JAX PULLED INTO the parking lot of Whiskey Bro's, wishing he knew what was going on in Jordan's mind. They'd had a moment back there in his gardens. An earth-moving-beneath-his-feet moment, but she'd been quiet ever since.

Her brow furrowed as she eyed the shady-looking biker bar and the plethora of motorcycles and trucks lining the lot. "Are you sure this is the right place?"

"Yeah. Didn't Finlay mention that her husband, Bullet, and his family own this bar? Finlay works here part time and runs her catering business out of the kitchen."

"No, she didn't, and neither did Trixie. Her husband's name is *Bullet*?"

"Yeah, and I know how that sounds, but you can relax. They're a biker family. Bullet's great-grandfather founded the Dark Knights motorcycle club, and the guys go by their road names. Bones is a doctor, Bullet is former Special Forces, and Bear is a hell of a mechanic and designs custom motorcycles. Rumor has it, Bear earned his road name when he fought a bear."

"Holy cow. What are their parents like?"

"Biggs and Red are two of the greatest people around. Biggs

had a stroke a number of years ago, and he no longer rides, but he's a tough biker through and through. If you meet him, you'll have no doubt that if there was trouble, he'd throw down his cane and jump right in, and Red is tough as nails, too, like her daughter, Dixie, but she's kind as the day is long."

Jordan looked at the entrance to the bar, where three burly, bearded men wearing black leather vests with Dark Knights patches on the back were talking. Her fingers curled around the edge of her seat. "I've never been around a biker gang. Are you sure it's safe?"

He put his hand over hers, squeezing it reassuringly. "They're a club, not a gang. They're just a bunch of guys who enjoy riding and living a biker lifestyle. Some of them are tattooed and bearded, and others are clean-cut with no ink. I promise you're safe. I can keep you safe anywhere we go, but the Dark Knights? They've been keeping this entire town safe for decades. Come on. You'll have fun."

"If you say so."

Jax put his arm around her as they walked up to the entrance, not because he needed to, but because he wanted her to feel protected. The guys standing by the steps looked over as they approached. "Good evening, gentlemen."

They nodded, saying a collective "Evening."

Jordan smiled nervously as they ascended the steps and went into the rustic bar. They were greeted by the din of conversation, music, and the *clack* of billiard balls. Jordan's gaze moved over the sea of black leather vests worn by people sitting at tables and milling around the pool tables and dart boards in the back of the bar, as a room full of curious eyes turned their way.

Trepidation wafted off Jordan like a shiver of cold air.

Jax put his arm around her, speaking low. "Give them a

break for staring. It's not every day a woman with movie-star good looks walks in."

She smiled. "There you go again, making me feel better."

"Come on. That's Bullet behind the bar. Let's find out where Finlay is."

Bullet was the most intimidating of the Whiskey brothers at six five and probably two fifty, with cold dark eyes that Jax had seen stop men in their tracks. He wore a black leather vest over a black T-shirt, revealing tattoos from neck to wrist.

"*That's* Finlay's husband? He looks like a biker named Bullet. Who's the cute brunette bartender?"

"Izzy Ryder. Before moving to Maryland, she worked in Boston with Finlay and at my buddy Jared Stone's restaurant. He owns Nova Lounge and about a dozen other restaurants around the world."

"You know Jared Stone?" she asked as they made their way across the scuffed and marred wooden floors toward the bar. "I guess I shouldn't be surprised, given your clientele."

"He's a cool guy. Have you been to Nova Lounge?"

"No. Todd's been talking about checking it out for months, but every time I get a reservation, I end up having to cancel."

Jax gritted his teeth against the comment trying to escape about her prick fiancé. "I'll take you there one night, and I *never* break a promise."

She raised her brows. "I don't think that's true, Mr. *Oops, I Flirted Again*."

Jax laughed heartily.

Bullet lifted his chin in their direction. "Braden," he said gruffly, his dark eyes sweeping curiously over Jordan. "Evenin', sweetheart."

"Hi," Jordan said with a smile.

"You two here for karaoke?" Bullet asked.

"You have karaoke?" Jordan asked excitedly.

"Yeah. It's a new thing Izzy insisted we do," Bullet said. "The chicks dig it."

"I *love* karaoke." Jordan looked at Jax. "Do you?"

"I do now. So you sing?"

"Oh, *God* no, but I love watching other people sing. I'd *never* get up onstage."

We'll see about that. "Bullet, this is my friend Jordan. She has an appointment with Finlay for a cake tasting."

"My wife mentioned you and your man were coming in." He looked curiously at Jax. "You're not...?"

I wish. "No. I'm here for moral support."

"My fiancé got tied up with work and couldn't make it to town," Jordan explained.

Bullet's brows slanted. "Too busy for *you*? Dude needs to get his priorities straight before walking you down the aisle, darlin'. Where I'm from, nothing comes ahead of a man's queen."

Jordan looked at the brawny biker a little dreamily, but at the same time, Jax noticed a shadow of sadness in her eyes. He wanted to take that pain away and said, "He's got a pretty important position."

Bullet scoffed and shook his head. Then he set a serious stare on Jordan. "Don't you worry, darlin'. You're in good hands with Jax." He looked toward the kitchen, where Finlay, a petite blonde, was coming through the doors. "There's my girl now. *Yo*, Lollipop! Get your sweet ass over here. You've got company."

Jordan bumped Jax with her shoulder, eyes wide with surprised amusement.

Finlay hurried over, carrying a folder and scowling at her husband. Her hair flounced over the shoulders of her pink-and-white floral blouse. "Brandon Whiskey, what did I tell you about hollering things like that in the bar?"

"What? *You've got company?*" Bullet chuckled. "Jordan's here to see you. Her guy couldn't make it, so Jax stepped in."

"Hi, Fin." Jax kissed her cheek. "How's Tallulah?"

"She's just the sweetest little girl on the planet. Thanks for asking." Finlay turned a warm smile on Jordan. "Hi, Jordan. Please excuse my husband. I love him to pieces, but there's a reason I'm looking for separate catering space."

"There's nothing to excuse," Jordan said. "He obviously loves you very much."

Finlay lowered her voice as if sharing a secret. "You should see him with our baby girl. Lulu turns that beast into a teddy bear. I have a table all set up for us on the other side of the room."

As she took a step away, Bullet said, "*Hold up*, Lollipop. I think you forgot something."

Finlay turned around, and he tapped his lips with his index finger, a slow grin lifting his beard. Finlay rolled her eyes as she went to kiss him, but her smile betrayed her.

Jordan whispered, "I love that."

"He's not so scary now, huh?"

They followed Finlay across the room to a table draped in a white tablecloth with a candle in the middle, two champagne glasses, and a bottle of champagne on ice. On each side of the table there were seven slices of delicious-looking cake.

"Wow, champagne?" Jordan exclaimed. "And that's a lot of cake. You didn't have to go to all of this trouble."

"I'm holding tastings in a biker bar," Finlay said. "I need to add *all* of the ambience I can for beautiful brides like you. And as far as the cake goes, you said your fiancé didn't enjoy sharing and that he was particular about sweets, so I gave you two slices of each cake and several choices instead of the standard four."

"That was nice of you," Jordan said. "He would have appreciated your efforts."

"No problem at all. Why don't you and Jax make yourselves comfortable, and I'll give you my spiel."

As they sat down, Jax wondered if Jordan realized how often she made excuses for Todd.

"Before I forget, I emailed you sample menus as we discussed, but nothing is set in stone," Finlay said. "We have plenty of time before the wedding, so you and Todd can take your time reviewing them and get back to me once you've had time to make some decisions."

"That's perfect. Thank you."

"Now for the cake," Finlay said. "I usually let couples do tastings on their own instead of hovering, but I'm happy to sit with you if you prefer."

Jordan looked at Jax. "I think we'll be okay, don't you?"

"Champagne, cake, and a beautiful woman? I think I can handle it."

"Great. In that case, let me give you this." Finlay handed Jordan the folder she was holding. "Inside you'll find a flavor menu and ingredient lists for each cake, just in case you have guests with allergies. I also included information about a few other flavors I can make in case you don't like any of these."

"I'm sure we'll love them all," Jordan said.

"Let's hope so. I'll come back to check on you, but if you need me, I'll be in the kitchen working my magic."

After Finlay walked away, Jax said, "Do you think she has

any idea that she just walked away from two of the biggest sugar fiends she's ever met?"

"*Shh.*" Jordan leaned closer. "Don't spill my secrets."

He poured the champagne. "Your secrets are as safe with me as you are."

She gave him a look that said she wasn't sure she was all that safe with him.

With that gentle reminder, he said, "I'm sorry you didn't get to share today with Todd."

"It's fine." Her jaw tightened. "It's just cake and a roof over our heads when we say our vows."

He put his hand on hers. "It's not *just* anything, and you don't have to pretend like it is. It's okay to be disappointed in the man you love. It doesn't mean you don't want to be with him, but stop acting like your feelings are expendable, because they're not."

She looked at him for so long without saying a word, he feared he'd said the wrong thing and was about to apologize when she said, "You're right. It's *all* important. My feelings, his feelings, the cake, the venues. He said it was just cake, and I guess I tried to convince myself of that. But I don't want to think about anything negative right now. I had a *great* time today, and that's because of you." She lifted her glass. "I appreciate you, Jax. Thank you for making this day—this whole week—so much fun."

They sipped their champagne, and he said, "The day is not over, my friend. There is cake to be eaten and karaoke to be crooned."

"*Crooned?* Really?" They both laughed, and she opened the flavor menu, leaning closer so he could see it, too. "Look, there's café latte cake. Layers of chocolate cake and roasted almond cake, brushed with Kahlúa and filled with chocolate espresso buttercream and dark ganache."

The joy in her eyes hit him square in the center of his chest.

She set down the flavor menu. "I'm definitely going to be in a sugar coma by the end of the night."

"Don't worry. I'll revive you."

"Who are you kidding? You'll be in one, too." Her gaze swept over the slices of cake. "I don't know where to start."

"That's easy. We'll start with the one closest to us." He stabbed a slice of carrot cake and held it up for her.

"You're *not* going to feed me." She picked up her fork and took a bite, closing her eyes and moaning with pleasure.

Listening to her moan was torture. "Now, *that's* a rave review."

She giggled.

He shook his head as he took a bite. "You weren't kidding. That's good cake."

"The frosting is perfect." She reached for another plate. "Let's try the red velvet."

They each took a bite, and she sank back in the chair, placing her hand over her heart. "I want to drown in a vat of that cake."

Wouldn't that be the perfect dessert? He picked up his glass. "Here's to the image of you in a vat of cake."

She futilely tried to hide her smile as she touched her glass to his, then finished her champagne. "I need more."

She reached for more cake as he refilled their glasses, and they continued their tasting journey, toasting, laughing, and having a wonderful time. They shared white cake with chocolate fondant, triple chocolate cake sprinkled with rose-infused syrup, layered with rose-petal buttercream, and chocolate-raspberry cake with buttercream filling, each more scrumptious than the last. Jordan raved about each one, and Jax loved that she went back for seconds and thirds. She sipped champagne, adorably chatty and a bit flirty, which he loved. He was getting glimpses of a carefree woman he had a feeling she rarely set free and hoped he'd see even more of her.

"What'd you think of those places we saw today?" She finished another glass of champagne and held it up for him to fill. Her cheeks were a little flushed, and man, that was a great look on her.

"I thought they were all gorgeous. Which did you like best?"

She shrugged. "They were all nice, but I didn't feel a connection to any of them. The Davenport was too fancy, the hotel felt impersonal, and the one in town was just…"

"Not for you?"

"Yeah, but I *did* connect with one place we saw."

"The café where you stole half my fries?"

She giggled. "Yes, that was yummy, but also your gardens. They were so beautiful."

"You're killing me. I'm a nice guy, but not nice enough to let you marry another man in my sacred garden."

"I wasn't asking—"

"I know you weren't, and the thing that's really effed up is that if you did want to get married there, I'd probably let you."

"I'd never do that to you. But *why* would you let me?"

"Because I can't be a dick to you. I want you to be happy."

She sighed. "You're too good to be true. I'll pick one of the places I saw. Todd won't care which one."

He wanted to wave a red flag, but he fought the urge to point out the obvious. "Which of the three did you like best?"

Her brow wrinkled in concentration as she took a bite of the chocolate mousse cake. Pleasure rose in her eyes. "This dark chocolate ganache is *so* good. Sorry, but chocolate trumps venues any day."

"Chocolate is deliciously *versatile*." He winked.

"You are such a flirt, but a gentleman flirt, which is nice." She pointed her fork at him. "You're a good egg, Charlie Brown."

He laughed. "So are you, beautiful."

"*No*, I'm really not. I mean I *am*, but that's because I play it safe. But in here…" She tapped her head, whispering, "I don't always play it safe. I have secret fantasies."

"Secret fantasies are my specialty. I could help you set them free."

"Not *those* kinds of fantasies."

The spark in her eyes told him she meant exactly that kind. "You don't have to pretend with me, Jordan. You're a beautiful, sensual woman, and it would be a shame if you didn't explore that as often and as thoroughly as you could. So tell me the truth. You have dirty fantasies, don't you?"

"*Fine*. I *do*, but I have other ones, too."

This just kept getting better. "I think I need a list."

"I'm not telling you my dirty fantasies. But I'll tell you some of my bad-girl fantasies."

"I'm all ears." *And hands, mouth…*

"I've never crashed a party or gotten drunk on fruity drinks."

"A night of partying doesn't make you a bad girl."

"Okay, those are tame examples. I've never gone skinny-dipping, and I really want to."

"Still not *bad*, sweetheart. In fact, it just makes you even more alluring. What else you got?"

She crooked her finger, beckoning him closer and whispering again. "I've never fooled around in a car or had sex on a beach."

Her cuteness was an aphrodisiac. "Still not bad, just wickedly naughty, which I happen to like very much."

"I can't believe I told you that." She looked at her champagne glass. "Is there truth serum in there? How did we even get on that subject?"

"I don't know, but I'm not sorry. Are you?"

"*No*," she said softly, her honesty hanging between them like Eve's forbidden apple. "*Cake. I need cake.*" She nervously dug into a slice of café latte cake and shoved it in her mouth.

What you need is me, sweetheart.

"*Mm*, Jax, this is it. This is *heaven*. Stop looking at me like that and taste this."

"Looking at you like what?"

She whispered, "Like you're thinking about watching me skinny-dip!" She held up a forkful of cake. "Now give me your mouth."

"I'll give you a lot more than my m—"

She shoved the cake into his mouth with a sassy smile. He wrapped his hand around hers over the fork, keeping it still as he swallowed the bite and licked the fork clean, turning her sassy smile hotter, sexier, purely *desirous*. Her gaze dipped to his mouth, and she licked her lips, drawing him deeper into her beautiful vortex. He longed to feel those luscious lips around his cock as he devoured her like she'd never been pleasured before and itched to drag her into a dark corner and seal his mouth over hers. To lift her up in that flirty little dress and take her against a wall, hard and deep.

Her tongue slid over her lower lip.

"Better stop doing that." *Before I take that lip between my teeth and tug so you feel the sting between your legs.*

"*Jax,*" she whispered lustfully. The desire in her eyes was inescapable, but she quickly looked away.

Come back. Get lost in us again.

"Cake," she panted out, and shoved another forkful in her mouth.

She was staring at the cake as if she were afraid to look at him. But there wasn't enough cake in the world to smother the inferno between them, and he wasn't ready to let it go.

"*Jordan.*" He put his hand on her leg, drawing her eyes to his. Deep wells of *want* and *need* gazed back at him, but she looked as tortured as he felt. He didn't want to cause her angst, so he tempered his desires and reached up, cupping her cheek and wiping chocolate from the corner of her mouth just as Finlay returned.

"How's it going over here? Did you pick a favorite?" Finlay asked.

He held Jordan's gaze as he said, "I've definitely found mine," and licked the chocolate from his thumb.

"I LIKE A man who knows what he wants," Finlay said. "How about you, Jordan? Did you find one you can't live without?"

"I think so," she said absently, imagining Jax licking chocolate from all of her loneliest places.

"Wonderful!" Finlay exclaimed, jerking Jordan back to reality. "Which flavor?"

Flavor. Shit. She looked at the cake, trying to focus on it instead of the lust billowing inside her, rattling her brain. But it was like trying to hold back a gust of wind. "I liked the café latte best, but I'm not sure I can make the final decision without consulting Todd."

Jax pressed his leg against hers under the table, sending a shiver of awareness through her. "Given how busy Todd is and what he said about *cake*, I think he'd be thrilled if you made a final decision. The *right* decision for *you*."

He was right. Todd didn't give a damn about the cake or the venue. She wasn't even sure he gave a damn about her anymore.

"That's okay. There's no rush," Finlay said.

"No, Jax is absolutely right. Todd doesn't have time to think about anything but work. If I wait for him to make a decision, the wedding will be postponed again."

"In that case," Jax mumbled for her ears only.

She couldn't help but smile. "I think I need a few days, if that's okay."

"Yes, of course," Finlay said. "We can talk after you review the menus. Are you two sticking around for dinner? I have a delicious special tonight."

"I'm sure Jax has plans," Jordan said at the same time Jax said, "Yes."

"My night *is* spoken for," Jax said, looking at her. "By my very beautiful friend."

Her stomach flipped. "What about Coco?"

"She was the one who suggested I hang out with you today. She's having a girls' day with Grandma. What do you say, Jordan? Should we try Finlay's special and have a cocktail?"

She didn't know if it was the champagne or Jax's interest bolstering her confidence, making her want to take a chance, to be bold and enjoy herself, but as she said, "I'd love to," it sure as heck felt good. "But no more champagne. That stuff is like truth serum."

"I was thinking Sex on the Beach."

"Jax." Her mind was sprinting to the beach.

"I meant the drink. It's a fruity cocktail. But if you'd rather…" He waggled his brows.

She swatted his arm.

Finlay giggled. "So we're having Sex on the Beach and tonight's special?"

As if she even had a choice? "Yes, please."

AFTER A DELICIOUS dinner and a couple of fruity cocktails, Jordan was flying high. They hadn't spent another second talking about the wedding, and that was unexpectedly and *marvelously* freeing. The bar had gotten crowded with all sorts of people, but bikers definitely outnumbered non-bikers. Even the men in the band that had been playing for the last hour were wearing Dark Knights patches on their vests. But after she'd observed the rough-looking guys clapping one another on the backs and listening to their humorous banter, her trepidation had given way to a night of fun. Jax was so attentive, she had a feeling he could make any place feel safe and special enough to bring out sides of her she hadn't even known existed, as he'd done tonight.

"You're up, Braden," a bearded guy said as he walked by the table.

"Come on, beautiful." Jax took her hand as he rose to his

feet, pulling her up with him.

"Where are we going?" She didn't want to leave yet.

"It's time to give you the full Whiskey Bro's experience."

He led her over to the pool tables, and a handsome clean-cut guy handed her a pool cue. "Here you go, darlin'."

"Thanks, but I don't play pool." She held the cue out for Jax.

"You do now." Jax nodded at the guy. "Thanks, Court."

As Court went to join a group of guys, Jax guided her to the head of the pool table.

"I'm happy to watch you play, but I don't know the first thing about pool."

He stepped closer, speaking so quietly, she had to lean in to hear him. "Observing can be fun in a more *intimate* setting, where we have the privacy to join in if we're so inclined. But for tonight's lesson, I'd like a more hands-on approach."

Her body heated at his seductive tone.

A sexy grin appeared on his handsome face, as if he felt the heat seeping from her pores. "Stick with me, sweetheart, and your new experiences will be endless and incredibly enjoyable."

She had a fleeting thought about asking him to adhere to their no-flirting rule, but he made her feel alive and seen and made her want so much *more* than she'd ever wanted out of life. More butterfly-inducing experiences, more laughter, more spontaneity. When she was with Jax, she felt like she was finally living, and she was going with it.

Hold on to your handkerchief, Jax. Two can play at this game.

"Okay, Mr. Braden. I'll be your willing pupil. Show me what to do with this big stick."

"Careful what you ask for."

"I could say the same to you." *Did I really just say that?*

"Unless you're about to hustle me out of a few bucks, I'm more than prepared for anything you have to give." He took her hand. "Let's get familiar with the cue." He touched her fingers to the tip. "This is the tip. You'll want to treat it delicately. Nobody likes a bruised tip."

The glimmer of wickedness in his eyes spurred her on. "You should probably show me the rest, because nobody likes just the tip, either." *Ohmygod!* Flirting with Jax was addicting.

"I can see I need to show you how to slow down and savor every moment of *every* experience. Preparing for your shot will lead to a more satisfying outcome."

Lord, he was *good* at flirting.

"First you need to chalk the tip." He picked up a small cube of chalk from the edge of the pool table. "Angle the cue, so you can see the tip, and then use deliberate movements, like this, to paint it." He put his hand over hers again, showing her how. "Don't twist it. You don't want to miss any spots."

"What exactly does it do?"

"The chalk provides friction, so the tip doesn't slide off the ball prematurely."

She couldn't resist saying, "We wouldn't want premature slippage."

"An experienced player knows how to avoid that." He set the chalk down and curled her fingers around the cue just below the tip. "This is the shaft. Get comfortable with it. Take a few slow strokes." He moved her hand up and down along the shaft. "*Mm.* You're good at that."

He was standing so close, he got her all hot and flustered. She could barely think straight. His hand tightened around hers, lifting the cue higher while simultaneously sliding her hand down to the thicker end.

"You'll grab the butt nice and tight. How does that feel?"

"*Good*" came out soft and breathy.

"Then let's get this show on the road."

He stood behind her, showing her how to line up her shot and helping her position her hand on the table. He took her by the hips, turning her slightly away from the table. His hands felt so good on her, her breathing became shallow.

"Now practice your stroke." His warm breath coasted over her cheek and his hips cradled her butt as they moved the pool cue forward and back. "That's it, nice and slow."

His body heat seeped through the thin material of her dress as he guided the tip of the cue toward the ball.

"You're a natural." He ran his hand down her arm. "When you're ready to strike the ball, don't slow down, and keep your follow-through straight and relaxed. A longer stroke will give you more momentum and will lead to a better outcome."

She turned her head and his face was *right* there, his eyes brimming with so much emotion she felt it clawing at her, reeling her in.

"Jax Braden!"

Jordan startled upright at the female voice. Jax's arm swept around her, tugging her against the side of his chest. The back of her head barely missed his face. "Whoa, baby. You nearly knocked me out."

"*Sorry.*" Her gaze shot to the tall redheaded waitress wearing knee-high leather boots, a black leather miniskirt, and a Whiskey Bro's T-shirt. Colorful tattoos decorated her arms, and she wore a big-ass grin.

"I was going to see if you wanted a drink, but after watching you two, I think I need one. Or maybe a cigarette, and I don't even smoke."

"Hey, Dixie," Jax said. "I was just teaching Jordan how to play. Jordan, this is Bullet's sister, Dixie Whiskey-Stone."

"Hi. I would love a drink, please." *Or three.*

"I bet you can use a *stiff one* right about now," Dixie said. "What's your pleasure?"

Jax held her tighter. "Sex on the Beach. Right, babe?"

Oh no, you didn't. Paybacks are hell, Jaxon. She slid her arm around him. "You said you wouldn't give away my secrets, Jaxie."

Mischief shimmered in his eyes. "I didn't tell her how much you like sand between your cheeks."

"*Hey* now," Dixie said in a singsong voice. "You're my kind of girl, Jordan."

"It's Jax. He's a bad influence."

Jax didn't miss a beat. "*Bad* wasn't the word you used last night."

"Oh yeah. That was *quick*." She lowered her voice. "Don't worry. It happens to a lot of guys."

Dixie burst into laughter. "I think I'll get that drink."

As she walked away, Jax backed Jordan up against the pool table, every inch of his hard frame pressing against her. "The only thing quick about me is how fast I'm falling for you."

Emotions whipped through her like a hurricane.

He leaned forward, speaking directly into her ear. "If you were mine, you'd know the only other quick thing about me is how fast I can make you come."

A needy sound escaped before she could stop it. The heat she'd seen in his eyes only minutes ago was nothing compared to the inferno staring back at her now.

"The mic is now open for karaoke," the leader of the band announced.

"That's us!" Jax shouted. He grabbed Jordan's hand, pulling her toward the stage, while she tried to remember how to walk.

"*Jax.* What are you doing?"

"Getting you up onstage." He tugged her closer. "You're too great a woman to be afraid to do *anything.*"

He ascended the steps, taking her up with him, and talked with the band leader, still clinging to her hand. Everyone was watching them. Anxiety prickled her limbs.

"Jordan, what are we singing?"

She looked at him like he'd lost his mind. "You're asking *me*?" She lowered her voice. "I can't do this."

He stepped closer. "I've never sang onstage either, but with you I'm willing to try anything."

He made her want to try anything, too.

"What song do you know all the words to?"

"*Um…*" She scrambled to think of something. "The song from *Mannequin.*"

"The movie?"

"Yes. I've watched it a million times. 'Nothing's Gonna Stop Us Now.'"

He grinned. "Perfect. I know that one."

A few minutes later, the band started playing, the din of the crowd quieted, and Jordan's nerves caught fire.

Jax squeezed her hand. "Look at me, not them."

His gaze remained trained on her as he sang about seeing paradise in her eyes and wanting to give her the love in his heart. He made her feel like every word he sang was solely meant for her. She didn't think as she joined in, singing about not caring if people said they were crazy, being together as the rest of the world fell apart, and never looking back. *God* she wanted that. As they sang the chorus, everything else—the people, the band, the music—faded away, leaving just the two of them, pouring out their hearts in a bubble of sizzles and sparks. Jax clutched her hand as he sang about sticking by her in good times and bad, and they belted out the chorus, so lost in each other, they lifted their joined hands, emphasizing their words, and she believed every one of them. When she was with him, she *felt* unstoppable.

As the last lyrics left their lips, the crowd rose to their feet clapping and cheering, and she threw her arms around Jax, laughing and feeling like her heart was going to burst.

"I want to kiss you so bad right now," he growled into her ear.

"*Jax*," came out as tortured as she felt. "I *can't*."

He held her so tight and felt so good, she never wanted him to let go.

But she knew she had to, and reluctantly, she said, "I think you'd better take me home."

JAX HAD A full-on war raging in his head as he drove Jordan home. He was glad he'd had only one cocktail, because Jillian was right. The connection between him and Jordan was bigger and more powerful than he was, and he really needed to keep his head on straight. But she was wrong about him doing something stupid. Honesty was never stupid, and life was too short to play games. As he parked in her driveway, screenshots of their time together flashed in his head of the long conversations in which she'd lain her heart bare. The tears, laughter, and intensely intimate moments were underscored by images of her radiating happiness as she sang her heart out on that stage. But on the heels of those images was the agony in her voice as she'd said she couldn't kiss him and the heaviness in the air around them now, burying them in silence.

He climbed out of the car and grabbed her bag from the trunk, trying to figure out how to navigate this thorny terrain. She took his hand as she stepped from the car, and her agonized gaze hit him like a knife to the chest. He drew her into his arms, and as she clung to him, two things became crystal clear. He never wanted to cause her pain again, and if she could look him in the eye and tell him she didn't feel about him the way he felt about her, he'd hand the design process over to his sister and get the hell out of town, because that was the only way he'd survive walking away.

Neither said a word as he walked her to the door, and then he couldn't hold back and said, "Jordan—" at the same time she said his name. "Go ahead, sweetheart."

"I'm sorry. I shouldn't have let you come with me today."

Yes, you should have. You should be with me every day. "Then why did you?"

"Because I *like* being with you. I'm happy when we're together, and even when we're not, just thinking about you makes me happy. I've had the greatest week of my life, but we were doing things for my *wedding*, and I thought about you a heck of a lot more than I thought about Todd, and that's wrong on so many levels."

"Doesn't that tell you something?"

"*Yes.* That I'm royally screwed up. But I've felt alone for *so* long, and since you came into my life, I never feel that way. You make me feel seen and heard and special. You listen like you care, and—"

"That's because I *do* care, and I see the real you. Every bit of you." He stepped closer and took her hand. "I know you might never feel whole if you don't get answers about Casey. I also know you might never find them, and you deserve to be with someone who can be there *for* you and *with* you as you grieve her absence."

Tears welled in her eyes. "*See?* This is exactly what I was talking about. I don't have to pretend with you. You don't just see me. You accept me for who I am, even if I have a big black hole inside me. I just wanted more of that, but I can't have it, and it's not fair to lead you on."

"*Why* can't you have it?"

"Because I made a promise to the person who was there for me when I needed someone a long time ago." She waved her left hand.

"But where is he *now*, Jordan?"

"It doesn't matter where he is. This is about me, and I'm not the kind of person who leads a guy on or has to remind myself that I shouldn't think about kissing another man every time we're together."

"Then *don't* go through with it. Don't walk down the aisle to a man who can't even find the time to see you. He hasn't reached out to you once in all the time we've spent together. I don't have to tell you what that tells me."

Tears slipped down her cheeks.

"Talk to me, Jordan. Why did you *really* put off your wedding four times? Was it scheduling issues or something else?"

She clamped her mouth shut, her lower lip trembling.

"What are you afraid of, sweetheart?"

"*Everything*" fell shakily from her lips.

He held her hand between both of his and brought it to his

lips, pressing a kiss to her knuckles. "Then let me help you get past the fear. I have been crazy about you since the first time we met, when you came into my office and tried to convince me that you were marrying the man of your dreams. I think we *both* knew even then that you were wrong, because you were looking him in the eye as you said it."

She tugged her hand free. "This is all so messed up."

"Tell me you don't feel for *me* what you know I feel for *you*, and I will walk away and *never* come back." *Don't say it, Jordan. You know you won't mean it.*

More tears sprang free. "I can't do this. I have to get my head on straight. I'm sorry, but I don't think we should see each other for a while."

"*Jordan—*"

"No, *please*." She dug her keys out of her purse and fumbled with the lock. "Just let me go."

Jax felt his heart ripping to shreds as she went inside and closed the door behind her. He stared at the dove door knocker, the symbol of hope bringing another spear to his chest. How was he supposed to walk away when everything he wanted was right behind that door?

Chapter Ten

JORDAN HAD THOUGHT she'd mastered the art of holding her shit together, juggling grief, loneliness, and emotions she didn't even understand as she made her way through each day. Boy was she wrong.

In one evening, she'd managed to bring her entire life toppling down around her, leaving her to question everything she thought she knew about herself.

Her fingers curled around Jax's handkerchief. She was sitting on the couch, where she'd been since three in the morning, when she'd left Todd a third unanswered message and had finally given up on trying to sleep. She looked at the applewood candles on the mantel, coffee table, and windowsills and the wedding gown designs and crocheted gloves still artfully displayed on the dining room table as if she were getting ready for a visit from a king and needed to have everything perfectly presented.

Jax's voice traipsed through her mind—*He hasn't reached out to you once in all of the time we've spent together. I don't have to tell you what that tells me*—bringing the sting of tears.

Her phone vibrated on the cushion beside her, and AUNT SHEILA appeared on the screen. She answered on autopilot.

"Hi."

"Hi, honey. I'm sorry to interrupt your time with Todd, but I wanted to see how your day went yesterday. Did you pick a venue?"

"He never showed up," she said flatly.

"Oh *no*. I'm so sorry, honey. Work again?"

"Mm-hm."

Tsk. Her aunt sighed. "I wish you had let me come down. Did you go alone?"

"No. Jax Braden went with me."

"Really? Isn't that unusual, for the wedding gown designer to go?"

Jordan shrugged, realizing too late that her aunt couldn't see her. "He's pretty unusual." Her voice cracked, and tears slid down her cheeks. She'd been crying on and off all night and hadn't thought she had any tears left.

"Oh, baby girl. Are you okay?"

"Yes. No." She swiped at her tears, not wanting to be a burden, but at the same time, wishing she could fall into her aunt's arms and let it all out. "I'm tired and overwhelmed."

"I'm not surprised. You've been running yourself ragged lately. I'm worried about you."

"I am, too." A sob broke free. "My life is out of control."

"No, it's not, honey. It just feels that way."

Jordan swiped at her tears. "I wish that were true, but I don't know which way is up anymore."

"Take a deep breath and tell me what you mean."

Between sobs and gasps, Jordan managed to tell her aunt everything, from the first time she and Jax met and how she'd postponed her wedding because of what she'd felt for him right down to the last thing she'd said to him last night. "I told you

I'm a mess. When did I turn into such a crappy girlfriend?"

"You are *not* a crappy girlfriend."

"I postponed my wedding because I felt something for someone else. That makes me awfully crappy."

"No, honey. It makes you smart for realizing you weren't ready to get married."

"Not smart enough." She wiped her tears. "I feel like I cheated on him by enjoying time with Jax."

"Don't be so hard on yourself. You've outgrown a man who has neglected you and taken you for granted for too long. Did you and Jax get physical?"

"No, of course not."

"Then that proves that you're not a mess, and to be honest, I'm surprised nobody caught your eye sooner. But you keep yourself in such a safe little box between work and Todd, you haven't let yourself experience very much outside of that."

"Because I'm *engaged*, and that's what I thought I should do."

"Honey, being in a relationship shouldn't feel like a prison sentence. If you were happy with Todd, you never would have given Jax a second thought, and keeping your circle so small tells me that some part of you knew that, even if you couldn't admit it to yourself."

"I should have ended it with Todd instead of postponing the wedding last year."

"You weren't ready, just like you weren't ready the three times before that."

"I was *terrified*. I still am. I've already lost so much. I didn't want to think about losing anyone else."

"I know, baby girl. Todd has been your *person* since you were nineteen. He was there for you when you needed him most, when you were at college starting over *again*. Kids are usually excited to get away from home, but you'd had your home ripped out from under you when you were so young. Everything that happened in the years between the time you moved in with us and when you moved back to Prairie View was just a means to an end for you. Prairie View is where you always wanted to be. But you've been feeling alone for years, and you've made excuses for Todd since shortly after he moved to New York."

"Because we had a plan," she reminded her.

"Yes, but the two of you also agreed to make joint decisions and support each other from afar, which is difficult for any couple. But somewhere along the way, Todd forgot those pieces of the bargain. And this will be hard to hear, but your mom's not around to tell you the hard truths, so I have to do that. You held up your pieces of the bargain, but I don't believe you could ever hold up the moving to New York part of it. I had hoped you could, and I know we encouraged you to do it, because we thought it would help you move forward with your life and finally stop holding out for the past to rectify itself. But now I wonder if we did more harm than good. We never meant to make things harder for you."

Jordan closed her eyes against a flood of tears. "You didn't."

"I'm sure we did, and it's okay to say that, Jordan. Gary and I aren't perfect. We love you, and we're just doing the best we can. But we've been worried about you for a very long time. We've watched you grow into a smart, compassionate woman, so much like your mother, I swear sometimes it's her words I hear coming out of your mouth."

"I hope it's not when I talk about messing up."

"Everyone messes up, honey. That's what makes us human

and allows us to grow."

"I'm so confused and scared." She swiped at her tears. "I think I'm with the wrong man, but how can that be when I've only known Jax for a week?"

"You haven't only known him for a week. You just told me that you postponed your wedding because of what you felt for him. But you do realize that this isn't about Jax, don't you? He's just the person who opened your eyes enough for you to finally admit what I think you've known for a very long time, which says a lot about him and even more about your feelings for him."

"I never felt with Todd what I do when I'm with Jax. That makes me feel guilty, but it's true. I know it's fast, and the circumstances are horrible, but if you met him, if you saw how he is with me, you'd see what I mean. He listens to every word I say, and he cares about *me*, not what anyone else will think of me, or him when he's with me. I feel like I can talk to him about anything. I feel safe with him."

"You don't have to convince me about how fast feelings can come on or how big they are. I fell in love with your uncle when I was twelve. But since he was twenty and saw me as the little girl down the block, I had to wait a decade for him to even notice me. Your father was less than thrilled about his baby sister falling for a guy who was older than *him*."

"Did he give Uncle Gary a hard time, or just you?"

"He got into a fistfight with your uncle."

"Ohmygosh." She tried to picture her laid-back, lean and fit uncle with his short gray hair and clear blue eyes, who would rather play Scrabble than watch football, defending himself against her brawny father. "I can't imagine them fighting."

"Because you remember how loving your father was. My

brother was very protective of all of us. But your uncle stood up to him, and he told your father he could beat him up every day of the week, and it still wouldn't stop him from loving me."

Jordan sighed. "You're so lucky. You guys are meant to be."

"And maybe you and Jax are, too. But again, this isn't about him. This is about you realizing that the ring on your finger doesn't match the love in your heart. As scary as all of this feels, if you decide to end things with Todd, you will *not* be losing him. He's not being ripped away from your life without warning like your family was. You are in control, and you will be the one making that decision. It'll be hard and hurtful because you love him, and you probably always will on some level. But, honey, you don't need Todd or Jax or any other man by your side to be whole. You've *already* proven that. But this is a lot to deal with, and we both know you live your life trying not to make waves for other people, which makes this even harder for you. Would you like to hear my suggestion?"

"Yes, please."

"I suggest you go against everything you've ever done and put *yourself* first. Take Todd's and Jax's feelings out of the equation and ask yourself if you're really ready to be done with Todd. If so, then give yourself a little space to decide whether you want to be closer to Jax. Because this is *your* life, and the only thing that matters is what *you* want."

Out of the whole situation, the thing that hurt and scared her most wasn't the idea of ending things with Todd. It was the thought of being without Jax.

Chapter Eleven

THIS IS SHIT.

Jax tore the mediocre sketch of Penelope Price's wedding gown in half, crumpled it up, and threw it at his office wall. He leaned back in his chair, fists to the ceiling, gritting out, "*Fuck.*" His elbows hit the desk, and he let his face fall into his hands. It was early Tuesday evening, three of the longest days of his life since Jordan had said she didn't think they should see each other for a while. Respecting her wishes and not contacting her was torturous. What the hell constituted *a while*? Because he was losing his fucking mind.

He heard something and looked up to find Glenna tiptoeing toward his desk, holding the jar of candy she kept on hand for Jonathan. "I'm just going to leave this here, and then I'm gone for the night," she said quietly as she set the jar on his desk.

"Have I been that bad?"

"You didn't hear it from me, but the word *intervention* has been tossed around the break room."

Shit. "I'm sorry." He needed to get the hell out of there before he lost the team he'd worked so hard to build. "When you get in tomorrow, I need you to cancel my appointments for the rest of the week. Then call my cousin Treat and ask him which of his resorts offers the most privacy, and book a bungalow or a suite for me and Coco. I'll be working remotely for a while, and I don't want anyone knowing where I am." He pushed to his feet and grabbed his jacket. "Glenna, that goes for my family, too. Don't share the information with anyone. Got it?"

"Of course." Her brows slanted. "For how long?"

"I don't know. Leave it open ended for now."

"Are you all right?"

No. I fucking suck. "I'm fine."

"You're worrying me. You never take time off when you have so many projects in the works. What about Jordan's dress? You told the team they were getting the designs this week, and the timeline is already short."

"It'll be taken care of."

"Am I rescheduling your appointments?"

"Only phone and video appointments for now. Schedule them a week or two out. I've got to go."

He left the office and called Jillian on his way to pick up Coco.

"Did you get my birthday present yet?" Jillian asked far too cheerily.

Damn it. He'd forgotten about their birthday and their party. "I need a favor."

"Is that a *no*? Because I can give you a few ideas."

"Jilly, this is serious," he said sharply.

"Sorry. What's up?"

"I need you to listen and not ask questions. Can you do that?"

"If I have to."

He knew better, but he had no other alternative. "I need you to finish the design for Jordan's gown. She just needs to make a few decisions and then it'll be ready to go. My team is expecting the designs this week."

"What happened?"

"It doesn't matter. Can you do it or not?"

"I have a huge project coming my way later this week, but you know I'll do it."

"Good. Thanks. One more thing. How pissed will you be if I miss our birthday party?"

"*Jax.* You can't ditch me on our birthday. We came into this world together, and we celebrate together every year. We made a pact."

"I know, but—"

"Unless you're about to tell me that you have the most important client of your life breathing down your back for an appointment on our birthday, you can take your excuse and shove it where the sun don't shine."

He gritted his teeth as he drove toward Heidi's house. "Damn it, Jilly. I can't stay here knowing Jordan is right around the corner. I need to go away for a while or I'm going to ruin everything I've built."

"*Jax.* We lost two of our brothers for a decade and we *just* got them back. I am *not* losing you for some undetermined length of time. What happened that has you running for the hills?"

He considered not telling her, but if he didn't tell someone, he was going to explode. "I fell for someone else's woman and thought I could handle it."

"You did *not* think you could handle it. You thought you could change her mind."

"No, I didn't. I thought she'd change her own mind if we spent more time together." *And I fucked myself over, because now I know what it feels like to spend time with her, to hold her in my arms when she cries and soak in the sweetness of her laughter when she's happy. I know her every smile and those little sexy sounds she tries not to make.* A stabbing pain sliced through his chest. That pain had become all too familiar the last few days and made him want to tear something apart. He hadn't believed Zev when he'd told him there was no greater pain than a broken heart, but now he knew the truth.

He rubbed his chest. "I don't want to talk about it, and don't give me shit. This is *my* mistake, and I had to make it or I'd never have forgiven myself for not trying."

"I'm not going to give you hell, but I'd like to give her a piece of my mind."

"*Jilly,*" he warned. "This isn't Jordan's fault, and you know it. Do *not* go after her."

"I won't," she snapped. "But *come on*. Her fiancé is a shit, and you're amazing. It's her loss. I hope you know that."

"Jilly. I don't need a cheerleader right now."

"I'm just pissed. I'll take over the design and manage the team, but you have to make me two promises."

He was hit with as much relief as he was regret. "Anything."

"Don't leave until *after* our birthday party. It's our thirtieth, and I don't want to celebrate without you. I know that sounds selfish, but it's only a few days from now, and you can take off the second it's over."

"And the second condition?"

"That you'll come back. Give me a timeline and stick to it."

"I don't know how long it'll take to get my head on straight."

"You can't do that to us, Jax. Think of Mom and Dad."

"I can't think right now. I promise I'll come back. That's the best I can do."

He ended the call, picked up Coco, and went home. He hadn't slept in days. Every time he closed his eyes, he saw Jordan's tormented tears. He headed out back to shoot some hoops and try to wear himself out, but being around his gardens just made it worse. He missed every shot and gave up.

Coco cocked her head, as if to say, *That's not like you.*

"Yeah, I know I'm off my game again." He sat down, and Coco climbed onto his lap, licking his face. He leaned back on the lounge chair, tucking one hand behind his head and looking up at the sky as he petted her. She'd stuck to him like glue since he'd come home Saturday night. He hated feeling like this and hated bringing his bad mood into Coco's world, but he was grateful for her comfort.

He lay there until the sun went down, replaying every minute of his last conversation with Jordan until it blurred together and he couldn't take it anymore. Then he headed inside and took a shower.

His phone rang as he was drying off, and Reggie Steele's name appeared on the screen. He answered it as he went into his bedroom. "Hey, Reggie. How's it going?"

"Not bad, actually. Is this a good time to talk?"

"Yeah, sure. Did you find something?" He pulled on boxer briefs and sweats.

"Yes, but I don't know how meaningful it is yet. I spoke to some people who were involved in the investigation, and it appears there was evidence of another vehicle at the crash site."

"That's good, right?"

"It would be if the evidence still existed. It never made it back to the station, and they buried the report, as if it never happened."

"Who is *they*? Aren't there protocols for that sort of thing?"

"Yes, but rules are only as good as the people who carry them out."

"How could they get away with that?"

"It could have been an honest mistake. I'd hoped to speak with the lead investigator, but he died a month after the accident. I asked around the department, but nobody's talking. I also looked at the age-progression photos, and technology has advanced tremendously since the images on file were done. I think we can get better ones."

"Do it. Let's get this out to the media and see what we can find." As he said it, he realized he shouldn't have. Jordan would never go against Todd's wishes, and if the other night had shown Jax anything, it was that even if he knew in his heart that she *wanted* him as much as he wanted her, she'd *chosen* Todd. That was a tough pill to swallow, but one he had to find a way to come to grips with.

"Slow down, Jax. I won't bring attention to this case without meeting with your friend and knowing it's what *she* wants. I don't want to give her false hope, and there are other factors to consider. If I start poking around and find that we're looking at shady cops and not just an honest mistake, there's a good chance this will blow up, and it could be hell for your friend. Even if I don't find anything unsavory with local officials, circulating new pictures to the media will bring out all sorts of attention-seeking psychos. Not only are we likely to get thousands of false sightings, but your friend needs to be prepared for the worst. And by worst, I don't mean finding a body. I mean coming up empty again despite putting forth our best efforts."

"I'm starting to understand why her aunt and uncle wanted her to let it go."

"None of it will be pleasant, Jax. It'll affect her ability to concentrate at work, her relationships. Nothing in her life will go untouched."

He thought about all the roadblocks Jordan had overcome. She hadn't even lost hope when her aunt and uncle had encouraged her to move on. She'd given up her dream of being a designer so she could move back to her hometown after college, and she put off her wedding multiple times, which couldn't have helped her relationship, all so she could be where Casey could find her. But given that she'd shut Jax down when he'd suggested they get age-progression photos and make a concerted effort to find Casey, he was ninety-nine percent sure that even if she wanted to take *this* risk, which she probably would, she wouldn't go through with anything that could have a negative impact on the people she loved.

More importantly, he'd gone too far Saturday night and caused a shitstorm of pain for her. Did he even have the right to ask? To be talking to Reggie about her family?

"That's a lot to consider." Jax paced, chewing on his last thought.

"There's one more thing you need to understand. Your friend might have given you the impression she would do anything to track down her sister, and she might have thought she meant it. But when reality hits, it's ten thousand times harder than anyone thinks it will be. Every bit of it. The waiting for answers, the highs of getting leads, and the devastation when they don't pan out. It could take years to get a resolution, if she gets one at all. I know you think closure is a good thing. We all do. But what if it was Jilly that had gone missing? Would you really be better off knowing she was dead?" Reggie paused, letting his words sink in. "Or would it be better to hold on to the hope that she was alive for the rest of your life because knowing she wasn't would tear you apart? *That's* what your friend could be facing."

It had been excruciating for his family during the ten years Zev and Beau were gone, never knowing if they were okay or when they'd be back. Could he handle losing any one of his siblings? No way in hell. But would he want to know if they'd been killed? His chest constricted. He didn't have the answer, and where Jordan was concerned, it wasn't his decision to make.

"You've given me a lot to think about. I'll talk to Jordan and get back to you."

"Let me know if she wants to move forward. I can make time one evening next week."

"Okay. Thanks, Reggie. I appreciate everything you've done."

After the call, Jax finished dressing and tried to decide how and *if* he should talk with Jordan. He didn't want to disrupt her life any more than he already had.

That was a blatant lie.

He wanted to take her in his arms and tell her all the reasons she'd made the wrong choice. But that option was no longer on the table. Hell, it never had been. He'd promised her he'd keep his flirting in check, and then he'd let his damn heart lead, and it had not only bared itself, but it had climbed onto a silver platter and launched at her. Only to be received like cold, pointy darts and batted away with tears. He had no fucking idea how to stop feeling like he'd been slaughtered and left to bleed out.

But damn it, this wasn't about him. This was about giving the woman he loved what might be her only opportunity to take steps toward finding her sister. She might give him hell, but that was a chance he was willing to take.

He made the call, but it went to voicemail after two rings, which he was pretty sure meant she'd sent it there. He paced as he left a message. "Hi. I'm sorry about the other night. I know you don't want to talk to me, and I'm trying to respect that. I'm not calling to try to change your mind. I want to talk to you." He stopped himself before *about Casey* came out of his mouth. This wasn't the type of information he should deliver in a voicemail. "Please give me a call when you get a chance. It's important."

He spent the next half hour wearing a path from one room to the next with Coco at his heels, replaying the message he'd left in his mind. It was too vague. How could she trust him not to try to convince her she'd made the wrong choice after he'd promised to keep himself in check and hadn't followed through? He started to thumb out a text, but it was too long and drawn out, and it all still sounded like a ploy to talk to her.

Of course it sounded like a fucking ploy. Three days was seventy-two hours too long to go without seeing her, but this was too important to leave up to chance. He put on sneakers and grabbed his keys. She could give him hell *after* he gave her the information about Reggie. Even if she didn't want to follow through, at least he'd know he'd done everything he could to help her find her sister. Coco followed him to the front door, tail wagging.

"Come on, girl. I need all the help I can get."

He came up with fifteen different ways to tell Jordan what he'd come to say, but the second he pulled into her driveway, those thoughts were obliterated by gut-wrenching emotions. He couldn't leave town. He wasn't even sure he'd be able to walk away from her fucking house after seeing her again.

Coco sat up, her ears perking, ready for an adventure.

"You think this is a good idea? Or am I about to get my balls busted again?"

She barked.

"Okay, girl. Here's the plan. If she gets mad that we're here, you do something cute. Got it? Distract her enough for me to say my piece."

Coco licked his chin, and he took a deep breath. "This is it, girl. All or nothing time."

He and Coco made their way up to the front door, that dove door knocker tugging at his heartstrings. What would happen to all that hope Jordan was holding on to when she married a man who didn't even like her talking about her sister? What would it do to her radiant soul to have her hopes, and her love for her family, permanently silenced? How would she survive that without resenting her husband?

Jax's gut twisted, his protective urges rising to the surface as he knocked on the door. He looked down at Coco, trying not to let the long stretch of silence eat away at him, but when seconds turned to minutes, his chest burned. It was one thing to ignore a voicemail, but she didn't seem like the kind of person who would ignore a personal visit.

He knocked again, his nerves strung so tight they felt like they might snap. Another long stretch of silence had him pulling out his phone to try to call her. As he navigated to her number, the front door opened. Jordan's eyes were red and puffy, and her nose was pink, twisting him up inside even more. Her hair was a tangled mess, and she was wearing a pink sweatshirt with HOPEFUL ROMANTIC written inside a white heart, white pajama shorts with pink hearts on them, and fuzzy pink bootie slippers.

"*Jax,*" she said in a tired, scratchy voice, her eyes filling with tears, driving that knife deeper into his chest.

Holy shit. Did I make a mistake by coming? "Sweetheart, please tell me I'm not the cause of those tears."

She opened her mouth to speak, but sobs fell out, shattering his heart like a landslide. He gathered her trembling body in his arms, silently cursing himself for convincing her to let him make her dress. He should have left well enough alone and walked away. At least then he'd be the only one hurting.

JORDAN CLUNG TO Jax, unable to believe he was there.

"I'm sorry, Jordan. I never meant to hurt you."

How could he think he was the one to hurt her when all she wanted was to be with him? She looked up through the blur of tears. "You didn't. It's over."

Confusion rose in his eyes.

"I broke up with Todd—" Sobs stole her voice, sadness and anger twisting together, Todd's hateful words slaying her anew. Coco whimpered, rubbing against her leg, sparking more tears. How did he know she'd need her, too?

Jax pulled her into his arms again. "I'm sorry." His words were filled with as much grief as relief.

"I just didn't expect it to hurt so bad."

"You were together for a long time. It's going to take some getting used to."

"Not for *him*. The arrogant, sleazy, two-timing bastard."

His jaw clenched, and she felt the rest of his muscles flexing, too, as if he were readying for a fight. "Why don't we go inside?"

She led him to the living room, but he stopped at the entrance, his concerned gaze moving over the shards of glass and chunks of broken candles on the floor by the fireplace.

"Coco, *sit*," he said sharply, and she plopped onto her butt beside him. "Was Todd here? Did *he* do this?"

"No. I did. I just haven't...I'll clean it up. Sorry." She headed for the hall closet, but he gently grabbed her wrist, drawing her back to his side.

"I'll get it. You stay with Coco. I don't want you getting glass in your feet."

She told him where the vacuum was, and as he cleaned up the mess, she loved up Coco, trying to pull herself together.

"Thank you," she said as he put away the vacuum. "I'm sorry I'm such a mess."

"Don't be sorry. You're beautiful, not a mess, and you have every right to be sad."

"You don't know the half of it." Anger bubbled up inside her again. "I'm sad one minute, and I'm *so* angry the next, I want to..." Her hands fisted.

"Throw something. I know." He stepped into her path, taking her hands and unfurling her fingers. "Do you want to talk about it?"

"*Maybe?* I don't know. It's embarrassing, and I hate to dump it on you."

"You're not dumping anything on me." He led her to the couch, and Coco climbed onto the cushion beside her, resting her chin on Jordan's lap. "I care about you, and you shouldn't keep that much anger bottled up. But I'm not sure throwing candles is the healthiest way to get rid of it."

"That's so embarrassing. I can't even believe I did it. I swear I'm not usually like this. But we were together for *so* long, and I know things weren't perfect, but I thought they were still good enough that if I ended things, he'd be sad or hurt, but when I told him I wanted to break up, he said *horrible* things to me."

"Is that because you told him about me?" The guilt in his voice was tangible.

"*No*. He didn't even ask why I was ending things, which also hurt and pissed me off. He just laid into me, saying he was relieved and that he'd only planned to marry me because I was the *marrying kind* and I would look good on his arm. He was so mean and spiteful, I felt like I was talking to a different person than the guy I knew."

Jax's jaw clenched. "I'd like to get my hands on that arrogant prick."

"He said he was sick of dealing with my issues anyway, and I couldn't figure out what he was talking about. I never complained to him about work or anything. I didn't even complain about spending holidays without him, or when he canceled our weekends together, until last weekend. I *did* get upset about that because I scheduled all those appointments for us, and you opened my eyes to how badly he was taking me for granted."

"I know I should say I'm sorry, but sweetheart, it would have killed me to see you marry a man who treated you so badly."

"I'm *glad* you got me to own up to the truth. I was miserable for a long time, but I was also scared of losing the one person who had been there for me for so long. But now I wish

I'd ended it *years* ago, because when I asked him what he meant by my *issues*, he said…" Tears flooded again, and she choked out, "*All that shit about your dead sister.*"

Jax gritted out, "Fucking asshole." He gathered her in his arms, holding her tight. "He's out of your life now, and he'll never be able to hurt you again."

"It gets worse," she said through her tears. "I called him Sunday morning, because I knew I was done and wanted to end things. But he didn't call me back until a couple of hours ago. He said he was too busy with his client in Atlanta. Then, at the end of our conversation, after all the other hateful things he said, he told me he never went to Atlanta. He said he took his secretary to Cabo for a long weekend. And he didn't stop there. The bastard told me about all the other times he'd taken women on trips. When I asked him why he cheated on me, he said it was because there are women you marry and women you *fuck*, and they're never one and the same." She dragged air into her lungs, pain slicing through her anew. "And I know he's not lying, because when I called his office yesterday morning, a temp answered, and she said she was filling in while his secretary was in Cabo. So many things make sense now. Like why he insisted on using condoms when I'm on birth control. God, I feel so stupid. How could I have been with him for so long and not known?"

"You are *not* stupid." Jax held her face between his hands, wiping her tears with the pads of his thumbs. "You are a smart, trusting woman, and what he did has *nothing* to do with you. Cheating is what weak people do to make up for their own inadequacies. Please don't waste your energy trying to figure out why he did it or if you could have done something differently, because a man as cruel and selfish as that couldn't have been deterred by anything."

A wealth of emotions pushed all that anger aside, filling up all her empty spaces. Jax was so good to her, so loving and tender, she wanted to climb into his arms and soak in his comfort. "As much as I hate you seeing me like this, I'm so thankful you're here."

"There's no place else I'd rather be." He tucked her hair behind her ear and caressed her cheek. "You know what I think, beautiful? We need to work on healing your bruised heart. Why don't I run you a bath so you can relax?"

God, this man...

"Can I just do one thing first?" she asked, stirring the butterflies that had been beaten down by those uglier emotions back to life.

"Anything."

She leaned forward and pressed her lips to his. His lips were even warmer and softer than she'd imagined, so perfect, she lingered, wanting more. When their lips finally parted, her heart was racing, and she was desperate to chase that entrancing feeling. He must have felt it, too, because he kept her close, sliding his hand into her hair as he brushed his lips over hers and whispered her name. His mouth came coaxingly down over hers in a slow, sensual kiss. Her body flooded with awareness. He tasted of lust and something deeper, and he didn't rush, didn't push too hard or linger too softly as his tongue swept over hers, like he was savoring the feel and taste of her, and *oh* how she wanted to savor him. "So sweet," he said against her lips before taking the kiss deeper, exploring every dip and curve of her mouth.

He kissed her so thoroughly, she came away dizzy with desire. Her eyes fluttered open, and she was spellbound by the raw emotions looking back at her.

"I've wanted to do that for eight and a half long months." He pressed his lips to hers in another sweet kiss. "I'd better go run that bath before I get carried away. Do you have any candles left?"

"Uh-huh," she said breathlessly.

"Candles?"

That sparked her brain into gear. *Geez! It was just a kiss. Pull yourself together.* "There are some on my dresser and in my bathroom, but you don't have to—"

He silenced her with another tender kiss. "I want to. Just point me in the right direction."

She pointed down the hall and watched him disappear into her bedroom in his gray sweatpants and a black T-shirt that clung to his broad back. Giddiness bloomed inside her, and she flopped against the back of the couch, grinning up at the ceiling and petting Coco.

How could the worst day of her life also be the best?

A few minutes later, Jax sauntered back into the living room. He walked behind the couch, put his hands on her shoulders, and leaned over her, eyeing Coco, who was lying on her back with her head on Jordan's leg as she scratched her belly. "I'll never get her to leave now."

"Good. I don't want you to leave."

He leaned over and kissed her forehead like he'd been doing it forever, and it felt that way, too. "Then how about if I order us some dinner while you relax in the tub?"

"You're spoiling me again."

"Sweetheart, I haven't even begun spoiling you." He came around the couch and took her hand. Coco followed them down the hall. He stopped at the entrance to her bedroom. "I'll wait out here for a few minutes while I order dinner in case you need anything."

"Okay." She went through the bedroom, and even though she'd known he was lighting candles, her breath caught at the sight of their flames dancing in the dimly lit bathroom. He'd put bubbles in the tub and laid a washcloth over the side and two fresh towels on the sink. She relived their kisses as she stripped off her clothes and sank into the warm water, wishing Jax were in there with her. The bubbles covered her body, and she had a thrilling thought about asking him to join her. But she couldn't do that.

Could she?

A little voice in her head said, *Yes, you can! The only thing standing between you and the man you want is your own inhibitions.* She'd been miserable for so long, she deserved a little happiness, and that wonderful man out there deserved to know how much she wanted him.

"Jax?" She closed her eyes, unable to believe she was doing it!

He opened the bathroom door just a crack. "I'm right here. What do you need?"

"You."

He peered around the door and grinned. "Me?"

"Mm-hm." She scooted forward in the tub. "In here with me, please."

She didn't have to ask twice. He told Coco to stay and closed the door, holding her gaze as he stripped off his shoes, socks, and clothes, and *holy mother of hotness.* His body was a work of art, all hard planes and defined muscles and an enticingly long, thick cock nestled between powerful thighs, all of which put Todd to shame. Her loneliest parts clenched with desire as he settled into the tub behind her, drawing her back against his chest.

He gathered her hair to one side and kissed her shoulder. "These freckles have taunted me since I first saw them."

Kind of like your mouth taunting me. She ached to have his mouth on hers again.

He put body wash on the washcloth. "Lie back and close your eyes."

She did as he asked, and he kissed her shoulder again, whispering, "So soft and beautiful." The feel of his warm lips trailing up her neck and his teeth and tongue on her skin had her vibrating with desire. He pushed the washcloth down her arm and over the crest of her breasts, the edge of it brushing her taut nipples, sending spikes of pleasure over her flesh. She sucked in a sharp breath, wishing it were his bare hands on her.

As if he'd read her mind, his hands snaked around her belly, palms to flesh. Need stacked up inside her as he caressed his way down her ribs and stomach and over her thighs, squeezing them just tight enough to draw a needy whimper. She felt his arousal hard and insistent against her back, heightening her own desires. His fingertips rested so close to where she needed him most, she knew he was trying not to rush her. But she needed *more*, and as she'd done with Jax so many times in different ways, she threw caution to the wind and covered his hand with hers, guiding it between her legs.

He moaned, low and rough, into her ear and nipped at her neck as his fingers slid through her wetness, zeroing in on the bundle of nerves at the apex of her sex. She gasped at the shock of pleasure spiking through her, and he growled. "Mm, you *like*…"

"*So* much," she panted out.

He pushed his fingers inside her, using his thumb on that sensitive spot. His other hand caressed her breast, and he rolled her nipple between his finger and thumb, showering her with scintillating sensations. She arched her back, rocking her hips as she rode his fingers. "That's it, baby. Soon that'll be my mouth between your legs."

His husky voice and dirty talk sent thrills racing through her. He bit her earlobe as he squeezed her nipple, causing a desperate moan to escape.

"You want to come, sweet girl?" He pushed his fingers in deeper, the thick invasion bringing another wave of intensity as he expertly found that other secret spot, teasing her slow and steady.

"*Yes.*" Her head lolled back, her breaths coming in fast, greedy spurts. He gradually quickened his efforts, every increase bringing a new rush of pleasure, taking her right up to the edge of release.

"You're so tight. I can't wait to be buried so deep inside you, you'll still feel me a week later."

Every stroke of his fingers hit the spot that caused her toes to curl, and his thumb expertly worked her clit, until she was panting, hanging on to her sanity by a fast-fraying thread. "*Jax,*" she pleaded.

He slowed his efforts again, driving her out of her ever-loving mind. Her body throbbed, aching for release. His other hand left her breast and fisted in her hair. He ran his tongue along the rim of her ear. "Give me your mouth."

Yesyesyes! She turned, and he took her in a rough, demanding kiss, taking and giving, then taking even more, devouring her until her senses spun. His fingers pushed deeper, stroking faster, his thumb applying unrelenting pressure to her most sensitive spot, creating an explosion of sensations. The world tilted on its axis, and she cried out into their kisses as her orgasm ravaged her. Jax kissed her harder, fucking her mouth with his tongue as he did with his fingers down below, and she freaking *loved* it. When she started to come down from the peak, he sent her right back up again to the edge of madness, and then the world spun away, and she felt freer and safer than ever before.

Jax stayed with her, loving her with his mouth and hands, until the very last pulse of her climax. She collapsed against his chest, and his strong arms circled her. He kissed her lips, cheek, and forehead and gazed deeply into her eyes, looking as drunk on her as she was on him.

He ran his hand down her back and squeezed her ass. "Sweetheart, you are fucking amazing."

He made her feel bold and sexy, awakening something darker and dirtier inside her. "I want *more*," she said shakily, *greedily*. "I want *you*."

"I want you more than I've ever wanted anything, but I don't have protection."

She was so greedy for him, she hadn't even thought about that. "I'm on birth control, but are you…? Have you…?" She didn't know how to have this conversation.

"I always use protection. You're safe with me."

"Thank God, because I need you so bad right now."

They both laughed.

"I need you, too." He grabbed her by the hips, turning her toward him. "Straddle me, baby."

He kept hold of her as she lowered herself onto his shaft, feeling every blessed inch of him until he was buried to the hilt. Her breath rushed from her lungs, and he gritted out, "Holy hell, baby. Don't move."

He wrapped one arm around her, holding her still as he rocked his hips up, taking her impossibly deeper, and dragged his tongue over her nipple. Titillating shocks skated over her skin. He sucked her nipple to the roof of his mouth, sending an erotic mix of pain and pleasure through her core. She grabbed his head, holding his mouth there. "Don't stop." He did it again, and her sex clenched tight and fast. *"Ohmygod."* She was *this close* to coming again. She'd never felt so much or craved so deeply.

He lavished her other breast with the same attention, sending her body into a frenzy of want and need. When he grazed his teeth over her nipple and used his fingers between her legs, teasing her clit, a loud moan flew from her lips. She tried to rock her hips, but he held her still, tight against him, until she was trembling with desire, pleading and panting for more. Only then did he release her from his grip, gritting out, "Ride me hard, baby. Make me yours."

He pulled her mouth to his, taking her in a deep, penetrating kiss as they began to move, quickly finding their rhythm. She rode him fast and frantic, every stroke of their hips causing a whirlwind of sensations. When he grabbed her hips, moving her faster, harder, he tore his mouth away. "Okay?"

"So good. Don't stop."

Not only did he continue thrusting powerfully and helping her move with one hand clutching her hip, but he moved his other hand between her legs again, sending her right up to the moon. She cried out, clinging to his shoulders, engulfed by pleasure. Bath water sloshed around them as their bodies bucked and rocked. This wasn't sex as she knew it. There was something miraculous between them that breathed new life into her lungs, caused explosions of pleasure inside her.

And she couldn't get enough.

Luckily, neither could he. He was all about *her* pleasure, and boy did he know how to bring it. He touched her like he knew her by heart, making her body sing in ways it never had before. She was right there with him, reveling in the feel of his muscles flexing, clawing at his shoulders, earning one gruff, sexy noise after another. His body felt familiar, as if they'd become one before, and at the same time, every touch and every kiss was as new as the first.

When she finally floated down from her high, her body quivering and shaking, his eyes held hers, dark and ravenous, as *"Again"* fell gruffly from his lips.

He wrapped her in his arms, holding her tight as he reclaimed her mouth, fierce and possessive, like he'd waited his whole life to kiss her and was never going to stop. His hips pistoned in time to her efforts, every stroke taking her higher. Their movements became rougher, his moans turned to growls, the sexy sounds making everything more intense. His hands curled around her shoulders, keeping their bodies tight, and with the next pump of his hips, they both cried out, enraptured by their passion as they catapulted into ecstasy. Fingers dug into flesh, moans and kissing sounds floated around them as their slick bodies moved in perfect harmony, until she collapsed against him in the tepid water. They kissed and clung to each other, their hearts slamming to the same frantic beat.

"Jesus, baby," he said low and gravelly against her neck, pressing a kiss there. He rested his forehead on her shoulder. "That was…"

Words flew through her mind—*incredible, magical, addicting*—but the only words she could manage were *"A lot?"*

He laughed and kissed her lips. "Too much?"

"Are you kidding? I didn't even know my body was capable of feeling so good. I've never been able to...*you know*...more than once, and once was often hard to achieve."

"That's the power of us, sweetheart." He kissed her again, sweet and slow. "And it'll be even better next time."

It was hard to imagine anything could feel better than what they'd just done, but she couldn't wait to put his claim to the test.

A LONG WHILE later, after enjoying a delicious pasta dinner and taking Coco for a walk, Jordan was tucked against Jax's side on the couch, with Coco curled up beside her. The lavender and peppermint candles they'd used in the bathroom cast shadows from their new perch on the mantel, the scent of hope wrapping around them like an embrace. She petted Coco's head, listening to the steady cadence of Jax's breathing. She'd never been so happy and relaxed with Todd, or maybe *ever* since losing her family. Was this what it felt like to be with someone who didn't look at her like arm candy? That thought brought a pang of hurt over how much time she'd wasted.

Jax kissed her temple. "Talk to me, sweetheart. You've had a hell of a day. Are you okay?"

She looked at him, wondering how one man could be as manly as he was tender and caring. "I think so. Right now I'm happier than I've ever been. I've never had *this*."

"You and Todd never cuddled on a couch?"

She shook her head. "He wasn't a cuddler. He was a lot

more attentive in college, but he liked going out and being entertained, which makes sense given his secret sexual proclivities. You know, I thought he was being protective of me, because he'd stay by my side and push me a little out of my comfort zone to attend parties. Now I think it was just to show me off. Not that I think I'm all that, but..."

"You *are* all that, sweetheart, and so much more."

Her heart filled up. "I love that you think so, but it's even bigger than just what he and I had. This whole evening with you has been wonderful and cathartic. I feel like I can breathe with you. I don't have to hide my hopes or insecurities. I've had to do that on one level or another with every relationship I've ever had."

"I'm glad you know you never have to pretend with me, and you don't have to with my family, either. I know you trust my parents, but my siblings and sisters-in-law are some of the most loyal and supportive people you'll ever meet, and you could use a little more support in your life. Girlfriends to confide in. But maybe don't talk about our bathtub habits."

She giggled. "Is once considered a habit?"

"No, but I'd like to make it one."

He nuzzled against her neck, and a thrill chased through her. She loved everything about them, but they were moving so fast it brought a little trepidation. Not that she wanted to slow them down, but she was just *aware* of it. "Can I ask you something?"

"Always."

How could one word make her feel so good? "How did you know I needed you tonight? I felt so betrayed, and you're the only person I wanted to talk to, but as I said earlier, I didn't want to unload on you. And then there you were, like someone tapped you on the shoulder and told you I needed you."

"It was hell staying away from you the past few days, and I guess you could say someone did tap me on the shoulder, giving me the excuse I needed to come see you." He shifted beside her, so he could see her face. "When you first told me about Casey, I reached out to a private investigator friend of my cousin's. Reggie Steele is one of the best in the business, and he called me today. That's why I came over."

"You did?" She sat up, her mind reeling.

"Yes, and I'm sorry I didn't tell you, but—"

"I don't care. I'm glad you did it. What did he say?" *Please let him find her.*

"He said there was evidence of another vehicle at the crash site, but the evidence was lost and never processed."

"What does that mean? Is that bad?"

"I don't know, and I'm not sure he does yet, either. But if you're interested in talking with him to discuss the possibility of moving forward with a new investigation, I can set that up."

"I am. When?" Her heart was racing.

"One evening next week."

"Any day. Whatever works for him. You'll be there, right? *Please?*" Her words came fast and anxiously.

"Of course, every step of the way. Finding Casey, or finding out what happened to her, has become as important to me as it is to you. But do you want to talk with your aunt and uncle first?"

"No. I won't do anything major without discussing it with them, but what would I say right now? That we're meeting with him? I don't even know what that means yet. I'm nervous, scared, and hopeful about meeting Reggie, which kind of makes me anxious, and I don't want to do that to them until I know what Reggie has to say."

"You're so careful not to make waves for them."

"They took me in and raised me when they didn't even want children of their own. They never made me feel like an imposition, but I have always tried not to be too much of a burden."

"So careful," he said softly. "I love that about you, and I think in this case, it's a smart move."

"Okay, good, because I don't know up from down right now. I can't believe you talked to a PI. Thank you." She threw her arms around him.

"One day you'll realize I would do anything for you."

His words were laden with so much emotion, her heart crawled out of her throat. "Will you stay with me tonight?"

He cocked a grin. "I wasn't planning on leaving."

"*Oh.* I guess I'm not used to that, either." Todd had always seemed in a hurry to leave.

"That makes two of us." He brushed his lips over hers. "I'm going to enjoy discovering new things with you."

"Oh, you are, are you?" she said playfully.

"Hell yes." He ran his hand along her thigh and brushed his scruff down her cheek. "Dinner was great, but I'm hungry for dessert. My girl spread out on the dining room table sure is enticing."

She gasped in surprise, but that didn't stop her neediest parts from throwing an anticipatory party. *"Jax."*

"Does that mean you've already christened that table?"

"Ohmygosh. *No.*"

A wolfish grin appeared, and he scooped her into his arms, both of them laughing as Coco jumped off the couch to follow them. Jax gave his pooch a serious stare. "You *stay.*" Coco plunked onto her butt, and Jax's eyes blazed back to Jordan. "So I can make *you* come."

He sealed his mouth over hers in a kiss full of dirty promises and so much more.

Chapter Twelve

THE MORNING SUN trickled in through the sheer curtains, illuminating Jordan's long legs and luxurious curves draped over Jax's side. Her head rested on his chest, and Coco was asleep, nestled behind her. If Jax could wake up like this every morning, he'd be the happiest man alive. This had to be *it*. The feeling his brothers talked about that had made them fall hard and fast for their significant others. Except Nick, who had walled his heart off so adeptly, he'd wasted years when he could have been with Trixie all along.

Jax wasn't going to make that mistake, and he sure as hell wasn't leaving town.

Last night had been the most intense sexual experience he'd ever had. They'd gone from the table to the couch to the floor and, eventually, to the bed. Being with someone he cared about brought pleasure to a whole new level, and it also intensified his need to cherish and protect Jordan. They'd stumbled into the shower to rinse off at two in the morning, laughing and kissing as they'd bathed each other, and the intimacy of taking care of her was just as magnificent as their lovemaking.

He ran his hand down her hip, wanting to show her how he felt in every way he could so she never had any doubts. He gently rolled her onto her back, and she made a mewling sound.

"Please don't go," she said sleepily.

"It took us months to get here, and I'm not losing another second." He moved over her, lightly kissing her lips. "The only place I'm going is *down* on you." He began kissing his way down her neck, and Coco jumped off the bed.

Jordan giggled, her cheeks pinking up. "I think she knew what you meant."

He'd seen that flash of innocence last night when he'd devoured her, and it had gotten him all twisted up inside. He'd never been a twisted-up kind of guy, and he loved that feeling, too.

He continued kissing his way down her body, her delicate fingers running through his hair. Man, he loved her touch, and he knew how much she loved his, because her breasts rose with each heavy breath. He slowed to lavish them with attention the way he'd already learned drove her wild, teasing with his tongue, grazing with his teeth, and sucking hard enough that she bowed off the mattress, sexy sounds spilling from her lips. Those needful sounds spurred him on as he tasted and nipped his way south, trailing his fingers down her rib cage and over the dip at her waist, bringing rise to goose bumps and earning more greedy whimpers. He clutched her hips, utterly bewitched by her curves, and couldn't resist taking a little love bite.

She sucked in a breath. "Do that again."

He did, only this time he moved one hand between her legs, teasing her wetness, and she made a long, low, *hungry* sound. He kissed her inner thigh, moving her leg over his shoulder and splaying his hand over her other thigh, holding it against the mattress as he slicked his tongue along her wetness. "So damn sweet." He sealed his mouth over her clit, working it to perfection, until she lost control, quaking against his mouth and then falling limp against the mattress.

His gaze swept up her body as he lowered her leg. She looked like an angel with her hair spread out on the pillow, eyes closed, fingers digging into the mattress.

"Open your eyes, baby."

Her eyes fluttered open, revealing deep pools of desire. He ached to be inside her, but that would have to wait. He wanted her out of her mind with need for him.

"Put a pillow behind you and scoot up. I want you to watch me feast on you."

Her eyes flamed as she followed his request, the flush on her cheeks deepening.

He pressed a kiss just above the very heart of her and went up on his knees, holding her gaze as he dragged his hand over her slick heat, teasing her with his fingers and wetting his palm. He fisted his cock, giving it a few tight strokes, and her eyes widened. *Oh yeah, baby. We're going to experience so many great things together.* "You like to see me touch myself?"

She nodded.

He continued stroking himself and used his other hand to drive her wild, caressing her clit with his thumb as his fingers worked their magic inside her. Her eyes closed and she bit her lower lip, her fingers clawing at the sheets.

"Eyes open, sweetheart."

She opened her eyes, and he quickened his efforts between her legs, still stroking his cock, bringing her right up to the edge of losing control, then slowing, leaving her panting and whimpering.

"Touch your breast."

Her hand moved tentatively to her chest.

"Don't be shy, baby. I'm stroking my cock for you. You're safe with me."

She palmed her breast.

"That's it. Now tease your nipple the way you like me to do it." She did, and her eyes closed. "Eyes on me, baby. You're so fucking sexy, I could come just watching you."

Her eyes locked on his and dropped to his fisted cock, a needy sound slipping free.

"Oh, you'll get it, baby. You'll get it good. But first I want more of you."

He lowered himself between her legs and slicked his tongue along her wetness, earning more sinful sounds as he loved her slowly, savoring her sweetness, coveting every needy moan and rock of her hips. But it was the emotions swimming in her eyes, the desperation and desire, bringing out his carnal desires. When her eyes fluttered closed, he drew back, reminding her to watch. Those baby blues hit him like a hook, reeling him in, making *him* want and need until he couldn't hold back. He gave her what she craved, sealing his mouth over her clit, sucking in fast, hard pulses, heightening her pleasure and keeping her at the peak until her entire body trembled and shook and his name flew from her lips like a prayer.

He eased his efforts, licking and loving her as she came down from the clouds, and then he kissed his way up her body, whispering between touches of his lips, "So beautiful...so sweet...so soft and feminine."

So mine.

Pleasure and so much more shimmered in her eyes. His heart thundered and swelled as he aligned their bodies, lacing their fingers together, but her cold, hard engagement ring brought reality rushing back. Just because he was ready to give her the world didn't mean she was ready to accept it. He lowered his mouth to hers in a merciless kiss, trying to chase that thought away as their bodies came together, and he poured all his emotions into the woman who was changing his world one sweet smile at a time.

Their bodies took over, and they found their rhythm, stealing his need to chase anything other than their pleasure. He lost himself in her warm, willing mouth, her softness molding to his hard frame, and her tight heat welcoming his cock like he'd finally found his home. He pushed his hands under her hips, lifting and angling so he could take her deeper. She made an appreciative sound and dug her fingers into his arms, rocking up to meet his every thrust. *So fucking hot.* Her thighs flexed, and he felt her orgasm mounting in her trembling body. He tore his mouth away, quickening his efforts.

"Let go, baby. Come for *us*." He reclaimed her mouth, but in the next breath her head fell back, eyes closed as she succumbed to their passion. Her body clenched tight and hot around him. He gritted his teeth, staving off his own powerful release, wanting to look into her eyes, to see her ravaged with pleasure as they crossed that bridge together.

He took her in a slow, sensual kiss as the last of her climax rumbled through her, and when their lips parted, he wanted to say a hundred romantic, unforgettable things. But as her eyes found his, soft and hauntingly sultry, his emotions took over, and he wrapped his arms around her, giving in to the whirlwind that had swept him up months ago. She was right there with him, clinging to him like she'd never let go. He felt her muscles tightening, unleashing the last of his restraint. Pleasure spiked through him, clawing up his core as he sent them both spiraling into ecstasy. Their kisses turned urgent and messy, hands groping, bodies thrusting, until they collapsed, sated and sweaty, to the mattress.

He held her close, burying his face in her neck. "*God*, what you do to me. I wasn't too rough, was I?" He kissed the crook of her neck and lifted his face, drinking in her blissed-out expression.

Her lips curved up, and she shook her head. "You were perfect. I might be a little sore later from using muscles that I'm not used to using, but that's a good pain."

"I'll have to give you a rubdown." He rolled them onto their sides, reveling in the feel of her snuggling against him, wishing they could blow off work and spend the day together. He wouldn't care what they did. He just wanted more time with her.

JORDAN WAS FLOATING on a cloud of happiness. Jax felt so good, she didn't want to move out of his arms, much less out of her bed, but she had to get cleaned up. His eyes were closed, and he looked so peaceful, but he held her tight, one hand on her back, the other on her bottom, as if he didn't want her to sneak away. She used to think she was asking for too much, wanting to feel desired and made a priority. But he did those things all on his own, making it easy for her to reciprocate and making her want to do so much more—in and out of bed.

"Jax." She kissed his chest. "I need to use the bathroom."

"Okay. I should let Coco out back, too." He tightened his hold on her. "But I don't want to move."

She loved that. "Me neither, but I need to before things get *messy.*"

He groaned, kissing her again. "Go ahead, beautiful." He swatted her butt as she climbed out of bed, and she glared at him over her shoulder.

"Next time I'll bite it."

She giggled as she went into the bathroom, closing the door behind her. She felt so alive, she bounced on her toes, doing a little happy dance. To think she could have gone her whole life without ever feeling the way she did with Jax. She looked in the mirror. Her hair was a mess and her skin was flushed, but for the first time in her life, she felt sexy and truly wanted. She touched her face, catching sight of her engagement ring, bringing betrayal rushing back like a bullet to her chest. The hateful things Todd had said echoed in her ears, bringing an onslaught of hurt. How could he have been so vicious after saying he loved her for so long? How could he have cheated on her? He'd sounded proud of it, too, which made her wonder who else knew about it. Did his parents know? His co-workers?

Humiliation nearly brought her to her knees, and she sank down to the edge of the tub. How could she have ever thought what they'd had was enough?

"Are you okay, sweetheart?" Jax asked through the door.

"Uh-huh" came out thin and shaky.

"Jordan?"

"Yeah. I'm okay." Her voice cracked.

The door opened, and Jax peered in, wearing only his sweats, his brow knitting. "Oh, sweetheart." He grabbed a towel from the rack and wrapped it around her, tucking the top into itself over her chest, as he lowered himself to one knee. "What's wrong?"

His thoughtfulness drew tears. "I don't *know.* I was fine,

and then I saw my ring, and it all came back. The hurt and anger, and the betrayal just cut so deep." She swiped at her tears.

He put his arms around her. "It's okay, sweetheart. Your entire world was upended, and even though you got the better part of the deal," he said with a teasing smile, "it's going to take some time for the hurt to go away."

"It didn't take *him* any time to move on," she bit out.

"Because he's an unfeeling prick. Thank God you're not like him."

"What will everyone think of me? I was engaged one minute, and I didn't even take a breath before jumping into bed with you. Don't get me wrong. I *wanted* to be with you. I still do. But how am I going to explain it? We *just* had dinner with your parents. They think I'm marrying *Todd*." Her voice escalated as reality hit. "I can't exactly say, *Oh yeah. That was last week. Now I'm crazy about your son.* They'll worry that I'm unstable, or that you're my rebound. Oh *God*. What if they think I'm with you because of who you are?"

"I *hope* you are into me because of the man that I am."

"I am, but you know what I mean. They'll think it's because you design gowns for celebrities. What if *everyone* thinks that? What if your staff thinks that? How can I face them? They'll assume I'm a gold digger."

"Jordan, slow down and take a breath." He took her hands in his. "Let's take this one step at a time. First, I'll cancel the billboard announcing our relationship."

She appreciated his levity, but she was too rattled for it to help.

"Seriously, babe. You shouldn't feel any pressure about us. We'll take things slow while we figure this out. We'll be cool in public, and I know it's not just what people will think or say. It's also a lot to deal with in your own head. We don't need to jump back into bed until you're ready."

She hated putting restrictions on them. "Okay. But you *know* this isn't about not wanting to be with you. I still want to see you. I just need to get my arms around this situation without feeling like everyone at my work, and your family, will judge me."

"I know. Let's start at the beginning. Have you told your aunt and uncle that you and Todd broke up?"

"Not yet."

"You should probably make that call. Do you want your co-workers to know that he was unfaithful?"

"Yes. I want to put *that* on a billboard so people know who he really is."

"That wouldn't embarrass you?"

"I'm already embarrassed that I stayed in an unhealthy relationship for so long. His cheating is just the icing on the embarrassment cake."

"But think about it, Jordan. Preparing always brings better outcomes. What do you want people to know about why it ended, if anything? It's okay to say you grew apart."

"That's the truth. I think I fell out of love with him a long time ago. I just couldn't own up to it until you opened my eyes."

"Okay, but why don't you think it over? I'll support whatever you decide, and when you're ready, you can take off your ring and figure out if you want to wait until your co-workers notice and ask about it, or rip the bandage off and tell them up front."

"I have to tell the ladies who made me the gloves, and Finlay and Isla. I feel so bad for wasting everyone's time." Her heart pitched. "And I'll pay you for the time you put into designing my gown." She pulled the ring off her finger and closed her fist around it, the finality of it drawing more unwanted tears. She swiped angrily at them. "I'm not crying about *him*. I'm just…"

He grabbed tissues from the counter, wiping her tears, then handing her another wad of them. "Todd was a big part of your life for a long time. You're allowed to mourn the man you thought he was and the relationship you had. It's also okay to be pissed off that you have to deal with the aftermath. It's all okay. And you're *not* paying me a penny. Knowing you're no longer going to be taken advantage of is payment enough."

"I can't believe you're not running in the opposite direction. How can you be so understanding?"

He brushed her hair away from her face. "I care about you, Jordan. I'd have to be a callous self-centered jerk not to want to help you heal."

"I hate how weak that makes me sound."

"Not weak. Just hurt, and don't waste your energy worrying about my family or my staff. They won't think you're into me for any reason other than my charming personality and sexual prowess."

She laughed softly. "I can't even roll my eyes at that, because it's partially true. They're probably used to women falling at your feet. Oh my gosh. *Jax*. The *auction*. I'm going to need to save my money so I can win you."

"You already won me. I backed out two days ago."

Her brows knitted. "After I told you I couldn't see you? Why would you do that?"

"Because the only woman I care about is sitting right in front of me, and I wasn't going to get up onstage and pretend otherwise."

"I don't even know how to respond to that."

"You don't have to respond. Just know it's true. I'm not going anywhere, sweetheart. You're stuck with me and all my charms."

She laughed softly. "Thank you for making me feel better, and just so you know, it wasn't your charms or your looks that first caught my attention. It was the energy when I walked into the room. That first time our eyes connected, I felt like I knew you, or I was supposed to know you, and then we talked, and yes, I got swept up in your charms. But what stuck with me for all those months was who you were and how I felt when I was with you. You were so inquisitive and open and easy to talk to. I immediately felt like I wanted to know you and for you to know me. I'd never experienced that before." She opened her hand, looking at the ring. "I should have returned this eight months ago, because those feelings were the reason I postponed the wedding the last time."

"You weren't ready to end things then."

"That's what my aunt said when I talked with her last weekend."

"Why don't I take care of returning this?" He took the ring out of her hand and put it in his pocket.

"Are you sure? I can deal with it."

"I know you can, but you've got enough to figure out." He hugged her. "Does he have any of your things at his place? Or is any of his stuff here that needs to be returned?"

She shook her head. "We lived out of a suitcase when we visited."

"Sorry, sweetheart, but that says a lot."

"I know. When I look back, I see all the signs I missed."

"I'd say I wish you and Todd had never gotten together, but if it weren't for that relationship, we might never have met."

That made it worth the pain. "Where does this leave us, Jax?"

"Where we probably should have started in the first place." He took her hand again. "Ms. Lawler, would you do me the honor of having dinner with me tomorrow night? I promise to flirt incessantly, maybe grope your leg under the table, and to leave you on your doorstep with nothing more than a good-night kiss."

That Braden charm gets me every time.

"I might also cop a feel, but I promise I won't step foot inside your house until you're ready for more. What do you say?"

"I think my neighbors might like the copping a feel thing a little *too* much."

"Okay, a *discreet* feel *in* the car."

She giggled, a little giddy thinking about making out with him in a car. That *was* on her bucket list. "I would like that very much, Mr. Braden."

He rose to his feet, bringing her up with him. "So, this taking-it-slow thing. Can it start *after* we shower together, or would you like me to leave now?"

She untucked the towel, allowing it to drop to the floor. "I might be a little confused right now, but it would be selfish of me to deny us a little something to remember on our lonely nights apart." She hooked her finger into the waist of his sweatpants, tugging him forward. "These need to come off now, please."

Chapter Thirteen

JORDAN COULDN'T STOP grinning Friday afternoon as she read Jax's text, feeling more like a giddy college girl than a professional woman. *Dear Ms. Lawler, thank you for accompanying me to dinner last night. I thoroughly enjoyed your company and the meal, but the strawberry cheesecake wasn't nearly as delectable as you, and that front-seat make-out session only whet my appetite. Did it whet yours?*

Warmth surged through her as she remembered just how *whet* her *appetite* had been when he'd kissed her senseless in the car after their date. It was crazy how much she'd missed him after he'd left.

She thumbed out a response. *Dear Mr. Braden, that is quite a personal question. While I'm not inclined to answer it specifically, I will say that it's a good thing I don't live in an apartment with thin walls, or the neighbors might have heard your name being cried out late last night as I imagined your fingers in place of mine.* Her heart raced as she sent the naughty message. She'd never sent sexy texts to Todd, and she was glad, because this was new and exciting, and it was *theirs*. She liked having experiences that were new for her and Jax, like making love in the bathtub, which Jax told her last night had been a first for him, too.

Her phone vibrated and her pulse spiked before she even read his response. *Dear Ms. Lawler, thank you for that visual. However, I won't be able to stand up from behind my desk for quite some time.* Jordan giggled. *Perhaps your right hand should now be named Jax, as I've called mine Jordan for the past several months. I, too, was strung tighter than a violin last night, and poor Coco searched the house for you when I imagined my hand was your mouth as I gritted out your name.*

Jordan's body flamed. She fanned her face, turning her chair away from her office door as she responded. *Dear Mr. Braden, I'm afraid this line of messaging has necessitated a change in panties, which I don't have on hand. Perhaps we should keep things a bit more professional.*

His response was immediate. *Dear Ms. Lawler, wearing panties is overrated. Feel free to forgo them on our next dinner date.* Her heart raced as she texted, *Dear Mr. Braden, I've noted your request and will take it under consideration.* Jax wasted no time. His message rolled in a minute later. *Dear Ms. Lawler, would you like to join me and Coco for a sunrise run tomorrow morning? I promise to keep my hands to myself. Fortunately, my mouth is not as easily controlled. Panties optional.*

Grinning, she typed, *Dear Mr. Braden, I would love to join you. However, I do have a request. If you plan on wearing your gray sweatpants, please wear tight undergarments. If you don't, and if I forgo wearing panties, it could lead to a sticky situation.*

"Hi, Jordan."

Jordan startled and leapt to her feet, turning to find Trixie standing in the doorway. Her long dark hair fell in natural waves over the shoulders of her pink Rising Hope T-shirt. A true Southern girl, Trixie always wore jeans and cowgirl boots, and she was holding Annabelle's lead, one of her adorable miniature therapy horses, who wore a pink Rising Hope vest and shoes.

"Trixie, hi." Jordan set her phone on the desk, trying to calm her runaway hormones.

"Did you forget about our meeting? I can come back if you're busy."

"No. I didn't forget. I was just"—*sexting with Jax*—"distracted. Come in. Sit down. It's great to see you. You look refreshed from your honeymoon."

"I have a feeling I'll look *refreshed* for quite some time. I swear Nick has the sexual energy of a twenty-year-old."

"Lucky you." Jordan wanted to gush about Jax, but Trixie didn't know she'd broken off her engagement, and she still wasn't comfortable sharing too much personal information. She'd told her aunt, and her aunt had been relieved that she'd finally ended her relationship with Todd. She'd also told Kelly and a few other staff members, but there were still more people who needed to know that her engagement had been called off for good, including the Knotty Hookers and some other residents with whom she was close. It *was* getting easier to tell people, and she wasn't sure if that was a good or a bad thing.

"And how are you, pretty girl?" She petted Annabelle, instantly feeling a little more relaxed. She'd noticed that Coco had the same effect on her. "Are you ready to bring smiles to our residents today?"

"Is she *ever*. She's in a great mood." Trixie sat down, and Annabelle stood dutifully by her side.

"She's always a sweetie." Jordan's phone vibrated as she went behind her desk to sit down.

"Sorry I'm late!" Jillian breezed into the office on sky-high heels, wearing a gorgeous two-toned cap-sleeved minidress with a white hourglass-shaped panel in the front, flanked by black sides.

"Hi." Jordan couldn't hide her surprise. "I didn't know you were joining us."

"Sorry. That's my fault," Trixie said. "I think I forgot to mention it."

"I'm doing a ride-along with Trixie today." Jillian settled into the chair beside Trixie. "It's kind of like a ride-along with the police, you know, to see what Trixie really does."

"Oh. How fun, but I'm afraid you might be bored during this meeting. We're just going over schedules." Her phone vibrated several times in rapid succession. "I'm sorry. I forgot to turn that off." She snagged it off the desk, hoping they didn't notice Jax's name on the messages.

"Someone must *really* want to reach you," Jillian said. "Maybe it's your fiancé."

"I bet Todd's counting down the days until your wedding," Trixie's gaze moved to Jordan's left hand, then flicked up, filled with concern.

"Um, let me just…" She opened one of Jax's messages, catching the word *panties* as she thumbed out, *Can't text. In meeting.* She sent the text and shoved the phone in her purse, remembering the nice things he'd said about Jillian and Trixie. "Sorry about that. It wasn't Todd. I broke off our engagement."

"Oh, *no*," Trixie said empathetically. "Cold feet again?"

"No. I'm done. I should have ended it a long time ago."

"Really?" Jillian sounded strangely enthusiastic. "Does my brother know?"

Trixie winced. "That's right. Jax was designing your wedding gown with you."

"He knows. I saw him the night it happened, and we had

dinner last night." Boy, it felt good to say that out loud.

"You did? *That's* interesting." Jillian scooted forward on the chair. "So, was this a friendly dinner, like let me comfort you in your time of need? Or was it *more* friendly, like *hey, baby, I can make you forget that guy ever existed?*"

Ohmygod.

Trixie's eyes bloomed wide. "Jilly!"

"What?" Jillian splayed her hands. "I'm just *asking.* If you hadn't been so busy mooning over your new husband at your wedding reception, you would have seen the sparks flying between them. They nearly caught the dance floor on fire."

"How did I miss *that?*" Trixie asked incredulously.

"Because you weren't *supposed* to notice it. I was still with Todd. It was totally inappropriate that I felt anything at all for Jax."

"Ha! Are you kidding me?" Jillian laughed. "You can't hide that kind of chemistry, and thank God. Jax had been *off* for so long, I thought he was losing his touch. But when I saw you two dancing, it all came together, and I realized you'd knocked my brother's socks off last summer and had knocked him completely off-kilter."

"You *did?*" Trixie's brow knitted. "I remember you calling Jax *charming,* but I didn't realize he'd had that kind of impact on you."

"He was—*is*—charming, but there was something bigger between us. Not that we did anything about it. I didn't even know he felt it for all those months."

"Like I said, big, explosive *fireworks,*" Jillian chimed in. "Everyone seems to find them except *me,* but whatever."

Jordan smiled at Jillian's eye roll. "I wasn't looking for fireworks. I cut our first meeting short because I felt so much for him, and then I spent the next several months trying to get him out of my head."

"How'd that work for you?" Jillian asked. "Because we Bradens are kind of unforgettable."

"Maybe Trixie could have warned me about that. Why do you think I postponed the wedding?"

"Oh my gosh," Jillian said. "It *was* because of Jax."

"That must have been so hard for you. Why didn't you tell me?" Trixie looked hurt.

"I'm not really used to sharing my personal life, and you consult for the company. I didn't want to complicate our relationship. But I was also uncomfortable about having feelings for Jax while I was with Todd, and I didn't want you to think bad of me."

"I wouldn't have. I understand not wanting to mix business with pleasure and all that, and I know we haven't gone out that often, but I consider you a friend," Trixie said. "You can always come to me. I won't let it make our business relationship weird."

"And don't blame yourself for having feelings for Jax," Jillian added. "I mean, he *is* my twin, which means he's pretty darn awesome."

"He is a great guy, but with everything that's happened, Jax and I are taking things slow. Thank you for not making me feel bad for how it all came together. It's been really hard to deal with. Not only did I feel horrible for wasting Finlay and Isla's time, but I also found out that Todd had been cheating on me for a long time."

"That scumbag," Jillian said. "I bet Jax wants to tear him to pieces."

"Jax can't go after him. He has a reputation to protect. But I could send Nick to teach him a lesson," Trixie offered. "Or my brothers. They love a good fight."

Jillian nodded. "That's a great idea."

"You guys, come on. I appreciate your support, but *nobody* is going to fight because of me."

"You obviously didn't grow up with brothers," Trixie said. "That jerk disrespected you, and where I come from, he'd never get away with it."

"Mm-hm," Jillian agreed. "Family protects family, which means anyone in our circle—and that includes *you*. So if you change your mind, we've got your back. Well, our brothers do."

"You can't imagine how much that means to me." She thought about Casey and debated telling them about her but quickly decided that conversation was too emotional to have at work.

"I guess this means we'll see you at our birthday party to-morrow afternoon," Jillian said.

"It's your birthday?" Jordan asked.

"Yup! Jax and I are turning *thirty*. I can't believe it, but I also can't believe that I still haven't found my soul mate, so there's that." Jillian rolled her eyes.

"Nick and I are throwing them a party. Jax hasn't men-tioned it to you?"

An uneasy feeling moved through Jordan. "No. But that's okay. Like I said, we're taking it slow, especially in public. There are still some people I need to tell that Todd and I broke up."

"He probably didn't tell you about the party because he didn't want to put pressure on you," Trixie said.

Jillian nodded. "Yeah, that explains it. I know Jax would want you there. But he'd definitely put your feelings ahead of his own. Our family can be a lot to deal with, and he's never brought a woman to a family event. Everyone would make a big deal out of it."

"That sounds like Jax." Jordan's heart warmed with thoughts of him. "He always puts my feelings first. I'll find some way to make it up to him."

"I bet you will." Trixie waggled her brows.

"It is his birthday," Jillian said in a singsong voice.

They all laughed, and Jordan thought of several naughty things to give the man who probably wanted for nothing.

Chapter Fourteen

"I THINK I can. I think I can." Jordan panted out the mantra as she and Jax ran through the park Saturday morning. She'd been so excited to see him and Coco, she'd barely gotten any sleep last night, and she was paying for it. Her legs felt like lead, and they were nearing the biggest hill, on top of which they'd watched the sunrise last time.

"I *know* you can." Jax winked.

He made running look easy, barely breaking a sweat. Jordan groaned, and Coco looked up, her tongue hanging out of her mouth as she trotted happily beside them.

"Talk to me. It'll keep your mind off running. How did it go when you told the ladies who made your gloves about breaking up with Todd?"

"Surprisingly well." Was she supposed to talk *and* run? "I offered to give them back the gloves." She panted for air. "But they said they made them with love for me, and the love still held."

"That's really nice. Are there many people left to tell?"

"Just a few managers, vendors, and residents I haven't seen yet."

"Good, and you feel okay about it?"

She nodded.

"I'm glad. I know it's hard. On a happier note, I spoke with Reggie. He'd like to meet with us next Friday for dinner in the city. Is there any way you can take that day off work?"

"Yes." This is really happening! "I have plenty of unused leave."

"Great. He wanted to know if you could bring pictures of your family around the time of the accident."

"Of course." She had all of her parents' old pictures, and her aunt and uncle had given her copies of theirs, too. "I'll go through them today and pick some out."

"Are you going to be okay doing that? Would you like me to be there with you?"

As much as she wanted him there, he hadn't mentioned his birthday, and she was sure Jillian had been right about him trying to protect her from the pressure that went along with attending. There was no way she'd let him miss his own birthday party because of her. "Thanks, but I'll be okay."

"Okay, but call if you need me, and I'll come over. I have a brief meeting in the city Friday afternoon before we meet with Reggie. I thought it might be fun if I arrange a tour of JRBD for you while I'm at my meeting. You can see how the big guys work."

"Are you kidding?" She gulped in air. "That would be *amazing.*"

"Great. I'll arrange it with Josh's assistant, Mia. We can fly back Friday night, or we can knock around the city and have a romantic weekend together, sleeping in separate hotel rooms if you'd like."

Her nerves prickled at the thought of hanging around the city, where she had mostly uncomfortable memories. "I've never found the city to be romantic."

"That's because you've been going with the wrong person. We'll play it by ear. See how you feel after meeting Reggie."

They came to the bottom of the giant hill, and as they started jogging up it, Jordan panted out, "I think I can. I think I...*can't.*" She stopped and bent at the waist, holding her side.

"Yes, you can." He moved behind her and grabbed her butt with both hands, pushing her forward. "Go, baby. I've got you!"

They laughed as she tried to jog up the hill with him pushing her from behind. Another jogger came over the top of the hill, and Jax dropped his hands, dramatically trying to act nonchalant by wiping his brow as he practically ran in place beside Jordan because she was running so slowly.

He lifted his chin at the other jogger. "How's it going?" As soon as the man ran past, Jax put his hands on her butt again, pushing her up the hill.

"Jax!" She turned around, cracking up.

A sly grin slid across his face, and he held up his hands, stalking toward her. "Do you want these someplace else?"

He was so *bad*, and she loved it, but there was a group of women jogging up the hill. "Not *here!*"

"Why not?" He ran toward her.

She squealed and sprinted up the hill, out of breath and gloriously happy as the daffodils came into view. Jax swept his arm around her, hauling her against him, his eyes glittering victoriously. "I knew you could do it."

He gave her a chaste kiss as she tried to catch her breath. "Be sure to"—she gulped air into her lungs—"tell the paramedics it's your fault when I pass out." She rested her cheek on his shoulder.

"Don't pass out before the sun rises, sweetheart."

She lifted her face as a sliver of sunlight peeked over the horizon, spreading ribbons of color rippling across the sky. Jax took her hand, leading her off the path, toward a blanket with a picnic basket lying in the grass beneath the leafy umbrella of an oak tree.

"Mr. Braden, *what* have you done?"

"I might not be able to wake up with you in my arms for a while, but that doesn't mean we can't enjoy breakfast together."

Butterflies fluttered in her chest. "You want to eat breakfast with me?"

"If I had it my way, you'd fall asleep every night in my arms and wake up between me and Coco every morning, and I'd have *you* for breakfast."

"That doesn't scare you at all, does it? Not the dirty part— the staying over part."

"No. As I said at Nick's wedding, life is too short to hold the important things in. I'm falling hard for you, sweetheart, but I have no problem going slow. You can take a week, a month, or a year. Take however long you need to heal and to trust your own judgment and mine. I know what I want, and I'm going to keep showing you and telling you exactly how I feel, because you deserve to know."

She needed someone to pinch her to make sure she wasn't dreaming. She was falling for him, too, for all the little things he said and did and for knowing how to nurture her heart in ways other people never had. He brought so much light and clarity into her life, it allowed her to take a new look at who she was, what she wanted, and what she had to offer. "How did I get lucky enough to meet you and then run into you again at the wedding?"

"I think they call that serendipity." He kissed her softly.

"Let's get comfortable, so we don't miss the rest of the sunrise."

She sat on the blanket, and he knelt by the basket on the other side of the blanket as Coco settled in beside her.

He opened a water bottle and handed it to her. "First we hydrate." He poured water into a dog bowl and set it down for Coco, and then he guzzled some water, too. She loved how selfless he was, caring for them before himself. He lifted a beautiful stained-glass dove wind chime from the basket and hung it on the lowest branch of the tree. He thought of *everything*.

"That's beautiful, Jax. Doves and wind chimes are signs of hope."

He tossed her a wink. "Only the best for my girl." He tapped the chimes, and Coco tilted her head curiously at the whimsical sound.

Jax knelt by the basket again, handing Jordan a warm thermos and two mugs. "That's peppermint tea. I know we usually have lattes, but trust me, there's a method to my madness."

"I love peppermint tea." *Peppermint. Another sign of hope.* She'd always noticed signs of hope around her, but Todd had rolled his eyes at her so many times she'd stopped mentioning them long ago. She thought about that as Jax set a bowl of kibble near Coco and a plate and napkins by Jordan. She hadn't known why she'd opened up to Jax about the signs of hope she'd noticed while they were together, but she just figured it out. Everything about him—his kindness, honesty, and yes, even those flirty, sexy innuendos and his exquisite follow-throughs—made her want to share everything about herself. But spotting signs of hope *was* a little odd, and she imagined it could get tiresome if she mentioned every little thing she saw, so this time she kept it to herself.

He set a banana-nut muffin on the plate, and then he added a cinnamon roll, a cherry-cheese tart, and a chocolate-almond croissant. Jordan's mouth watered at all those delicious options. *Four. Another sign of hope.* "Are you a little hungry this morning?"

"That's a dangerous question now that I've had a taste of you."

She giggled. "I meant for *food*."

He put his hands on the blanket on either side of her legs and crawled up her body. Her chest felt like there were hummingbirds in it as he caged her in, his dark eyes sparkling with as much happiness as desire. "Good morning, Ms. Lawler."

His seductive voice coasted over her skin. "Good morning, Mr. Braden."

"Do you realize we're literally surrounded by hope right now?"

"You noticed?"

"It was purposeful. I told you there was a method to my madness. I wanted that for you." He brushed his lips over hers. "I looked up the symbols of hope, because I want your *every* morning to start with it." He kissed the corner of her mouth, his words taking her breath away. "And I want you to end every night feeling as safe and happy as you can be." He gazed deeply into her eyes, and she felt herself getting lost in them. "And when you're ready, we'll add *sated* to that nightly list."

"I want that, too." So much, she ached for it.

"When you're ready."

"I *want* to be ready."

"There's no rush. You'll know when the time is right." As he pressed his lips to hers, she hoped that was true.

LATER THAT AFTERNOON, Jordan sat on her living room floor surrounded by her mother's sketch pads, photo albums, and loose pictures of her family, memories coming at her from all sides. They were good memories, and it was a good feeling, even though she missed them. She wished Jax were there so she could share them with him. She wanted him to see her mother's creativity jumping off the pages of her sketch pads and the light in her father's eyes as he carried Casey on his shoulders, holding one of her tiny hands, his other arm slung over their mother's shoulder, holding *her* hand. She wanted to put a face to their names and let Jax see her mother's beautiful smile, her arm draped protectively over Jordan's shoulder, her hand on Jordan's belly.

Her phone rang with a call from her aunt. She answered and put it on speakerphone. "Hi!"

"Hi, honey. I wanted to see how you were holding up."

"I'm having an amazing day. I met Jax for a run this morning, and he surprised me with a picnic breakfast, which we ate while we watched the sun rise."

"He sounds wonderful. Is he with you now? Should we chat later?"

"No. We're still taking it slow."

"He's okay with that?"

"He's okay with everything. I never realized how much thought I had to put into my relationship with Todd until now. Being with Jax is so easy and natural, it makes me see how stressful things were with Todd."

"Life has a funny way of showing us things we don't want to

see."

"It's so true, and being with Jax, being happier, has changed me. I'm realizing how much I neglected myself in my relationship with Todd, too. You were right, I had put myself in a safe little box, and I think I did it to keep from wanting something else."

"And now you're going for runs and having picnics."

"More like going for very slow jogs." She laughed. "And I had a great day all by myself. I went shopping and had lunch in town at this cute little café, and now I'm going through old pictures."

"You sound like a whole different person."

"I feel like it, too. Want to know something else that's kind of weird?"

"Sure. I like weird stuff." Her aunt giggled.

"I told you that I can talk to Jax about Mom and Dad and Casey."

"Yeah, you mentioned that."

"Well, as I'm looking through these pictures, I'm *not* crying, and almost every time I looked at them when I was with Todd, I bawled my eyes out."

"You looked at them with Todd? I thought he had a hard time revisiting your old memories."

"He did. I didn't mean with him. I looked at them when we were apart, but I'm not crying now, and I think that's because I don't have to hide my feelings about them anymore. And that's not just because of Jax. That's because of you and Uncle Gary, too."

"Oh, Jordan, that's great news."

"Yeah, it feels really good. You should see the picture I just found from a Fourth of July parade. I think it was the year before the accident."

"I want to see it! Hold on. I'll FaceTime." A few seconds later her aunt's smiling face appeared on the screen. She was petite and wholesome looking, with fair skin, honey-blond hair, and bright blue eyes, so different from Jordan's big, burly dark-haired father. "*Whoa.* Happiness looks good on you. You are positively radiating."

"That might be the sugar high from the ice cream I had after lunch."

"No. I've seen you eat enough ice cream to recognize the difference. You look like you did when you were a little girl and your daddy would surprise you with a new dress."

Jordan's hand moved over her heart. "I miss that. Not the presents, just that feeling when he walked through the door. Me and Mom and Casey would *all* run to him, even if he was empty-handed."

"He loved you all so much. He used to say that his world was gray before your mom came into it, and she brought rainbows and sunshine, even on rainy days."

"I love knowing that."

"It sounds like Jax is doing the same for you."

That made Jordan feel good all over, because she was thinking the same thing.

"Now show me that parade picture."

Jordan held it up, and her aunt's expression warmed.

"Look how little you and Casey were, and your parents look so young. It's hard to believe we were ever that young. That picture *was* taken the summer before the accident. We were there visiting that weekend. I took that picture, and I can still hear my brother telling me not to mess it up. Casey sure did idolize him." They were wearing matching flannel shirts. "Look at her chin resting on his head, one spindly arm wrapped around his neck like he was *hers*."

"She wanted to *be* him."

"Yes, she did. Can we look at more pictures?"

"I would love to!" Jordan set her phone down to free her hands, and they looked at several more pictures. Her aunt shared stories for nearly every one of them.

She pulled out a picture of her father sitting in a rocking chair, holding a baby bundled up in a blanket. He was looking at her with a serious expression. "Do you know who he's holding—me or Casey? I can't tell the color of the baby's hair."

"That's you, and it was taken about a week after you were born. I stayed with you guys for the first two weeks after each of you was born to help out. Neither of you was a great sleeper. Your father was so worried about why you weren't sleeping, every night before you went to bed, he'd have a very serious talk with you about how you were safe and tell you he would never let anything happen to you. That's what he's doing in that picture."

"That's so sweet. I can't believe I never knew that."

"Talking about your parents and Casey was hard for all of us for a very long time. As adults we could compartmentalize it, but it was too hard for you. You used to break down in tears whenever we talked about them, and you'd get angry if we talked in the past tense about Casey. Even three years after the accident, you were adamant that one day you'd move back to Maryland and you guys would be together again. That was one reason we encouraged you to move on with your life. It was so hard knowing you were hurting so much. I'm glad we can talk about them now."

"Me too." She glanced at the picture of her father. "You can see how much he loved me."

"That man lived for you and your sister and mom. But he was a *little* overprotective. The first few nights after you came home from the hospital, he slept on the floor beside the crib with his arm through the slats and his hand on you. He was afraid you might stop breathing and he wouldn't know."

"That's an awful thought."

"Unfortunately, that's a reality for many young parents." Her aunt lowered her eyes, and when she lifted them, there was sadness there. "Uncle Gary and I lost our baby to SIDS when she was three days old."

"I didn't even know you had a child. I'm so sorry. I thought you said you didn't want children."

"We didn't after that, because we weren't sure we could survive losing another baby." Her aunt teared up, and so did Jordan. "It turned out we could, because we lost Casey and your parents, and we're still here. But we are *not* going to cry or be sad over what we cannot control. Not when we have so many reasons to be grateful, right?"

"Yes, but I am sad for you and Uncle Gary. That must have been awful."

"It was, but we got through it, and we were lucky enough to be a big part of your family's life from the day you were born. Your parents made sure of that, and we're so thankful they did."

"So am I."

"I know, honey. No more sadness, okay? Life is too short to spend it crying."

Or to leave the important things unsaid. Jordan nodded, trying to rein in her emotions. "Thank you for taking me in and caring for me. I love you and Uncle Gary so much."

"Oh, honey. We adore you, and we loved raising you. Do

you know what your father would say if he were here right now?"

"What?"

"He'd tell you to live every second as if it were your last. You're a careful, patient woman, and I respect that, but don't let your life pass you by. This moment that we're living in right *now* might be all we will ever get, which is why I'm so happy to see you taking control of your life. Taking risks that are making you happier instead of settling for what I know felt safe and familiar but in reality was holding you back."

"I hate that I wasted so much time with Todd."

"You can't think about it that way, honey, or it'll always upset you, and if I've learned one thing over the years, it's that holding on to regrets only drags us down. It doesn't help us heal or grow. You have to learn to forgive yourself and be proud of having the courage to make a change. You are finally grabbing your brass rings and experiencing more of what life has to offer."

"I'm definitely experiencing more, but I don't feel like I'm grabbing my brass rings and making them *mine*. I'm hanging on to them while they're still tethered, so if I let go, they won't drop. It's safer that way."

"I know how scary it is to make big life changes and feel like you're making them alone."

"But that's just it. I don't feel alone anymore. I felt alone because I was in a one-sided relationship, and I couldn't talk about the family I lost to Todd or to you and Uncle Gary. But I'm not in that situation anymore."

"Then what are you afraid of?"

"I don't know. Being hurt, being judged."

"You've been hurt and judged before, honey, and you not

only survived, but you came out stronger. We don't know what will come our way in an hour, much less tomorrow or next week. If you feel like you've already wasted years, then let that fuel your determination not to waste another second of your life, because once that second is gone, there are no do-overs."

"You're *right*. What am I waiting for? I'm going to do the things that make *me* happy, and the heck with anyone who doesn't approve."

"Good girl. That's the spirit."

She popped to her feet. "Aunt Sheila, I'm sorry, but I have to go."

"Are you okay?"

"I'm better than okay. I'm *amazing*."

Her aunt smiled. "Yes, you are, but your uncle and I have always known that."

Jordan looked at the woman who had raised her and loved her like her own child, finally understanding that she hadn't been a burden to her but a blessing. "Thank you for loving me through all my hard times."

"Sweetheart, you're easy to love."

"For the first time in my life, I actually believe that's true."

JAX HAD ALWAYS looked forward to family gatherings. Especially since Beau and Zev had come back into the fold, bringing with them Char and Carly. But as he watched the four of them playing horseshoes and stealing kisses from their significant others while Graham and Morgyn cheered them on, it only made him miss Jordan more. He turned away just as

Nick's dogs, Goldie and Rowdy, darted past, chased by Beau's dog, Bandit, and Coco. Bandit had something in his mouth, and Nick, manning the barbecue with their father and holding Pugsly, his old, partially blind pug, was hollering at Bandit, calling him a thief. A few feet away, their mother was laughing at him with Trixie and Jillian. It was easy to imagine Jordan among them, chatting with the girls and tossing flirtatious glances his way.

One day…

He had a feeling she would have loved the party. Nick and Trixie had gone all out. The front of the barn was decorated with a big HAPPY 30th BIRTHDAY banner, and balloons danced from long strings tied to the fencing around the pastures and the drink and snack tables. They'd set up enormous easels around the yard displaying poster-sized pictures of Jax and Jillian. There was a picture of them as babies, propped up with pillows in their father's recliner. They wore matching onesies. Jax's had BIG BROTHER across the chest, and Jillian's had HE'S NOT THE BOSS OF ME. Jax wore a small smile, while Jillian's mouth was wide open, like she talked as much then as she did now. Another easel held a blown-up copy of the picture his parents had shown Jordan of his and Jillian's first backyard fashion show. There were a handful of other pictures from their youth, including pictures of Jax and Jillian making costumes for school plays. Jax was sitting at a sewing machine, and Jillian was leaning over his shoulder, brows knitted, mouth open, probably giving him directions. She'd always been mouthy, but he loved that about her. There was a picture of Jax playing high-school basketball, with Jillian on the sidelines, her fist in the air, cheering him on, and pictures from each of their first runway shows, as well as a few candid shots taken behind the scenes.

But his favorites were the pictures of them with the rest of their family and of him and Coco when she was a puppy.

He wondered what Jordan's birthdays had been like with her family before the accident, and after with her aunt and uncle.

"Hey, Jax!" Morgyn called out, and she and Graham headed his way.

Jax turned around just as Zev slung an arm over Carly's shoulder, pulling her in for a kiss. Beau and Char snuck up behind them and smacked them on their butts, making everyone crack up as Zev and Carly chased them around the yard.

Morgyn caught up to Jax. "Amber wants you to know that Lindsay will be at her wedding."

"She's cute," Graham reminded him. "And a wedding planner."

"Do you want her to set you up?" Morgyn asked.

Jax said, "No thanks," at the same time Jillian hollered, "No, he does *not*!"

Jax looked at his sister. "What do you...?"

"Everything." Jillian stalked toward him.

"How?"

Jillian smirked. "Doesn't matter."

"Are you—" *Bluffing?*

"Ha! Yeah, right," Jillian countered. "You know me better than that."

"Jillian—" *I told you to stay away from her.*

"Don't *Jillian* me. I do what I want and I know what you need."

Jax cursed.

"How do they know what they're talking about?" Morgyn

asked.

"Who the hell knows? It's twin talk," Graham said. "Half the conversation goes on in their heads."

"Jilly!" Nick growled, glowering as she strode over. "He doesn't need to be a rebound."

"Shows how much you know." Jillian closed the distance between them. "He'll be her rebound, her dunk shot, her *anything*, because he's crazy about her."

"How does Nick know who they're talking about?" Morgyn asked. "He's not their twin."

"Who knows? Jax, who are you talking about?" Graham asked as Carly and Char walked over and Beau and Zev raced toward them.

Jax held Nick's protective stare. "Jordan Lawler, and Jilly's right."

"Trixie's friend?" Char asked.

"Jaxie has a *girlfriend*? Guess she likes old pretty boys." Zev threw his arm around Jax's neck, putting him in a headlock, cracking up as he tousled Jax's hair.

"Jealous that you'll always be older and uglier than me?" Jax bent his knees and flipped Zev over his shoulder. Zev landed on his back with a *thud*, and Jax dropped down, pinning his arms with his knees.

"What'd you do? Buy a blow-up doll from Char and name her Jordan?" Zev threw Jax off, and they grappled in the grass, laughing hysterically and talking shit to each other, just like old times.

"Come on, you guys." Beau tried to pry Jax off Zev.

Jax looked at Zev, the glint in his brother's eyes telling him he had an ally, and they both went after Beau, tackling him to the ground.

"Get 'em, Beau!" Char yelled. "You've got this, baby!"

"No, he doesn't," Carly chimed in. "Zev is squirrely!"

"Cut the shit, you animals," Nick bit out.

"I love when he gets all growly," Trixie said.

Nick grabbed Zev's arm, trying to peel Zev off Beau, but Jax plowed Nick to the ground. Graham piled on, and the dogs ran toward them, barking up a storm. Everyone was cracking up as the guys wrestled and gave each other grief. The girls cheered for their men, Jillian cheered for Jax, and their parents just shook their heads.

The dogs took off, and their father shouted, "Time-out!"

Everyone froze. Jax had Graham pinned, but Nick had a vise grip on Jax's arm.

"I think Jax has a visitor," their father said.

They all followed their father's gaze to the driveway, and Jax saw Jordan heading across the lawn toward them. He jerked his arm free and headed for her, but their eyes connected, and the sheer force of the impact stopped him in his tracks. He felt like he was in one of those nineties teen movies, watching the girl of his dreams coming toward him in slow motion as she tossed her hair over her shoulder, looking a little unsure and so damn beautiful in her pretty yellow dress and denim jacket, he couldn't look away. The dogs vied for her attention, and she reached down, petting them.

"Hi," she said a little nervously, snapping him from his stupor. "Were you guys *fighting?*"

"No, just messing around." He raked a hand through his hair and looked down at his clothes, which were covered with dirt and grass, and started brushing them off.

"I hope it's okay that I came by."

"It's more than okay." He leaned in and kissed her cheek.

"How did you know I was here?"

"Jilly told me. I had a meeting with Trixie yesterday, and she was with her. Why didn't you tell me it was your birthday?"

"You have enough on your mind. You don't need to face an inquisition from my family."

She glanced over his shoulder and lowered her voice. "What if I want to?" She didn't give him a chance to respond. "When I was going through pictures, I was wishing you were doing it with me and wishing I was here with you, and I realized how foolish I was being. There's this *incredible* man who makes me happier than I ever dreamed possible, and I'm keeping us apart. Waiting for the fear of the unknown to go away and for an appropriate amount of time to pass so nobody—including myself—can judge me about moving on too fast."

"I don't mind waiting, sweetheart."

"I know you don't, but *I* do. I've wasted enough time being unhappy, and if you meant all the wonderful things you've said to me, then keeping us apart makes you unhappy, too, and you sure don't deserve that. I don't care what anyone thinks. You shouldn't have to hold back when you want to kiss me, and you shouldn't have to celebrate your birthday—or anything else—without me." She whispered, "You do want me here, *right?*"

"Hell yes. Every minute of the day and night."

"Then happy birthday, Jax." She stripped off her jacket and thrust out her chest. Her dress had a deep V-neck, and the two sides of the top tied in a bow between her breasts. Just below the bow was a sexy triangular cutout. "I'm ready to commit and tell the world that I'm yours and you're mine, and we'll see where this goes."

"You're *mine?*" He hauled her into his arms, happier than he'd ever been.

"That's what the bow is for. I'm your present."

"Damn, baby. Then I've got only one thing to say. *No take-backs.*" He crushed his mouth to hers, and cheers rang out around them. Their lips parted on a laugh, and he looked over his shoulder. His entire family was watching them from about ten feet away. The girls and his mother were mooning. Beau and Graham gave him a thumbs-up, cheering for them. Nick's and his father's brows were knitted, but they were nodding their approval.

"Way to go, old man!" Zev called out.

"Happy birthday, Jax!" Jillian hollered. "There *better* be a man wrapped up in one of those boxes for me!"

Everyone laughed, and Jax turned back to Jordan. "Are you sure you want to be part of all *that?*"

"Yes, more than anything, and I *do* care what your family thinks. I want to tell them about Todd and my family, so it's all out in the open. You've shown me how it feels to be completely honest with myself and others, and I don't want to hide *anything* anymore."

"Then you'll never have to hide anything again."

JAX WAS IN awe of Jordan's courage. A little more than an hour ago, she'd barely known his family, but here she was, fearlessly sharing her most difficult, personal stories and answering their questions. His family was compassionate and empathetic, and just as supportive as he'd hoped they'd be.

"I'm sorry for taking over the party. I didn't want to hide anything from all of you, and Jax has been so wonderful, I didn't want him to have to explain my past. I know I come with a lot of baggage, but hopefully you'll see there's more to me than what I've lost."

"Honey, everyone has baggage," his mother said. "And in this family, nobody walks alone. That means, when our burdens get too heavy, we're all here to help carry you through."

"I'm going to manifest you finding your sister," Morgyn said.

"Morgyn knows all about the energy of the universe," Char explained. "If anyone can work that kind of magic, it's her."

"Thank you. I appreciate all the help I can get," Jordan said. "But now that you know my life story, I'd love to know a little more about each of you. Jax gave me a brief introduction to your amazing lives."

"How much time do you have?" Carly asked. "There's a lot to tell."

The girls started talking over each other, and Jax shared knowing looks with Beau and Nick. Jax leaned closer to Jordan. "I'm going to get a drink. Would you like one?"

"No thanks, I'm okay."

He kissed her temple. "I'm really glad you're here."

Beau, Nick, and their father followed him over to the cooler, and Jax prepared himself for whatever shit he was about to get. He handed beers to each of them and met his father's serious gaze. "Don't worry, Dad. I didn't push her to end things with Todd. The guy dug his own grave. All I did was treat her the way you taught us to treat a woman."

"I never doubted that, son."

"Then what's that look for?"

"You're taking on a lot, meeting with Reggie and potentially opening up her sister's case again," his father said. "On one hand, I'm so damn proud of you, and on the other, I'm worried for both of you."

"We know the odds are against us finding her, and I'm sure it'll be agonizing in many ways if she decides to reopen the investigation. But Jordan believes her sister is alive, and there is nothing I won't do to help her try to figure out what happened. I'll make sure she's supported every step of the way, no matter what."

"And we'll make sure you are," Nick said. "Sorry about the shit I said about being a rebound. I didn't know she'd been into you since last summer, too."

"No sweat."

"Do you want me and Char to go with you to New York?" Beau asked. "We've both lost people we love. We could be a comfort to her."

"I appreciate that, but I think we've got this." He talked with them for a little while longer, catching stolen glances from Jordan. She was glowing as she chatted with the girls.

When he finally went back to the table, Jillian was talking a mile a minute. "There are ten bridesmaids, and Katrina wants unique designs for each one."

"New project?" Jax asked as he sat beside Jordan and slid his arm around her waist.

"Yes, and I want to take it on, but I'm starting Johnny Butthead—I mean *Bad's*—project soon, and once I start, I won't have much free time."

"Do you mean *the* Johnny Bad? The rock star?" Jordan asked.

"Yes, but he's a real self-centered *you-know-what*. He's already rescheduled twice. As if *my* time isn't important." Jillian rolled her eyes.

"Most rock stars just need a stylist, but he wants a custom wardrobe, and Jilly isn't used to working with divas," Trixie chimed in.

"More than one diva in a room is too many." Jillian wiggled her shoulders. "But as I was saying, I want to take on the bridesmaid gowns. If *only* I knew someone who could help me design them."

"What about Jax?" Jordan asked.

"He's all about bridal gowns, and he's totally booked. But there *is* someone else at this table who could help me." Jillian and the other girls all looked at Jordan.

Jax chuckled. "I think she means you, sweetheart."

"Me?" Jordan looked at him like he was crazy.

"Yes!" Jillian exclaimed. "Jax showed me your sketches. I'm sorry, your *doodles*. I love your style, and he said you're great to work with. So why not give it a try?"

"This is a once-in-a-lifetime opportunity. I think you should do it," Trixie said.

The other girls chimed in with their encouragement.

Jordan shook her head. "That sounds amazing, but I'm not a professional designer. I don't have any idea what I'm doing."

"Yes, you do." Jax held her a little tighter. "You're an excellent designer, and you'll have Jilly to guide you."

"Thanks, but when would I even do it?" she asked nervously. "I work full time, and you and I *just* got together. Don't you want time for us?"

"There will always be time for us," Jax promised. "I want you to realize all your dreams. Besides, you *doodled* the designs in the sketchbook. I'm sure you can find time if you want to. The question is, do you think you'd like to try it?"

She looked at Jillian. "Are you serious? You're not just being nice?"

"I'm not *that* nice." Jillian laughed. "I've been thinking about it since Jax showed me your sketches. You don't have to decide tonight. We can get together in a few days to talk more about it, and if you decide to try and it ends up being too much, or you don't enjoy it, then you can stop. No hard feelings."

"Won't that leave you in a bind with your client?" Jordan asked.

"No, because I'm taking credit for you coming here today, which means my overbooked brother owes me one." Jillian flashed a cheesy grin.

Jordan turned to Jax. "I can't do that to you."

"You're not. I'd help her no matter what, and she knows it."

"In that case…" Jordan's eyes lit up. "I'd *love* to try. But, Jilly, you have to promise that if you don't like my designs, you'll tell me."

Jillian gave her a deadpan look. "Do I seem like the kind of girl who holds back?"

"Jilly couldn't hold back if her life depended on it," Carly chimed in.

"Okay, then," Jordan said. "I'll give it a try."

"*Yay!* This is so exciting." Jillian told Jordan about her client and her client's vision for the bridesmaids' dresses, and the two gabbed up a storm.

As the evening wore on, Jax showed Jordan around Nick and Trixie's ranch, pulling her into an empty horse stall and kissing her breathless. She gushed over the animals almost as much as she loved the poster-sized pictures of him and Jillian. His family told her stories about when they were growing up, and she soaked it all in. When they sat down to eat, Graham and Morgyn told them about a new passive tiny house community they were developing with Graham's business partner, Knox Bentley, whose wife, Aubrey, was one of the founders of LWW Enterprises and the force behind one of Char's books being made into a movie.

"They finally finished filming," Char said. "You'll all have to come to the red-carpet premiere. I'll let you know when I get the date."

"We're all so proud of you, Char. We wouldn't miss it for the world," his mother said.

"Think you can clear your schedule to be my date for the premiere, Ms. Lawler?" Jax asked quietly.

"I'd clear my schedule to be your *anything*, Mr. Braden."

If she only knew the doors that opened.

"We want to make time to go to Silver Island before the fall to check out Zev and Carly's diving expedition before they go back to Colorado." His mother reached for his father's hand. "I might even take a diving lesson or two."

"About damn time." Zev chuckled.

As Zev and Carly updated everyone on their expedition progress, Jax pulled Jordan closer and said, "He and Carly spend the warmer months diving off the coast of Silver Island and winters in Colorado."

"I know. Carly told me. She and the girls filled me in on everyone." She put her mouth beside his, whispering, "I *love* them."

This was exactly what he'd wanted for her, support from people who wouldn't let her down and would cheer her on every step of the way. "I guess that means you're having fun."

"Are you kidding? Your family is amazing. I feel like it's *my* birthday, and you and your family and the opportunity with

Jilly are my gifts."

She was the amazing one, putting her heart on the line for them, and he was desperate to get her in his arms and show her just how much he appreciated her courage.

"Speaking of gifts." He ran his hands down her back. "I can't wait to unwrap mine."

Chapter Fifteen

THANKS TO JAX whispering naughty things in Jordan's ear for the last hour, as their evening with his family wound down, her body was like a bundle of live wires. Driving to his place in separate cars only revved her up even more, his dirty promises lingering in her mind. She knew he'd make good on every one of them.

Jax stalked toward her like a panther on the prowl as she got out of her car, and he caged her in against the cold metal as Coco bounded into the yard. His mouth covered hers hungrily, their tongues colliding urgent and greedy. He tangled his hands in her hair, angling her mouth beneath his and devouring her like he'd never get enough. She had loved kissing him since the first time their lips had touched, but there was a new fire raging inside her. A bolder greed and deeper devotion from setting herself free from the expectation of others, and that freed the aching *need* to be closer and the confidence to take what she wanted. She bowed off the car, grinding against his hardness, craving more of him, drawing a groan from his lungs.

"It's crazy how much I miss touching you," he growled against her lips.

"Good, because I'm sure as heck going to touch you."

A wicked grin split his lips, and he recaptured her mouth in another fierce kiss. He kept one hand fisted in her hair, the other moving swiftly over her body, groping, caressing, driving her out of her freaking mind. They stumbled toward the house, stopping every few steps to paw at each other or take their kisses deeper, until they were both delirious with desire.

Jax fumbled with his keys and threw the front door open. Coco darted past, and after he kicked the door closed, he wasted no time reaching for the bow on Jordan's dress. She held his gaze as he untied it and pushed the spaghetti straps down her arms, freeing her bare breasts. He made a growling sound as he dipped his head and slicked his tongue over her nipple while undoing the three buttons at her waist. The dress puddled at her feet. His gaze ignited as it slid down her naked body.

"You said panties were optional," she said as innocently as she could, fluttering her lashes.

"If I'd've known you were naked under there, we never would've left Nick's barn."

He reached for her, but she giggled and pushed at his chest. "Uh-uh, birthday boy. I need *you* naked."

She tugged his shirt up, and he took it off as he toed off his shoes. She opened his jeans, and he stripped them, and his socks, off. His erection bobbed enticingly, and her mouth watered as she brought her lips to his chest, kissing the hard planes and teasing his nipple with her teeth. She sucked and nipped and ground her belly against his arousal.

He grabbed her hair, tugging her head back, his eyes blazing into hers. "Your mouth is going to make me come undone."

His voice dripped with raw, untamed desire, making her even more determined to unleash his animalistic side. She untangled his fingers from her hair. "No touching, until *I* say you can, *Mr.* Braden." She had *no* idea where that had come from, but she loved it!

"I fucking adore this side of you, *Ms.* Lawler."

"Me too. It's *new*." She whispered that last word. "Just for you."

She brought her mouth back to his hot skin, tasting her way down his body, the heat of his stare spurring her on. Every time he reached for her hair, she batted his hands away. He groaned through clenched teeth, and it was the sexiest sound she'd ever heard. She grinned up at him as she slicked her tongue along his abs, grabbing and groping his ass. His hips rocked forward, and she continued teasing him, kissing and touching him every-where *except* where he wanted it most. She loved the sinful noises he made and the way his muscles flexed with restraint.

When she licked closer to his cock, her cheek brushing along the length of it, he gritted his teeth. "Jesus, baby. You're killing me."

"We wouldn't want that." She fisted his hard length, drag-ging her tongue from base to tip and over and around the broad head, savoring the feel and taste of him, earning one needful moan after another. His eyes remained trained on her, chin low, jaw clenched so tight it had to hurt. She squeezed her thighs together to stave off her own neediness as he slid lower against the door, to the perfect height for her to take him in deep. His eyes flamed as she stroked and sucked, desire blazing between them. He reached for her head but stopped himself, clutching her shoulders instead, letting her set the pace.

"*God*, you fucking own me, baby."

She quickened her efforts, squeezing tighter, sucking harder, feeling his thighs flex. His hips thrust harder and faster, his body shaking with restraint. She wanted to feel his power, his *possession*, and moved his hand to her hair. He grabbed hold, but even ravaged by desire, he was still taking care of her. Those dark-as-night eyes sought her approval. With that in her heart, she nodded and loved him with everything she had, until his hips bucked so hard, he lost all control, gritting out her name as he came. She stayed with him, his body jerking through the aftershocks, until his hands slid from her hair to her jaw, massaging it as she released his cock.

His eyes pooled with emotions as he lifted her to her feet, and she said, "Happy birthday."

He kissed her, slow and sweet, and touched his forehead to hers. "I've never come so hard in my life."

"I've never sucked so hard in my life."

They both laughed softly, and their mouths came together in a kiss so divine, she never wanted it to end. His hand slid down her back, and he cupped her butt with one hand, pushing his other hand between them and zeroing in on that spot that had her going up on her toes. In one swift move, he turned them, pinning her against the door, and dropped to his knees, feasting on her like a ravenous beast. She grabbed his hair, already so close to the edge, her vision blurred. He was a master with his mouth, and it didn't take long before she was crashing into her own release and crying out his name.

He stayed with her, every slick of his tongue sending prickles of heat along her oversensitive flesh. When she finally came down from the peak, he rose to his feet, taking her in a deep, penetrating kiss, her body still riddled with sensations.

He drew back, his eyes on fire. "You still with me, sweetheart?"

"Uh-huh."

"Ever been fucked in the moonlight?"

Holy cow. Hello, second wind. "No. Have you?"

"Not *yet.*" He lifted her, guiding her legs around his waist as he carried her out the patio doors. The cool air brought goose bumps despite their body heat. "Kiss me *hard.*"

Damn, he knew how to use his words.

She crushed her mouth to his, their tongues tangling as he carried her into the pool and their bodies slipping and sliding in the heated water. They kissed and groped as he carried her deeper. The buoyancy brought curiosity, and Jordan wanted to explore. She broke away and swam to the side of the pool, holding on with one hand and crooking a finger at Jax, beckoning him to her.

He swam underwater, clutching her hips as he came up behind her, his chest brushing her back and his cock pressing against her entrance. "I want the world to hear you cry out my name so they know you're *mine.*"

Her body ignited. "I had no idea I liked to be talked to that way. What does that say about me?"

"It says you want to be mine." He drove into her in one hard thrust, and they both cried out.

"*Again,*" she pleaded.

His hips shot forward, sending pleasure rippling through her, and they found a savage rhythm that had them moaning, pleading, and cursing as pleasure torched through them. She knew she'd hear those erotic sounds in her dreams. She clung to the side of the pool, her body quaking as Jax gathered her in his arms, his heartbeat thundering against her back. He kissed her shoulder, murmuring, "I can't get enough of you."

He turned her in his arms, and as his loving eyes came into focus, he said, "Stay with me tonight," and for the first time since she'd lost her family, she knew without a shadow of a doubt that she was *exactly* where she was meant to be.

JORDAN FELT LIKE she was dreaming, but she was fully awake, lying in Jax's arms, cocooned by his warm body and masculine scent in his giant plush bed, with Coco snuggled at their feet. When they'd gone to bed last night, she'd felt as comfortable as if she'd been there before, even though his bedroom was bigger and roomier than any bedroom she'd ever known, with dark wood furniture and massive windows, splashed in hues of blues and grays with a touch of white. It was masculine, calming, and *open*, just like Jax.

"Good morning, beautiful." He stretched, his arousal pressing against her belly. "You look wide-awake. Guess I didn't wear you out well enough last night."

He kissed her forehead, and then those sexy dark eyes that made her want to do *everything*, found hers. "You've got to be kidding. I slept like a bear hibernating for the winter."

"I'd like to hibernate inside *you* for the winter." He nuzzled against her neck, making her giggle. He moved over her, and she reveled in the weight of him. "You made me the happiest man on earth when you showed up at the party yesterday."

"If you only knew how nervous I was."

"But you couldn't stay away, could you? Because I'm the pig in your blanket, the chocolate in your croissant, the creamer in your coffee."

She laughed.

"You know it's true."

She wound her arms around him, grinning like a fool.

"Well, you do have a creamy cannoli."

"*Hey* now." He wiggled his hips. "I love that you play along with me."

"You make me want to take chances and say *yes* to everything, and after meeting your family, I can see why you and your brothers and Jilly all went after your dreams. Your whole family is so supportive, they make *me* want to take life by the horns and go after everything, just like you do."

"I told you they were awesome."

"I haven't known many people like that other than my parents, until you came along and reminded me what life could be like. That's one of the reasons I was so drawn to you. Well, that and *this*." She grabbed his butt, earning a seductive growl.

He nuzzled against her cheek. "Spend the day with me."

"I was hoping you'd ask. You're kind of addicting."

"Only kind of?" He nipped at her lower lip. "I'm going to have to fix that."

As he lowered his lips to hers, Coco jumped off the bed. "Should we put her out first?"

He laughed softly. "I'm trying to seduce you and you're thinking about Coco. She has a doggy door."

"I can't help it. She relies on you to take care of her."

"And I'd never let her down." He laced their hands together, and as he gazed into her eyes and their bodies became one, he said, "And one day you'll realize that you can rely on me, too."

AFTER A LUXURIOUSLY lazy morning of making love,

eating breakfast on the patio, and strolling through Jax's gardens, they headed to Jordan's house so she could change clothes before going out for the afternoon.

"I'll be quick." She gave him a chaste kiss and headed for her bedroom.

Jax went into the living room and found sketch pads, pictures, and photo albums spread haphazardly on the floor, as if Jordan had left in a hurry. He crouched to get a better look, taking in pictures of a young, beautiful Jordan, with eyes that sparkled like the afternoon sun. There were dozens of pictures of her, some with her family, some without, each one cuter than the last. She had her father's smile and her mother's hopeful eyes. He studied a picture of Casey, with a mix of golden brown and blond hair and her mother's dazzling blue eyes.

Where are you, sweetheart? Little girls don't just disappear.

He picked up a picture of Jordan sitting next to her father on a picnic blanket, holding a baby. Jordan's hair was pinned up in pigtails with pink bows, and she was wearing a frilly pink-and-white dress, white tights, and shiny white Mary Janes. Her father wore a flannel shirt, jeans, and work boots, just as Jordan had described. He was a big, burly man. His arm was wrapped protectively around her shoulders, pride shining in his eyes, and Jordan was absolutely beaming.

Jax looked through more pictures, and in every one of them, her father had been either holding Jordan's or Casey's hand, carrying them, or he had his arm around them. He was obviously very protective. Jax wanted to know more about the man who had been so in touch with his daughters he'd fed their needs for fancy dresses and flannel, the man who probably saw his car rushing at a tree and thought only of his girls and his beautiful wife.

"Sorry that took a few minutes," Jordan said as she came down the hall.

He looked up from where he sat among the pictures, at the incredible woman whose parents had poured their hearts and souls into raising her, and emotions overtook him.

"I'm sorry about the mess. I rushed out yesterday." She dropped to her knees in skinny jeans and a peach off-the-shoulder sweater and began gathering the pictures. "It'll just take a second for me to clean up."

Jax took her hand, pulling her onto his lap. "I want to know more about you and your family. I want to know the stories behind these pictures and the secrets behind your smiles."

"I don't want to bore you with my family's stories."

"Bore me, sweetheart. Take me on a picture tour of your childhood. Then you can show me around Prairie View, and I can see that from your eyes, too."

"Are you sure you want to do that?"

"It's exactly what I want to do, unless it'll be too difficult for you."

Her eyes lit up. "It won't. I *want* to talk about them. But I might have to call my aunt to ask about some of the pictures that I don't know the stories behind."

"Good, because I want to meet her and your uncle." There it was, that radiant light in her eyes that lit up the room. But now he knew that light had once been even brighter, and he was going to do everything in his power to help bring that brightness back.

Chapter Sixteen

JORDAN STARED OUT the window of the cab, her thumb twitching against Jax's hand as they made their way through stop-and-go traffic in Manhattan. He wished he knew what was going through her mind. The week had passed in a flurry. Busy days and sexy texts had led to dinner dates and late-night walks, and at the end of each evening, neither wanted to say goodbye. They'd fallen into each other's arms. Sometimes at her place and other times at his. Their steamy nights gave way to midnight conversations about everything from silliness and childhood memories to how nervous Jordan was about meeting with Reggie, and all of the *what-ifs* that went along with it. She hadn't said she was nervous about being back in the city, but he had a feeling that added to her anxiety. He was glad he'd arranged for her to tour Josh's design facilities and hoped it would distract her from her worries while he took care of business.

He squeezed her hand. "Are you okay, sweetheart?"

"As okay as I can be when I'm meeting your cousin who just happens to be a world-famous fashion designer and then meeting with a PI about my long-lost sister. I feel like I'm going to pass out or throw up. Are you sure I look okay?" She'd changed her clothes three times before they'd left Maryland that morning, and when they'd checked into the hotel this afternoon, once she'd come down from the awe of the luxurious penthouse suite, she'd considered changing again.

He leaned in and kissed her. "You look gorgeous, and you could have come in jeans and you would have looked just as beautiful. And don't worry, sweetheart. If you pass out, I'll catch you, and if you throw up, I'm sure Josh has a few extra clothes in the design closet."

She bumped him with her shoulder, smiling.

"There's no reason to be nervous about meeting Josh and Riley. Don't think about their fame. They're just normal people who design clothes, and you'll want to be best friends with Mia. She's a riot." He lowered his voice as the cab pulled over in front of JRBD's offices. "And I'll be with you every step of the way with Reggie. If things get too difficult, we'll leave. He won't be offended. He's a professional, and you're in charge."

"I know you will. We've been so wrapped up in my stuff, I didn't even ask if you were ready for your meeting."

"More than ready." He paid for the cab, and as they stepped onto the sidewalk, he put a hand on her lower back. "Ready to have some fun?"

She shouldered her tote bag, eyes brightening. "I still can't believe I'm meeting *the* Josh and Riley Braden."

"Hey, I don't hear you gushing like that over *your* Braden."

She grabbed the front of his suit coat with both hands, grinning as she said, "Yes, you do. Every night as I cry out your name."

He swept his arm around her and kissed her. "*Damn*, I like you, you sweet, sexy thing. Do I really have to wait until tonight to show you just how much?" They'd decided to stay in the city and fly home Sunday, and he was looking forward to showing her a great time.

"Yes, you do." She giggled and gave him a quick peck.

They went into the building and headed for the elegant mahogany and granite reception desk. After a quick conversation with the perfectly coiffed receptionist, they waited for Mia to come get them.

"This is *exactly* as I pictured it," Jordan whispered excitedly.

"This is just the customer service area. Wait until you see the rest."

The elevators opened, and Josh and Mia walked out. Josh was dressed impeccably in a fitted navy suit, his six-three frame dwarfing Mia, even with her spiked heels. His short dark hair was side parted, and his serious brown eyes were moving appreciatively between Jax and Jordan.

"Jax, it's great to see you." Josh extended his hand, and when Jax took it, he pulled him into an embrace.

"You as well," Jax said. "It's nice to see you again, too, Mia."

Mia rolled her eyes. "Are you trying to impress your friend with your professionalism? Get in here and hug me."

Jax laughed as he hugged her. "Mia, Josh, this is Jordan Lawler."

"It's such a pleasure to meet you both," Jordan said excitedly. "Jax has said great things about you, and I appreciate you allowing me to visit."

"Jax has told us wonderful things about you, too," Josh said. "I understand you're *quite* the designer."

"Oh my goodness," she said incredulously. "Jax exaggerates. I have no formal training. I just draw what I like."

"In our business we call that innate talent," Josh said warmly. "My wife is looking forward to meeting you as well, although she's tied up in a meeting at the moment, which I'm due to attend. Jordan, I'll leave you in Mia's capable hands and catch up with you shortly, and, Jax, I'm sorry we couldn't get together for dinner tomorrow night, but our flight home leaves this evening. Let's get together soon."

"Absolutely," Jax said. "Thanks, Josh. Give my love to your family."

As Josh walked away, Mia said, "The meeting he's going to is about their upcoming fall line. Play your cards right, and you'll get a sneak peek at it."

"That would be amazing." Jordan looked like she was going to burst from excitement.

"I'm going to head out to my meeting, too. Mia, thanks for showing Jordan around."

"We're going to have a blast," Mia assured him.

Jax put his hand on Jordan's back. "Enjoy yourself, and I'll come find you when I'm done." He gave her a quick kiss.

Mia sighed. "You are one lucky lady. You get to smooch Jax *and* you're meeting the hottest PI around for dinner."

"You know Reggie Steele?" Jordan asked.

"Yes. I've known that tall, dark stud for quite a few years," Mia said.

As she and Jordan headed for the elevator, Jax heard Mia say, "I'd like to know Reggie a whole lot better, so feel free to give him a smack on his very fine ass and tell him it's from me."

Jax chuckled and headed out to hail a cab.

Half an hour later he strode into the offices of RZS Wealth Management. A pretty blonde wearing a black pencil skirt and a low-cut white blouse came out to greet him. "Mr. Newmen?"

"Yes, but it's pronounced New*man*."

"I'll be sure to remember that for next time." She smiled flirtatiously. "I'm Anna, Mr. Karns's assistant. I'll take you to his office."

He followed her to an office with the door slightly ajar. She knocked twice, then opened it just enough for Jax to get a good look at the guy he'd already checked out online. Todd Karns was born with a silver spoon in his mouth. He was fairly good-looking, with brown hair and eyes that were a little too close together and were currently trailing appreciatively down Anna's body.

Scumbag.

"Mr. Karns, Mr. New*man* is here to see you."

"Thank you, Anna." Todd rose to his feet, revealing a mediocre suit as he came toward Jax with his hand extended. "Mr. Newman, Todd Karns. It's a pleasure to meet you."

Jax ignored his proffered hand and strode past him, eyeing the framed pictures of Jordan behind his desk, which told Jax he hadn't been man enough to announce their split. "She is stunning."

"Yes, my fiancée is quite beautiful."

"*Hm.* She didn't mention you were into fantasies." Jax casually unbuttoned his suit jacket.

"Excuse me?"

"Perhaps I should clarify my name."

Todd arched a brow. "Jordan S. Newman?"

"No. That would be Jordan's *new man.* Jax Braden, and it is *not* a pleasure to meet you."

"What the...? The fucking dress designer?"

"*World-renowned* wedding gown designer, thank you. I believe this is yours." Jax put Jordan's engagement ring on the desk. "It wasn't nearly worthy of her magnificence, but then again, neither were you. I suggest you take down those pictures or you're going to be awfully embarrassed when the world finds out she's mine."

Todd's eyes narrowed. He was breathing so hard, he looked like a two-year-old ready to throw a tantrum. "You can *have* her and all of her fucking issues."

"There's that arrogance she mentioned. I didn't think anything could make you uglier, but damn. There it is. You might want to watch your mouth when talking about Jordan, unless you want to see your entire life crumbling down around you in a *very* public way."

Todd scoffed. "Good luck trying to get off with that cold fish."

Jax rolled his shoulders back, closing the distance between them, eyes trained on the asshole before him as he spoke low and controlled. "I heard about how bad you were in bed. That must suck. I don't know how Jordan suffered through it. In the future, you might consider giving your partner as much attention as you do your ego." He smirked. "Then again, without the basic equipment, there's not much you can do. And the truth is, it wouldn't matter if you knew what to do in bed, because there are men worthy of being husbands, and then there's you." Jax headed for the door and turned back to say, "Enjoy your loose morals, because I sure as hell am enjoying my girl."

"JAX, YOU SHOULD see their fall line. It's *exquisite*, and they let me pick out a few outfits, which they're sending over to our hotel. I couldn't *believe* it. But when I tried to say no thank you, Josh insisted." Jordan was talking a mile a minute on the cab ride to see Reggie, but she was too excited to slow down. "He's so nice, and Riley told me all about how she had a crush on Josh when they were younger and how nervous she was when she went to work for him. Can you imagine that? She's loved him her *whole* life. That's what fairy tales are made of. And Mia? Ohmygosh, she's a trip. That girl speeds around like she's on roller skates, and you can tell how much everyone respects her. The whole thing—the place, the people—was beyond wonderful, but none of it compares to *you* for making it all possible. It was invigorating being around all of that activity and seeing the world I used to think I wanted. I made the right choice staying in Maryland, because this might be *too* much for me. How can I ever thank you for this, and for talking to Jilly about my designs?"

"Your happiness is all the thanks I need." He leaned in for a kiss. "How are you feeling about meeting with Reggie?"

"I'm more nervous than a mouse in a snake pit, but I'm not letting myself think about it until we're at the restaurant." Although it had hovered over her all day like a rain cloud waiting to break open.

"That gives you about five minutes."

Oh boy. "I'll take it. How did your meeting go?"

"As well as I expected it to. Your ring has been returned."

Her stomach knotted. "You went to see Todd? I thought you'd mail it. How did it go?"

"I'm not sure he was thrilled, but it's done."

"What does *that* mean? You didn't fight, did you?"

"I think you know me better than that. If I were Nick, I'd have punched the smug look off his face, but I prefer to handle things with a little more couth. The right words can go a long way. He knows you're done with him, and that's all that matters."

Relief swept through her. "You *are* very good with your words." She leaned closer, whispering, "Among other things." That earned a sexy smile. "Thank you for looking out for me." The cab pulled over to the curb, and anxiety prickled her chest.

Jax covered her hand with his. "Remember, you're in charge, sweetheart. If it gets uncomfortable, we can leave."

She nodded, too nervous to speak. She grabbed her tote as she climbed out of the cab and took a deep breath. "Before we go in, I want you to know that no matter what Reggie says or what happens, it means the world to me that you set this up." She went up on her toes and kissed him. "Thank you."

"We make a good team, babe. I'll always have your back." He lifted their joined hands and kissed her knuckles.

Jordan was a nervous wreck as they headed into the restaurant. Jax gave the hostess their names, and she pointed to a handsome dark-haired man sitting at a table by the windows. As they made their way over, Jordan had the strange thought that Reggie *looked* like a private investigator, with his dark suit and serious expression.

He smiled as they approached, softening his harsh edges as he pushed to his feet, slate-blue eyes meeting first Jax's, then hers. "Jax?"

"Yes. Thanks for meeting us." Jax shook his hand.

"Thank you for coming into the city. My schedule's been hell lately. And you must be Jordan." He offered his hand, and when she took it, he covered it with his other one. "It's nice to meet you. I'm sorry for all you've been through."

"Thank you. I appreciate you looking into Casey's disappearance."

They settled into their seats and ordered drinks, and Reggie got right down to business. "Jordan, I will do everything I can to find out what happened to Casey, *if* you want me to. But as I told Jax, this will not be easy."

He went on to warn Jordan about how difficult opening up the search could be for her and her family. He explained the pros and cons of social media with missing person cases and that Jordan and her family could become targets for people trying to swindle money from them in exchange for information, or worse.

Jordan held Jax's hand, thankful for his strength. "That's all a little scary, but everything about Casey's disappearance has been scary. People don't just vanish." Saying it out loud brought all her pain to the surface.

"That's exactly right." Reggie's tone was dead serious. "Which is why you need to prepare yourself for the very real possibility that we could take this public and go through everything I've just mentioned and still not find any answers, or find a different answer from the one you are hoping for."

Jordan swallowed hard. "I have spent almost twenty years without answers. I know Casey may not be alive. But I truly believe she is, and I won't give up hope until I have an answer." It dawned on her that she hadn't asked the most important question. "How much do you charge for something like this?"

"My fees have already been taken care of."

"I don't understand." She looked at Jax. "Did you pay him? Because I have savings. I can pay for this, and I can take out loans if I need more money."

"I'm sure you do and can," Jax said. "But this is my gift to you and your family."

"Jax, I can't let you do that."

"It's already done, sweetheart. Reggie has a no-take-back rule, too."

She couldn't help but smile at his *rule* reference, but Mia had confirmed what Jax had told her, that Reggie was the best in the business, and she knew his time didn't come cheap. "Reggie, I can pay you directly."

Reggie splayed his hands. "Sorry. It's in the contract."

She gave Jax a deadpan look. "I know you mean well, and I won't turn your help away, but she's my sister, and I'm pitching in to pay for this."

"Let's not waste Reggie's time with those details. We can discuss it in private later," Jax suggested.

"Fine, but I have a good memory, Jax, so don't think we're done talking about it."

He eyed Reggie. "I told you she was sharp." He turned a more comforting gaze to her. "How do you feel about what Reggie has said?"

"I still want to do it, but given his warnings, I can't make any final decisions without talking with my aunt and uncle." She turned her attention to Reggie. "Can you tell me what, if anything, you've already discovered? Jax said there was evidence of another vehicle at the crash site, but it was never processed."

"That's right, and unfortunately, I don't have an answer as to why. As I mentioned to Jax, I didn't want to start overturning stones until I was sure you and your family were ready for the potential fallout."

"I appreciate that."

"I did review the case in detail, and if you decide to move forward, I'll revisit the people and groups who were questioned at the time of Casey's disappearance."

"Groups?" Jax asked.

"Yes, there was a religious group that was camping twenty miles from the crash site and a cult that has a compound about fifty miles away."

"What kind of cult? Are they dangerous?" Jordan asked.

"Neither of those groups has had any run-ins with the law. The cult is called Free Rebellion. They're anti-government and not religiously affiliated."

"So, what does that mean?" Jordan asked. "They're tax evaders? Can't they be arrested for that?"

"I don't know the extent of what it means yet, but the compound and the campsites for the other group were searched when Casey went missing. According to the files, they found no trace of her with either group. There are other groups as well as known pedophiles in the area. I'll check those out too."

Jordan took a drink, not wanting to think about the latter.

"If you decide to move forward, I'll retrace the steps of the original investigation and exhaust every possible avenue in case anything was missed, and in addition to using every usual tactical outlet to spread the news, I'll also have my brothers, Jesse and Brent, who are members of the Dark Knights motorcycle club, get in touch with all the chapters across the country. They've got dozens of members in each chapter, and they keep their ears to the ground with seedy operations that have been connected to deleterious activities."

"Is that the same club Bullet Whiskey is in?" Jordan asked.

"Yeah," Reggie answered. "Jesse and Brent are in the Harborside chapter. There are a few more things I want to discuss. I told you I won't do anything publicly until you give me the okay, but I had an updated age-progression photo privately made, and I'm hoping you brought the pictures I asked for.

Sometimes we can get a closer representation using an artist who takes the other family members and their age progressions into account."

Jordan opened her tote and handed him the large manila envelope with the pictures in it. "They're in here. Will I get them back?"

"Yes, and Jax has already arranged for copies to be made and the originals to be sent back to you within forty-eight hours."

She turned to thank the man who kept tripping up her heart, but before she could say a word, he squeezed her hand and nodded, as if to say, *I told you I've got your back.* He was always one step ahead, taking care of her before she even realized she needed it. She had a feeling this was how her mother felt with her father, and that not only made her feel good, but it also made her realize that sometimes it was okay to be taken care of. That realization made her feel stronger and even more determined to follow through with the search.

Turning back to Reggie, she said, "Can I see the age-progression photo?"

"Of course, but please take a moment to prepare yourself. It might be harder to see than you expect."

"I see Casey in my mind almost every minute of the day. I think I'm as prepared as I can be."

He reached into his jacket pocket and pulled out an envelope. As he handed it to her, he and Jax shared a worried glance.

Jordan took a deep breath, and Jax moved his chair beside hers and put his arm around her, as if he knew she was trembling inside. She withdrew the paper and carefully unfolded it. Her hands visibly shook as she looked at the image of a girl who was as much a stranger as she was a part of her. The girl in the picture had Casey's almond-shaped eyes and perky nose, but gone was the baby face Jordan had held so dear, replaced with slimmer cheeks and slightly fuller lips. Jordan tried to fit the girl in the picture to the one in her mind, but it was like trying to put a square block into a round hole.

"It's a little jarring, isn't it?" Jax asked.

"More so than I expected. It's like looking at someone that sort of looks like my sister and being told this is her, but it doesn't feel like her."

"That's where I think the artist can help," Reggie said. "Little tweaks go a long way."

"Can I keep this?"

"Yes, that's for you. Why don't we order dinner and we can finish talking while we eat?"

JORDAN'S MIND WAS still reeling when they got back to their opulent hotel suite.

"You were awfully quiet on the way home. Would you like to talk about it?"

"There's just so much to consider. I want to look for Casey, but after everything Reggie said, is it fair to do that to my aunt and uncle? Or to you?"

"Sweetheart." Jax took her hand. "I'm the last person you need to worry about. There's nothing I can't handle."

"Did you hear what Reggie said right before we left? He said being with you adds a whole different list of worries. People know who you are, and even though Casey's not your sister, if you're with me, that could make you a target for all the weirdos he warned us about and more."

"I'll make sure we are all protected, including your aunt and uncle."

"I can't ask that of you. You've already done so much, and we just got together. You could change your mind about me, and then you'd have gone through all of this for nothing."

His brows slanted. "I don't know how many more ways I can show you how much you mean to me, but I've been around the block, Jordan. I know what we have is special."

"That's not what I meant. I know it is, too. I've felt it for months, and it's even stronger now that we're together. But people *change*. Their wants and needs change, and all those things Reggie mentioned are *big*. It could be too much for you, and then you'll feel locked in."

He stepped closer. "I know you're scared. We're new, and you're fresh out of a relationship with someone who didn't appreciate or accept all of you. But I'm *not* him. Jordan, I'm with you because I *adore* all of you. I might have been attracted to your looks when you first walked into my office, but by the end of that meeting, I had gotten glimpses into your heart, and now that I know it intimately, you're stuck with me, babe."

There went that lump in her throat again. "I've hidden it for so long."

"I know, but when I look at you, it's your compassionate, loving heart I see. I don't want arm candy, sweetheart. I want the whole pajama-wearing, tousled-hair, smeared-eye-makeup, I-think-I-can shebang. I want to be there to hold you when you cry, whether it's because you miss your family or because we watched a sappy movie. I'm in this *with* you, Jordan, through laughter, tears, anger, whatever comes our way."

"You never get angry."

"Eventually I will. I'm not perfect. But more importantly, I want to help you find Casey, not pretend she never existed. Okay? So don't worry about me. I'm not going anywhere."

"I believe you now, but what if they *don't* find her? I won't want to stop looking."

"Then we won't," he said emphatically.

"That might wear on you, and what if they find her…?" She couldn't even bring herself to say the word.

Jax put his arms around her and kissed her forehead. "Then we'll get through it together. The *only* thing about this that scares me is you ending up brokenhearted, and people who care about each other don't leave when things get rough. When you're feeling empty, I'll fill you up. When you're scared, I'll protect you, and when things get so frustrating, you feel lost or unsure about why you started looking in the first place, I'll be there to remind you."

Emotions swamped her. "I don't know what I did to deserve you, when all I bring to the table is baggage."

"No, sweetheart. You bring your loving, adorable, funny self, and that's all I want. You make my life better, brighter, and happier just by being in it."

She let her face fall to his chest. "Can I keep you forever?"

"Hey," he whispered, bringing her eyes back to his. "Careful what you wish for. I've got a no-take-back policy, remember?"

Chapter Seventeen

JAX HAD GONE all out and gotten them the penthouse suite with a sunrise view, and they'd taken full advantage Saturday morning, watching the sun come up over the skyline from the warmth of their bed. Jordan swore the sun was more vibrant than ever, but that might just be a reflection of how happy she was that everything was falling into place. Even after she'd told her aunt and uncle all the things Reggie had warned her about, her aunt had said, *I think you need to do this*, and her uncle had added, *Maybe we all do*. Before they'd called Reggie to give him the okay to move forward with the search, she and Jax had talked about finances, and he'd agreed to let her help pay a small amount each month toward Reggie's fees. It wasn't much, but it was enough to let her know he respected her need to pitch in but that he also was in this with her for the long haul.

She'd have bet those were the reasons everything felt brighter today, but then she and Jax made love, and as he gazed into her eyes, confessing that he was falling fast and didn't ever want to stop, she realized *he* was the force behind that vibrant beauty and the lightness she felt. He was peeling back all her protective layers, allowing her to flourish and take control of the parts of her life she hadn't held the reins to for a long time, while also nourishing the parts of her that she hadn't known so desperately needed it.

They fell back to sleep tangled up in each other's arms, and when they woke up, they ordered room service and enjoyed a leisurely breakfast in bed. By the time they'd left their suite, it was almost noon. They took a ferry to Governors Island, where they rented bikes and spent the afternoon looking at art, enjoying delicious coffee and homemade ice cream, and seeing everything the tiny island had to offer, including Slide Hill: home of the longest slide in New York. Jordan sat between Jax's legs, squealing as they flew down the twisty slide. "I feel like a kid again!" she said as he helped her to her feet.

"Damn, baby, being a kid looks good on you." He took her hand. "Let's go again!"

They ran to the line, kissing and laughing, and after riding the slide a few more times, they took the ferry back to the city and spent the rest of the afternoon at Summer on the Hudson, a local festival. They listened to live music while dancing in the grass and held hands as they perused the festival attractions. They met a number of talented artists and craftsmen, and Jordan was especially taken with jewelry made by an upbeat, hippyish brunette named Heaven Love. She'd had so many unique pieces that Jordan adored, Jordan had bought Jillian a beautiful pair of earrings as a belated birthday present.

When they came upon a karaoke stage, Jordan dragged Jax up to sing, just as he'd done to her at Whiskey Bro's, and they sang "Glad You Exist" by Dan + Shay. As they sang about a hello turning into much more and getting so caught up in moments it felt like the world disappeared and it was only the two of them, they could have been singing about *that* very moment. When they finished the song, Jax hauled her into his arms and kissed her right there onstage as onlookers whooped and cheered.

Afternoon bled into evening, and they went back to the hotel to shower and change for dinner. Jax surprised her with reservations at HanGawi, a Korean vegetarian restaurant. They sat on pillows on the floor, and the vibe was so serene, Jordan felt far away from the busy city they were in, as if they'd stopped time and found their own private oasis—a brief reprieve from the worries she'd carried for so many years and knew she'd carry every day to come until she found out for sure what happened to Casey.

They shared the most delicious meal of stuffed shitake mushrooms, dumplings, and a mix of vegetables, rice, and wild mountain greens. When they finished eating, they had tea, and Jordan felt like they'd been in New York for a week instead of a day. How was that even possible? With Todd every day had dragged on forever. He'd been so busy with work—*or other women?*—during her visits, she was realizing that she'd never really relaxed. With Jax it was easy to relax. Everything felt natural, and he made her feel safe enough to let her worries go, knowing she'd pick them up again when she was ready. Was this sense of freedom and safety part of what truly falling for someone felt like?

Overcome with happiness, she reached for Jax's hand. "You were right, you know."

"About what?"

"This city. This amazing day. It feels like an entirely differ-ent place from the one I've been visiting for years." She scooted closer, wishing she could climb into his lap. "Before today, I'd never even heard of Governors Island, and I've been wishing I could go back to that night at Whiskey Bro's and kiss you onstage. I like you, Jax, and I like who I am when we're together."

"I'm glad you feel that way, because I got you a little something so you'd always remember this weekend." He reached into the pocket of his button-down and withdrew a linen bag with a drawstring enclosure.

Her pulse quickened. "When did you have time to buy something without me seeing?"

"At the festival, when you went to use the ladies' room."

"That was very sneaky of you, Mr. Braden."

He opened the bag and pulled out a necklace with a gorgeous white-gold, rectangular sunrise charm. The sun was brass, and it was rising over mountains etched into the white gold, just like the sun's rays, which stretched all the way to the edges of the charm.

"*Jax.* I love it. Thank you." She hugged him, whispering, "If we weren't surrounded by people, I'd show you just how much I love it."

Sparks flickered in his eyes. "Maybe we need to add *get sexy in a restaurant* to your naughty bucket list."

"Well, we *did* check off skinny-dipping, so there's room for more."

"Next time I'll book a restaurant with higher tables *and* tablecloths."

A thrill shivered through her, and she leaned closer, loving how he pushed her boundaries. "You are the *naughtiest*, and you make me want to be just as naughty."

"You haven't begun to see naughty." He put the necklace on her and kissed her. "This is one of Heaven Love's pieces, and I chose it because sunrises are signs of hope *and* new beginnings, and I'd like to think we've got a beginning worth remembering."

Her heart filled to the brim, and she pressed her hand to the charm. "We definitely do. I'll never take it off."

He kissed her. "Are you ready for our next adventure?"

"There's *more?*"

"Babe, this is the city that never sleeps. Are you ready to get wicked?"

"With you? *Always.*"

He squeezed her thigh. "We'll get wicked all right, but first I'm taking you to *see Wicked* on Broadway."

She gasped. "*Really?* I've never been to a Broadway show. Am I dressed okay?" She looked down at her royal-blue dress.

"You look gorgeous, and it doesn't matter what you wear. You're always the most beautiful woman in the room."

He sure made her feel that way.

A LITTLE WHILE later they were in the theater, but while Jordan sat on the edge of her seat, mesmerized by the performance, Jax couldn't take his eyes off her.

She leaned closer, eyes on the stage, whispering, "This is incredible."

"*Mm-hm.*"

She glanced at him, and her brow furrowed. "You're not even watching the show, are you?"

He slid his hand to the nape of her neck, pulling her closer. "Baby, you're all the wickedness I need." Her sexy grin brought his lips to hers.

When the musical was over, she was one of the first to her

feet, applauding and looking stunningly beautiful. When they made their way out of the theater, he took her hand and headed around to the back door.

"Where are we going?"

"To meet the actors and have them sign your playbook."

"We can do that?" She quickened her step just as raindrops began to fall, and they joined a crowd by the stage door. She grinned up at the sky, turning her rain-streaked face toward him. "I *love* the rain. I don't know why, but it makes me happy."

"You make me happy, baby." He gathered her in his arms, and as he kissed her, the sprinkle turned to a downpour. They came away laughing. "The cast may not stick around to sign autographs in this."

As the rain pummeled them, she said, "I don't need autographs. I just want you."

They ran out to hail a cab, kissing and laughing, and when they finally climbed into one, they were drenched. Jax put his arm around her, holding her close. "Now's your chance to make out in a car."

Her eyes widened, and she stole a glance at the driver. Then her gorgeous eyes narrowed seductively, and a vixenish grin slid into place. She straddled his lap, and their mouths crashed together. Jax's fingers dove into her wet hair as she rocked and gyrated, making him hard as stone. He pushed his hands up her thighs, beneath her dress, grabbing her ass with one hand and using his other thumb to tease her through her panties into a needy, *greedy* frenzy. He slipped his thumb beneath the thin, damp material, touching her where she needed it most.

She broke their kiss, her head dipping beside his as she whispered, "*Jax.*"

"You have about three minutes before we're at the hotel. I want to feel you come before we leave this cab. Give me your mouth, baby. *Now.*"

She didn't hesitate, and he quickened his efforts, masterfully massaging her clit as they feasted on each other's mouths. Her body tensed, and he grabbed her hair with his other hand, keeping their mouths fused, swallowing her sexy sounds as she came and pushing his fingers inside her to feel the clench and pulse of her tight heat. When their lips parted, he growled in her ear, "You are so damn sexy. I cannot wait to make all your dirtiest fantasies come true."

She climbed off him as the cab pulled over to the curb, and she kept her face down as they headed into the hotel and made their way to the elevator. When the doors closed behind them, he moved in front of her. She was so fucking beautiful and sweet, he could barely stand it. He wanted to protect her, love her, and fuck her in equal measure.

He moved her wet hair from her face and tucked it behind her ear, caressing her cheek. "You're mine and I'm yours. There's nothing to be embarrassed about."

"I've never done that before."

"I know, but it was on your naughty bucket list." He brushed his lips over hers, running his hand up her thigh. "I like doing new things with you, but if it's too much, just tell me."

"It's not. I like doing new things with you, too, but that doesn't mean I won't be embarrassed."

"Then how about checking something off *my* bucket list?" The elevator doors opened to their penthouse suite.

"What do you want to do?"

"I'll show you." He took her hand, leading her through the suite and onto the balcony, the lights of the city sparkling beneath them.

She put a hand on the railing. "Even with the rain, this view is amazing."

"*Mm-hm.*" He turned her back to the railing and pressed his body to hers, kissing her shoulder as he reached beneath her dress, hooking his fingers into the hips of her panties. "Time for these to come off." He stripped them down her legs, and as she stepped out of them, he guided her other hand to the railing. "Hold on tight, sweetheart."

As he dropped to his knees, she said, "Out here?"

"Penthouse, baby. Nobody can see us." He buried his face between her legs and she arched and moaned, making his cock throb. Her sexy sounds carried into the night as she shattered against his mouth. He pushed to his feet and shoved his pants down to his ankles, lifting her into his arms and turning them so her back was against the glass door. Their mouths collided, lightning scorching through him as he pounded into her, their moans and pleas getting louder as their passion mounted. Her fingernails dug into his shoulders, sending exquisite pain and pleasure tearing through him.

Her head fell back. "*Jax,*" she pleaded.

"That's it, baby. Let go for us."

He pumped faster, *harder*, and sealed his teeth over her neck, sucking until she cried out. Desire stacked up inside him, throbbing and pounding. Heat seared down his spine, and an explosion of sensations engulfed him. Sinful sounds flew from their lips, their bodies bucking and pulsing, until they had nothing left to give. Jordan went boneless in his arms, her breath hitting his cheek in desperate puffs.

"God, baby" was all he could manage, euphoria clouding his ability to string words together.

"I like your list," she panted out.

He laughed softly and kissed her again, both of them smiling. The rain curtained the balcony as he held her until their breathing calmed, and then he held her longer, not wanting to separate.

When he finally put her down, he helped her smooth her dress and picked up her panties before taking care of himself. He gathered her in his arms again, and as he lowered his mouth to hers, his phone vibrated several times in fast succession, and he uttered a curse.

"You'd better get that. It might be important."

He pulled it out and saw several texts from Jillian. "It's Jilly." He opened and read them. *Have you seen this?* She'd sent a picture of a leading gossip website with the headline *WILL BRIDAL GOWN DESIGNER JAX BRADEN BE MAKING HIS OWN BRIDE'S GOWN SOON?* above a picture of Jax and Jordan kissing onstage at the festival, though her face was hidden by his hands and their kiss. Jilly had also sent a picture of a Google search of his name, showing several similar headlines.

"What is it?"

He showed her the texts.

"Oh *no*. How did they even know we were here?"

"Someone must have tipped off a photographer."

As he pocketed his phone, she said, "Who would do that?"

He gathered her in his arms, unable to quell his smile.

Her jaw dropped. "*You* did it?"

"I wanted the world to know you were mine, but given the situation with Casey, I asked the photographer not to take pictures of your face. So at least now the world knows I'm taken. Is that okay?"

Her eyes lit up, and she was grinning as hard as he was. "It's unbelievably okay, and Reggie is reopening the case, so people will find out anyway. But tell me the truth. Did you want to rub it in Todd's face?"

He held up his finger and thumb about an inch apart. *"Maybe a little."*

She laughed. "How did I go from planning a wedding I didn't want to being with a man I don't want to live without?"

"Can't live without me, huh?" He kissed her neck. "Tell me more."

More melodic laughter fell from her lips. "What'll it get me?"

"Now you're learning, sweetheart. How about a warm bath and a back rub?"

"Only if you're in the tub with me."

"It'll be a hardship, but I *think* I can handle it."

Chapter Eighteen

THE COOL, RAINY spring had given way to a warm, dry summer. Jordan could hardly believe it was July already. Was it weird that she missed the rain? In the three weeks since she and Jax had been in New York, rain had become their *thing*, drawing them together, bringing with it a wealth of good memories. They opened the windows on rainy evenings to listen to the peaceful sounds of the rain falling. Coco had even become attuned to it, seeking them out to snuggle when the rain came. It wasn't something they decided or had talked about. It just happened, sort of like the way their lives had blended together.

Reggie had checked out the groups he'd mentioned and reinterviewed dozens of people, and although he'd come up empty, he'd not only breathed new life into Casey's case, but he'd made it go viral. It was all over social media and on every news outlet, as was Jordan and Jax's relationship. They, along with her aunt and uncle, were bombarded by the media, and as Reggie had warned, there had been a few crazies claiming to be Casey, which had rattled them all, because some of them had looked like her. Thank goodness for DNA tests. Most of those people backed down the minute the tests were mentioned, but some of them who had gone through testing had the gall to claim the tests were faulty.

It was exhausting.

But as Jax had promised, he made sure they were all safe. He and Jordan had been staying at his house, and he'd hired Elite Security to watch over Jordan and both of their families. It was strange knowing someone was always parked nearby watching, but things were starting to calm down, and she knew they were doing the right thing by bringing new attention to Casey's disappearance.

Jordan had met with Jillian for lunch a few days after they'd returned from New York to discuss the bridesmaids' dresses project, and Jillian had set up a meeting with Katrina Bailer and her bridesmaids for the following week. Jordan had been coming up with designs ever since, and luckily, Jillian liked the direction she was taking.

She focused on the bridesmaid gown she was sketching, listening to Jax and Nick joke around as they played basketball, while Jordan, Trixie, and Jillian sunbathed.

"Get 'im, cowboy!" Trixie hollered from the lounge chair next to her.

Jordan finished the hemline she was sketching and looked up just as Nick and Trixie's dogs, Goldie and Rowdy, darted past, chased by Coco. Pugsly was asleep on the lounge chair with Trixie. She watched Jax dribbling the ball, and he blew her a kiss. As Nick looked over, Jax made a beeline down the court and shot the ball, making a basket.

He did a fist pump. "That's how it's done, baby!"

Jordan cheered, while Nick grumbled, and Trixie yelled something about her man taking it easy on his little brother.

"Can you guys keep it down?" Jillian said from her lounge

chair. "I'm trying to catch some *z*'s over here."

"Maybe you should try sleeping at night," Trixie said.

"That's when she's most creative." Jordan and the girls had become much closer, and when they'd had lunch with Tempest and her adorable baby, PJ, last week, Jillian had explained that she gets her best ideas in the middle of the night—and Jordan had been so taken with PJ, she'd fantasized about her and Jax having their own family one day.

Jillian shielded her eyes from the sun, looking at Trixie. "Maybe you should try going a week without sex."

"Ha!" Trixie scoffed. "As if I'd *ever* want to do that."

"Then you understand. We're the same, Trix. We just have different addictions." Jillian lay back and closed her eyes.

Jordan giggled. She wouldn't want to go a week without touching Jax, but then again, she wouldn't want to go without designing, either. She'd only been designing bridesmaid gowns for Jillian for the past ten days, and she was fairly addicted herself. Jillian had loved most of her ideas, and she was learning a lot from her. Not just about designing dresses. She was also learning how wonderful it was to have girlfriends to share her life with. She didn't tell them the dirty details of her sex life with Jax, but it sure felt good to be able to tell them how amazing he was in every other way.

"Watch this, Jordan!" Jax hollered as he dunked the ball.

"Woo-hoo! Way to go, Jaxie!" she cheered.

"*Jaxie?*" Jillian and Trixie said in unison.

Jordan laughed. "It just came out. I don't know where it came from. I never call him that."

"Oh, *Jaxie, more, harder!*" Trixie teased, speaking in a sexy voice.

"Shut up!" Jordan laughed.

"Move your ass, *Jaxie*, before I whip you into next week."

Nick's deep voice rumbled through the air.

"Hey, Jaxie!" Jillian hollered. "Want me to have Glenna order you new business cards?"

Trixie laughed.

"Would you guys *stop*!" Jordan couldn't help laughing. "Sorry, Jax."

As Jax blocked Nick's shot, he said, "They're just jealous, baby. Ignore them."

The dogs bounded over, and Coco jumped onto Jordan's lounge chair. She set her sketch pad on the table, bringing Coco onto her lap. "Hi, sweet pea." She kissed her furry head. Most days, she could hardly believe *this* was her life, loving a man who supported her dreams and truly enjoyed being with her, surrounded by friends and a family who treated her like she was one of their own. They'd had dinner with Jax's parents last weekend, and they'd all gone for a walk around their neighborhood afterward. She had a feeling her parents had a hand in bringing her and Jax together. She didn't know if that was even possible, but she wanted to believe it, because it was so much better than believing they were just gone and not watching over her.

"Are you guys still planning on going to Ridgeport next weekend?" Trixie asked.

"Yes. I can't wait to see my aunt and uncle. I miss them." They'd video chatted with them several times, but Jax really wanted to meet them in person, and Jordan was excited for them to get to know him better and to get to know the person she'd become because of him.

"Do you want us to watch Coco while you're gone?" Trixie asked.

"Thanks, but we're taking her with us." Jordan hated being away from her as much as Jax did. She ruffled Coco's fur.

"Right, princess? Aunt Sheila and Uncle Gary are excited to meet you, too."

"They'll love Jaxie," Jillian said with a grin. "Everyone does. Except me at the moment. I still can't believe he hired Elite Security, the company owned by Brett and Carson Bad, Johnny Butthead's cousins, after the guy put me off *again*. I mean, that security guy parked out front is freaking hot, but still."

"Johnny must have something important going on for him to keep canceling. Maybe he lost his voice, or he's sick," Jordan suggested.

"I doubt it. The gossip magazines claim he's postponed his tour again due to personal scheduling issues, which probably means he's in a room with fifteen women and doesn't want to leave." Jillian rolled her eyes.

"Or maybe he knocked someone up and he's trying to avoid a scandal," Trixie said.

"Wow, you guys go right to the worst places. My mind doesn't work that way. Although since Todd cheated so much, maybe it should."

"I hate the bastard," Jillian said.

"If I ever see him, I'm going to give him hell," Trixie added.

"Where have you two been all my life?" Jordan looked at Jax, huddled with Nick, the two of them sneaking glances over their shoulders at her and Trixie. "Um...What do you think *that's* all about?"

"I don't know, but it can't be good," Trixie said as the guys stalked toward them.

Jordan's pulse quickened at Jax's wolfish grin, but something in his eyes told her he was up to no good.

Nick said, "Time to get wet, sugarplum." As he reached for Trixie, Jax lunged for Jordan.

The girls flew off their chairs, squealing and laughing. The dogs went wild, chasing them and barking.

"Don't you dare!" Jordan hollered just as Jax caught her around the waist and threw her over his shoulder like a caveman. Jax laughed, heading for the pool, as she squealed and flailed, and Nick scooped Trixie off her feet.

"Nick Braden, you won't get sex for a week!" Trixie threatened.

They were all laughing as Jordan and Trixie fought to break free and the guys jumped into the water, taking them down with them.

Jax took Jordan's hand underwater, and they broke through the surface near Nick and Trixie, laughing and kissing. Jordan clung to him as his powerful legs kept them afloat.

"You're *crazy!*" she hollered.

"Crazy for you, baby." He kissed her again, the four of them cracking up.

"Hey, lovebirds!" Jillian stood at the side of the pool in her pink bikini with her hands on her hips, scowling. "Once again I'm left out in the cold."

Nick and Jax exchanged a glance, and then they both went after Jillian. She screamed and the dogs barked and chased them as they ran around the yard. Trixie and Jordan were laughing and cheering Jillian on as she zigzagged, barely escaping Nick's grasp, only to get caught by Jax. He threw her in the pool, and he and Nick jumped in after her.

Jax swam underwater, slithering up Jordan's body, and kissed her as he broke the surface. "Having second thoughts about our crazy family?"

"*Yes.* Second, third, and *fourth* thoughts. Each one happier than the last."

Chapter Nineteen

JILLIAN'S DESIGN STUDIO was buzzing with excitement as bride-to-be Katrina Bailer and her ten bridesmaids giddily looked over the dress designs Jordan had come up with. Jordan stood off to the side with Jillian, trying not to let on that she was a nervous wreck, but her sketches were pinned up on a design board with all those keen eyes scrutinizing them. She'd been working like a fiend the last six weeks, sketching, tweaking, and meeting with Jillian and her sewing team to make sure she had everything perfectly called out, and now she felt like *she* was standing in front of those women naked instead of wearing one of her favorite original Jillian Braden dresses—a red figure-hugging shift with gathers under her breasts, a slim, deep V-neck, and capped sleeves. Jax called it her power dress, and she felt powerful in it. Jillian was also wearing one of her own designs—a burgundy tank dress, a shade lighter than her hair, with a gauzy cape and a sparkling silver belt.

Jordan took a deep breath, reminding herself that Jillian was thrilled with her designs. Jordan absolutely loved working with her. Jillian was a perfectionist, forthright, and unafraid to tell Jordan when something should be done differently. Jordan had always respected her as a designer, but her professionalism brought that respect to a whole new level. Especially since outside the design studio, Jillian was funny, quirky, and unfiltered, and she had become one of Jordan's closest friends and a trusted confidant. Although she still kept the dirty details of her sexy times with Jax to herself, they talked about everything else in their lives.

Katrina and the girls all turned around at the same time. Eleven beaming faces had Jordan holding her breath. She touched her sunrise necklace, throwing a silent prayer out to the universe. *Please don't hate them.*

"They're exactly what we hoped for," Katrina said, and her friends nodded eagerly. "But can we make a few small changes? We want to go a little shorter with all of them, and Tina wants hers to be sleeveless. Caroline really likes the cape you're wearing, Jillian. Can we add that to her dress?"

Jillian turned to Jordan. "What do you think? Are you comfortable with those changes to your designs?"

Jordan hadn't expected to be asked, but the answers came as easily and naturally as they did at her other job. "I don't think the length is an issue for any of them, and going sleeveless will work." Tina was petite and rail thin, and she needed a little extra something to create the illusion of curves. "But, Tina, how would you feel about changing the neckline? You have a beautiful figure, and I think if we go sleeveless, a sweetheart neckline might be more flattering. And since we're going shorter, I think adding a little lift beneath your bust, like the dress I have on, would accentuate your waist and hips. Let me show you." She went to the design table and quickly sketched the outline of two sleeveless dresses. One with a modified scoop neck and the other with a sweetheart neckline and lift beneath her bust.

"*Wow.* You're right. Once you take away the sleeves, it would be kind of shapeless. The sweetheart neckline is so much better, and the lift is perfect. You guys have to see this." Tina waved her friends over.

As they admired her sketches, Jillian whispered, "You're *good.*"

It was thrilling to have the clients like her ideas, but Jillian's compliment was like getting a gold star, and Jordan couldn't wait to tell Jax. He'd been as supportive about her working with Jillian as he was about working with Reggie. They'd had an amazing visit with her aunt and uncle, and they'd already made plans for another visit.

Their lives were full of family and friends, barbecues, and low-key dates away from prying eyes, and she was loving it. Thankfully, the need for security had died down, and they were enjoying their privacy. They'd been running together a few days a week, catching sunrises, and sometimes they went out to the garden to watch the sunset with Coco. They hadn't said those three important words yet, but they were always right there on the surface, ready to leap from her heart to his ears.

After Katrina and her friends left, Jillian turned to Jordan and clapped her hands together. "That was spectacular! Are you ready to take on another project?"

Happiness bubbled up inside her. "You want to keep working with me? But I thought since Johnny Bad put off his tour, it freed up your time and you wouldn't need my help anymore."

"He did, but the clients love you, and we work great together. I have more than enough work to keep us both busy, and you are insanely talented. What do you think? I know you were worried about having enough time for your full-time job and for you and Jax. Do you think you want to continue?"

"Are you kidding? Am I dreaming? Is this real? Of course I want to continue."

"Yay!" Jillian cheered and hugged her.

"I *love* working with you, Jilly, and fitting it in has been relatively easy. I don't feel any added pressure, and I think it's because I'm having so much fun, it doesn't feel like a job. The people at my other job keep telling me that they've never seen me happier than I've been these last few months."

"As much as I'd like to take credit for that, I think it has more to do with my brother than working with me. He moons over you like my other brothers did when they fell for their wives."

"That makes two of us. I'm crazy about him. Did I tell you that Jax came to have lunch with me one day last week, and now the Knotty Hookers call him *Gentleman Jax*, because he was so charming."

"Jax told me all about those naughty old ladies. Did you know one of them asked him if he was a gentleman in the streets and a freak in the sheets?"

"*Yes!* That was Ruth. She's so brazen. Did he tell you how he responded? He said *Jordan comes to work every day with a smile, doesn't she?*"

"That's my twin." Jillian shook her head, laughing. "I want to meet those dirty-minded ladies."

"You can meet them when you thank them for your present, which I almost forgot to give you." She went to the design area Jillian had set up for her and fished Jillian's gift out of her tote, handing her the gift-wrapped box.

"I love presents," Jillian exclaimed. "Did they make you something, too?"

"Yes. It's in my bag, but it would ruin the surprise if I

showed it to you."

Jillian tore open the box, and her brows knitted as she held up the tan crocheted tubelike object with DESIGNING DIVAS crocheted in black down the center and a small crocheted bag on either side. "*Um.* Jordan…?"

"Isn't it great?" Jordan tried to keep a straight face. "It's a pencil holder and two eraser bags."

"I don't think they thought through the design." Jillian held it between her legs, and they both cracked up. "Unless you've got it wrong and they made us willy warmers."

"I *know.* You should've seen me trying not to laugh when they gave it to me. I'd give mine to Jax, but it'd be too small." Jordan doubled over with laughter.

"Maybe I should bring it when we go to Amber's wedding and see how those Oak Falls boys measure up." Jillian wiggled her hips, making the tube flop from side to side. "Line up, cowboys! Let's see who's packin' more than *this!*"

They laughed hysterically.

After getting their laughter under control, they made plans to meet later at Tully's Tavern, a local pub, to celebrate their decision to continue working together.

By the time Jordan got to Jax's house, she was bursting at the seams to share her news. She saw him talking on the phone by the pool in his swim trunks—*Yum*—and hurried outside. Coco sprinted to her, and as Jordan loved her up, Jax looked over, his expression serious.

She pushed to her feet as he ended the call. "Is everything okay?"

"That was Reggie. He got an anonymous tip yesterday about a girl who escaped from that cult in West Virginia."

"Really? Does he think it's Casey? I thought he searched the compound and there was no sign of her." *Please, please be her!*

Jax shook his head. "He doesn't know. He said not to get our hopes up because it all sounded sketchy. He left his business card with everyone he interviewed on the compound, and a woman contacted him, but she wouldn't give her name. She said the girl's name was Sullivan Tate, but she goes by Sully. She said she came to the cult years ago with one of the leader's underlings when he'd returned from a trip out west. He said she was his niece and his sister couldn't afford to take care of her. She thought she *might* be around Casey's age, but she couldn't be sure, and she said she looked a heck of a lot like the age-progression pictures."

Goose bumps chased over Jordan's flesh. "*Jax.* What if it's her?"

"I hope it is, but Reggie said this could be someone sending him on a wild-goose chase because he ruffled a lot of feathers when he was there."

"I have so many questions. Why did she run away? How did she escape? She must have been scared or abused or something. People don't just run away."

"We can't jump to conclusions. Reggie put an alert out for Sully using what little information he had. He's heading back to West Virginia with an investigative team to see what they can find out."

Jordan's mind raced. "Did she give him the name of the guy? Sully's uncle?"

"Yes, but he died a few years ago of cancer, and the woman said that a lot of members change their names when they join the cult. They're encouraged to leave their old lives behind, so she wasn't sure if that was his real name or not. Reggie will get to the bottom of it."

"I know, but why would *anyone* want to be in a cult? Why is the woman who called him there?"

"She didn't give her name, and he couldn't even say if she was a member of the cult."

"I don't know what any of this means. Is it good? Is it even real? I want to hold on to the hope that it is. I got chills when you first told me, but even if it's not Casey, there's still some girl out there all alone and probably terrified."

"Since she escaped, she probably had help, so maybe she's not alone or scared, but safe and relieved."

Jordan took a deep breath. "You're right. I'll hold on to that. I want to hope it's her. I know we've had tons of false leads, but the location is right."

"Reggie said to treat it like all the other leads. Don't believe it until we hear from him that it's real. This could be another attention seeker."

"You're right. We should think of this like all the others. My heart is racing."

He gathered her in his arms, running his hand down her back. "We knew this was going to be a roller coaster."

"I know. I'm glad we're doing it. If they find Sully and she's not Casey, then maybe she belongs to someone else, or maybe she really is that guy's niece and she just wants to get back to her family."

"That's right. Reggie will let us know." He kissed her. "How did your meeting go? Did they like the designs?"

"They loved them, with a few minor tweaks."

"That's *awesome*, babe. I knew they would. We need to celebrate." He palmed her butt. "Starting right now." He kissed her neck, sending warmth down her chest.

"*Mm.* I like this celebration." She leaned her head to one

side, giving him better access. "We have more than one reason to celebrate. Jilly asked me to keep working with her, and I accepted."

"That's fantastic. I'm so proud of all you've done. I guess I'd better watch my back, or you might become more famous than I am."

"Hardly."

"I have faith in you, baby. I want to see you soar." He kissed her as he backed her up toward the house, rubbing his body against hers. "In more ways than one."

She giggled. "I told Jilly we'd meet her at the tavern at eight."

"That gives us just enough time for a few mind-blowing orgasms."

She feigned a pout. "Just a *few*? Guess I won't have time to get on my knees for you first."

His eyes flamed. "The hell you won't." He scooped her up and carried her into the house.

She giggled. "That's more like it, *Mr. Braden*."

Chapter Twenty

"I CAN'T BELIEVE how big she's getting." Trixie passed her phone around the table at Tully's Tavern, showing off pictures of her one-year-old niece, Emma Lou. "I miss her so much."

"You'll see her at the wedding, babe." Nick pulled her closer. "We'll spend extra time with them."

Jax looked at the pictures of Emma Lou with Jordan, imagining their own babies, with Jordan's blue eyes and her sweet smile that would have him wrapped around their little fingers.

"Emma Lou gets cuter every week," Jordan said dreamily. "Can you imagine waking up to that little face every day?"

"I sure can." Jax nuzzled against her cheek. He'd noticed subtle changes in Jordan these last few weeks. Like the way she sounded when she talked about the future, as if she knew they'd always be together, even though they hadn't said I love you or talked in specifics about their next step. He'd also noticed that when she told the others about the call from Reggie tonight, there was a calm confidence to her tone, which he was sure came from knowing their family and friends supported their search.

"I can't wait for all of you to start having babies," Jillian said, taking the phone from Jax. "I'm going to be the *best* auntie!"

"Don't you want a family of your own?" Jordan asked.

Jillian shook her head. "I don't do diapers, and I definitely don't do puke. Besides, babies keep you up all night, needing to be fed and changed and all of that, and I work at night. *I* need to be fed and cared for."

"Wouldn't that make it easier since you're up already?" Jordan asked.

Jillian looked at her like she'd lost her mind. "Definitely *not*. My muse would run and hide, and I might never get her back."

Everyone laughed except for Jordan.

"That *might* change one day," Jordan said. "Before Jax and I got together, I couldn't think about moving forward with any part of my life, much less having kids." She gazed lovingly into his eyes. "But with him, I want *everything*."

"Bet he loves that." Nick smirked.

You have no idea how much. "Damn right I do."

As Jillian handed Trixie her phone, Jordan said, "I can't wait to meet that little cutie pie."

"I can't wait to introduce you to everyone back home. You'll love them all," Trixie said.

Jax hugged Jordan against his side and kissed her temple. "I'll be keeping her away from your single brothers and their wandering eyes."

"Better hold her tight," Jillian warned. "All of Dash's football buddies will be there, too."

"There's no way anyone could steal me away from Jax," Jordan insisted. "What we have is too special."

"And it always will be." He kissed her again.

Jillian made kissing noises. "Not that I'm jealous or anything." She rolled her eyes. "But seriously, where are all the hot single guys tonight? I hate to think I got all dolled up for nothing."

"You live to get dolled up," Jax reminded her. She looked as beautiful as ever, even if a little dressy for the local tavern, in a white blouse with a plunging neckline and billowing sleeves, which she'd paired with a cute black miniskirt.

"Girlfriend, you asked, and now you shall receive." Trixie motioned over Jillian's shoulder to Travis Helms, her and Nick's close friend and neighbor. He was a single father with an adorable little girl, and he ran a horse ranch specializing in miniature horses.

Jillian looked in his direction, then leaned across the table, whispering, "Did you *invite* him?"

"Yes, and you're welcome." Trixie wiggled her shoulders.

"Are you nuts? He's a tall, dark, and delicious *DILF*! He'd be fun for a night, but he's looking for a *wife*, and I'm *not* stepmom material," Jillian whispered harshly, seconds before Travis arrived at their table.

"Hey, y'all." Travis eyed Jillian appreciatively. "Hey, city girl."

Jillian spoke flirtatiously, flipping her hair over her shoulder. "How's it going, cowboy?"

"It'd be better if you let me take you for a spin on the dance floor."

Jillian eyed his cowboy boots. "Can you even dance in those things?"

He peeked under the table at her sky-high heels. "Can you?"

He offered his hand. Her eyes narrowed, and she took his hand, rising to her feet. "Try to keep up, cowboy." As they walked away, Jillian looked over her shoulder, mouthing, *Just one night!*

"Would she really get together with him for *just* one night?" Jordan asked.

"I don't want to know," Nick and Jax said in unison. They raised their glasses as if they'd just made a toast and took a drink.

"Come on, sweetheart. I want to dance with the sexiest woman in here." Jax pushed to his feet, bringing Jordan up with him.

"Us too!" Trixie nudged Nick, and they all headed to the dance floor.

Colorful lights rained down on Jordan as she swayed her hips and shoulders seductively, a far cry from the nervous way she'd danced with him at Nick and Trixie's reception. Their bodies moved in perfect harmony. It seemed they were always in sync, with their thoughts, their hopes, and their lovemaking, which was out of this world. He drew her closer as they danced, bringing them thigh to thigh, chest to chest, the temperature rising between them, stoking the fire that had taken root nearly a year ago, when he'd first set eyes on his beautiful girl and was always simmering just beneath the surface.

He spoke into her ear as they danced. "How long do we have to stay?" She giggled, and man, that carefree sound still drove him crazy.

"A little while longer. You can't keep me in the bedroom all the time."

"Who said anything about the bedroom?" He nipped her earlobe.

"Why, Mr. Braden, where were you thinking?"

He met her lustful gaze. "If you call me that, we might just have to stop at my office on the way home."

She arched a brow. "Promise?"

"Hell yes." He pressed his hips forward, letting her feel what the thought of it did to him.

The song ended, and Jillian said, "Bathroom break!" She grabbed Trixie's and Jordan's hands, tugging them off the dance floor.

"Fucking Jillian," Nick growled as Travis joined them.

Jax watched as his girl, his love, his *life*, glanced over her shoulder, blowing him a kiss. "I'm so in love with that woman I can barely see past her."

"I sure as hell hope you're talking about Jordan and not Jilly," Travis teased.

Jax glowered at him.

"Have you told her yet?" Nick asked.

"No. After everything she went through and all the attention on Casey's case, I'm waiting for the right time."

JILLIAN DRAGGED THEM into the crowded ladies' room. "You guys, Travis is packin' major heat, and *boy* can he dance."

"How do you know what he's packing?" Jordan asked as Trixie got in line to use the bathroom and she and Jillian made their way to the mirrors.

Jillian gave her a deadpan look. "Don't pretend you have no idea, little miss dirty dancer. I saw you and my brother practically having sex on the dance floor."

Jillian had her there. She loved dirty dancing with Jax, feeling his body all revved up for her.

Two blondes and a brunette barreled into the ladies' room giggling and got in line for the stalls. "Did you guys see Jax

Braden?" the brunette asked.

"He's so fucking hot," one of the blondes said.

Jordan stole a glance at them in the mirror, feeling proud that he was hers.

"He's even hotter in bed. Didn't I tell you about the foursome we had?"

Jordan grabbed the edge of the sink as the room spun, their voices turning to white noise. A foursome? Her sweet, charming, sexy Jax? His voice trampled through her mind. *I've been snagged by plenty of women.* Flashes of them having sex in his pool, on the balcony in New York, and making out in the cab pummeled her. She couldn't catch her breath and stumbled backward.

Jillian grabbed her arm, tugging her out the door.

Jordan put her hand on the wall to steady herself. "Is it true?" The pained look on Jillian's face sliced through her heart.

"I don't know. *Probably.* But you should talk to Jax."

Gutted, Jordan choked out, "I need air." She hurried toward the front of the bar and raced outside. Her heart thundered against her ribs as she ran through the parking lot to the sidewalk, trying to catch her breath, but her head was spinning, as she imagined him with that girl—and two others.

"Jordan!" Jax was sprinting toward her. "Sweetheart." He reached for her hand, his face a mask of worry and grief.

She stepped back. "Is it true? Did you have a *foursome*?"

His jaw clenched. "I've never lied to you, and I'm *not* going to start."

"Did you?"

"Yes, but let me explain."

She turned away, shaking. "I'm so stupid. I was with Todd for years, and I had no idea *who* he was. Why did I think I knew you at all?"

"Because you *do* know me." He moved in front of her. "I've never hidden a thing from you."

"Except a *foursome*, and God knows what else." She swiped at tears.

"I didn't *hide* it, Jordan. You never asked if I'd been with more than one woman at a time. Ask me *anything*, and I'll tell you the truth. I'm an open book with you, and I have been since day one."

She shook her head. "I don't even know what to ask. When was it?"

"Last year, before we even met."

That made her feel a little better, but the thought of him with three women made her nauseous. "I get that it was before we met, and everyone has a past, but I was duped by Todd for so long. I don't want to find out years from now that I overlooked red flags. Were there *more*?"

"*Foursomes?* No. Just that once. *Threesomes?* Yeah, a couple, when I was younger. But I was *single*, baby. It didn't matter what I did, because I wasn't cheating on anyone."

Her breath rushed from her lungs, her knees weakening. "I fell in love with you thinking I was *enough*, but how can I ever be? I can't compete with multiple women, and I don't *want* to."

"That's good, because I don't want anyone but you."

"*Today*, maybe! But what about tomorrow? Or next year?"

"Ask me how many women I've been with since we met last summer."

"I don't think I want to know."

"Yes, you do, baby. I haven't been with *any* other woman since I met you eleven and a half months ago. You weren't even mine, and I didn't think I had a chance in hell of ever *seeing* you again, but just the *thought* of you was enough to flick a switch inside me and turn off any interest in anyone else. I didn't even want to look at another woman."

"Wh…? Is that true?" She shook her head, trying to process what he'd said.

"Yes, Jordan. You can ask Nick. He knows. I have been crazy about you since you first walked into my office, and I know how outlandish it sounds when I say I wasn't with anyone else for all those months. But it's as real as the fucked-up gossip you just heard." He stepped closer, taking her trembling hands. "I would *never* hurt you, and if I had known we were destined to meet, I probably never would have been with those women. But I promise that I have never, and will never, lie to you."

"I know you won't. I trust you. I'm just…shocked."

"I'm sorry. I can't change the shit I did before we met, but you are the *only* woman I've ever had in my house and in my *bed*. You're the only woman I've introduced to my family and my dog. And you are the *only* woman I have ever fallen in love with, and I know with every iota of my being that you are the only woman I will ever *be* in love with. Because whether you knew it or not, when you walked out of my office last summer, you took the biggest part of my heart with you."

Fresh tears tumbled down her cheeks. "Don't you hate me for freaking out?"

"No, baby. I love that you're willing to stand up for yourself, because you should never have to compete for anything. Especially my attention, and if I've ever given you a reason to feel like you're not enough, then I need to work harder."

She gulped air into her lungs, trying to stop the tears from falling. "You haven't."

"Good, because I love *you*, Jordan Lawler. I love everything about you. I love your sensitive, hopeful heart, your sweet laughter, and your brilliant brain, and I love the way you love me. All I want is to make your life wonderful, so please don't throw us away because of something that happened before we knew each other. I chose *you*, baby, and I would choose you a million times over. You have always been, and you will always be, more than enough for me."

"I love you, too." She wanted to tell him she loved him more than life itself and that she'd fallen into a deeper, truer love than she ever imagined possible, but she was too over-whelmed to say another word, so with her heart in her throat, she went up on her toes and kissed him.

Chapter Twenty-One

SEPTEMBER BLEW INTO Pleasant Hill with cooler temperatures, painting everything in its path in vibrant fall colors. Jordan rushed around her office gathering her things an hour earlier than usual, excited to go home and watch London's Fashion Week with Jax. They'd bought new sketch pads and pencils, and they were going to make all the goodies her family used to make. It would be another *first* for them. She loved their firsts.

She picked up the card he'd had delivered along with a bouquet of daffodils earlier in the week, after she'd run two miles straight for the first time on their morning jog. The front of the card was white with I'M SO GLAD YOU ARE MY PERSON written in black above a big red heart and two smaller pink hearts beside it. She opened it and read what he'd written. MY BEAUTIFUL SWEETHEART, ONE DAY YOU'LL FIND THIS CARD TUCKED IN THE BACK OF A DRAWER, AND WE'LL STILL BE HAPPILY IN LOVE. FOREVER YOURS, JAX.

She set the card back on the desk, thinking about how much her life had changed. Thanks to Jax, she was getting stronger every day in every way. The insecurities of being with a man who had cheated on her had finally faded away, and although the search for Casey felt like a roller coaster, with new leads that looked hopeful then turned to dust, and there were times she broke down in tears feeling like she'd never get any answers, Jax was always there to remind her it was okay to be sad or angry and to hold her until she was strong enough to carry on. The phone call about the girl who had escaped from the cult had led Reggie on a wild-goose chase. The man was untraceable and had been using a fake name, and Sully hadn't turned up anywhere. But Reggie continued to follow up on every lead, no matter how far-fetched, and he made sure the search for Casey didn't fall out of the spotlight. This week he was chasing down a trucker who two guys claimed they'd seen with a girl who looked like Casey a couple of weeks ago.

"Knock, knock." Ari Lexington stood in the doorway holding a Tupperware cake container and wearing a bright blue three-piece suit over a black crewneck.

"Well, don't you look handsome. Big date with Bess tonight?"

"Yes *and* the Knotty Hookers, which I'm not thrilled about. They'll flirt with me all night, and I don't want my Bessie to get the wrong idea."

Jordan smiled. "They finally wrangled you into dinner?"

"Thanks to you, they wrangled Bess into watching London's Fashion Week with them, and Ruth said if I wanted to join them, I had to dress the part. Now, I don't know much about fashion, but my great-niece took me shopping, and she said this would be perfect. I don't know about the shirt. I was brought up to wear collared shirts."

"That shirt is perfect. I'm so glad you're all going to watch together. You'll enjoy the show, even if you don't know much about fashion. Did you make a cake for dessert?"

"No. This strawberry shortcake is for Jax." He handed her the cake carrier.

"For Jax? What's the occasion?" Jax had met several of the residents over the last couple of months when he'd come to pick up Jordan for lunch, or stopped in to say hello, and he and Mr. Lexington had gotten along fabulously.

"He makes you happy, and I don't know how many people are thanking him for that, but I wanted to."

Jordan got choked up. "Mr. Lexington, are you trying to make me tear up?"

"No, but I want you to know that we're all pulling for you two. Even if you *did* inadvertently rip me off from a night alone with Bessie."

She set the cake on the desk and hugged him. "Thank you for always thinking of me."

"Rosa used to say that good people are easy to love and impossible to forget. You're a good person, Jordan, and Rosa would have loved you."

That made her feel good all over. "I'm sure I would have loved her, too."

"Well, I'd better get going. Enjoy the show tonight."

"Thank you. You too."

When Jordan finally left the office, cake in hand, and was settling into her car, her phone rang with a call from Jax. "Hi, handsome. I'm just leaving work."

"Great. I'm running a little late from my meeting, and I left something important at my office. Would you mind stopping by and picking it up? Glenna knows where it is."

"Sure. I'll stop on my way home. See you in a little bit."

"Okay, I love you."

"I love you, too." He told her he loved her every morning,

every time they talked on the phone, and every night before they went to bed, and she knew she'd never tire of hearing it, *or* saying it.

She drove to his office, humming to the songs on the radio. Glenna was elbow deep in files behind the front desk when she arrived. "Hi, Glenna. Jax asked me to stop by and pick up something he left here. He said you'd know what it was."

"Yes. It's in the showroom. Would you mind grabbing it?"

"Not at all." She hurried into the showroom and found Jonathan and a pretty blonde.

In one hand, Jonathan held a gorgeous white silk sleeveless knee-length dress with a fitted bodice that was embellished at the back with distinctive cutouts and a low neckline. The waist was cinched, and the full skirt had two rows of black lace cutouts. White elbow-length gloves with black lace cutouts on the forearms were draped over his other forearm, and in his hand was a gorgeous pair of Christian Louboutin heels. Jordan's thoughts stumbled. That was a dress she'd designed.

"Good evening, mademoiselle," Jonathan said. "It will be our pleasure to help dress you tonight."

"Jax had my design made?"

"Yes, and don't worry—it has *your* name on the label."

Tears sprang to her eyes.

"Get those tears out now, sweetie, because this is Sarah Whiskey, the hair and makeup guru I told you about, and once she works her magic, you won't want to mess up your makeup."

"Hi, Sarah. Thank you. I can't believe Jax did this." She tried to blink away her tears.

"Love brings out the best in all of us," Sarah said. "We should get started so you're not late."

The next forty minutes passed in a whirlwind. The dress fit

perfectly, and Jonathan was a riot, giving his two cents as Sarah did Jordan's hair, which, as Jonathan suggested, she wore in an updo with a few tendrils framing her face. Glenna, Emiko, and Roberta came in to watch as Sarah worked her magic, and she told them about her three young children and her husband, Dr. Wayne "Bones" Whiskey. Jordan was shocked to learn that she'd escaped abusive parents and an abusive relationship and that she'd been pregnant when she'd met Bones.

"Life has a way of bringing the right people together at the right times," Sarah said.

Jordan could only hope that Casey had been so lucky. Maybe she'd been raised by a loving couple.

Jonathan took loads of pictures as Jordan was transformed into a woman so beautiful, she didn't recognize herself. She thanked them profusely, and Jonathan walked her out to the car, fixing her dress after she settled into the driver's seat.

"Honey, you are the brightest star in Jax's sky tonight and every night. Give your big hunk of deliciousness a little extra love from me. He did *good*."

"I will. Thank you so much, Jonathan, and please thank Sarah again for me. She's an amazing woman."

She drove home to Jax's with a smile plastered on her face and raced through the front door, only to be stopped in her tracks once again, blown away by the sight of a red-carpet runway lined with lights leading to the living room, which was decorated with strings of twinkling lights and vases of red and white roses and daffodils. Jax stood at the end of the runway wearing a white tuxedo with black lapels and holding a microphone. Coco sat beside him wearing a white tuxedo collar, her tail wagging.

"Welcome home, sweetheart. Please make your entrance

runway worthy." Jax lifted the microphone, flashing the smile that made her heart turn over in her chest. "Ladies and gentlemen, tonight we are graced with designer Jordan Lawler wearing one of her original gowns."

Jordan teared up as she made her way down the runway, toward the man who had not only rocked her world but had become it. Behind him she saw a long table draped in white, covered with enough enormous pretzels, pigs in blankets, and lime gelatin salad to feed an army. "I can't believe you did all this."

Jax pulled her into his arms and kissed her. "I'd do anything to see your smile, sweetheart. I hope you don't mind, but I can't take credit for the food. I hired Finlay to cater since she missed out on the business from your wedding."

"I think it is wonderful. *You're* wonderful!" She threw her arms around him and kissed him.

"Finlay brought whipped cream, but I put it away for us to enjoy later." He brushed his scruff along her cheek. "I look forward to eating it with *my* favorite dessert."

Her body threw a little party, and she was about to suggest she have *him* as an appetizer when the front door opened, and her aunt walked in wearing the V-neck tulle gown with embroidered shooting stars on the skirt that Jordan had sketched. Uncle Gary was behind her, dressed to the nines, along with the rest of Jax's family and their significant others. All the girls were wearing Jordan's designs.

She couldn't believe they'd all flown in to be there, and Jax had somehow found the time to have all of her sketches made into gorgeous gowns. There was no holding back the happy tears spilling down her cheeks as the couples strutted down the runway and Jax described each of the Jordan Lawler originals they were wearing, as if they were at her own private fashion show.

JAX'S HEART FILLED up as he watched the people he loved most embrace the woman he wanted to spend the rest of his life with. Jordan glanced in his direction, joy radiating from her beautiful eyes as their families raved about her dresses, and Jillian tried to convince her to quit her job and design full time. But Jordan would have no part of leaving behind the family she had at Pleasant Care Assisted Living.

Jax's father sidled up to him. "That's not the same lonely young woman who came to dinner at our house four months ago."

"I'm not the same lonely man, either."

"Should we start planning another wedding?"

"As much as I want to say yes, the answer is no."

"Now, *that* surprises me."

"Take a good look at her, Dad. You're the one who taught me that sometimes it's not about being in the limelight but about helping others shine. These last few months, she found her true self, and she just found her *tribe*, as Morgyn calls it. I want her to enjoy that without the pressure of planning a wedding." Jordan glanced at him again, and their gazes held, that magnetic pull drawing him in as it always did. "Excuse me, Dad. I'm having withdrawals."

His father laughed. "You are definitely my son, because I was thinking the same thing about your mother."

Jax headed for Jordan and slid his arm around her waist.

"Excuse me, ladies. Would you mind if I steal the designer for a few minutes?"

"From the look on my niece's face," Sheila said, "I don't think it would matter if we said we did."

"We won't be long." He guided Jordan away from the others, talking low. "Would it be in bad taste if we snuck into the bedroom?"

"Yes." She wound her arms around him, tickling the back of his neck with her fingertips. "Mr. Braden, you have outdone yourself tonight. What can I possibly *ever* do to top this?"

He held her closer. "One day, when you're ready, you can marry me."

"Jax...?" she said incredulously.

"I know it's too soon, but life's too short to hold in the important things."

A wealth of love shone in her eyes. "Do you know how much I love you?"

"I think I have a pretty good idea."

"How can you when there aren't enough words in the English language to describe it? I don't just love you with all my heart and soul. You've become a part of me, one I never knew was missing, and I look forward to becoming your wife one day." She went up on her toes and kissed him, whispering, "And you know that whipped cream you have hidden away for us? I call dibs on eating it off *you* first."

He loved her so much, he ached with it. "Are you flirting with me, Ms. Lawler?"

"Not flirting. Just stating a fact."

He lowered his lips to hers, kissing her passionately. His phone rang in his pocket, and he groaned as she broke the kiss.

She took a step back, fanning her face. "Answer your call. I need ice water before I combust and the whole house goes up in flames."

She blew him a kiss, and as she headed back to the party, his phone rang again. He pulled it out and saw Reggie's name on the screen. They spoke every week, and they'd been through such a roller coaster the first few weeks, he no longer got a hopeful high or a gut-wrenching low when Reggie called. "Hi, Reggie."

"Jax, are you with Jordan?" His voice was strong and calm.

"Yeah, we're with my family. Is everything okay?"

"I'd like Jordan to be the first to hear this news, but you should be with her. Can you FaceTime?"

Jax's gut clenched. "Yes, but, Reggie, should I prepare her?"

"You can't prepare her for this. Why don't you get Jordan and call me back on video?"

Jax ended the call, his feet rooted to the ground as his gaze drifted to Jordan on what was clearly one of the happiest nights of her life. He felt like he'd swallowed shards of glass, but he forced his legs to move. He went to her and whispered in her ear, "It's Reggie. Let's take it in private."

Her smile faded, fear rising in her eyes as he led her toward the den. He glanced at Beau, remembering when he'd gotten the news about Tory. Beau must have read his thoughts, because he caught up to him and said, "What happened?"

"Reggie wants to talk on video." Jax held Jordan tighter.

Beau's brows slanted, his jaw clenching. "I've got you."

He followed them into the den, and Nick appeared in the doorway, eyes narrow, jaw tight. "What's going on?" As Nick said it, Jordan's aunt and uncle appeared behind him. Had he been that transparent in his worries?

"Is everything okay?" her aunt asked.

Jax had never been more grateful for support in his life, but he'd also never realized support could feel suffocating. Or maybe that was his worry about what Jordan was about to hear. As grateful as he was, all he wanted was to be alone with her while they heard Reggie out, to protect her from whatever was coming her way, to comfort her without others watching.

"We're about to call Reggie, but I think it's best if it's just us." He looked at Beau. "Would you mind…?"

"Whatever you need, man." Beau ushered everyone away from the door and closed it behind himself, leaving Jax and Jordan alone.

"Do you know what's going on?" Her voice was thin and shaky.

"No. Reggie didn't say. Let's sit down and we'll call."

He grabbed a box of tissues from the shelves, and they sat on the couch. With his heart slamming against his ribs, he took Jordan's trembling hand, and holding the phone in his other hand, he called Reggie on FaceTime.

When Reggie's serious face appeared on the screen, Jordan squeezed Jax's hand so tight her nails cut into him, and she blurted out, "Is Casey dead?" Tears spilled from her eyes.

Jax put his arm around her, praying that wasn't the news Reggie had to share.

"No, Jordan. Casey is very much alive and safe. We've got her."

Sobs fell from Jordan's lips, and she doubled over against Jax's chest. He held her close. "She's *alive*, baby. Casey's alive." He kissed the top of her head, tears burning his own eyes, as her body heaved with sobs. "What happened, Reggie? Where is she?"

"Casey *is* Sully, Sullivan Tate. The girl who escaped from

the cult. She was picked up in West Virginia by a trucker, Chester Finch, who was heading home to Colorado. He'd seen the news and thought she looked like Casey, but he wasn't sure, and she didn't want to go to the police or see a doctor because she was afraid of being sent back to the cult. Chester and his wife, Carol, took her in and convinced her to let them take her to Redemption Ranch, which is in Hope Ridge, Colorado, and run by a Dark Knights family—Tommy, who goes by the road name Tiny, and his wife, Wynona, Whiskey. The Finches knew she would be safe and protected and could get the medical help she needed while we determined whether she was Casey. The Dark Knights had been apprised of the ongoing search for Casey early on, as I mentioned to you, and Tiny called me. The DNA tests confirmed her identity a few hours ago. The leader of the cult and several of his underlings were arrested, and many others are being held for questioning. It'll be all over the news tonight, but we've kept the Finches, and Sully's whereabouts, out of the reports. There's no chance of anything leaking to the media. Consider the ranch her safe house."

Jordan sat up, wiping her eyes. "Is she okay?"

"She's doing well, considering everything she's been through, and Redemption Ranch is a good place for her to get the help she needs. They're a second-chance ranch. They rescue horses and help people with social and emotional issues or difficult pasts—victims of abuse, ex-cons, recovering addicts— heal and find their new path. They have a medical team and therapists on staff. It's an excellent program, and a good place for her to heal."

"Carly's friends with the Whiskeys. They helped her through a really hard time when she was younger," Jax said. "I trust that she's in good hands there. Reggie, does Casey know who she really is? When can Jordan see her?"

"Does she remember what happened or how she got to the cult?" Jordan asked.

"She doesn't remember how she got there, but our working theory is that the guy who brought her there—the one who was reported by that anonymous caller—had happened upon the accident, saw an opportunity, and took it. She knows what we've told her about who she is, but she doesn't remember her life before the cult, and she only knows herself as Sully."

More tears flooded Jordan's cheeks. Jax drew her closer, kissing her temple. "It's okay, sweetheart." He looked at Reggie. "In your experience, do those memories ever come back?"

"They can, and that's what I'm hoping for. Sometimes a victim will *say* they don't remember anything when they really do, and they can withhold those details for a hundred different reasons. But Sully is going through therapy with Wynona. She's a highly respected therapist and excellent at working with all types of trauma victims. She said Sully's a tough girl. A real fighter."

Jordan smiled through her tears. "That sounds like Casey...*Sully*. I guess I have to get used to that." Her smile faded. "I don't know much about cults, but I've heard some horrible things. Was she mistreated?"

"The leader of the group is being charged with numerous accounts of rape and sexual assault. As far as we know, he's the only one who laid a hand on Sully."

"Oh, *Casey*." Jordan closed her eyes, head bent forward, clinging to Jax's hand. "*Sully*." She looked up through damp eyes. "Does she have children?"

"No. It appears she had a guardian angel. There was a midwife who was secretly giving her and a few of the others birth control shots. We think she's the anonymous caller."

"Who is she?" Jax asked. "We'd like to thank her, and the Finches, too."

Jordan nodded in agreement. "Yes, please."

"The midwife's name is Gaia, and we have her in protective custody. I'll make arrangements so you can thank her, and the Finches are in a safe house until we're sure they're not in any danger. But I can arrange a call so you can thank them. Jordan, Sully would like to meet you, but given that she doesn't remember a life with you in it, it might not be the reunion you're hoping for."

"I don't care if she doesn't know me. I'll know her." She wiped her eyes. "I can help her to remember. Can we go tonight and meet her tomorrow?" she asked hopefully.

"Yes. I highly suggest that you leave as soon as you can. The media will be all over you two and your families. They're bloodhounds. You'll want to alert your employer, and, Jax, I suggest you buckle down on security for everyone."

"I'm on it." Jax pulled out his phone and texted Brett Bad about beefing up security for both families.

"Can you fly out of a private airstrip?" Reggie asked. "They'll be watching all the airports."

"My cousin Victoria has a private plane. We'll make arrangements with her to leave tonight."

"Perfect. I'll set up the meeting for tomorrow."

"Can my aunt and uncle go with us?" Jordan asked.

"Yes, but I worry about overwhelming Sully. Having a family she doesn't recognize barrel in can be scary regardless of how tough she is. I suggest you meet her first, and as far as your aunt and uncle go, I'd play that by ear."

Jax promised to call after they'd made their travel arrangements, so Reggie could coordinate their visit. His mind was racing, thinking about how he could help Jordan through what would likely be a long, emotional, *complicated* journey.

"Reggie, I don't know how to thank you for everything you've done," Jordan said.

"I'm just glad your sister is alive and well. Besides, I think the thanks goes to Sully for saving herself, and to Chester and Carol Finch and the Whiskeys for keeping her safe and off the media's radar."

After they ended the call, nervous laughter fell from Jordan's lips as they stood up. "Casey's *alive*. I'm going to see my sister! It doesn't feel real, but at the same time, I've been hoping to find her for so long, it feels more real than anything ever has."

"It's *real*, sweetheart, and the sooner we make flight arrangements, the sooner we'll get there."

"I have so many questions. I hope she'll eventually want to come home."

"Let's not worry about what's to come. Let's be happy about the gift we've all been given. She's obviously going to have a lot to deal with, and so are you and your family. But you need to know that I am willing to do whatever you want or need. If you want to stay in Colorado for a few weeks or months, we can rent a house there, or stay at Beau and Char's inn. We'll do whatever will make this easiest for the two of you."

"You would upend your life like that for me?"

"Are you *really* asking me that?"

She laughed. "I'm sorry. Of course you would." She threw her arms around him. "I love you so much. Thank you for believing in me and for pushing me to follow my heart. We need to tell my aunt and uncle and your family!"

"Let's do it." He reached for her hand.

When they opened the door to the den, *everyone* was standing there with worried expressions.

The din of their families' conversations silenced, and her aunt rushed forward. "What happened?"

"They found Casey! She's alive and well. She doesn't remember us, and she goes by Sullivan Tate now. *Sully.* But she's *alive!*" Jordan exclaimed with a rush of fresh tears. "She's in Colorado at a place called Redemption Ranch, and we can see her tomorrow."

Her aunt threw her arms around her, and her uncle embraced them both as cheers of relief rang out and everyone talked at once.

"I know everyone at the ranch. Birdie Whiskey is my business partner, and her family is like family to me. I'll call over there and introduce you," Carly said.

"Or we can just go with you," Zev offered.

"You can stay with us at the inn," Beau said.

"What can we do to help?" Graham asked.

"I'll make your flight arrangements. When do you want to leave?" Jillian asked.

"Do you want us to come with you?" Jax's mother asked.

"We'll watch Coco," Nick said. "Unless you want us to come with you, too."

"I knew the universe would come through for you." Morgyn hugged Jordan. "Now it's time to manifest healing."

Jordan looked a little overwhelmed, her gaze bouncing from one person to the next.

Jax stepped forward and said, "First and foremost, Sully's whereabouts and name must stay out of the media. That means no talking to family or friends about where she is, where we're going, or any of it." There were murmurs of understanding.

"Carly, *yes* to the intro, but give us a few minutes to wrap our heads around this. Beau, sounds good. We'll stay at the inn until we figure out a plan, thank you. Can we use your truck so we don't leave a trail with a rental receipt?"

"It's in the shop. I'll have Cutter get Char's car ready for you." Cutter was one of Beau and Char's friends.

"Thanks. Jilly, call Victoria. We need a private plane and a private airstrip, and please let her know to keep it under wraps. Sheila and Gary need flights, too. We need to leave ASAP." He looked at Gary. "Does that work for you?"

"Yes." Gary nodded.

"Great. Zev, Mom, thanks for offering to go, but we don't want to overwhelm Casey with too many people. Nick, watching Coco is great, and, Graham and Morgyn, if you could turn the manifesting of healing to overdrive, we'd appreciate it."

"*Jax*," Jordan said as quickly as his words had come.

"Yeah, babe? Sorry, I know it's overwhelming."

"It is. A good kind of overwhelming. But I don't want to put everyone out just because you're with me. I can handle this. I can make flight arrangements and find a hotel, and—"

"Honey, we aren't helping because of Jax." His mother stepped out from between his brothers. "We're helping because this is what family does, and we consider you family." She looked at Sheila and Gary. "All of you, and Casey, too."

Jordan looked like she was going to cry again, and Jax reached for her hand.

"I'm okay," she said with tears in her eyes. "I'm better than okay. I'm *not* going to cry. I'm *not* going to…" Tears slid down her cheeks. "I *love* you, and I love your family, and we found Casey, and now *she* has family to help her carry her baggage, too. I'm sorry I'm crying. I'm just so darn *happy*."

"It's okay, babe. Life's too short to hold the important things in." As Jax wrapped her in his arms and his family began scrambling to make their arrangements, he found a sense of peace among the chaos. Not only had Jordan found her sister, but he'd also found his perfect fit. He gazed into her teary eyes, overflowing with love for the woman who had stolen his heart more than a year ago, and as a sweet sigh escaped her lips, he said, "I'm darn happy, too."

Chapter Twenty-Two

JORDAN GAZED OUT the window of Char's car, trying to focus on the Colorado landscape whooshing by as Jax drove toward Redemption Ranch, but she was too nervous to concentrate on anything. With the exception of a few hours on the plane, she hadn't slept a wink. Her muscles ached, and her mind hadn't stopped whirling since they'd gotten the news about Casey. *Sully.*

She had always considered herself to be strong, and she'd tried hard not to be a burden on anyone, but it was nice not having to pretend to be that resilient with Jax. Last night as the arrangements were being made, he'd taken her out to the garden and had just held her in the moonlight, away from everyone else, somehow knowing she'd needed a little extra care.

As promised, Carly had called and introduced them to Tiny and Wynona Whiskey. Tiny sounded gruff and direct but friendly, and Wynona was warm and compassionate, reassuring them that Sully was safe and being well cared for. They'd explained how they used physical work on the ranch as part of their therapy practice, providing a purpose for those who were a little lost. Four of their five children also worked on the ranch. Jordan liked knowing her sister was surrounded by a good family. But she sure hoped she and Sully could be family again, too.

Jax reached across the seat and took her hand. "How are you holding up, sweetheart?"

"Okay. I'm just nervous."

"I'm so nervous I feel like I could throw up," her aunt said from the back seat.

Jax rolled down her aunt's window, amusing everyone. Jordan was thankful for the levity. Then again, she was grateful for everything about him.

"I'm sure Sully is nervous, too," Jax said. "As Wynnie said, a transition like this is not going to be easy for her or for the three of you. Just remember to take it slow and not to expect too much."

"That's the hardest part. We don't know what she's been through or what her life was like," Jordan said. "I want to be there for her, but how can I if she has no idea who I am? She doesn't know she can trust me."

"Seeing you might trigger memories," her uncle chimed in.

"I know Wynnie said that could happen, and I'm hoping it's true. But what if she never remembers?" Jordan hated thinking about that, but she knew it could happen.

"Then you'll develop a new relationship and get to know each other as the people you've become. This can be whatever the two of you want it to be." When the entrance to the ranch came into focus, Jax tightened his hold on her hand. The main gate had a wooden beam with an iron *RR* across the top—the first *R* was backward—and there were three enormous men standing in front of motorcycles blocking the entrance. Two of them stood with their boots planted on the pavement, wearing black leather vests, their arms crossed over their chests. The third, a dark-haired bearded man, wore jeans, cowboy boots, and a black T-shirt, and he was walking toward the car.

The man strode up to Jax's window and peered into the car. He was handsome, even if slightly intimidating with piercings in his ears, septum, and nostril, and tattoos on his neck and arms. His dark eyes moved over their faces, a smile lifting his beard. "Mornin', folks."

"Hi, I'm Jax Braden, and this is Jordan Lawler and Sheila and Gary Matheson. Tiny and Wynnie are expecting us."

"Welcome to Redemption Ranch. I'm Devlin Whiskey, but you can call me Dare. It's nice to meet all of you." His gaze moved to Jordan, and that smile reached his eyes. "Bet you're eager to see your sister."

"Very much so." Jordan got choked up.

"She's in good hands, and we haven't had any media hounds sniffing around. But we've got Dark Knights posted around the ranch, keeping watch." He motioned to the two guys moving their motorcycles away from the gate. "Why don't you follow me down to the main house. My parents are looking forward to meeting you."

As he walked away, Jordan turned to see tears in her aunt's eyes. "I'm glad I'm not the only one who can't hold it together."

"That's okay. We came prepared." Her uncle handed her a wad of tissues.

"Thanks, Uncle Gary, but Jax filled my pockets with tissues this morning."

They followed Dare onto the property, passing pastures, barns, riding arenas, and parked in front of an impressively large house made of stone, wood, and glass with a sign out front that read REDEMPTION RANCH THERAPEUTIC SERVICES. Jordan recognized Wynona and Tiny standing out front. They looked just like Carly had described them. Wynnie was a pretty middle-aged blonde with a shag haircut and a warm smile. She wore a blue blouse tucked into jeans and cowgirl boots. She had to be at least five six, and Tiny *towered* over her. He was a mountain of a man with a thick gray beard, gray hair trapped beneath a red bandanna tied around his head, and as many tattoos decorating his arms as his son had. His T-shirt was stretched tight over his pendulous belly, which hung over the front of his jeans, and on his feet were well-worn cowboy boots.

Dare parked by the curb. Tiny clapped him on the back, a smile warming his features as they talked. Dare waved to Jordan and Jax as they climbed out of the car, then drove off.

Jax took Jordan's hand, speaking quietly into her ear. "Breathe, sweetheart. It's going to be okay."

"Hi. I'm Wynnie, and this is my husband, Tiny. Welcome to our ranch. We're so happy to meet all of you."

"Hi. I'm Jordan. Thank you for taking care of my sister." Jordan tried not to sound too anxious, but she really wanted to say, *Can I see her?*

"It's our pleasure, darlin'," Tiny said.

"This is my aunt and uncle, Sheila and Gary Matheson, and this is my boyfriend, Jax."

"Hi, Jax Braden. It's nice to meet you." He offered his hand.

"Son, I've known who you were before *you* knew who you were." Tiny laughed at his own joke as he shook Jax's hand. "Hal Braden and I go way back. He's a good man, and he sure is proud of the rest of you Bradens."

"I forgot Hal knows everyone." Jax turned to Jordan and the others. "Hal is my father's cousin, Josh's father. He owns a ranch not far from here, in Weston."

Her aunt and uncle introduced themselves, and Wynnie said, "Sully's been through a lot, as you can imagine. Our son Callahan, who goes by the name Cowboy, has taken on the role of her protector. I hope you don't mind that she's asked him to stay in the room while you two get to know each other."

"I don't mind, but is she afraid of me?" *Please say no.*

"No, sweetheart. She's not afraid of you. She simply wanted someone who felt familiar in the room to help settle her nerves. She's a tough bird. It's hard to imagine her afraid of anything. But as a therapist, I know that's what she's showing us right now. In here"—Wynnie put her hand over her heart—"it might be a whole different story. Only time will tell."

"I'm fine with whatever she needs to feel safe." Jordan glanced at Jax. "I know how comforting being near the right person can be."

"I'm sure y'all have been through hell and back worrying over Sully," Tiny said. "Why don't we go inside so you can set your eyes on that little darlin'?"

He held the door for them as they walked into the spacious building, which looked more like a resort than offices, with high ceilings and exposed wooden rafters. The doors opened into a large two-story gathering space with several couches and chairs, bookshelves, various tables with puzzles and other things on them, and a massive stone fireplace. A second story ran around the perimeter with several doors visible. There was a hallway to their left, and to their right was another open area with enormous farmhouse-style tables. Just beyond, Jordan saw a kitchen and another hallway.

"This is what we call the main house," Wynnie explained. "On this level are our traditional therapeutic service offices, and staff residences are upstairs. We also have meeting rooms and a movie room. We all eat together as often as we can, clients, therapists, and ranch hands included."

"That's wonderful," her aunt said.

"The people who come to us have typically felt alone for a long time," Wynnie explained. "We do everything we can to help alleviate that feeling."

"Has Case—*Sully* been enjoying her time here?" Jordan asked.

"I'm going to let Sully answer that directly. I try not to assume those types of things. Why don't I take you to meet her, and Tiny can show everyone else around."

Jordan turned to Jax and her aunt and uncle. "I hope I don't say the wrong thing."

"Follow your heart." Her aunt glanced at Jax. "It's been guiding you perfectly lately."

"She's right, babe. Just be yourself, and remember, we've got nothing but time." He kissed her. "I love you."

"I love you, too."

As she and Wynnie headed down a hallway, Wynnie said, "You and Jax sure are sweet together."

"Thank you. He's wonderful."

"And from what I hear, you are, too." She stopped outside an office with her name on the door and took Jordan's hands. "Honey, I know you're scared. Is there anything I can help you with before you meet Sully?"

"Is there anything I shouldn't say? How will I know if I say the wrong thing?"

"I would tread lightly when asking about her life. Let her know you love her and you care, but don't push. She'll let you know if you say something that bothers her. She's a firecracker."

"She always was. Thank you, Wynnie."

"You're very welcome. We have many therapists and coun-selors on staff. If you or your family would like to talk, we're here."

"I appreciate that."

"Are you ready to meet Sully?"

"Yes, please." Jordan's heart was beating so hard, she was sure Wynnie could hear it.

Wynnie opened the door, and Jordan saw a tall, thin girl pacing. Her slightly frizzy golden-brown hair hung to her waist. She wore a loose purple batik shirt, cutoffs, and scuffed and worn brown leather boots. But they weren't cowgirl boots—they were more like combat boots. Her back was to Jordan, and she stopped pacing and looked up at the broad-shouldered muscular man standing with his arms crossed, chin low, eyes on Sully.

Cowboy.

He had hair the color of wheat and a beard a shade darker. He nodded at Sully, and she turned around. Her hair fell in front of half of her face, but half was all Jordan needed to recognize her younger sister. Her frantic heart nearly leapt out of her chest, and tears sprang to her eyes.

"Sully, this is Jordan." Wynnie stepped aside, allowing Jordan to walk into the room. "Jordan, this is Sully, and my son Cowboy."

Cowboy's gaze flicked to Jordan, and he gave a single curt nod. "Nice to meet you." His attention quickly returned to Sully, serious and unfaltering.

"Hi." Jordan's lower lip trembled as she tried to keep her emotions at bay. It took everything she had not to run to Sully and throw her arms around her.

Sully's brows knitted. "Hi, Jordan."

Her lips curved up, bringing a quick and painful memory of Casey saying goodbye when Jordan left for camp the year she went missing. Casey had cried and begged to go with her, and Jordan had told her not to cry and had promised they'd see each other soon. She must have buried the memory of those promises along with her parents, but now they brought a rush of tears.

"I'm sorry." Jordan dug tissues out of her pocket and wiped her eyes.

"It's okay to cry." Sully stepped closer. "They said you're five years older than me. You must remember everything."

"I do. Every second." She dragged air into her thickening throat.

Sadness rose in Sully's eyes. "I don't remember you. But I'd like to."

Her voice was confident and compassionate, opening the floodgates. Tears flowed like rivers down Jordan's cheeks. She opened her mouth to speak, but she was too overwhelmed. "I'm sorry, but I've missed you so much. I thought I'd never see you again."

Sully embraced her, a little awkwardly, drawing deeper sobs. "You should never be sorry for your feelings. It's the one thing we have that's truly ours."

"You sound like the older sister." Jordan wiped her eyes as she stepped out of her arms and realized Wynnie had left the room. Cowboy still stood sentinel a few feet away, watching them like a hawk.

"I've had a lot of practice taking care of younger kids," Sully said with a small smile.

Jordan struggled to rein in her emotions. "I'd like to hear about that one day, and maybe I could tell you about our family, too."

"I think I'd like to hear about your family. Do you have time to talk now?"

Her use of *your* cut like a knife, but Jordan tried not to let it show. "Yes."

Cowboy pulled a chair out at the table for Sully, and after she sat down, he gave her shoulder a reassuring squeeze and planted himself a few feet away, her formidable bodyguard. Jordan had the sense that he'd jump in front of a charging bull for her sister. She was glad Sully had someone she trusted, and after all the nice things Carly had said about Cowboy, she was glad he was watching out for her.

Jordan told her about their family and about her life after the accident. Sully asked a lot of questions about their parents and their aunt and uncle, and Jordan showed her pictures of everyone. She watched her closely, hoping for a hint of recognition, but didn't see any. She tucked that disappointment away and told Sully she could have the pictures, hoping they might spark a memory. When Sully asked what her life was like now, she desperately wanted to tell her about the years of heartache, when she'd hidden her feelings about finding her, and her difficulty forming friendships, and her broken engagement with Todd, and how being with Jax had changed all of that. But her sister was dealing with enough, and so was she, so Jordan let those negative thoughts go and told her about Jax and his family and how wonderful they were, and that she hoped one day Sully would get to know them, too.

More than an hour later, as they said goodbye, Sully said, "Can you come back tomorrow? Maybe we could take a walk and talk?"

"Yes. I'd like that very much. Would it be okay if I hugged you goodbye?"

Sully nodded, and as they hugged, she said, "You felt like a stranger when you first walked in, but you don't now."

And just like that Jordan was crying again.

Sully smiled. "You must have gotten all the emotional genes in the family."

"I was always the crier, and you were the tough one. I guess some things never change."

Jordan left the room feeling like a piece of her that had been missing for too long was finally within reach.

Jax and her aunt and uncle came toward her as she walked into the main room, and Wynnie and Tiny were right behind them.

"How did it go?" her aunt asked.

"Good." Jordan pulled more tissues from her pocket to dry her tears. "The pictures didn't help her remember anything, and we didn't talk about her life, but she wanted to know about mine."

"That's a start," her uncle said.

"Yeah, and she asked me to come back tomorrow."

"That's wonderful, baby." Jax kissed her temple. "How are you feeling? Are you okay?"

"I feel so many things right now. I'm thankful that she's okay." More tears fell. "And hopeful that she'll regain her memories, but I'm scared because I know it might never happen. But most of all, I feel like I've been blessed with two new beginnings." She looked at the man who had shown her what true love was and how good it felt to give and receive that love and said, "It took us months to see where we were always meant to be."

"It took *you* months," Jax said with a sexy grin. "I knew from day one."

God, she loved him. "Yes, and a wise, thoughtful man once told me that love has no timeline. That impossibly charming man was right, and I know that however long this takes, and whatever it becomes, it will be what it was always meant to be, too."

Ready for more Bradens & Montgomerys?

I hope you enjoyed Jax and Jordan's story, and meeting Jordan's sister, Sully. Grab Jillian Braden and Johnny Bad's story, **ROCKED BY LOVE**, below, and then turn the page to get Sully and Cowboy's story in **FOR THE LOVE OF WHISKEY**.

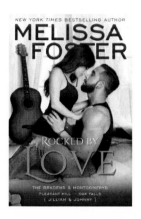

He's a rock star with a secret. She's a fashion designer with a nose for bullshit.

When Johnny Bad hires Jillian Braden to design his tour wardrobe and cancels for the umpteenth time, she's had enough. Jillian is determined to set him straight, but she isn't at all prepared for what she finds, or for the type of help Johnny really needs. Come along for the hilarious, sexy ride as Jillian and Johnny get caught up in a storm that just might be bigger than both of them.

Are you ready to fall for Sullivan "Sully" Tate and Cowboy Whiskey?

The Whiskeys: Dark Knights at Redemption Ranch.

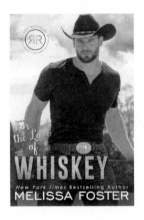

When Sullivan Tate escaped from a cult, leaving behind the only life she'd ever known, she thought she'd already endured the most difficult things she'd ever have to deal with. She knew she needed to figure out who she was, but she hadn't expected to fall for overprotective and sexy-as-hell Callahan "Cowboy" Whiskey along the way. How can she give her heart to a man who has always known exactly who he is, when she's only just begun figuring that out about herself?

Fall in love with the Steeles on the sandy shores of Silver Island, home to coffee shops, boat races, and midnight rendezvous

A man who has lost it all and carries a torturous secret, a single mother with everything to lose, and the little girl that helps them heal. Fall in love with Jock and Daphne in TEMPTED BY LOVE, the first book in The Steeles at Silver Island series.

Ready for hilarity and heat?

Start the Seaside Summers series FREE in digital format

Fall in love at Seaside, featuring a group of fun, sexy friends who gather each summer at their Cape Cod cottages. They're funny, flawed, and will have you begging to enter their circle of friends.

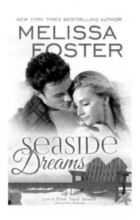

Bella Abbascia has returned to Seaside Cottages in Wellfleet, Massachusetts, as she does every summer. Only this year, Bella has more on her mind than sunbathing and skinny-dipping with her girlfriends. She's quit her job, put her house on the market, and sworn off relationships while she builds a new life in her favorite place on earth. That is, until good-time Bella's prank takes a bad turn and a sinfully sexy police officer appears on the scene.

Single father and police officer Caden Grant left Boston with his fourteen-year-old son, Evan, after his partner was killed in the line of duty. He hopes to find a safer life in the small resort town of Wellfleet, and when he meets Bella during a night patrol shift, he realizes he's found the one thing he'd never allowed himself to hope for—or even realized he was missing.

After fourteen years of focusing solely on his son, Caden cannot resist the intense attraction he feels toward beautiful Bella, and Bella's powerless to fight the heat of their budding romance. But starting over proves more difficult than either of them imagined, and when Evan gets mixed up with the wrong kids, Caden's loyalty is put to the test. Will he give up everything to protect his son—even Bella?

Have you met The Whiskeys: Dark Knights at Peaceful Harbor?

If you're a fan of sexy, alpha heroes, babies, and strong family ties even to those who are not blood related, you'll love Truman Gritt and the Whiskeys.

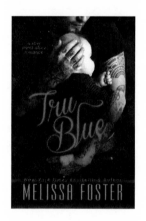

There's nothing Truman Gritt won't do to protect his family—including spending years in prison for a crime he didn't commit. When he's finally released, the life he knew is turned upside down by his mother's overdose, and Truman steps in to raise the children she's left behind. Truman's hard, he's secretive, and he's trying to save a brother who's even more broken than he is. He's never needed help in his life, and when beautiful Gemma Wright tries to step in, he's less than accepting. But Gemma has a way of slithering into people's lives, and eventually she pierces through his ironclad heart. When Truman's dark past collides with his future, his loyalties will be tested, and he'll be faced with his toughest decision yet.

New to the Love in Bloom series?

If this is your first Love in Bloom book, there are many more love stories featuring loyal, sassy, and sexy heroes and heroines waiting for you. The Bradens & Montgomerys is just one of the series in the Love in Bloom big-family romance collection. Each Love in Bloom book is written to be enjoyed as a stand-alone novel or as part of the larger series. There are no cliffhangers and no unresolved issues. Characters from each series make appearances in future books, so you never miss an engagement, wedding, or birth. You might enjoy my other series within the Love in Bloom big-family romance collection, starting with the very first book in the entire Love in Bloom series, SISTERS IN LOVE.

See the Entire Love in Bloom Collection
www.MelissaFoster.com/love-bloom-series

Download Free First-in-Series eBooks
www.MelissaFoster.com/free-ebooks

Download Series Checklists, Family Trees, and Publication Schedules
www.MelissaFoster.com/reader-goodies

More Books By Melissa Foster

LOVE IN BLOOM SERIES

SNOW SISTERS
Sisters in Love
Sisters in Bloom
Sisters in White

THE BRADENS at Weston
Lovers at Heart, Reimagined
Destined for Love
Friendship on Fire
Sea of Love
Bursting with Love
Hearts at Play

THE BRADENS at Trusty
Taken by Love
Fated for Love
Romancing My Love
Flirting with Love
Dreaming of Love
Crashing into Love

THE BRADENS at Peaceful Harbor
Healed by Love
Surrender My Love
River of Love
Crushing on Love
Whisper of Love
Thrill of Love

THE BRADENS & MONTGOMERYS at Pleasant Hill – Oak Falls
Embracing Her Heart
Anything for Love

Trails of Love
Wild Crazy Hearts
Making You Mine
Searching for Love
Hot for Love
Sweet Sexy Heart
Then Came Love (Previously Summer of Love)
Rocked by Love (Previously Winter of Love)
Our Wicked Hearts
Claiming Her Heart

THE BRADEN NOVELLAS
Promise My Love
Our New Love
Daring Her Love
Story of Love
Love at Last
A Very Braden Christmas

THE REMINGTONS
Game of Love
Stroke of Love
Flames of Love
Slope of Love
Read, Write, Love
Touched by Love

SEASIDE SUMMERS
Seaside Dreams
Seaside Hearts
Seaside Sunsets
Seaside Secrets
Seaside Nights
Seaside Embrace
Seaside Lovers
Seaside Whispers
Seaside Serenade

The Real Thing
Only for You
Love Like Ours
Finding My Girl

HARMONY POINTE
Call Her Mine
This is Love
She Loves Me

THE WICKEDS: DARK KNIGHTS AT BAYSIDE
A Little Bit Wicked
The Wicked Aftermath
Crazy, Wicked Love
The Wicked Truth

SILVER HARBOR
Maybe We Will
Maybe We Should

WILD BOYS AFTER DARK
Logan
Heath
Jackson
Cooper

BAD BOYS AFTER DARK
Mick
Dylan
Carson
Brett

HARBORSIDE NIGHTS SERIES
Includes characters from the Love in Bloom series
Catching Cassidy
Discovering Delilah
Tempting Tristan

More Books by Melissa

Chasing Amanda (mystery/suspense)
Come Back to Me (mystery/suspense)
Have No Shame (historical fiction/romance)
Love, Lies & Mystery (3-book bundle)
Megan's Way (literary fiction)
Traces of Kara (psychological thriller)
Where Petals Fall (suspense)

Acknowledgments

There are so many things I want to say about this book. I never write about heroes or heroines who are in relationships with someone other than the main character of their book, but with Jax and Jordan, I had to, and I hope you're as thrilled with their story as I am. I'd like to give you a little peek into how Jordan and her sister's story came to be. I began writing Sullivan "Sully" Tate's story in 2013, and I set it aside because of other projects and a feeling that it wasn't quite her time yet. When I met Jordan, I knew in my heart that she was the older sister in Sully's original story. I am excited to bring you Sully's story, FOR THE LOVE OF WHISKEY, in which you'll learn about her life and see her get her own happily ever after with Callahan "Cowboy" Whiskey, in The Whiskeys: Dark Knights at Redemption Ranch.

I am inspired on a daily basis by my fans and friends, many of whom are in my fan club on Facebook. If you haven't yet joined my fan club, please do. We have a great time chatting about the Love in Bloom hunky heroes and sassy heroines. You never know when you'll inspire a story or a character and end up in one of my books, as several fan club members have already discovered.
www.Facebook.com/groups/MelissaFosterFans

To stay abreast of what's going on in our fictional boyfriends'

worlds and sales, like and follow my Facebook fan page.
www.Facebook.com/MelissaFosterAuthor

Sign up for my newsletter to keep up to date with new releases and special promotions and events and to receive an exclusive short story featuring Jack Remington and Savannah Braden.
www.MelissaFoster.com/Newsletter

And don't forget to download your free Reader Goodies! For free ebooks, family trees, publication schedules, series checklists, and more, please visit the special Reader Goodies page that I've set up for you!
www.MelissaFoster.com/Reader-Goodies

As always, loads of gratitude to my incredible team of editors and proofreaders: Kristen Weber, Penina Lopez, Elaini Caruso, Juliette Hill, Lynn Mullan, and Justinn Harrison, and my *last set of eagle eyes*, Lee Fisher.

I am forever grateful to my family, assistants, and friends who have become family, Lisa Filipe, Sharon Martin, and Missy Dehaven, for their endless support and friendship. Thank you for always having my back, even when I'm deep in the deadline zone and probably unbearably annoying.

Meet Melissa

www.MelissaFoster.com

Melissa Foster is a *New York Times, Wall Street Journal,* and *USA Today* bestselling and award-winning author. Her books have been recommended by *USA Today*'s book blog, *Hagerstown* magazine, *The Patriot,* and several other print venues. Melissa has painted and donated several murals to the Hospital for Sick Children in Washington, DC.

Visit Melissa on her website or chat with her on social media. Melissa enjoys discussing her books with book clubs and reader groups and welcomes an invitation to your event. Melissa's books are available through most online retailers in paperback, digital, and audio formats.

Made in United States
North Haven, CT
06 June 2022

19898089R00217